Praise for

'Jesse Blackadder has all t[...]
fiction writer, achieving a fin[...]
atmospheric detail and suspenseful story ... she posits the
ephemeral nature of humans against a weighty sense of history
and an ageless landscape, something she does with an incisive
grace that truly elevates her story ... she doesn't hit one
wrong note' *Sunday Telegraph*

'Within the rich tradition of positioning the previously invisible or
marginalised centre stage, *The Raven's Heart* is a complex political
intrigue counterbalanced by the protagonist's increasingly
poetic sensibilities ... a welcome and audacious piece of work'
Australian Book Review

'I found the story utterly intriguing and completely
unputdownable ... the writing is evocative and powerful and
I haven't enjoyed a book in this genre so much since *The Little
Stranger* by Sarah Waters' *Good Reading*

'Jesse's novel is gripping from the first few pages. Her writing and
research paint an intriguing, intimate glimpse into Queen Mary's
life and character' *Courier Mail*

'Jesse Blackadder does a wonderful job in this novel of
allowing the historical aspect to come through without
overtaking the plot ... Her prose is both sexy and chaste, ruthless
and tender, bringing out these elements in all her characters ...
Sarah Waters' fans are sure to enjoy this new historical fiction'
Lambda Literary

'Blackadder's prose is sumptuous and expressive; perfectly pitched in terms of time and never anachronistic ... Her sense of place is marvellous – her descriptions are powerful but never overwhelm the action. And her pacing is a perfect blend of action and exposition that never drags or lags. Historically accurate and meticulously researched, Blackadder's facts are a jumping off point for her fiction and never jar the reader or seem out of place. Altogether an engrossing read, *The Raven's Heart* is sure to please both history buff and fiction lover' *Out in Print*

'Each character is well drawn, with a depth of personality that truly makes them believable. Couple that with colourful descriptions of clothing, surroundings, and castle life, and it does make for a fascinating read ... a compelling, well-told tale with plenty of plot twists and excellent dialogue to keep readers interested' *History and Women*

'It is not often I say this about a book, but this one grabbed and held me from the first page. Ms Blackadder is a masterly writer with active and descriptive prose ... Anyone who enjoys reading about this era will love this book and it will create a new fascination for the tragic queen. I can honestly say I look forward to Ms Blackadder's next novel' *Historical Novel Review*

Jesse Blackadder lives on the caldera of an extinct volcano in northern New South Wales and is fascinated by landscapes, adventurous women and very cold places. She wrote *Chasing the Light: A Novel of Antarctica* as part of a Doctor of Creative Arts at the University of Western Sydney. Jesse was awarded the 2011–12 Australian Antarctic Arts Fellowship (which allowed her to voyage to Antarctica); and she won the 2012 Guy Morrison Prize for Literary Journalism for her essay 'The first woman and the last dog in Antarctica'.

See more at
jesseblackadder.com

Also by Jesse Blackadder

After the Party
The Raven's Heart

CHASING
THE
LIGHT

A NOVEL OF ANTARCTICA

JESSE BLACKADDER

FOURTH ESTATE

Fourth Estate
An imprint of HarperCollins*Publishers*

First published in Australia in 2013
by HarperCollins*Publishers* Australia Pty Limited
ABN 36 009 913 517
harpercollins.com.au

Copyright © Jesse Blackadder 2013

The right of Jesse Blackadder to be identified as the author of this
work has been asserted by her in accordance with the *Copyright Amendment
(Moral Rights) Act 2000.*

This work is copyright. Apart from any use as permitted under the
Copyright Act 1968, no part may be reproduced, copied, scanned, stored
in a retrieval system, recorded, or transmitted, in any form or by any means,
without the prior written permission of the publisher.

HarperCollins*Publishers*
Level 13, 201 Elizabeth Street, Sydney NSW 2000, Australia
31 View Road, Glenfield, Auckland 0627, New Zealand
A 53, Sector 57, Noida, UP, India
77–85 Fulham Palace Road, London W6 8JB, United Kingdom
2 Bloor Street East, 20th floor, Toronto, Ontario M4W 1A8, Canada
10 East 53rd Street, New York, NY 10022, USA

National Library of Australia Cataloguing-in-Publication data:

Blackadder, Jesse.
   Chasing the light : a novel of Antarctica / Jesse Blackadder.
   ISBN: 978 0 7322 9604 9 (pbk.)
   ISBN: 978 1 7430 9782 3 (ebook)
   Women – Travel – Antarctica – Fiction.
   Antarctica – Fiction.
A823.4

Cover design by Philip Campbell Design
Cover image by Victor Lyagushkin
Typeset in 11/15 Baskerville BE by Kirby Jones
Printed and bound in Australia by Griffin Press
The papers used by HarperCollins in the manufacture of this book are a natural, recyclable
product made from wood grown in sustainable plantation forests. The fibre source and
manufacturing processes meet recognised international environmental standards, and carry
certification.

6 5 4 3 2   13 14 15 16

Dedicated to

The women who journeyed to Antarctica in the 1930s
on the Christensen fleet:
Ingrid Christensen
Mathilde Wegger
Lillemor (Ingebjørg) Rachlew
Ingebjørg Dedichen
Caroline Mikkelsen
Augusta Sofie ('Fie') Christensen
Solveig Wideroe

My mother, Barbara Walsh (1941–1988),
whose journey ended too soon

And my partner, Andi, who came along on this
journey from beginning to end

AUTHOR'S NOTE

This novel has been inspired by events in Antarctic exploration that took place in the early 1930s and by the people involved in those events.

I have used real names for many characters, including those of the earliest women to reach Antarctica.

However, this is a work of the imagination, and many of the events and dates have been significantly changed, as have some of the names. The characters, though prompted by real people, are imaginary. In the afterword you can find a more factual recounting of their stories.

FOREWORD

by Diana Patterson, first female station leader in Antarctica

In early 1995 I had just commenced my year as leader of Davis, one of Australia's three Antarctic research stations. I was pleasantly surprised when a member of our summer team suggested that we plan a celebration of the sixtieth anniversary of the first landing by a woman in Antarctica. While I was aware that in the early 1930s much of this part of East Antarctica was discovered and mapped by Norwegian whaling fleets, it came as news to me that the first landing by a woman was made roughly thirty kilometres to the north of the station. That we should honour the occasion, acknowledging the history of women in Antarctica, was a far cry from prior experience of a hostile and negative attitude to the presence of women by some male expeditioners.

We duly celebrated the landing and throughout the polar winter our small team took a special interest in locating the site and learning more about the 'first' woman. Our curiosity was rewarded and by year's end we had a name, face and location and, unexpectedly, belated recognition in Norway of the achievement. Local place names such as the Vestfold Hills and Four Ladies Bank in Prydz Bay acquired more meaning as we now knew their derivation came from the same voyage of discovery.

Despite this I was left wondering about the presence and experience of the Norwegian women on the whaling vessels. The few photos I saw could have placed them on an Atlantic cruise ship rather than an Antarctic whaler. I was therefore delighted to learn that Jesse Blackadder had been inspired to write an Antarctic novel based on these pioneering women. With so much focus on the stories of the Heroic Era of Antarctica, of the race to the South Pole and national scientific expeditions, the exploration of Antarctica in the 1930s is a story that has been overlooked.

Although I have now made numerous voyages to Antarctica myself, I found reading *Chasing the Light* an enthralling adventure story. To me it was like undertaking a new journey in a different era, my companions three women with very different personal circumstances, each with their own motivation for setting forth across the Southern Ocean. Motivation that I could well relate to with my own desire to venture south five decades later. While the race to the South Pole was well over, how would the race to be the first woman to step foot in Antarctica be resolved?

It is often said you cannot visit Antarctica and not be changed by the experience. The immense landscape, the fury of blizzards contrasting with the tranquility and silence of the pack ice on a still evening, all contribute to that change which occurs within. Less mentioned is the impact of the interpersonal encounters when you become part of a small community within the confines of a ship or a base on land. Just how the change is manifest is unpredictable, no less so in the 1930s as it is today.

In *Chasing the Light* Jesse Blackadder has made a superb contribution to Antarctic literature and adventure writing.

PROLOGUE

England, 1914.

Dr Marie Stopes held the chunk of raw coal in her hand, hefting its weight. She'd chiselled it from deep underground in the colliery tunnel, and kept it on her desk as a paperweight long after the other samples had been packed and stored in wooden drawers at the university. It contained an intricate leaf-fossil pattern, and fitted nicely in her fist.

She needed it today. The *British Museum Natural History Report* had arrived in the morning post.

It should have been a bag of Antarctic rocks sitting there on her desk, not a report. Marie gripped her piece of coal so hard that her knuckles turned white. It wasn't done to think ill of the dead but she cursed Robert Falcon Scott. He and his four men had died to bring those rocks back from Antarctica, imbuing them with far more than their own physical weight. A decade ago she'd been the one to teach him what to look for – how dare he send them to someone else?

According to the eminent Dr Seward of Cambridge, Scott's rocks were imprinted with the fossilised patterns of leaf veins, indicating that trees had once grown on Antarctica. But it should have been her to make the finding. Trained for precisely that purpose, her eye should have been the one to pick out the traces of ancient *Glossopteris indica*.

Marie had wanted to go with Scott. Wanted to chip the rocks from the seam near the Beardmore Glacier in the

Queen Maud Mountains of Antarctica for herself. In the Manchester coal seam she'd known the thrill of levering out chunks of the earth to reveal its secrets. She'd found clues to the origins of the continents and saved them from being burned in factories and fireplaces across Britain. Without her, Scott wouldn't have brought the rocks back at all. Wouldn't have known what to look for.

Another woman, one more charming and persuasive, might have convinced Captain Scott to take her, but there was little place for charm in Antarctica and, it seemed, no place for a palaeobotanist either, if she happened to be female.

They had danced at their first meeting. Marie knew it wasn't her strength, but at the fundraising ball for the *Terra Nova* expedition it had been the easiest way for her to speak to him. She'd accepted his invitation and though he was short and slight, he was good on his feet and a firm leader, the kind you felt no hesitation in following.

But he tricked her. While they danced, he described the expedition and her fingers tightened on his arm. He was going to the place where the answers to her life's work lay. Etched in Antarctica's rocks, where no life now survived, might be the imprints of earlier life, evidence of how the continents had once embraced in a lover's grip – the fabled Gondwanaland.

'Take me,' she'd said, with her usual bluntness and lack of forethought.

'But, my dear, it's impossible.' His smile was all charm. 'A woman cannot go to Antarctica.'

'It was impossible for me to be Britain's youngest Doctor of Science, but it was done,' she said.

He shook his head. 'You've no idea of the hardships.'

'I've been down Manchester collieries in winter looking for fossils,' she replied. 'Which was easier, on the whole, than convincing the University of Manchester to employ a female academic. You have no idea of my endurance.'

The music ended and he stepped back. There were many influential wives for him to dance with and husbands still to fete, for the expedition funds were far from raised, she could see.

'I will give you an answer, but not till the night's end,' he said. He bowed his head and excused himself.

The sly fox had told her his decision only after she'd pledged a donation to the trip and in this she caught a glimpse of his ruthlessness.

'But I'll have my men collect your rocks,' he said, by way of consolation.

'Oh, really?' she'd snapped. 'And how will your men know what rocks are of use to me, Captain Scott?'

'I will learn them myself,' he said, his face serious. 'I'll come to the university and you can teach me. I can give you three days, Miss Stopes.'

'*Dr* Stopes. It's only taken me a decade to learn palaeobotany. I'm sure you'll pick it up in three days.'

He was unperturbed. 'I'm a fast learner.'

Scott had stuck to his word and come to Manchester. She'd been rude when he arrived but he was interested and diligent in learning and she sent him away with a rudimentary knowledge of what to look for. She'd not have guessed, from his cheerful demeanour, that he was a man who'd rather die than lighten his load by casting away those specimens.

For as it transpired, Robert Falcon Scott was on an inexorable path to his own death in a tent in Antarctica, on his bitter return from the South Pole, to which Roald Amundsen, the Norwegian, had beaten him by a month. Scott and his men had taken a day to gather the rocks on their way back. A precious day, as it turned out. They carried them all the way to their last camp, thirty-five pounds of specimens slowing their steps. Freed from their weight, might they have made the last eleven miles to One Ton Depot, and their salvation?

But though he was committed to her rocks, Scott had let her down in the end. By the time he died, eight years had passed since they'd met and he left no instructions to send the rocks to Marie. Instead, at the height of the public's grieving over Scott's death, the rocks went to Dr Seward of Cambridge.

The door to her study creaked open, startling her back into the present.

'My dear?' Reginald poked his head inside, his eyebrows raised.

In the years since meeting Scott, Marie had married, thinking it a simple enough transaction. She needed a man with a mind as sharp as her own, and Reginald at first seemed to fit the bill, being a Canadian geneticist. He had wooed her with wit and intelligence at a university dinner in Missouri while she was visiting America and she'd foolishly thought two days was enough to take her measure of the man, agreeing to his proposal at once, though stipulating that she would keep her own name.

But though they were both clever, neither Reginald nor Marie knew about love. Their marriage bed was as ice blown as Antarctica. She was ashamed to admit it but they hadn't consummated their union. Reginald, seeming unaroused by her in any way, was impervious to hint, suggestion or seduction. Marie had no idea what to do about it. Their marriage was heading the way of Scott's expedition, crawling towards a slow, frozen death.

It was a method of birth control, she supposed. She couldn't afford to fall pregnant, not now, with the success of her work imminent.

'Lunch is ready,' he said. 'Are you coming?'

'In a moment.' Marie looked down at the rocks again. She waited until she heard the click of the door and exhaled heavily.

Ernest Shackleton was now planning an assault on Antarctica, in a ship called *Endurance*. The papers had reported the week before that he aimed to be the first man to sledge across the continent, a plan clearly formulated in a hurry once the South Pole was no longer a prize to be won. Another flurry of fundraising had begun.

Marie had composed a letter explaining the theory of Gondwana and asking to be included on his trip as a palaeobotanist. In a cruel twist, the reply had come just this morning, in the same post as the British Museum's report.

Sir Ernest Shackleton begs to thank Dr Marie Stopes for her letter, but regrets there are no vacancies for the opposite sex on the expedition.

She pounded the chunk of coal on the table, ripping the page containing Seward's words and smearing them with black. Damn them. Damn the lot of them.

NORWAY
Early 1930s

CHAPTER 1

It was a night so silent that every ski stroke rasped like a bow drawn across a cello string, sounding a rough and steady note, calling out their path to any trolls or wolves or errant gods that might watch from the dark of the trees. The white fur of Ingrid's collar was warm against her cheek. Her breath billowed in clouds, the gasp of it in time with the scrape of the skis. The mountains rose steeply to the velvet black of the Norwegian winter sky.

Up ahead, Lars checked and held up his hand, arcing to a graceful stop. Ingrid glided to his side, pivoted and sliced to a halt. She pulled off her goggles and rested on her stocks, breathing hard.

'There,' Lars said, pointing.

Ingrid turned her head to look. Against the stars, a curtain of pale green light shimmered, almost winked out, surged again. The light spilled around them onto the snow, reflecting eerily as though each snowflake mirrored back the aurora. The land seemed to dance.

The lights spun and pulsated and died away. In their wake Ingrid felt the silence in her bones, as if the aurora had revealed the true size of the Arctic winter night. She inhaled slowly. In that moment she felt nothing but herself, nothing but a woman in the snow, a woman in the wild dark night without thought or responsibility. The unaccustomed pleasure of it burned in her chest like ice. She hadn't felt this way since her honeymoon. Not since she'd become a mother.

'I'm glad we came back,' Lars said. 'I suppose I can thank Unilever for something.'

His words jolted her from her absorption in the moonlit snow. To celebrate their twentieth wedding anniversary, she and Lars had left their six children at home and travelled to Espedalen to repeat the adventure of their honeymoon – night skiing in the mountains to see the aurora borealis. It wasn't only a romantic gesture. It gave Lars something to do while his fleet lay idle in Sandefjord Harbour instead of working the Southern Ocean whaling grounds as it had for the past three seasons. She'd hoped he might leave business behind him.

He reached out a mittened hand for her. 'They've got us over a barrel, you know.'

Ingrid took his hand. 'What do you mean?'

'Unilever's big enough to put us all out of business.'

At the worry in his voice, Ingrid turned to look at him. In Sandefjord, in front of the children and around his business associates, Lars had made light of Unilever's power to lay up Norway's entire whaling fleet for the season and she'd believed his public assurances that he wasn't concerned. Although Lars normally talked about his work with her, perhaps he hadn't shared the extent of his private fear.

'But isn't the layover just for this year?'

'I'm worried Unilever will build up its own fleet,' Lars said. 'I hear they're trying to buy up ships from smaller companies that can't outlast the layover. Then they'll become my competitor as well as my customer.'

The cold air seemed suddenly menacing and Ingrid shivered. 'What will we do?'

'We've got to find southern whaling grounds for Norway so Unilever can't run a fleet cheaper than we can. Paying concessions to the English to hunt in Antarctica is ruining us.

Next year I'm going down there to confirm our own territories. I can't keep sending other men – I've got to do this myself.'

The northern lights pulsed again, distracting her, and in spite of her worry, Ingrid felt a matching flare in her veins. This was the moment, after her twenty patient years, after her cheerful mothering, after her steadfast support, that he'd remember the adventurous woman he had married, and the promise he'd made her. She took a deep breath, drawing in air to the bottom of her lungs, and tried to imagine an even deeper cold.

'I suppose we'll go on *Norvegia*?' she asked.

'Hjalmar said *Norvegia* tossed like a tin toy in the storms last year,' Lars said. 'I don't want to take any risks. I'll go on *Thorshavn*.'

It took a moment for his use of the singular to sink in. 'You couldn't go without me,' she said.

The aurora flickered once more and she strained to read his face. Half her lifetime ago, when they skied these runs as newlyweds, she'd felt they were a single person, moving in unison, united in body and mind. There was nothing they couldn't do together. Nothing they didn't know about each other.

'Lars?'

He shook his head. 'We can't both go.'

'But you promised.'

He tried to draw her closer. 'Ingrid, my sweet. We weren't parents then. Besides, think of those men on the ships. They don't see women for months and then you come along. There'd be a riot.'

She pulled her hand out of his, outraged that he could joke. 'You promised,' she repeated.

'But the children,' he said, and it wasn't a question.

'We've left them before. What's different now?'

He pushed back his hood. 'None of my boys show any promise in running a whaling empire. I want us to have another child.'

Lars's long face was pale against the snow, his eyes unfathomable. Ingrid doubted he had come to her bed as a husband more than a handful of times since their last child was born five years earlier. The heat of their early marriage had cooled over time and she'd been busy enough not to miss it too much. She felt a rush of rage, deep and elemental, the rage of a woman who has borne enough children and wants something for herself.

'I'm thirty-nine, Lars.'

'So there's no time to lose.'

Around her the night was dark and huge and she started to shiver in earnest. 'You'd leave me with a newborn and go south for – what? Four months?'

They looked at each other and then Lars shrugged. 'Let's get moving. It's too cold to stand still.'

Ingrid bent her knees, leaned into the stocks and pushed off hard, suddenly wild to get away from him. She was flying, the air freezing her cheeks, her body moving without thought, the grace of skiing unlike anything she knew in her ordinary life. Above her the black sky; below, the snow crunching as her skis sliced through it.

She could hear the grating of Lars's skis behind her and she leaned lower, speeding up so he couldn't overtake her.

She'd thought, when they first skied together on their honeymoon, that their marriage would always be like that, the one in front laying down the path for the one behind to follow close, their skis fitting into the grooves left by the other. Back when she was too young to understand how suddenly a divergence could crack between them, like a crevasse opening up in the snow.

24

Ingrid slid out of the heavy front door and shut it behind her to stop Ranvik's warmth escaping into the winter night. She stood on the back step, took a few deep breaths till her lungs adjusted, and then stepped out into the snow. It was overcast, but the moon had risen somewhere above the clouds and there was enough light to see by.

She and Lars had returned to their home in Sandefjord in time for Christmas and neither of them had spoken further of the next season and the Antarctic trip. In public Ingrid was as kind to Lars as ever, but she turned away from him when he came to bed late at night, her legs clamped together to close off any idea of another child.

The snow crunched under her boots as she walked around the house, skirted its curtain-darkened face and headed across the white expanse of snow, down towards the water's edge. She dug her hands into her fur-lined pockets, feeling the chill nipping at her fingertips.

It was January, the time of long nights and bone-deep cold and the water of the fjord freezing around the boats. The town of Sandefjord, a cluster of buildings and docks at the fjord's head, closed in on itself in the dark season when the men followed the light down to the whaling grounds of the Antarctic. Winter was a place of women and children, with no comfort for those wives through the long hours of darkness, save for the little ones brought in to warm their beds.

But this winter, with the fleet laid up, Sandefjord was full of restless whaling men with nothing to do, their agitation rippling through the air.

The sea ice was glassy and perfect and she wished she'd brought her skates. In that smooth motion, like skiing, she could forget herself. A light snow began to fall, floating and insubstantial, the flakes suspended on Ingrid's fur collar for a moment, then suddenly vanishing. She stopped and tilted her head backwards to watch them. She looked for a glimmer of the aurora, but the sky was heavy with cloud.

Ingrid could still remember the first time she'd seen the aurora as a child. She'd found her way out of the house looking for her mother and she recalled the sensation of the thick snow crunching and how she sank ankle-deep with every step.

She had followed the white path leading to the gate, some instinct telling her that the single line of footsteps breaking the snow belonged to her mother. As she toddled her thick-legged way along it, she glanced up at the brilliance in the night sky above and her mouth opened in wonder. She tilted her head back and overbalanced, falling with a soft crunch on her bottom. The snow cushioned the impact and she laughed.

The aurora had flared again, lighting up the snow around her. Ingrid stretched out her hand, entranced, and tried to grasp the glittering colours. Her fingers closed on snow and she grabbed handful after handful, opening her hand each time to find just pale ice. As the aurora faded and the snow returned to its usual white, Ingrid remembered her purpose. She clambered to her feet again. Another few steps and she was at the gate. It was high, but she reached up, found a handhold in the wood, and pulled herself up from the ground, marvelling at how it felt to move through the air. Poised between sky and snow, she reached higher. Her hand flailed, her foot slipped and she fell, landing on her back.

The snow rose around her protectively. Footsteps crunched down the path towards her, getting louder in her ears, and then she was lifted from the ground's icy embrace. She started to cry.

'What are you doing, little Viking?' her father, Thor, asked, wrapping his arms around her.

Ingrid strained against his grip. 'Mommo?'

'Mommo has gone with the Snow Queen.' Thor hoisted her onto his hip and turned for the house.

Over his shoulder Ingrid could see the next luminous wave of light, this one a green curtain drifting across the sky. 'Mommo!' she cried, her arms outstretched.

Ingrid shivered at the memory, so long ago but still vivid. She came from Vikings on both sides. It was in her blood to know the deep winter of the Poles and the gift of the aurora to make the long night bearable.

She'd grown up, too, with the legend of the Snow Queen, ruler of the snowflakes, whose kiss made people forget so she could lure them to her ice palace in the far north and keep them prisoner. It seemed Ingrid had known even as a child that she was one of those who could never resist the siren call of the snow.

The flakes began to fall more heavily and Ingrid shook her head. The memory of Mommo was one she didn't want to call up. She turned towards the house. Through a crack in the curtains she could see the light in the upstairs bedroom. She pulled her hood around her face and started back up the path.

Since Wall Street had crashed in 1929, the world was changing so rapidly that Ingrid had trouble keeping track. She'd always stayed informed about the whaling industry, on which their fortunes rested, but now that she realised the depth of Lars's worry – and that he'd kept it hidden from her – she made an effort to pay greater attention to it when they returned to Sandefjord.Whale oil had become the cheapest fat to use in producing soap and margarine, and while other industries foundered, deep-sea whaling in the Southern Ocean boomed straight after the crash. The newly formed British company Unilever had become a buyer of such might that it could control the price of whale oil in Europe. But after the record catches of the last few seasons, there was a glut of whale oil and even Unilever, churning out Sunlight Soap and Stork Margarine, couldn't keep up. The Norwegian whalers had no choice but to capitulate when Unilever 'suggested' that the entire fleet lay up for a season so it could use the backlog.

In January's short daylight hours the view down the fjord from Ranvik was grim. When Lars left in the early morning to walk to his offices in town, the darkness was still thick. Even once the sun rose, Ingrid still felt hemmed in by her home's dark wooden walls.

One morning, several hours after he'd left, Ingrid went looking for the children, desperate for some activity. The eldest three were lazing by the fireplace with books, in the kind of winter stupor that infuriated Ingrid. She left them to their sloth, gathering the three younger ones with promises of treats. She dressed them up warmly, put them in the motorcar and set out towards town. She was the only woman in Sandefjord who drove, one of the many privileges that set her apart.

She parked near the waterfront. Lars had warned her not to go to the docks, not with the anger felt by out-of-work whaling men, but she had begun showing her resentment towards him in small acts of defiance.

In Ingrid's lifetime Sandefjord had grown from a small whaling and sealing port nestled around the harbour's edge into the centre of Norway's whaling industry in the Southern Ocean, with Lars and his contemporaries investing ample funds to extend the docklands and build a business centre. Lars's pride was the Whaling Museum, which he'd designed, funded and built in honour of his father.

For the past few years Sandefjord had bustled with activity, but this season the factory ships and their broods of catchers lay limply at anchor in the harbour, scrubbed and repaired, crisply clean, forlorn. However, the docks were far from empty. Nearly four thousand whaling men, a good number of them employed by Lars and all accustomed to toiling through the long Antarctic summer, were marooned in Sandefjord's winter. In the middle of the day, when the sun rose for a few hours, they gravitated seaward to stand in small knots, staring up at the idle ships.

When Ingrid reached the docks she let the older children run ahead, their feet thudding against the well-trodden boards jutting out in long reaches from the shore. Cato, the youngest, was still content to clasp her hand, but Soren and Sofie raced each other to the dock's end, where their father's fleet was moored. Ingrid followed them, looking up at the resupply vessel *Thorshavn*, ready for its maiden voyage, and the three gleaming factory ships, *Thorshammer*, *Solglimt* and *Falk*, less than three years old, purpose-built to navigate to the far end of the world. Lars tried to keep some of his men employed with cleaning and maintenance but there were only so many times you could polish a ship that wasn't sailing.

Ingrid turned her face skywards towards the snowflakes drifting down. Her anniversary trip with Lars had reawakened her old passion for the far south. When she thought of him boarding the fleet in the following season, her fists clenched involuntarily.

'Ouch!' Cato squirmed. 'You're hurting me.'

'Sorry, my darling.' Ingrid looked down at him. At his age, Lars had been going out on his own father's ships. Her husband was right; none of his own sons showed that promise. At five, Cato was plump and sweet, still a mother's boy. Soren, aged ten, was interested in sport, while fourteen-year-old Lars Junior was bookish. The girls, Motte and Bolle, were more than old enough for marriage. Sofie, the twelve-year-old, was the only one who showed her father's interest in the sea, but being a girl, there was no future for her in that.

'Come on,' Cato said, tugging at her.

Ingrid was aware of men falling silent as she passed. She held her head high, nodded politely in their direction and kept a tight clutch on Cato's hand. It was Lars who'd represented the Norwegian whalers in negotiations with Unilever, and Lars whose name was known all over Sandefjord as the one who'd agreed to cave in. 'The black day for whaling' was what Sandefjord's whalers called the day Lars had convinced them to let the fleet lay up for the whole season. But Ingrid thought it good for the men to see her and remember that Lars was also a father with his own children to feed. Not that the Christensens were in danger of going hungry. The only economy they'd instituted under Ranvik's graceful roof was eating margarine – and as the main producers of the whale oil that comprised it, they would have been eating the stuff no matter what the world's economic conditions.

Ahead on the dock she could see *Norvegia*'s prow. Next to the new ships, the coal-powered *Norvegia* looked old fashioned, her wooden sides battered and marked, her masts rising like toothpicks against the bulk of the factory ships, her squat funnel laughably small. But on her unassuming lines rested their hopes. For three seasons now, under command of Captain Hjalmar Riiser-Larsen, heir apparent to the great Norwegian explorers Nansen and Amundsen, the little ship had gone south with the whaling fleet in search of Antarctic lands and seas that Norway could claim as its own.

Soren and Sofie, running ahead, had reached *Norvegia* and were dancing up and down on the dock, waving. Ingrid picked up her pace to reach them, pulling Cato past a group of men who stood together in sullen silence. Their eyes seemed to burn into her and as she drew level with them she heard the wet sound of spittle hit the ground.

Norway's whaling men were usually polite and the shock of it stopped her in her tracks. Ingrid turned on her heel to face them, pulling Cato close.

'Is there something you wanted to say to me?'

They all stared at the ground but for one, younger than the rest, who refused to look away. Ingrid took a few steps closer.

'I don't think I know you, Sir.'

'I'm Erik Petersen,' he said, without lifting his cap.

'Mrs Ingrid Christensen. You look like a man who'll speak his mind.'

He shrugged. 'Your youngsters are fat and well, while ours are thin. We hear your husband's doing very nicely from Unilever while we're laid off with nothing.'

Ingrid swallowed. 'I can assure you,' she said, working to keep her voice steady, 'that we're getting nothing from Unilever either. My husband is working day and night to make sure the fleet goes next year, or we will all truly starve.'

'What's to stop us starving this season?' he demanded, his voice rising.

From the corner of her eye Ingrid could see movement and a quick glance confirmed that other men were gathering around them. Lars was right, she realised, in trying to keep her away from here. She hadn't realised how strongly sentiment was running against him.

'Mama!' Cato said, tugging at her arm.

She straightened. 'Mr Petersen, if you or your family are in need, then come and see my husband in person.'

A menacing murmur rose around her and Cato shrank against her legs. Ingrid sensed the circle closing; felt a prickle of sweat under her arms.

'What about the rest of us?' a voice called above the muttering. 'You'll feed all of us? Or just bolt your doors up there while we freeze?'

Ingrid turned, trying to find the speaker. Some instinct told her not to show fear. 'Why yes, I will feed you all if that's what's needed,' she said, projecting her voice.

There was silence and then a voice rang out from the back. 'How dare you!'

Ingrid tried not to show her relief as the men parted and Hjalmar pushed through to join her in the centre of the circle. But when she saw Sofie and Soren holding his hands, their faces afraid, her heart sank. It was a terrible gamble for Captain Riiser-Larsen, as now Lars Christensen's three youngest were all at the crowd's mercy. She hoped his judgment was sound.

'When has Lars Christensen *not* looked after his men?' Hjalmar said loudly, turning on the spot to look at the crowd. 'It's not his fault the fleet is grounded. He's kept the industry going through two years of depression. You should be grateful. Shame on you, speaking this way to his wife and children!'

Ingrid saw some of them shift their feet and look away, embarrassed. In the main they were good men, she knew; just desperate.

'My husband and I will organise more assistance for the men of our fleet,' she called, pressing the advantage. 'There'll be food here tomorrow for all families.'

'You heard her,' Hjalmar said. 'Be here tomorrow, or send your wives. Now let Mrs Christensen and her children pass.'

The men stepped back, some of them shamefaced. Hjalmar gestured for her to precede him. Soren and Sofie took her arm and Cato clutched her hand tighter as she forced herself to walk calmly through the crowd in the direction of town. Ingrid felt between her shoulder blades the gaze of every man watching their retreat.

'I want to go home,' Cato said, his lip trembling.

'What a good idea,' Hjalmar said brightly. 'I think it's time for hot chocolate, don't you, Mrs Christensen? I'll come up the hill with you and have one too. Now, children, who can be the first to the shore?' He gave them a gentle push and they took off with a squeal, half pleasure, half terror.

'Did you mean what you said about food?' he asked when they were out of earshot.

'Of course!' Ingrid said, more sharply than she intended.

'You'll need more than a one-off. Perhaps a soup kitchen?'

'Sandefjord men won't go to a soup kitchen.'

'You lose your pride when you're hungry, especially if your children are hungry. They'll send the women. And perhaps you should stay away.'

Ingrid raised her chin. 'On the contrary, I should come more often. If we're talking a soup kitchen, I'll be here running it. If they see me every day, this kind of talk can't get out of hand.'

'I'm not sure of that,' he said. 'But it would be a good investment for your husband to keep them fed.'

'They're people, Hjalmar, not an investment.'

'Of course. I know just how they feel, anyway. Bored and cold and chafing to go south. Remember, Ingrid, we chase the sun. Some of these men haven't seen more than three hours of darkness for years. They don't know how to cope with the long nights any more.'

'Well, all our hopes rest on you next season,' she said. 'Find us some coastline that Norway can claim.'

'It's no good if Lars doesn't have a buyer for the oil.'

One thing she'd learned from Lars was that appearances were everything in business. Ingrid covered her worry with a laugh. 'Unilever will need oil again by next year,' she said, more confidently than she felt.

'Let's hope so.' Hjalmar pulled his long-stemmed pipe from his pocket. 'I need something to do, Mrs Christensen. The Air Force has some work for me and, to tell the truth, I wouldn't mind flying. I can't sit here drumming my fingers all year either.'

Ingrid's heart sank. Even Hjalmar was abandoning them. It occurred to her, for the first time, that the whole whaling industry really might fail, not just the small operators. Other industries around the world had fallen after the Wall Street crash, but whaling had cushioned Norway from the worst of its effects until now.

Lars would survive, she felt sure. Although whaling was his biggest investment, his interests included shipping, the stock market and hydro electricity, and he was never short of a new idea. But without whaling, she would never have a chance to travel south.

She looked over at Hjalmar as he began fiddling with his pipe. I should have married an explorer, not a businessman, she thought. It was an old regret, stretching back to her teenage years, but it had resurfaced this winter.

Then Cato came running back to her, his cheeks flushed, the fright of the crowd forgotten. He threw himself against her legs. 'Mama! Sofie's teasing me!'

Ingrid bent down and put her arms around him. He snuggled in, pressing his face to her neck, burrowing into her as if the rest of the world didn't exist. She breathed in his sweet, soapy scent.

She wished it were enough. It never had been.

CHAPTER 2

Mathilde looked down at the straggle of snowdrops clutched in Ole's small fist, their petals drooping.

'Here, Mama,' he said.

'Thank you, darling.' She reached for them.

Ole drew his hand back. 'Not for you. For Papa.'

Mathilde checked herself and took a breath against the pain of the words. 'We'll take them tomorrow.'

'No. Now.' Ole looked up, his chin jutting out. Mathilde had to look away from that stern expression, a miniature of his grandfather glaring at her.

'But we went yesterday,' she said.

'Now.'

Mathilde sighed and the fight, what little there was of it, ran out of her. 'Oh, all right. Where's your sister?'

The three of them left the house by the back path, bundled up against the cool afternoon. Ole held the gate open for her and then ran ahead, trailing petals. Aase clutched her hand. Mathilde could have walked the path with her eyes closed. Every step of their way was imprinted on her body, along with the feeling of Aase's childish weight at the end of her arm, and the hole that lived in her chest, weighing down her footfalls.

At the cemetery Ole brushed the snow off the gravestone and laid the bedraggled bouquet next to Jakob's name. Both children turned and wandered off while Mathilde stared at the unchanging surface of the black granite. She wished she could weep. At least tears would bring some kind of temporary relief, a sense of something happening. A second winter had almost passed since Jakob was killed in Venezuela – a place that sounded so exotic she simply couldn't form a mental picture of it – and it had been no easier than the first. Time heals, everyone said, but time was doing no such thing. Time led to more time, more empty time stretching ahead, years of time to be filled.

In an attempt to help herself and the children move on, Mathilde had cut back on their daily cemetery visits. Now it was only every second day they climbed the hill to lay flowers or nuts or sweets on Jakob's grave. But it seemed the children couldn't imagine a life beyond this either. All three of them were frozen fast in the small world of Sandefjord. It was just as well that her mother's grave was on the island of Nøtterøy, Mathilde thought. It would have been too hard to have all her losses laid in the same ground.

Ole and Aase eventually came back to her. Ole took her hand with a sternness she would have found heartbreaking if she'd had any heart left to break.

'Let's go to Grandpa's,' he said, tugging at her.

'Not today.'

'Please!' the children begged in unison.

She gazed down at their faces. They looked afraid at the prospect of another long, dark afternoon alone with her and the fact of their fear cut into her. They pulled, one on either hand, and against their combined weight she stumbled and took a step. Their faces lit up at their success and she took another and another, and before she knew it the steps had led out of the cemetery and down the steep hill and then along the winding street to the house of Jakob's parents, Ole Senior and Gerd.

Gerd's face was unsmiling when she opened the door to

Mathilde. She looked out and up at the afternoon sky. 'I didn't expect you.'

'Grandma! We found snowdrops!' Ole said, dropping Mathilde's hand and pushing forward. 'Have you got buns for us?'

Gerd gave them the smile she reserved for her grandchildren and they pushed past her into the house.

Mathilde was marooned on the doorstep. She made a hopeless movement with her hands. 'I'm sorry. They wanted to come. I couldn't seem to stop them.'

Gerd opened the door wider and gestured for her to come in. Mathilde passed her and went through to the parlour, warm and smelling faintly of cooking, so unlike her own, and she wondered if she should agree after all to leave the children with their grandparents. Gerd asked often enough. Perhaps not realising the children were the only thing keeping her alive. Or perhaps she did realise.

'You should start teaching again,' Gerd said when the maid had poured out coffee and laid down a plate of fruit buns, lavishly spread with margarine.

Mathilde took a mouthful of coffee, scalding herself. Their visits, like all of her days, ran to a routine and she had to steel herself to repeat the same sentences. 'Soon,' she murmured. It was a lie: she'd never sing again, let alone teach anyone else.

'The Christensens were here today,' Gerd continued. 'Asking after you. Ingrid said you don't answer the door.'

'Of course I do,' Mathilde said. 'I must have been out.'

'They want you to come to dinner next weekend. She asked me to pass on the invitation.'

'I don't think so,' Mathilde said. 'I'll be with the children.'

'We'll have the children here,' Gerd said. 'It's a hard time for us too, Mathilde, without Jakob. We'd like to see more of the little ones. You should go.'

Mathilde put down the bun she was nibbling. Her hand was thin and her wedding ring hung so loosely on her finger that she had to be careful not to lose it. 'I'm not ready for dinner parties.'

Gerd poured her more coffee. 'You can't go on like this. It's not healthy for the children.'

Mathilde nodded and sipped her drink. She could feel it travelling down her throat, hot and alive, and her body felt dead in comparison.

'Leave them here tonight,' Gerd said.

Without the children to fill her empty kitchen, Mathilde was terrified of the merciless night approaching. She looked up at Gerd in mute appeal.

'Have a rest,' Gerd said. 'A break from cooking. Put your feet up. Read a book.'

'No, I –'

'You'll be fine. Go on, while it's light. Come back for them in the morning.'

Mathilde hardly knew how she came to be standing out on the street in the gathering twilight, alone, the fur of her collar failing to keep out the cold, and the front door of the Wegger house firmly closed. She wondered if she'd come back in the morning to find her in-laws had left in the night and spirited the children away, leaving a barred door and an empty house.

She shook her head to dispel the thought. Foolish. Ole Wegger was one of Sandefjord's pillars, one of the town's coterie of powerful businessmen, a tight group with fingers in the pie of every industry and interests stretching far beyond Sandefjord, or even Norway. Not the sort to slip away in the night.

Poor dead Jakob had expected to be one of them, though his progress had been slower than he'd hoped. She wondered if he'd have succeeded. Jakob was a good man, and clever, in his way, but he was old fashioned and, she had to admit, staid. You only had to look at Lars Christensen to see his entrepreneurial mind and inexhaustible energy. Jakob's own father, Ole, was another powerhouse of ideas and drive, but Jakob wasn't like that.

She felt weariness stealing over her at the thought of Lars and Ingrid, their busy household, their dizzying achievements, their flock of attractive children. It was true; she shushed Ole and Aase and crawled under the table when Ingrid came knocking. The glare of her sympathy was too brilliant.

A motorcar came down the road, its headlights boring into her, and the toot of its horn made her jump. She stepped onto the pavement to let it pass. The long twilight lay heavily on the afternoon, the temperature dropping. She could see down to the docks, crowded with Sandefjord's whaling ships. Every last one had been forced to stay in port for the season. Sandefjord's married women all had their husbands for winter.

Mathilde started walking, her hands thrust deep in her pockets, her head down. The air was full of white dots, minuscule precursors to snowflakes. She reached the house and opened the front door. She'd let their one maid go after Jakob died, ostensibly for the cost, but in reality because she couldn't bear another adult observing her. It should be possible, she thought, to turn on the electric lights, to start the fire, to cook something. There was nothing physically stopping her. But stepping into the empty house sucked the life out of her. When the children were there with her, she was numb and heavy, without energy. In their absence, her grief became acute; paralysing.

By the bed, Jakob glared at her from his photograph. He jutted out his chin just as Ole had today, but in truth Ole was carved from the same block as his grandfather, while Jakob, sandwiched between them, was simply the means to an end. Mathilde let her coat fall to the floor, kicked off her shoes and sat on the edge of the bed, looking at his photograph. What would he have her do to start something resembling a life again, she thought, with a slight stirring of the emotion she remembered as anger. But he had no answer for her, not even a smile, just his slightly anxious face and the way he clenched his teeth together to appear strong. She'd let him keep his pride and together they'd maintained the fiction that he was stepping up to his father's expectations and would one day be his equal.

Did he ever know that she loved his vulnerability? Her favourite times were those when he came to her in the privacy of their room and let his guard down. Sometimes, when worry kept him awake, he'd allow her to draw his head down to her breast and hold it there while she sang him a lullaby. It was something they never referred to outside the marriage bed, but it was the time she loved him most, she thought.

Mathilde pulled the covers back and slid into the bed's cold embrace, not bothering to undress. A widow at thirty-six; not what she'd expected. She'd always been conventional in her life's hopes, believing if she didn't ask for too much, she'd have more chance of it coming to her. She wouldn't have cared if Jakob had never risen higher than managing some unimportant arm of his family's empire. She could have been perfectly happy with the four of them living in their little cottage on the hill, taking Ole and Aase on the boat trip to Nøtterøy to visit her family every few months and making do with a single housemaid for the rest of their lives.

But just weeks after Jakob's accident Mathilde's mother had died too, and her father had hastily remarried, taking in a flock of step-children and a wife who wanted little to do with Mathilde. Whatever haven she thought her old family home may have offered was gone. Gerd and Ole, her parents-in-law, were the closest family she had left.

She reached out, took hold of the picture and brought the hard rectangle of the frame to her chest. As she wrapped her arms across it, slowly the cold thing began to warm. Perhaps Gerd was right. Mathilde wondered if she even remembered how to sing after so long. Jakob had loved the lullaby that Mathilde sang to put the children to sleep, the one that whispered of the dangers in the dark forest and the safety behind the stout walls and the heavy door, barred fast. She took a breath and opened her mouth.

A single note came out, pure and shocking, and she stopped and swallowed. There wasn't room in the house for beauty. Not yet. She tightened her arms around the picture and lay down.

Spring would be coming soon. The snowdrops were already poking their heads through the ground. Daylight was inching back into her life and Mathilde dreaded its coming. Spring meant she'd have to do something to rebuild her life without Jakob. Another winter like this would kill her.

CHAPTER 3

Lillemor glanced around to see if there was anyone famous in the lounge before she sat down. A week earlier Virginia Woolf had been taking tea by the fire. Last month Eleanor Rathbone, whose parliamentary speech about clitoridectomy in India was still being talked about two years after she'd given it, had smoked a cigarette in this very chair.

But it was a quiet afternoon in London's Women's Service House. Over in the corner Freda was dozing by the fire. As far as fame went, Freda's was long gone. Unhappiness was carving permanent grooves on her face and she looked much older than her fifty years.

Lillemor took a deep breath, relieved to be away from the sight of the slums and food queues that had sprung up all over London since the crash and showed no signs of disappearing. She crossed over to the fire and sank into the firm leather of the Chesterfield armchair next to Freda. The maid was by her side in moments with a decanter of whisky, a box of Havana cigarillos, her mail and the day's newspaper on a platter.

Lillemor stretched her legs out and lit a cigarillo, trying to dismiss the thought that they were all play-acting. Barred from the world of men's clubs, she – and all of them – could only guess how to act in the inner sanctum of London's only club for women. But warming cold feet by the fire, relaxing into the leather and enjoying one of the small, slender cigars that had become so scarce of late – well, surely that was what the men did too, wasn't it?

Lillemor pursed her lips and sent a stream of fine Havana in Freda's direction, until those sad eyelids opened. Lillemor clipped another cigarillo and passed it over.

'And how was your day at work, dear?' Freda asked after the first puff. 'Hand out plenty of dutch caps?'

'Fifteen. Much good may it do those poor women.' Lillemor stared at the fire and shivered. Her charity work in the Mothers' Clinic kept her occupied and feeling useful, but she couldn't see it having much effect. 'Things aren't getting any better, Freda. What's going to happen to them?'

'We all die in the end.' Freda swallowed the last of her whisky and waved for another. 'Don't start on me,' she said, giving Lillemor a warning look.

'Why not? Otherwise you'll sit here and drink yourself to death.'

'I'd rather do that than ladle slop for people who feel even worse than me. I admire you, Lillemor, but I can't do it. I suspect you won't do it much longer either.'

'I'll be doing it forever at this rate.' Lillemor reached for the tray of letters and picked up the opener to slit the first one.

'Still getting your post here? Anton will think you've got something to hide.'

Lillemor ignored her. Freda had had much more of Lillemor's attention before she married Anton the previous year, and was now making her disdain for him clear.

The letter was from Sarah Clegg of Women's Service House, inviting her to meet Miss Amelia Earhart on her brief visit to London.

Apologies for the short notice, Sarah wrote, *but I'm sure our members will leap at the chance to meet Miss Earhart in person for afternoon tea at the House tomorrow before she returns to America after her epic solo flight across the Atlantic.*

She'd scribbled a postscript: *Lillemor, my dear, could you bring your camera and take some photographs? The press will be here but we'd love some snaps for the album.*

'Have a look at this.' Lillemor passed the letter to Freda and picked up the newspaper.

Freda read it and shrugged. 'Photographer, eh? I suppose you'll have to go.'

'Oh, don't be so tedious,' Lillemor said, unfolding *The Times*. 'Of course I'm going. Surely you want to meet her?'

'Not really.' Freda looked away.

Lillemor tried to catch her eye. 'I believe the English phrase is "Buck up old chap".'

'It's Muriel's birthday today,' Freda said.

'Oh, I'm sorry.' Lillemor reached over and laid her hand on Freda's arm. The English would never do such a thing but they were both expatriates – Lillemor from Norway and Freda from Australia. They could take the occasional liberty.

'Ladies! Have you seen who's coming for tea?'

They both jumped. Marie had approached without their hearing her. She sat down in the third chair at the fireplace, waving her invitation.

Lillemor smiled at her. Though she must have been Freda's age at least, Marie Stopes was still notorious for her radical books on sexuality and contraception. Lillemor had particular reason to be grateful for her work.

'Isn't it exciting?' Marie said.

'Wonderful,' Freda muttered. 'Another brilliant creature for Lillemor to worship.'

Lillemor rolled her eyes and gave Marie a rueful grin to mask how the comment smarted. Freda knew her too well.

'Oh, stop it!' Marie waved her hand at Freda. 'You can't keep Lillemor all to yourself. Why shouldn't she worship Amelia

Earhart? The woman's just made the whole world sit up and take notice.'

'Exactly,' Lillemor said.

'You've got to stop hanging around other women who've achieved something and get out there for yourself, Lil,' Freda said.

'It's all right for you; you've made your firsts.' Lillemor drew away from Freda. 'And anyway, what's wrong with wanting to do something first for its own sake? I notice men never get castigated for it.'

'I wanted to climb,' Freda said. 'Earhart wants to fly. Marie wanted to write. What comes first is the thing you love doing.'

Lillemor was silent. If anyone other than Freda had spoken to her like that, she'd have walked off. But Freda was the closest thing she had to a best friend here in London, and Lillemor had learned to put up with Freda's bluntness. She waved to a passing maid and gestured for another round of drinks.

'Don't let Freda deter you,' Marie said at last. 'You're a young woman in a new era. Don't give up.'

The drinks arrived and Lillemor was pleased for the momentary distraction. She accepted another single malt, but it failed to quell the flutter of anxiety in her belly. She was thirty, not that young, and time was running out.

It was six years since she'd seen the photograph that had set her on this path. An image of Louise Arner Boyd on her first trip to the Arctic in 1926. Dressed in heavyweight clothing and grasping a rifle, Louise was standing in the embrace of a dead polar bear, hung by its neck so it towered above her, its full size apparent. The photograph was titled 'The girl who captured the Arctic'.

That damned woman had come into her massive inheritance when she turned twenty, and could simply outfit herself as a polar explorer and head to Greenland. Lillemor was at once jealous and admiring. She wanted to be the one standing there with a hunting trophy and a rifle, gazing calmly at the camera, dressed for anything. But Arner Boyd had claimed the Arctic as her own, going back there on several more trips and even now planning further exploration. Freda had encouraged Lillemor to apply to be included, but Lillemor knew there was only room for one 'Arctic Diana', as the press had dubbed Boyd.

Lillemor had to go south if she wanted to be first. The South Pole had long been conquered, but the British still spoke about Robert Falcon Scott in reverent tones, as if he had beaten Amundsen after all. The maps of the southern land were still mostly blank and in spite of the rush of discoveries made before the war, most of the continent was unseen by humans. All she had to do was make landfall and she could be 'the girl who captured the Antarctic'.

But she had no chance of being included in a British expedition. They still held to their quaint model of gentlemanly exploration, running fundraising evenings, setting sail in old wooden ships and leaving their women well and truly behind. Her own countrymen were more pragmatic, travelling south in enormous steel vessels and paying for their travels by harvesting whales. The Americans, like Richard Byrd, simply flew.

Perhaps it was the Americans she should emulate. They seemed to have a knack for making things happen. Look at Miss Earhart.

The late spring afternoon was closing in on London by the time Miss Earhart walked into the lounge. They'd waited nearly two hours and the second round of tea was being served. Lillemor strained to spot her through the crowd.

Miss Earhart looked tired but exhilarated. Just two days earlier she'd landed her Lockheed Vega in a pasture in Ireland. She'd come across to London by boat to celebrate being the first woman to fly solo over the Atlantic. The picture in *The Times* had shown her in a flying outfit, dashingly handsome in her leather bomber jacket and pants, with her goggles and helmet. Lillemor felt a stab of disappointment when she saw Miss Earhart was dressed in a plain dark frock with a pale shirt underneath. She could have been any of them, though at least she was bareheaded among the crowd of cloche hats.

Sarah Clegg had organised this reception at Women's Service House in her own record-breaking time so that London's leading suffragists, with little to do now they'd had the vote for four years, could feel important again. It naturally fell to her to step forward and hold her hand out to Miss Earhart. They shook hands like men, and to Lillemor's eyes the gesture still looked a little shocking.

If Miss Earhart was uncomfortable with a roomful of women staring at her, she showed no sign of it. She nodded and smiled at Sarah and glanced around the room at the rest of them. She had short, tousled hair and freckles scattered across her nose. She looked exactly like the tomboy Lillemor had imagined her to be.

'Here they come,' Freda said, fanning herself. 'I don't know why Sarah invited me. I can't think of a thing to say to the woman.'

'You'll be fine,' Marie said. 'Why don't you suggest to Miss Earhart that she take Lillemor and fly to Antarctica?'

Lillemor's heart was racing. 'Don't you say anything,' she said. She put her shoulders back to appear taller and made herself smile as Sarah led Miss Earhart up to them.

'Miss Earhart, I'm pleased to present Miss Du Faur, the first woman to climb Mount Cook in New Zealand and the first person ever to climb Mount Dampier,' Sarah said.

Trust her to have memorised Freda's achievements, Lillemor thought, as though Sarah could reflect in Freda's glory. But she couldn't help a moment of jealousy as Miss Earhart's face lit up.

'Why I've heard of you, of course, Miss Du Faur,' she said. 'A real adventurer. Not like me, who only has to sit on her bottom and stay awake.'

Sarah and Lillemor laughed politely. Freda shook Miss Earhart's hand. 'We all know it took much more than that,' she said without smiling.

There was an awkward pause. Since her Muriel had died in such terrible circumstances, Freda had lost her ability to make pleasant conversation. For a moment Lillemor saw, in Miss Earhart, how Freda must have been, delighting and scandalising the world as she scaled New Zealand's wildest peaks in her skirts and knickerbockers. But that was twenty years ago and Freda was an old woman now, or at least looked like one.

Sarah smiled determinedly. 'It's an honour to introduce you to our famous author, Dr Marie Stopes,' she said, presenting Marie. 'You've no doubt heard of *Married Love*?'

'Of course I know your work very well, Dr Stopes,' Miss Earhart said, 'since my husband's company publishes your book in the United States. He says your work has changed the world. So much more important than flying.'

Marie shook Miss Earhart's hand. 'On the contrary, your adventures are so important for our younger women. I'm too old now to do such things, but women like Lillemor will be following the trail you've blazed.'

Sarah smiled and gestured to Lillemor. 'This is Mrs Lillemor Rachlew, from Norway, who's doing such wonderful charity work here in Dr Stopes' Mothers' Clinic.'

Miss Earhart held out her hand and Lillemor took it, wishing desperately for an interesting way of announcing herself. She had one claim on Miss Earhart's attention only, and in her nervousness she blurted it out at once. 'We're so thrilled you made it safely. My countryman Bernt Balchen, I believe, gave you some assistance.'

'You know Bernt?' Miss Earhart said, interested. 'What a darling man. He did the most wonderful refurbishment of Old Bessie so she could make the trip. And he threw the press off my trail.'

'Really? How did he do that?' Sarah asked.

'Oh, he pretended he was flying Bessie to the Arctic himself, and they left him alone. Worked wonders. I got to take off without the pack snapping at my heels. What an aviator! You must be so proud.'

'Yes,' Lillemor said, hoping there'd be no further questions about Bernt, who she'd never, in fact, met.

Miss Earhart turned to Freda. 'Are you still climbing, Miss Du Faur?'

Freda shook her head. 'The war made it hard, and my dear friend was ill for the last few years.'

'Yes, very sad,' Sarah said hastily. 'And now, Miss Earhart, do come and meet Mrs Furness.'

She directed Miss Earhart firmly away from them. Lillemor took Freda's arm and gave it a squeeze. She'd only met Freda after Muriel's death and though she'd heard their relationship was fairly discreet, most of the women involved in the suffrage movement were keen to distance themselves from lesbians. Many lesbians themselves stayed safely undercover, Lillemor knew, and plenty of women from the club acted scandalised when Radclyffe Hall dressed in a suit, took her lover, Lady Trowbridge, to the Lyric Theatre without any apparent shame.

'Well,' Lillemor said, 'you never told me her husband published your books.'

'You never asked,' Marie replied. 'I'm surprised she remembered though. She's certainly a rising star. Come on, Freda; let's get a cup of tea. Why don't you take some photographs, Lillemor?'

Lillemor remembered that her camera was in her bag and cursed herself for not having had it ready. She'd bought the Beau Brownie when she applied for Mawson's expedition, but had hardly used it, though its workings were simple enough. It was time she got more confident with it. She took another cup of the damned tea that the English always served on such occasions and a tasteless cucumber and margarine sandwich, wishing for a strong Norwegian coffee and a cake with some substance to it.

She watched Miss Earhart being steered around the room. There was something different about her, something more than dress, and Lillemor studied her to see what it was. The English women held their bodies stiffly upright, as though the posture had been bred into them over generations. They took small steps and kept their elbows close to their sides. They held their teacups at breast level, and took polite sips.

Miss Earhart had a lanky elegance about her, moving her body as though she was unconscious of the space it took up. She reached without forethought to take a sandwich and ate it in a few bites. She laughed often, her face opening up and her wide grin showing the gap between her front teeth.

Lillemor liked Americans. She liked the way they took on everything with their loud confidence, secure in the knowledge that their way was best. She envied Bernt the chance to work in

America and rub shoulders with the great aviators like Amelia Earhart and Richard Byrd, while she merely did the kind of charity work that a diplomatic wife of means should do.

Lillemor looked across the room. Miss Earhart had turned to reach for a sandwich and their eyes met. For a moment she was unattended. This was her chance.

Lillemor straightened up and approached her. 'Miss Earhart?'

'Please,' Amelia pressed a hand on her arm, 'it's Amelia. We're more casual in America.'

Lillemor opened her bag and took out the camera. 'Sarah asked me to take some photographs. Do you mind?'

'Of course not.' Amelia put down her cup of tea, clasped her hands and grinned in a practised manner.

Lillemor balanced the Beau Brownie, peered down into the viewfinder and pressed the lever. She looked up. 'I want to be the first woman in Antarctica,' she said.

Amelia nodded. 'Excellent. Bernt told me about flying over the South Pole. Antarctica sounds like an extraordinary adventure. How do you intend to get there?'

'That's the problem,' Lillemor said. 'No one will take a woman. I asked to be included in Mawson's Antarctic expedition in 1929 but he didn't even bother replying.'

'Did you offer him money?' Amelia asked, with a smile.

Lillemor shook her head. 'I have some means, but not that much.'

'Could Bernt help you?'

Lillemor shrugged. 'I'm not an aviator. I'd just be luggage.'

'I was just luggage on my first Atlantic flight,' Amelia said. 'I hated it. Better to find a way where you can be doing something. Do you have any skills?'

What Lillemor was best at was making men do her bidding, but it wasn't working in relation to Antarctica. She wondered if

Amelia had the same skill. She wished she dared propose that she and Amelia fly to Antarctica together, a female Norwegian–American duo matching the feat of Bernt Balchen and Richard Byrd in overflying the South Pole, but she didn't have the nerve.

'I can make soup and feed the starving. But there's not many of them in Antarctica.'

'What about photography?'

'I suppose I can use a Beau Brownie,' Lillemor said.

Amelia gave her such a thump on the shoulder that Lillemor jumped. 'Excellent! You must go as a photographer, Mrs ...'

'Call me Lillemor. I prefer my own name.'

'Me too. The press tries to call me Mrs Putnam, but I won't have it.' Amelia leaned close. 'Become the best photographer you can, Lillemor. Learn to write too. The public is hungry for stories of far-off places. I fund most of my flying through public relations, with the help of my husband. You may convince a newspaper to support your cause.'

Sarah bustled over. 'Excuse me, Lillemor, if you don't mind. Miss Earhart hasn't met everyone yet.'

Lillemor stood back. 'Goodbye, Amelia.'

Amelia winked. 'I'll look forward to reading about you.'

She walked away and Lillemor gazed after her. Amelia carried in a new era on her slight shoulders. She'd crossed the entire ocean between England and America. The first woman and only the second person to do it. Was that what glowed out of her in such a way, Lillemor wondered. Amelia had touched the very sky, and it showed.

CHAPTER 4

'Please stop this,' Lars said in the dark, across the chasm that their marriage bed had become.

Ingrid stayed still, facing away from him.

He sighed heavily. 'I know you're awake.' His hand reached across the sheets towards her.

She drew away from him. 'I don't want another child.'

'Can we at least discuss it?'

'No.'

Lars threw back the blankets. 'God! You could drive a man to desperate acts.'

'What, Lars?' she snapped. 'Force? Infidelity? What did you have in mind?'

He gave a bitter laugh. 'Infidelity? I'm afraid that's your side of the family.'

She kicked out across the bed, catching him in the shin. 'How dare you!'

'You can't deny your father's bastards are all over town. I don't think even he knew how many.'

'You know nothing about it,' she said.

He sat up and faced her. 'When I took over the firm, do you know how many of Thor's women were on the books quietly receiving a cheque every month? Five, Ingrid. I thought I'd spare you the details, but perhaps I should have told you then.'

Ingrid got out of bed. 'Perhaps you should follow his example.

Get yourself a mistress and see if she can give you a better son than the ones you've got.'

'You're twisting what I said.'

'I'm not. You want to keep me like a brood mare till you get your perfect young stallion. You've got six fine children, Lars. Enough!'

'And you've never wanted for anything,' he said. 'I've never said no to you, no matter what you've asked for. So I say to you, enough!'

Ingrid stamped across the room. 'I should have waited for Amundsen rather than marrying you!' She slammed the door behind her, not caring if she woke the children.

'Amundsen was never going to marry you!' Lars bellowed after her.

'That's what you think,' she muttered, pulling her dressing gown closed and heading downstairs.

She wished it was snowing. She wanted to run outside and get lost, disappear into it like her mother had. But it was a spring night out there, far too warm and pleasant.

She halted in front of her father's portrait on the wall of the big lounge room, his long face a white blur in the dark. For all his faults, he was the only man who hadn't broken a promise to her.

She remembered her fifteenth birthday. Thor had promised her a surprise and no matter how much she'd pestered, he wouldn't reveal it. He'd smiled enigmatically and told her to be patient. When she tried again, he simply raised an eyebrow. 'I hope you can show you're worthy of it.'

Ingrid refused to let herself hope the surprise might be her mother returning. Nothing eventuated on the morning of her birthday, just a handful of presents of the ordinary kind, and a twinkle in Thor's eye. She'd been packed off to school without ceremony and found it hard to concentrate on her lessons. The attentions of her friends, usually so welcome, became irritating so that she snapped at them and walked home alone.

Her sister Alvhild was at the gate, jiggling from one foot to the other, when Ingrid got to the house, her face chilled from the autumn air.

'You'll never guess who's here,' Alvhild said.

'Who?'

'I'm not allowed to tell.'

'Well, be quiet then.' Ingrid pushed past her and started down the path.

'You'd better put on a smile,' Alvhild taunted, following close behind. 'Father will be cross if you're in a temper.'

Ingrid rounded on her. 'Shut up, I said!'

'Ingrid!' Her father's voice was loud and Ingrid shrank. She hated to cause his anger but sometimes she couldn't help it.

'Father?'

He glared at her from the doorstep. 'I thought you were adult enough for this, but perhaps I was wrong.'

'I'm adult enough,' she said, raising her chin. 'For what, anyway?'

He shook his head in resignation. 'Only to meet one of our greatest living Norwegians.'

Her irritation fell away at once. 'Who? Nansen?'

A man stepped out from behind her father. He was too young to be Fridtjof Nansen, her long-time hero, and she felt a stab of disappointment.

'She's not a dissembler, that's for sure,' the man laughed. 'I'm sorry to be such a letdown, Miss Dahl.'

'Let me introduce Roald Amundsen, who has kindly consented to join us for your birthday dinner,' her father said. 'Go and change, and I trust your manners will improve before you rejoin us.'

Chastened, Ingrid escaped to her room. Roald Amundsen, having at last found the fabled route through the Northwest Passage, was almost as famous as the great Nansen, anyway. She flicked through her wardrobe looking for something to wear, but her best outfit was a child's dress, frilled and ruffled. She was fifteen and this was her night. She was too old for such a frock.

Ingrid crept quietly into her father's bedroom. Her mother's dresses still hung in his closet, dusty and unused. She rifled through them. She knew what she was looking for, and felt a thrill when her fingers met the white silk. She took the dress back to her room, flung off her school clothes and drew the dress over her head. She pulled her auburn hair out of its plaits and brushed it with her mother's fine hairbrush, until it cascaded over her shoulders. She squeezed her feet into a pair of her mother's shoes that were half a size too small and then faced the mirror.

She'd grown in the past six months and in an adult's dress she could see the woman she'd become. The white silk showed off her long red hair and small waist. She wanted to show Amundsen how capable she was, not how pretty, but she didn't know how. She longed for her mother with a sudden pang. She'd lived without her for years now, but Thor hadn't seemed to notice that she'd become a young woman and that some female guidance, as she stepped into womanhood, would be a welcome thing.

Ingrid ran her hand down the sides of the dress, squared her shoulders and went downstairs. The surprise on Roald Amundsen's face made up for her father's shock and his unspoken promise of later punishment. She saw, for the first time, how a man looked at a woman when he appreciated her and it was a heady experience. She felt her colour rise as it seemed he couldn't look away from her and she was grateful when her father proposed a toast to Amundsen's Northwest Passage success and they drank it enthusiastically. Amundsen must have been well over thirty, twice her age, but she couldn't help sneaking sideways glances at him.

'Your father tells me you want to be an explorer,' Amundsen said as they sat for dinner and the servants began bringing in the first course.

'Ingrid is *kjekk og frisk jente*,' Alvhild broke in importantly. 'Wants to be a girl *and* a boy.'

Amundsen picked up his glass. 'I understand such girls can be adventurous without losing their womanliness,' he said to Alvhild. 'A very good thing, I would say.'

When Ingrid looked up, Amundsen gave her a quick wink and she smiled gratefully. 'I want to go to the South Pole, Mr Amundsen.'

He smiled back at her. 'Antarctica is a very long way off. What about the North Pole? It will be won very soon, I think. I'm planning to reach it myself, and there are plenty of others trying too.'

Ingrid shook her head. She'd known for years that the tale of her mother going with the Snow Queen was no more than a story told to a child, but it had left her with a lingering dread of that region.

Amundsen put his glass down on the table. 'It's a very long way and very expensive to go to Antarctica, but I tell you what, Miss Dahl. I hope to go there too. If you still want to be an explorer when I set out for the South Pole, I'll take you with me.'

Ingrid kicked her sister triumphantly under the table and then remembered to nod in a ladylike manner and smile at him. 'I'd like that very much, Mr Amundsen.'

'We'll see,' her father had said, and then the talk turned to other things. But Amundsen had taken her hand most warmly at the end of the evening and the memory of his lips brushing her knuckles was the marker that her childhood was over.

For four years she'd waited for news that he was setting out for the South Pole. Lars Christensen, from the biggest ship-owning family in Sandefjord, tried to win her attention all that time, waiting each day to walk her to the school gates on his way to work, and accompanying her home each afternoon. But the thought of Amundsen, fuelled by his occasional friendly replies to her letters, caused her to keep Lars at arm's length.

Ingrid was almost nineteen when Amundsen wrote to say he was leaving Norway in Nansen's old ship *Fram* to try again for the North Pole. He said he still planned to head south when he came back from this trip. The thrill she felt on receiving the letter disappeared as she realised this meant waiting at least another couple of years.

Lars tried to comfort her. 'Never mind,' he said. 'I'll make it up to you.'

'I'm not getting married,' she told him. 'I'm going south with Amundsen, after he's claimed the North Pole. I don't care how long it takes.'

He shrugged and turned up again the next day, and the next. Thor looked on Lars with favour, she knew, for though he was a long way down the procession of Christensen sons, Lars showed more promise than any of his older brothers. He had the mark of a man who knew what he wanted, and how to get it.

He took the bold step of kissing her goodbye one evening and before long he'd drawn her into dizzying pre-marriage embraces that took her by surprise and rocked her resolve. They started meeting in secret at the far end of her father's garden in a secluded rock hollow and Ingrid found it harder and harder to resist him. One night when their caresses threatened to sweep her into uncharted territory, she pushed him away.

'Don't be like that,' he said. 'I want to marry you.'

'You know I won't say yes.' She could feel her chest rising and falling with her breath, and tried to stop it.

He stroked her long hair and coiled it gently around his hand. 'But Amundsen's gone south,' he said. 'Without you.'

She pulled away from him, sliding her hair out of his grip. 'Don't be silly. Everyone knows he's gone north.'

Lars shook his head. 'It's in the newspaper. Frederick Cook has beaten him to the North Pole. Amundsen's sent word that he's going to Antarctica instead, to race Robert Scott to the South Pole. Even his own crewmen didn't know. He sent Scott a telegram from Madeira saying, *Beg to inform, heading south.*'

Ingrid's lip trembled and she was alarmed to find she was about to cry in Lars's presence. She turned away. 'I don't believe you. He promised to take me.'

He took her hand and squeezed it. 'I'd never lie to you, Ingrid. But listen, I have an idea.'

She refused to look at him, but he continued. 'You and I will go to Antarctica too. I've already commissioned our ship. She's called *Polaris*, after you, my north star. Tomorrow I'll take you to the shipyards to see her. When she's finished we'll sail south and continue my father's search for Antarctic whaling grounds. You don't need to wait for Amundsen. He'll be too old to go south again, anyway.'

She turned to look at him and he drew her into his arms. 'Nothing about us will be ordinary,' he said, and pressed her body against his.

He'd won her. What choice did she have? Amundsen had left her behind and there was no other route to Antarctica that she could see. She and Lars wed within a few months.

The following year Amundsen reached the South Pole, beating Robert Scott in a race that became a legend. The explorer never married, though it was said he didn't lack for female companionship. Ingrid liked to believe he stayed a bachelor out of disappointment that she hadn't waited for him. There was no evidence for the idea, except the warmth in his eyes on the occasions she saw him over the years when Lars would invite the great explorers around to dinner or show them off at parties. Nansen, Amundsen and Riiser-Larsen: Norway's three famous sons.

She'd been bereft when Amundsen fell victim to the land of the Snow Queen four years earlier. He was a genius in the air but on a search-and-rescue mission in the north his flying boat disappeared into the fog. The fact of her long marriage to Lars and her six children didn't stop her jealousy when she read in the papers that an American heiress leading her own expedition to the Arctic had put her boat and all her personnel in the service of the rescue effort. Ingrid suspected Amundsen had been romantically involved with her. Louise Arner Boyd, an unmarried woman with a personal fortune that almost dwarfed Lars's, had spent three months and thousands of dollars sailing back and forth between Spitsbergen, Franz Josef Land and Greenland. She didn't stop until the Arctic winter came down and any hope that his party might turn up, sheltering on some remote shore of the Barents Sea, was gone.

It seemed cruel that Nansen had died too, only a couple of years later. Norway's greatest men from the days of exploration, gone. Only Hjalmar remained. One of Amundsen's best friends, and her last link to him.

Outside the window the moon had risen and Ingrid could see the long stretch of Ranvik's lawn running down to the fjord. It was true; her marriage to Lars Christensen, Consul for Denmark, shipowner and businessman, had been extraordinary in many ways. Not only was her husband the richest man in

Sandefjord – or one of the richest at least – but for twenty years she and Lars had shared almost everything. She'd counted herself lucky when she saw the unions of her contemporaries evolve into sterile affairs, where husband and wife lived in separate orbits. She'd thought that could never happen to them.

She rubbed her eyes and yawned. It was late and she was tired. She'd made her point to Lars. She wasn't going to give up on this one. She'd never forgiven Amundsen for breaking his promise, as Lars well knew.

CHAPTER 5

The knock at the door was so loud and sudden that Mathilde jumped. She'd been sitting in a trance, staring at her coffee as it cooled and a faint, milky film formed across its surface. She glanced around, animal-like, ready to scramble under the table. Sometimes people came around to the kitchen window to peer in and rap on the glass. She'd tested it herself, going outside and standing in the flowerbed to check. She was fairly certain her hiding place was safe.

The children needed no instruction now to ignore the door and stay silent in their rooms. The knock came again and she slid off her chair, crawled under the table and crouched. She could feel breadcrumbs and other nameless grit under her knuckles. She didn't mind. It was like a cave, comforting, the light dimmer than in the rest of the kitchen. If she shifted onto her bottom and leaned her back against the solid leg of the table, she could sit there for hours. Why not? Why sit upright in a chair, anyway? Under the table, where a wounded animal might creep, felt like the right place for her. There were no expectations under there and no scrutiny.

For a third time, the heavy knock came and a man's voice called out, 'Anyone at home?'

Mathilde tilted her head, trying to recognise the voice. From down the hallway came footsteps and she saw Ole's shoes stop at the kitchen door.

'There's someone here, Mama,' he said in a dangerously loud voice.

Mathilde gestured at his feet to go back to his bedroom but they stayed firmly planted. She leaned across and twisted her neck so she could look out from under the table and see his face. His arms were crossed and he stared down at her.

'Go back to your room,' she mouthed.

He turned, but in the opposite direction, and began walking up the hallway towards the front door. Mathilde could feel the vibration of each step, tiny shivers that ran through the floorboards and into her body through her hands and feet, the points where her weight was concentrated. She was trembling, though whether from the crouch, or real terror at what might be waiting at the door, she couldn't tell. Sweat started to break out on her skin.

Ole's footsteps stopped at the door. 'Who's there?' he called in his high voice.

'Hans Lund,' came the answer. 'Is your mother home?'

Mathilde thought frantically. The name seemed distantly familiar, but she couldn't place it. She willed Ole to say no and the man to go away, but she heard the squeak of the key in the lock and the door's protesting groan as her son dragged it open. It felt as if the whole world rushed in on the draught.

'Could you wait a moment?' she heard Ole say, and then his footsteps retraced their path down the hallway. His brown lace-up shoes halted in the kitchen doorframe.

'Mama, there's a man with two fish at the door,' he said, and without waiting for a reply the feet disappeared in the direction of his bedroom.

Mathilde felt a flash of rage. She'd punish him, afterwards, and he wouldn't dare disobey her again. She had an image of caning his bottom, the way his father had done after some serious transgression, and the image was so vivid and satisfying, it wasn't until the man at the door cleared his throat in an attention-getting cough that Mathilde shook her head and crawled out from under the table, suddenly afraid he would walk down the hallway and catch her there.

'I'm coming,' she called, stumbling a little over the words as she bent and brushed the crumbs from her knees and hands where they had made strange dents in her skin. She ran a hand over her hair and it felt matted, like a dog's. She wondered if she'd brushed it that day, or the past one. A man with two fish. Shouldn't take a minute.

The hallway seemed infinite, the daylight streaming in and hurting her eyes. The man-shaped silhouette provided a welcome shadow against the glare, so that by the time she reached the doorway and the shape materialised into a big blond man in a fishing jumper, Mathilde realised she'd been staring at him. He was freshly shaven and his eyes were some light shade of sea.

'Mrs Wegger?' he said. 'Forgive me just arriving but I have something for you.' He extended a parcel with the wrapper pulled back. Two trout glistened. 'I had so many, and Mrs Christensen thought you might like some.'

'Did she send you?' Mathilde asked.

'No, that is, I asked her. That's all. I brought them myself.' He offered them again and this time Mathilde gathered her wits and took the parcel.

'Thank you,' she said, and took a step back. He stood, looking up at her from the step, his cap in his hands, and she wished he would go. The silence was becoming awkward when she heard a clatter in the hallway behind her.

'Hello,' Aase said, poking her head around Mathilde's skirt. 'I'm Aase. I've just put the kettle on.'

'Well, aren't you a clever young lady?' he said, leaning forward. He straightened again and looked at Mathilde.

'Would you like a cup of coffee?' she asked, when it was becoming rude not to.

He ignored the uninviting tone of her voice. 'That would be most kind,' he said, stepping forward.

She led the way to the kitchen. Ole had dragged a chair across to the high cupboard. He was standing on it holding one of the best cups and saucers, and for a moment as he turned to face her, she saw the look of entreaty upon him, a look that he must have worked hard not to show her before. For the past year his face had been a mask of determination and she'd forgotten his vulnerability. The reminder of it sliced into her.

She turned. Hans Lund, whoever he was, was standing in the kitchen doorway, clutching his cap and looking as desperately uncomfortable as she felt. What possessed him to come into the kitchen of a grieving widow to try to make small talk? Aase was behind him, her face alight. Mathilde put the fishy parcel down on the sink. She'd have to remember how to cook trout, and the task seemed overwhelming.

'How do you take your coffee, Mr Lund?' she asked.

'Black, sugar.'

Mathilde gestured to a chair and Hans sat down. The children's speed and activity was shocking. She stood, surrounded, as they rushed to and fro with cups and spoons and napkins. Steam began to rise from the kettle.

'Would you like me to fillet them?' he asked.

Mathilde turned her body away from his and concentrated on pouring the boiling water into the coffee pot, smelling the sharp scent of it. The steam rose into her face and she hoped it was that making her eyes water, and not the simple offer of help from another human being. She couldn't do it, not yet. If this big man with his work-worn hands started to fillet the trout in her sink, his knife would slice through the straining stitches that kept the remnants of her life together, and the whole lining would fall apart, the innards gushing out like the viscera of a fish, and she would never get it packed away neatly again.

'There's no need,' she said, when she could trust her voice. 'I'll bake them whole.'

'Very good,' he said.

She took the coffee pot to the table and set it down in front of him. 'Forgive me, Mr Lund; it's been a difficult time,' she said. 'Have we met before? Should I know you?'

His face fell a little. 'I knew your husband, God rest him. You and I have met a few times at church.'

And what are you doing here now? she wanted to ask, but instead poured out the coffee, set the cup and saucer in front of him and pushed the sugar bowl towards him. Aase and Ole watched as he spooned sugar into his cup and stirred.

He looked up and blinked under the intensity of their stares. 'I know it must have been hard and I thought I should call on you. It gets lonely over winter.'

'But it's spring now,' Aase said.

'I thought you might be ready for some company,' Hans said.

Mathilde was filled with a sudden weariness that made her want to lay her head on the table in her arms. It was too soon: couldn't he see that? And it would always be too soon. She'd never be ready to have a man come into her kitchen and sit there sipping coffee, appallingly alive, while she was finding it harder and harder to recall Jakob's face. The sound of his voice was long gone, having slipped out of her grasp the way a dream does upon waking.

Hans took a few great gulps of coffee and stood up abruptly. 'I mustn't keep you,' he said. 'I'll be on my way.'

The children crowded out into the hallway in his wake and by the time Mathilde had gathered her wits they were at the front door. She followed them and reached the door as he went down the steps. 'Thank you for the fish,' she said.

'Pleasure.' He bobbed his head. 'Mrs Wegger, could I call on you again?'

She wanted to snap 'No!' and shut the door, but before she could speak Aase said, 'We're making a cake tomorrow.'

'Very well,' he said, putting on his cap. 'I'll look in tomorrow. Goodbye.'

'Goodbye,' the children chorused. Mathilde watched him turn away, watched the set of his shoulders as he walked down the path and wondered if he was smiling. She'd find out who'd sent him, she decided, and give them a piece of her mind.

CHAPTER 6

Lillemor slid the key into the door, turned it and stepped inside. She stopped and drew the air into her nostrils. Anton tried to surprise her with his homecomings, but his presence charged the atmosphere of the house so it vibrated with his need. Her lips curled into a smile as she took off her coat and hung it on the rack. The absence of servants was a second clue, but it was always the air that alerted her first. She unwound the scarf from her neck and drew off her gloves, finger by finger, her skin coming to life.

'How do you always know?' His voice echoed, rich and deep, from the stairwell. He was sitting on the step, watching her through the banister.

She kept her head lowered. 'I can smell you.'

'You cannot. I've showered. Thoroughly. I defy anyone to smell me.'

She took a deep breath, filling her chest, allowing it to swell visibly. 'I can sniff you out anywhere, Anton.'

'Come here,' he said.

She knew enough of him to move slowly. She finished sliding the glove from her little finger, readying herself. He'd been away for three weeks; his desire would be strong. Hers was already rising to meet it. She slid the shoes from her feet, turned and crossed the floor in her stockings, raising and placing her feet like a dancer. At the bottom of the stairs she took hold of the railing, curling her fingers around it, sliding her hand along the polished wood as she ascended. If she approached him the right way, she could make him moan aloud before they even touched.

Lillemor had no illusions that she was beautiful. That wasn't why men hummed around her. It was elemental. They knew, somehow, that she was a woman whose passion could match their own. She didn't need to flirt. Sometimes she didn't even need to meet their eyes. They came to her, drunk on some scent that emanated from her. It mattered nothing how conservatively she dressed or how she kept her eyes down. In a roomful of strangers she only had to look up and there'd be male eyes waiting to catch hers.

Women, on the whole, were bemused. She'd seen Sarah Clegg studying her covertly, her brow wrinkled. Sarah was far prettier, and yet men turned from her to Lillemor with rude eagerness.

Freda, with a more knowledgeable eye than most, understood it. 'Watch yourself,' she'd said at the opening night of *For Services Rendered* at the National Theatre. 'If those Bloomsbury bohemians catch a glimpse of you, they'll snatch you for their own. I'm a retired old Sapphist now – you're safe with me – but there's no telling what they'll do if they get you in their clutches.'

The thought hadn't been entirely unappealing but Lillemor knew it was time for her to marry. Her allure to men – and women – wouldn't last forever. She needed the resources a good marriage would bring. She'd been having a discreet affair with forty-five-year-old Anton Rachlew, the Norwegian naval attaché in London, which had proved an unexpectedly passionate diversion. She wanted him with a strange chemistry that took no account of the difference in their ages or the whiff of wife and children about him, but she was resolved to put it aside and set her sights on marriage. If she could be unemotional about the match, she could snare herself an ambassador, perhaps, or some wealthy businessman smart enough to come through the depression unscathed.

When she advised Anton of her decision, he surprised her. He said he'd leave his wife and children and marry her. Lillemor put it down to the emotion of the moment, but he returned the next day in a taxi with his suitcases. Lillemor extracted one more promise from him before she agreed to the registry office ceremony – that she could keep much of the freedom she'd been accustomed to.

'It's a new era for women,' she'd said. 'Even England can't keep us down forever, so don't think for a moment that you can.'

Lillemor schooled herself not to think of his wife or his children. She presumed they'd have no desire to meet the siren who'd stolen their father and split their family.

She came to a stop in front of Anton, seated on the stair, his face at the height of her belly. She leaned forward, reaching out to tip his chin up, and brought her lips close to his. His breath caught as she lingered, kissed him, parted her lips. He was a navy man, with all the discipline that entailed, and so when he did shudder, Lillemor felt an answering shiver of excitement.

She drew back. 'There's a very good show opening tonight at the National.'

He was on his feet in a fluid motion, gripping her hand, the softly-softly game over. He pulled her against him, his kiss demanding, and in a moment they were both breathing hard.

A younger man might have picked her up and carried her but Lillemor was a tall woman and Anton knew his limitations. He took her hand and pulled her up the stairs, into the bedroom and onto the bed. The first time, as had become their ritual, they would barely remove their clothes. Afterwards, when he'd recovered, he would undress her and the second time would be slow and tender. He'd quickly learned the things Lillemor had shown him and he was good at them.

When they were done, they lay next to each other easily. Lillemor longed for a cigarette, but Anton detested them and she didn't smoke in his presence. She looked down at her rumpled clothing and smiled. She loved the pleasure of their prolonged lovemaking, but she loved the rough and fast of their first reunions too. Though they were never so fast that she didn't have time to fit her cervical cap.

Freda was right; Marie Stopes and her birth-control clinics had changed the lives of women like Lillemor. Had she been born a decade or two earlier, it would have been much harder to avoid pregnancy. She'd incorporated the act of fitting the device into their lovemaking, letting Anton nuzzle her fingers afterwards. From his response she judged that his first wife, a serving girl he had married for the convenience of it, had no inclination towards sexual adventures.

Anton undid his buttons and pulled his twisted shirt off. Lillemor sat up, adjusted her clothing and leaned back against the bed head. 'Shall I ring for dinner?'

He shook his head. 'I've got a surprise for you. An old friend of mine is in town – Captain Hjalmar Riiser-Larsen. I thought you might enjoy dinner with a polar explorer.'

'You know Captain Riiser-Larsen?'

'Of course. Known him for years.'

'You never told me that. He was in Antarctica – when? Just a year and a half ago.' Lillemor shook her head. 'I should have met you earlier, Anton, instead of wasting my time with Mawson!'

He grinned. 'Well I'm glad you didn't meet Hjalmar any earlier. He's divorcing. Lucky I've made an honest woman of you, or he might have swept you off to Antarctica on his next trip.'

Lillemor stared at him. 'Don't tease me.'

His face became serious. 'I'm not. All jokes aside, I think you should ask if you can go with him.'

'You wouldn't mind?'

He paused. 'I trust you, Lill. He's a handsome devil, but I know you'll be true. Won't you?'

'Of course,' she said, and kissed him again. 'What am I going to wear? Something dashing and adventurous – but what?'

Anton leaned back and laughed as she clambered from the bed and threw open the door of her wardrobe. Devastatingly feminine? Or should she be like Louise Arner Boyd and go to dinner in pants?

Anton was right; Hjalmar was a ladies' man. But Lillemor had prepared herself for the delicate balance of keeping her husband proud of her and his friend attracted to her without arousing jealousy or suspicion. She'd opted for an attractive but businesslike straight skirt with a pale shirt and a single-breasted jacket, and met his appraising welcome with a firm stare and a wide smile. His quick, almost unconscious glance down her body confirmed that her effect on men hadn't waned with marriage. She put aside the sneaking thought that if she had married him rather than Anton, she'd have an open ticket to Antarctica.

'My God, Rachlew, how did you convince this lovely creature to settle down with you?' he asked as they took their seats. 'I'd have thrown my own hat in the ring if I thought she'd settle for someone as old as you.'

Anton laughed but Lillemor could hear that the comment had hit home and she patted his hand. 'Why Captain Riiser-Larsen, none of us know where Cupid's arrow will strike,' she said. 'Anton swept me off my feet and I have eyes for no one else.'

She felt Anton sit a little taller in his chair and she flashed them both a smile as the waiter approached with champagne.

'Congratulations on your last voyage,' Anton said to Hjalmar. 'You were in the paper here every other week it seemed.'

Hjalmar raised his glass. 'Only because Mawson and I kept bumping into each other. The whole of Antarctica to sail in, and who should I meet?'

'From the sound of the newspapers I thought you'd avoid each other.'

'Quite the contrary. When we saw *Discovery* we blew the horn and they came sailing up close and invited me to come on board. Mawson introduced me to Captain Davis and showed me all over the ship. We agreed I would only explore west of forty degrees and he only east.'

Anton shrugged. 'I'm sure Mawson is a gentleman. But a handshake between two men on the ice doesn't mean much to the bureaucrats back home. Now the real bickering over claims is underway.'

'Unfortunately that's true,' Hjalmar said. 'I'm sorry, Mrs Rachlew; this must be dull.'

'Not at all,' Lillemor said. 'I'm fascinated by Antarctica. Did Anton mention to you that I applied myself to go on Mawson's expedition?'

'Really?' he asked, raising his eyebrows. 'What happened?'

'Nothing! According to *The Times*, twenty-five females applied and Mawson refused to take a single one of us.'

'What was his reason?'

'He said he thought the sleighing would be too arduous,' Lillemor said. 'But he was kind enough to say that under proper conditions he thought women could probably do as well as men. I doubt he has had many dealings with Norwegian women, or he'd never say such a thing.'

'Well, he's a fool,' Hjalmar said. 'A woman has a civilising influence on polar journeys. I was on Miss Arner Boyd's ship during the search for Amundsen. You've heard of her?'

'Of course.'

'She was braver than some of the men on board. Not to mention her generosity in giving up her own voyage to look for Amundsen. It would have cost her a fortune.'

'By the sounds of it, she has a fortune to spare,' Lillemor said dryly.

The three of them laughed and Anton gestured to a nearby waiter. Lillemor was relieved that they turned their attention to the food. The fact that Hjalmar had been on Louise's ship was one more thing to annoy her about the woman.

When they'd ordered their food, Anton cleared his throat.

'All jokes aside, my wife is determined to go to Antarctica. I thought you might be able to help.'

'I'm grounded myself this season,' Hjalmar said. 'Along with the whole Norwegian whaling fleet, thanks to Unilever.'

'But you'll be going next season?'

'I hope so.'

Lillemor met his eyes for just the right amount of time. 'It mightn't be a bad thing for Norway to be able to claim the first woman on Antarctica.'

'It wouldn't hurt our territorial claims at all,' Anton said. 'Britain would have a much harder time ignoring Norway's explorations if the papers were full of a woman having been on board. And it would show Mawson up as an old-fashioned fart.'

Hjalmar was nodding and Lillemor sipped her drink and kept quiet. If she were a man, even without skills, she could simply have asked to go on the expedition, or paid her way. It took all her self-control to act as though she was indifferent to the outcome of the evening. But she was relieved to find that

Hjalmar was progressive. He'd have no problem, she thought, in taking her on a sledging run or an exploratory ski trip. She had to keep her flirtation subtle so as not to alarm him.

By tomorrow, if they pressed him with enough wine, Hjalmar would almost start to think the idea had been his. She allowed him a smile more coquettish than before, while dropping her hand to Anton's thigh to distract him. The trick was to ensure both men finished dinner feeling flattered.

Inside she sighed. What a game to be played.

CHAPTER 7

While Sandefjord blossomed, Ingrid kept her body off-limits to Lars all through spring. Flowers sprang up, the sky was blue and clear, the children fished and swam and picked berries. But the cool that had set in between Lars and Ingrid was impervious to the season. Lars travelled to Oslo and London, desperately negotiating with Unilever and the other whaling companies. Ingrid didn't go with him.

The lingering chill wasn't only between them; in town some businesses closed their doors and boarded up their windows and people turned away from Ingrid in the street. It was the soup kitchen and the food handouts, she surmised. The whaling folk were proud people and accepting charity galled them. Lars and Ingrid didn't go to their hunting lodge that year, a decision that they made without discussion once the snow began to melt and the hills around Sandefjord rang with shots. There were plenty in Sandefjord who had greater need to hunt and fish.

Lars had been in Oslo for a few days when Ingrid heard voices in the hallway one afternoon. She came down the stairs to see who was there. Lars was standing by the door grinning like a schoolboy. She looked at him questioningly.

'The layover's finished, thank God,' he said. 'I've been meeting with Unilever all week and the fleet will sail again this season.'

He caught her by the waist and tried to swing her around as if she were eighteen again, their first playful moment in half a year. Ingrid realised in a flash how much she'd missed it. It was dangerous to layer ice into a marriage; it could harden and lock solid. She laughed too and put her hands on his shoulders. When he came in to kiss her she didn't turn her face away but met him, coming home to the familiarity of their lips together.

'That's good,' he said, keeping his hands on her waist. 'It's been too long, my dear.'

They hugged. In his grip she felt the depth of his worry and the fear he'd kept hidden from her. She regretted her distance. She should have known it wouldn't work on him. Theirs was a partnership built on kindness. How could she have forgotten?

Lars released her. 'Hjalmar is back from London and I've asked him to come for dinner. There's so much planning to get the ships and the scientific program ready and only a few months to do it. I've invited Aagaard too.'

'Good,' she said. 'We need to talk over so many things.'

He hesitated. 'Don't keep fighting me on this. My mind is made up.'

She drew back, the disappointment a pain in her chest. He reached for her hand and she kept it limp.

'It's just too risky for us both to go,' he said.

It took all Ingrid had to summon a smile. She didn't speak, but nodded at him and turned away in case he saw the tears threatening. 'I'll speak to the cook about dinner.'

'Excellent,' he said. 'Let's eat outdoors; it's such a lovely day.'

Ingrid wanted to pound her fists and kick the wall. But there wasn't time. She had to instruct the servants, oversee the setting of the table out on the terrace, organise the nanny to make sure the children were clean and neatly dressed, and change her own outfit. She helped Lars with his cufflinks and when he went downstairs, she sat at the dressing table and took out her eyebrow pencil. Her eyebrows had mysteriously disappeared after her fourth child and drawing them back on was a twice-daily task.

She looked into the mirror. Forty years old. She was growing heavier. On the wall of the bedroom in their wedding picture Lars was a dark-haired man with earnest eyes and Ingrid a slender young woman with a curved waist and a long neck. She hadn't looked like that for a long time now. Even her red hair was starting to fade.

The tears came then, no matter how much she wiped under her eyelids and clenched her jaw to keep them back. She got up and walked around the room, tipping her head back to stop them falling down her cheeks and smearing her makeup.

If Lars went to Antarctica with such a rift between them, and was gone for months, what would happen when he came back? Their companionship was a precious thing and perhaps not impervious to her cold treatment. She would have to yield on this.

Ingrid rubbed her eyes and forced the tears back. She'd look even older than her forty years with swollen, red-rimmed eyes. She sat down again abruptly, shook her head and aimed the eyebrow pencil again. She took a breath to keep her hand steady.

This was the choice then. Lars and their marriage, not Antarctica. But if she stayed behind while he went south, she wouldn't give him another child. It was time he knew what that kind of loss felt like.

The six children were all at home for dinner. Hjalmar was popular in their household and they never tired of his exploration stories, which Ingrid suspected were embroidered for their benefit. Lars had invited Bjarne Aagaard, the Antarctic historian he'd commissioned to write of their explorations a few years earlier. But Bjarne was opinionated and outspoken, and Ingrid hoped he wouldn't turn the party sour.

Their long table was set up on the terrace in the sunshine when the guests arrived and they assembled outdoors. When the oysters were finished, Ingrid served Hjalmar and Bjarne generous plates of roasted grouse heaped with vegetables, before gesturing for a servant to serve the rest of them and pour the champagne.

'Thank you, Mrs Christensen,' Hjalmar said, as she placed it in front of him. 'Delicious. I'm sick of English food.'

'Have you been to the South Pole?' Cato burst in, unable to contain himself any longer.

Hjalmar reached over and ruffled Cato's hair. 'No, sweet child. Just in London this time. But last time I went to Antarctica I saw land that no man had seen before, and I planted your mother's flag on it. I saw penguins and whales, and a leopard seal nipped the end of my nose!'

'Tell! Tell!' Cato and Soren chorused. Sofie gave them an older sister's disdainful look, but she still turned to Hjalmar in fascination as he began the next story.

'I suppose you'll be looking out for whales?' Bjarne asked when there was a break.

Hjalmar shrugged. 'We usually make note of them. That's the Consul's business after all.'

'Tell me,' Bjarne said, 'have you noticed any reduction in their numbers?'

Hjalmar shot a glance in Lars's direction. 'I really couldn't say. It seems to me their distribution varies from season to season. There were plenty last season.'

'Exactly,' Bjarne said. 'The largest catch in recorded history. How long do you think the species can sustain such hunting?'

'You sound like one of those socialists in the north,' Lars said.

Bjarne pressed his lips together. 'If those socialists in the north hadn't destroyed the Mehamn whaling station, whaling would still be allowed here in Norway and the stocks would be exhausted.'

Lars shook his head. 'Now you're being disingenuous. You know as well as I do they tore down that whaling station only because they believed – with no proof – that whaling was damaging their fishing trade. It had nothing to do with the whale stocks.'

'The fact remains, the Norwegian fleet killed more whales last year than in the past two hundred years put together. You can see what's going to happen in the Southern Ocean.'

'Well, there you and I are in disagreement,' Lars said. 'I've assessed the numbers of whales and taken the advice of scientists – our harvest can be sustained, they assure me. I've given employment to four thousand men and no one in Norway has to live near the stench of a whaling station any longer. Surely that's not a bad thing?'

'Employment that will collapse in a few years. We've seen already what's gone on with the layover! How many companies closed this year?'

Lars put his hand on Bjarne's arm and gave him a warning look. 'Whalemen have just had the most welcome news of the year. I'll be employing extra men next season, so those who've lost jobs elsewhere can find new ones with me. We'll have to agree to disagree on this. It's time for a toast. To Norwegian whalers and seamen!' Lars raised his glass.

'Norwegian whalers and seamen,' Bjarne said after a moment, raising his own glass, his mouth set.

They drank and Ingrid forced a smile. She wasn't ready to think of the months Lars would be away and the emptiness of the Norwegian winter without him.

'I have a surprise for you,' Hjalmar said, wiping his mouth and laying down his napkin. 'I'm bringing a photographer this year. I want a proper record of any new discoveries we make.'

Ingrid sat up, relieved at the change of subject. 'Well, that's good news. We only have such basic photographs from your earlier voyages.'

'Knowing you, he'll be someone famous,' Lars said. 'Not Frank Hurley?'

'I'm taking Mrs Rachlew.'

The pain in Ingrid's chest was so sharp and sudden that her hand flew to her sternum. Lars stared at Hjalmar, his brow furrowed.

'You know her husband of course,' Hjalmar continued. 'Anton Rachlew, the Norwegian naval attaché in London. Perhaps you've met the lady herself? She was Miss Enger before they married recently.'

A face flashed before Ingrid's eyes. Lillemor Enger. They'd met in Oslo, some years earlier. Charismatic and predatory, Ingrid recalled. A woman who knew how to get what she wanted, it seemed.

'I didn't know she was a photographer,' she said, her voice tight.

'That will be quite a turn-up for the history books,' Bjarne said. 'Is her husband travelling with you too?'

'I haven't worked out the details yet,' Hjalmar replied.

'Good.' Lars's voice was hard. 'You're the captain, Hjalmar, but on this matter I have the last word. Find yourself someone else.'

Ingrid looked down at her plate, feeling the heat rise in her cheeks.

'Lars, surely you're not so old fashioned,' Bjarne said. 'A landing place named for a Norwegian woman who has stepped there herself – well, it would be much harder for the English to ignore.'

'That may be, but I have indeed met Mrs Rachlew and she attracts scandal like a magnet. Hjalmar, you don't want a woman like that on your ship.'

Hjalmar shrugged. 'You're in charge.'

Ingrid's heart was still pounding when Bjarne turned to her. 'What do you think, Mrs Christensen? Is it time for a woman to go to Antarctica?'

'Why not?' she said, keeping her voice even. 'Miss Arner Boyd has been leading her own expeditions to Greenland for years now. But it seems like the Americans are far more progressive than the Norwegians when it comes to women.'

'I think Lars should take a woman down himself,' Bjarne said. 'I'd be most interested in a female perspective on the whaling activities. Don't you think, Mrs Christensen, that a woman would be more likely to see the hunt for what it is? An overfishing of a limited stock that can only end in collapse?'

Ingrid took a breath. 'Now, Bjarne, I can't agree with you there. Lars is too good a businessman to do that.'

She glanced at Lars and saw a quick, grateful look in return. She rose and pushed her chair back. 'Hjalmar, I'm sure you and my husband have much to discuss. Children, it's bedtime. Bjarne, why don't you come with me for a walk down to the seashore?'

He took the hint. 'That's most kind of you, but I should be getting home. Consul, I look forward to hearing more about your voyage when you've finalised the details.'

They all rose and the children filed inside. As Ingrid closed the terrace door behind Bjarne, she heard Hjalmar say, 'Of course, I'll find someone else if you wish. Now ...'

In truth there was nothing for Ingrid to do once she had ushered the children from the terrace and sent Bjarne on his way. There were servants to clear the dishes and bring aquavit and cigars for the men when they moved in to Lars's study. There were servants to undress the younger children and ready them for bed, and servants to turn down the covers in the marriage bedroom and draw the curtains against the light of the long summer evening. When she'd kissed the younger children on their warm, clean cheeks and stroked their hair on the pillows, Ingrid stood in the hallway at a loss. In the past she would have joined the men again, listened to their discussion, made suggestions. She felt at a loss.

Motte came up behind her in the hallway. 'Mama, we're going for a paddle. Come with us?'

Ingrid slipped her arm into Motte's and they went outside, kicking off their shoes before stepping onto the grass. Bolle, the chubby one, was standing by Lars Junior, her arm flung affectionately over his shoulder. As she turned to see them coming, Bolle's face went blank. Ingrid sighed. She knew her eldest daughter, Motte, like a slice of herself, but why pretty Bolle ate so much, ruined her looks and always rebelled against Ingrid, and why Lars Junior hunched his shoulders and stammered, she couldn't understand, nor easily tolerate. She must be a poor mother, she knew, for not loving them equally, but it seemed beyond her.

As the three of them ran ahead towards the beach, Ingrid skirted around the rocky outcrop that lay at the bottom of the stairs and climbed up the small knoll that overlooked Ranvik's stretch of sand. She settled herself on the warm rock of the headland and faced south, the sea wind in her face.

She and Lars had moved to Ranvik as a young couple and at first the house seemed too large and too grand, with its commanding view of the fjord and the rocky headland separating it from Sandefjord like a haughty shoulder. They were the first to know what ships were coming in, but some older, primal part of Ingrid felt the danger of being the lookout, the first place that invaders spied. Lars had to have all the new inventions – phone, car, electric light – and there was no hiding Ranvik's illuminated brilliance through those big windows overlooking the water. Lars had chided her for such foolish fears and Ingrid tried to ignore them. Eventually she did fall in love with Ranvik the way she'd fallen in love with Lars, relaxing into its solid embrace. It became their foundation, the constant in their lives as the world tipped and changed around them, as new decades came and went, as their children were born and as Sandefjord grew from a sailing port to a steamship port to a fuel-powered ship port.

Cato would be six soon and when he'd slid out of her she'd felt the relief of it in her bones, knowing that he was the last. She could never have been one of those farm women who carried a dozen or more and watched half of them die along the way. Six healthy children. Lars should be content.

Ingrid turned her head to the sun, so the glare of the light on the water dazzled her. She could feel a light breeze from the ocean on her face, blowing from the south, the direction of Antarctica. When she could feel the light burning her eyes, she closed them, so the backs of her eyelids were red and warm.

The children's laughter drifted up towards her and she wished she could switch off their sounds and find the silence she craved. The six of them always wanted something from her; always crowded her with warmth and noise and energy. Sometimes she had to go out in the snow just to get away from them and try to find some quiet place for herself.

She and her mother were alike in that, she thought. Ingrid was still young when Alfhild had begun wandering in the snow on nights lit by the moon or the aurora borealis, disappearing from the house for hours at a time.

At first Thor had laughed. 'I'm off to look for the Snow Queen,' he'd say, pulling on his jacket and boots. He'd return leading a shivering and elated Alfhild by the arm. But her absences grew longer and Thor stopped joking when he had to go searching for her. She seemed unaware of how frozen she was when he brought her back, her lips dark and her eyes far away.

One night he was gone for many hours looking for her. He finally returned after dawn, carrying his wife into the kitchen where Ingrid was sitting eating porridge the cook had made. There were claw marks on his cheeks and although Alfhild was limp in his arms, her blue eyes were wild, lit with a strange, inner glow.

'Mommo's not well,' he'd said to Ingrid. 'I'm taking her to the doctor. Stay inside.'

Mommo had never come home again. Thor said, 'Your mother's gone with the Snow Queen,' in answer to any question. It wasn't till Ingrid was ten that he revealed the truth. He'd told her in anger, dragging her inside yet another time from her contemplation of the patterns of light on snow in the garden. 'Don't turn into another mad woman like your mother,' he'd bellowed, shaking her. It turned out that Alfhild had been committed to an asylum, and by that time there was no prospect she would ever come out.

The last time Ingrid saw her mother was a few months before Cato was born. One final try to elicit recognition in those faraway eyes. She'd failed, and Alfhild had died not long afterwards.

Ingrid opened her eyes again and stared at the flickering light on the water, squinting till she could see only patterns of light and dark. If she did it long enough, the burning after-image of the light stayed with her for minutes, blinding her to everything else. If she did it long enough, she could sometimes see her mother.

An image wavered in the light, then clarified. It was Alfhild, but not as the gaunt, demented creature she'd visited in the asylum. She was a young woman, her skin alabaster white, her eyes aquamarine. She was suspended in the water like some nymph creature of the deep, her pale hair floating around her like a cloud.

What was it Alfhild had gone seeking when she followed the light? Ingrid leaned forward, mentally reaching for her. A yell came from below and a splash. Ingrid blinked, startled. Lars Junior had fallen over in the shallows and from his prone position was splashing his older sisters. Bolle bent down, scooped up a handful of wet sand and threw it at him. Laughter drifted up to her. The moment was gone.

She rubbed her eyes, feeling her head start to ache. Such glimpses of her mother were invariably frustrating, for she was always just out of reach. But this time, for once, something remained and Ingrid felt her veins humming.

Alfhild had gone mad looking for something out in the snow. If Ingrid had learned anything from her mother, it was the danger of never finding what you were seeking. Had Alfhild appeared to remind her that if she gave up on her dream now, she'd never go to Antarctica?

Ingrid got up quickly and dusted herself off. Her mother had given her an idea.

When Lars came to bed, so late that the long dusk had deepened to true darkness, Ingrid pretended to be asleep. He undressed quietly. She heard the swishing of fabric as he draped his clothes neatly over the chair and pulled his socks off. He went to his side of the bed, lifted the covers silently and slid in. After a few moments of expectant silence he sighed, turned away and pulled the light covers up to his shoulder.

Ingrid waited a few heartbeats more and then slid across the sheets until her skin met the warmth of his back and she curled around him. He was a small man, and their bodies had always fitted well together. She wrapped an arm around his waist and he responded, easing back into her. His hand reached for her and he exhaled when he found she was naked.

'Ingrid?'

She pushed him onto his back, slid on top of him and kissed him, feeling his astonishment.

She broke their kiss. 'You've made some good deals tonight,' she said softly.

'What?'

'Now I have a deal.'

He tried to move but Ingrid shifted her weight to keep him still.

'Yes?' he said warily.

'The first man to the South Pole was Norwegian, and your expeditions are the first to see many new lands in the south. Norwegian names are all over Antarctica. The first woman to land there *must* be Norwegian.'

'So everyone seems to think,' he said, his voice resigned. 'Even Bjarne!'

For the first time in months Ingrid felt a moment of hope. 'It will happen, Lars, this season or next. Someone will do it soon, and the chance will be lost. If I'm the first, your reputation and your business will benefit, and Norway will benefit too.'

'Where does the deal come in?'

'I'll come with you to Antarctica and while we're on board, we'll try to make a child.'

He lay very still underneath her and Ingrid waited, conscious suddenly of her ageing skin and the fact that she was straddling him.

'Do you have any idea what you'd be in for?' he asked. 'It's a rough voyage and whaling can be revolting close up.'

'I can skin an elk, for God's sake,' Ingrid said. 'I won't be squeamish.'

'It's a few years since either of us have skinned an elk,' he said. 'But you don't want to be alone on a ship full of men, especially as I'll be busy. You'll need a female companion.'

Ingrid kept her delight in tight check. 'What about Mrs Rachlew? She can take photos.'

Lars shifted and slid out from under her. He sat up and switched on the bedside lamp. The sudden blaze of it was shocking.

'There are so few chances to be first at anything these days,' he said, looking down at her. 'If you want your name to be remembered, you mustn't take Mrs Rachlew. She'll want the glory herself. You need someone who'll let your name shine, the way Balchen let Richard Byrd take the honour of flying first to the South Pole, though he was the pilot.'

Ingrid felt a rush of relief. 'Very well. I'll find another woman who'll stay in the background, and I'll try to get you a child upon the sea. A deal.'

'A deal, my dear. Though we should keep it quiet. If the British hear about it, they might try to get one of their own women down there before us.'

'We'll be like Amundsen,' Ingrid said, 'and announce it only when we're leaving.'

They hugged, and then Lars drew back, his face serious. 'But I have a condition too. I need us to be friends again. I can't bear how it's been.'

'Me neither,' she said. 'Come here.' She drew him down, and they kissed again, body to body. Ingrid wanted to lose herself in the feeling, so long had it been. But a mistake in timing now, an early conception, would be the end of it. She pulled away from him.

'Not until we're on board,' she said, rolling away. 'Something to look forward to.'

Lars started to laugh and after a moment Ingrid joined in. He switched off the light and they lay there in the dark, their hands entwined.

'I'm not taking Bjarne, though,' he said, after their laughter died away. 'That man's become obsessed with whaling and I don't think he'll ever finish the history of Antarctica. I'm going to find a new historian.'

Lars fell asleep quickly, but Ingrid lay awake. The chances of conceiving a child were slim, she thought, and a risk she was ready to take. She'd heard of the Stopes birth-control clinics causing scandal across the world, and knew they trained women in using the time of their cycles to avoid conception. She would learn the technique and apply it on the voyage. Her ageing body might not still be fertile at any rate.

She was too excited to sleep. In just a few months she would leave the darkness behind and follow the light around the girth of the world. She sent a quick thank you to Alfhild, and felt something like the flicker of the aurora deep inside; the feeling that had come upon her the night of their anniversary. She would go there, at last. Perhaps she would finally discover what it was Alfhild had gone looking for out in the snow.

CHAPTER 8

Mathilde halted at Ranvik's imposing gates and tightened her grip on the children's hands. There was no need to be intimidated by Ingrid, she reminded herself. The woman was known all over Sandefjord for her kind-heartedness. It was just that the volume of it could be hard to take.

She could hear distant shouts of children's voices. How many did the Christensens have now? Six, she was fairly certain, apparently immune to the illnesses and accidents that beset other children of the district, whose fathers were farmers and whalers. The Christensens were short, but handsome. The signs were there that Ingrid would be a solid woman in her later years, but she still had much of the beauty of her youth. Not needing to work hard – or at all – did wonders for keeping a woman looking young.

Mathilde shook her head to try to remove such uncharitable thoughts. The anger that had carried her this far was wavering in the face of Ranvik's grandeur and she stood up straight to bolster herself. She would just calmly speak her mind to Ingrid about Hans Lund, take a cup of coffee, let the children play for a few minutes and then go home. They'd had social visits with the Christensens before, back when Jakob was still alive and it never occurred to her to question the normality of daily life. Back when the difference in their social standing hadn't seemed so wide. Ingrid needn't know that this was the first time Mathilde had stepped into another house, apart from that of her in-laws, since Jakob died.

Ole pushed the gate open and they walked up the tree-lined drive. Flowers grew in the soft grass on either side of the path and the light was pleasantly dappled. Strawberries gleamed through the green, but when the children tugged at her hands to pick them, she pulled them up hard and they marched along the drive. When they reached the front door, she took several deep breaths and knocked.

The servant who opened the door told them Mrs Christensen and the children were at the beach and that she could walk down to meet them. Mathilde's shoulders slumped, but she took the children's hands again and continued around the side of the house and onto the open lawn. They set out down the slope, skirting around bushes and trees. The sounds of distant laughter grew gradually louder, until they came around the side of a large rock above the beach.

The children were gathered around Ingrid, who was crouched down, her bare feet ankle-deep in the sand. A large fish was flapping desperately in the centre of the circle and it seemed Ingrid was instructing one of the children on how to kill it.

'Put your foot on its head if it won't keep still, silly,' she was saying. 'No, like this.'

She took the boy's wrist, wrapped his hand around the cleaver and raised it high. 'Hold on tight. Now bring it down hard and fast, like I showed you.'

The cleaver fell but the boy lost his nerve at the last minute and flinched. The blow glanced off the fish, which flapped again frantically. The other children laughed and jeered at him.

'Oh, for God's sake.' Ingrid took up the cleaver and with a sharp blow parted the fish's head from its body. 'Don't let it suffer.'

The boy twisted away from her, his face crumpled, and began to cry. Ingrid looked up and saw Mathilde and her children.

'Mathilde!' she called. She stood up. There was a streak of fish blood on the apron she had tied over her white dress, a dress that Mathilde would be too frightened to wear out of the house if she ever came to own such an expensive thing. Ingrid's red hair was tumbling out of its clasps and she bent to wipe her hands in the sand.

'My dear, I stink of fish,' she said. 'Cato just hasn't the stomach to kill them, I'm afraid.' She looked at Mathilde's children, standing on each side of their mother. 'Hello, Ole. Hello, Aase. Would you like to do some fishing?'

They dropped Mathilde's hands with cruel speed and ran to Ingrid. She waved at someone else in the rabble and another boy stepped forward, pulled some reels from a basket and took the children down to the waterfront.

'Thank goodness you came along,' Ingrid said, pushing her hair back with her forearm. 'I've had enough fishing for today. Coffee?'

'Thank you,' Mathilde managed.

'Let's go up,' Ingrid said. 'Here, I promise not to get my hands on you!' She slipped her arm through Mathilde's elbow. 'It's so good to see you. It's been a long time. I've thought of you a lot.'

She chattered brightly as they climbed the grassy slope and made it to the stairs of the terrace without Mathilde having to say a word. Ingrid called for a servant, ordered coffee and disappeared to wash her hands. 'I'll be back in just a moment,' she said, untying her apron.

The light was brilliant, glinting off the water, and Mathilde shifted herself to face away from it, pulling her hat down low. She could feel herself crumbling.

'There, that's better.' Ingrid stepped out to the terrace again and seated herself. She looked at Mathilde for a long moment.

'There's something I want to talk to you about. But first, how have you been keeping?'

'Really quite good,' Mathilde said, forcing a smile.

'It can't be easy,' Ingrid said, and patted her hand.

The servant arrived with the tray of coffee, to Mathilde's relief, and she took a few minutes through the pouring and serving and nodding and stirring to remember why she had come.

'There's something …' she said at last.

'Yes?'

'A man. Mr Lund. He keeps visiting. He comes every day for afternoon tea.'

'Don't you like him?' Ingrid asked.

'I don't know,' she said. 'But I'm not ready. So I want you to tell him not to come any more.'

Ingrid looked at her with a perplexed expression. 'I don't think I know Mr Lund.'

'He told me you'd said I would like some fish.'

Ingrid laughed, and then put her hand out in apology when Mathilde stayed silent. 'I'm sorry. I think your Mr Lund may have used my name to get you to open the door.'

'He says he works for your husband.'

'That's probably true. Half of Sandefjord works for my husband,' she said, and picked up her coffee. 'Mathilde, how long has it been?'

'A year and a half,' she said. 'Not long.'

'But you're a young woman.'

'I'm not ready to entertain men in my kitchen!'

'So tell him not to come any more.'

Mathilde shook her head. 'You don't understand. He's very determined.'

'Don't open the door. He'll understand that.'

'My children like him. They open the door to him, even when I tell them not to.'

They sat in silence for a few moments. Ingrid ate a small slice of cake. Mathilde finished her coffee and set it down on the saucer. She looked down at her hands, lying in her lap limply and suddenly lost the battle to keep her tears under control. Her shoulders began to shake. Ingrid, staring down at the fjord, didn't notice for a few moments until Mathilde gave an audible sob.

'Oh, my dear,' she said, putting a hand on Mathilde's shoulder.

Mathilde thought she might have got through it if Ingrid hadn't touched her. She leaned forward and put her hands over her face, the dreadful sobs beyond her control to halt.

'Now listen to me.' Ingrid drew Mathilde back up to sitting and patted her cheek. She lifted a napkin and wiped Mathilde's eyes and nose. 'This is no good. Not for you; not for them.'

'You don't know what it's like,' Mathilde said, struggling to regain herself.

'No, I don't,' Ingrid said. 'But I can see you need some help.'

'I just need to be left alone. I'm all right on my own.'

'I doubt that,' Ingrid said. 'But this is what I wanted to discuss with you. What about a holiday?'

The concept was so alien that at first Mathilde had no idea what Ingrid was suggesting. She looked at her blankly.

'Lars and I are going on a cruise,' Ingrid said. 'Come with us.'

Mathilde recoiled. 'What about the children?'

'They'll be perfectly happy with their grandparents. I'm leaving my children too, so they can come here and play together. Come on, Mathilde. It will be a great adventure. You need it.'

'Where to?' Mathilde asked, in spite of herself.

'You won't believe it,' Ingrid said. 'Antarctica!'

Mathilde laughed, a response as sudden and surprising as her tears. 'Antarctica,' she repeated. It was as impossible to imagine as Venezuela.

'It might be just what you need,' Ingrid said. 'Somewhere quite different. New people. Nothing to worry about.'

Mathilde was filled with an urge to get away from Ingrid. She'd been right to avoid her. The woman was capable of anything in the name of kindness.

She rose to her feet. 'That's kind of you, Ingrid,' she said. 'But I really can't go on a trip right now. I'm sure you'll have a wonderful time.'

Ingrid stood too. 'Think about it, Mathilde.'

'I'll get the children,' Mathilde said, stepping back. 'Thank you for the coffee.'

She turned before Ingrid could say anything more and hurried down the lawn to find Ole and Aase. What on earth had made Ingrid even think of inviting her to go with them? She must have had a dozen female friends better suited to such a trip.

Mathilde found herself shaking her head in disbelief as she strode onto the beach. Antarctica. As if she needed another winter.

She'd forgotten how fast word could travel in Sandefjord. The next morning, before she'd even planned how to busy the children and herself for the day, there was a knock at the door. Mathilde stamped down the hallway, annoyed at Hans Lund for coming so early and determined to see him off. But when she threw open the door, it was Ole and Gerd.

'Oh,' she said, standing still.

'Hello, Mathilde,' Gerd said. 'Can we come in?'

'Of course.' Mathilde stepped back.

They both smiled at her oddly as they came into the house. She followed them down the hallway and into the kitchen. Gerd went to the stove and started the coffee preparations herself.

'Let me,' Mathilde said, making her way over. 'Sit down, please. I'll call the children.'

'No need,' Gerd said. 'We want to speak to you first.'

Mathilde looked from one of them to the other. 'What is it?'

'The Christensens called us last night, on the telephone. Said you'd been around for a visit.'

'That's what you wanted, wasn't it?' Mathilde asked.

'Yes, my dear,' Gerd said. 'It's very good. We were thrilled. Ingrid told us she invited you on a trip.'

Mathilde busied herself with the cups. 'Oh, she said something about it. Somewhere ridiculous.'

'Antarctica,' Ole said.

She turned. They were both staring at her. 'What is it?'

'We think you should go,' Gerd said, straight to the point as ever. 'It's a wonderful opportunity. You need the rest, Mathilde, and what excellent company you'll have. It's such a generous offer.'

'I couldn't possibly leave the children.'

'But we'd love to have the children.' Gerd reached out to catch her hand. 'They need a change too, Mathilde. It's not right to keep them cooped up here like this.'

Her grip was so hard that Mathilde's fingers started to hurt, and she shuffled awkwardly. 'I don't want to go.'

Ole stood and laid a hand on her shoulder. It felt as heavy and unyielding as Gerd's grip on her fingers.

'You're in a bad way,' he said. 'And not getting any better. You need a change, Mathilde.'

Mathilde felt like a child. 'You can't make me.'

'It's for your own good,' he said. 'You'll thank us, once you're away.'

Gerd tugged at her hand. 'We're terribly worried about you. At this rate you'll end up in a sanatorium. Wouldn't you rather go on a cruise with Lars and Ingrid?'

Mathilde's shoulders sagged. She'd forgotten, in her grief, how Lars and Ole and a few other powerful men ran Sandefjord. She'd thought herself so far below their notice that they wouldn't bother with her. But she was bound to the Wegger family now; the mother of its male heir. They'd allowed her to think she was her own creature only while she caused no bother.

'It will be wonderful,' Gerd said. 'They're leaving on a passenger liner in December for Cape Town, and then on to Antarctica. A great adventure. I'd go myself if I could.'

'I'll let Lars know to book your tickets,' Ole said, when she didn't speak. He gave her a gentle shake. 'Aren't you the lucky one?'

They let go of her. Mathilde sat down, her legs weak.

'Bring the children to dinner tonight,' Gerd said. 'We'll celebrate. We're so thrilled to have them to stay. I promise you, we'll look after them so well they'll hardly notice you're gone.'

Satisfied, they ignored her silence and made their farewells. Mathilde sat unmoving as they let themselves out. The sound of the door closing behind them shuddered through the house.

All she wanted was to savour her retreating memories of Jakob before they ceased to exist. She needed the children with her to recall him fully. Looking down into their faces, she could see him written there. She knew she wasn't mothering them well in her grief, but she relied on them to keep her tethered to the world, to tug her back into it when she was ready. Now Gerd and Ole wanted to part her from the children and cast her adrift in a world of ice. Couldn't they see it was the very thing most likely to unhinge her?

For a moment Mathilde thought wildly of Hans Lund. She could marry him, perhaps, and then Jakob's parents wouldn't have such power. They could take the children, go somewhere else, make a new life. But even as she thought it, she knew it was impossible. The children bound her to Jakob's parents and there was no escaping the web of connections they had created.

She shook her head; straightened herself. She'd just refuse. That was all. They couldn't force her onto the ship. She imagined locking the door, buying a dog, refusing to let the children leave the house.

Aase and Ole. The looks on their faces when Hans came knocking, the way they ran down the hall to open the door, the entreaty in their eyes when they asked to go out. She couldn't do it, couldn't imprison them in her grief.

A sanatorium, Gerd had said. It hadn't registered in the moment she spoke, but as Mathilde sat there she realised what had been threatened. The ice or the madhouse. Both places without her children. These were her choices.

CHAPTER 9

The letter from Hjalmar was waiting for Lillemor in the front hall. She picked it up and paused before opening it. She realised she was shaking, and put a hand on the bureau to steady herself.

Since she'd first had the idea to go south, she had planned her Antarctic assault with the same care as Amundsen or Scott. The challenges and logistics were different, but her determination was as strong. Lillemor had read every account of polar exploration she could find. She knew her north and south, she knew the great journeys, the triumphs and failures. She knew Scott's dying words on his way back from the Pole, and Amundsen's pedestrian ones as he set down the daily details of his race to beat the Englishman.

Every journey of exploration faced challenges before setting out. The real explorers were those who could navigate through them. Captain Riiser-Larsen had agreed to take her, she reminded herself. The only obstacle in their way was Unilever and its determination to grind down the Norwegian whalers until they were more desperate sellers of oil.

She picked up the letter opener and slit the envelope in a single motion. The paper slid out and she unfolded it.

I'm terribly sorry, Mrs Rachlew, Hjalmar wrote. *It seems Consul Christensen wants his wife to be the first woman to visit Antarctica. Ingrid and a female friend are sailing with us on the resupply vessel* Thorshavn, *which is ferrying me south to meet up with* Norvegia. *The Consul has forbidden me to take any female passenger myself.*

Lillemor threw the paper to the floor in disbelief and fury, and gave an impotent half-roar of the kind a woman was reduced to making when another opportunity was denied her.

Anton came running out of the parlour at the sound. He stopped when he saw her, then came closer and picked up the letter. He scanned it quickly.

'Oh, darling,' he said.

She kept out of his reach. 'Those damned Christensens. Them and their great ancestors and their pure Viking blood!'

She thumped the bureau with her fist and groaned aloud, thinking of what had been snatched from her. Anton flinched. He hadn't seen her temper yet, she remembered. She forced herself to take some deep breaths.

'I bet Ingrid Christensen doesn't give a damn about Antarctica,' she said. 'It's just the latest season's holiday. Last year Rio, this year Antarctica, next year bloody Tahiti. And so much for your friend Hjalmar. Doesn't he rule his own ship? What kind of captain is he?'

'The kind whose explorations are funded by someone else,' Anton said. 'In this case, Christensen. Hjalmar wouldn't be exploring without the Consul's backing.'

'Well, he's a sop then. I don't care if he's being funded. He should have stood up for himself.'

Anton reached out a hand. 'I'll make it up to you. We'll go somewhere ourselves; have our own trip.'

'It's not just a trip!'

'I'm trying to help,' he said quietly.

She pushed him away. 'I'm going out.'

'I'll come with you.'

'I need to be alone.' She turned and pushed blindly at the door, out into the English summer afternoon.

She wasn't a crier, so she wished for gloomy English darkness and a cold London fog to close around her and express her misery. But as she strode along the street, the world refused to cooperate. Children played and carriages and cars went about their business and birds sang. London seemed as merry as if the crash had never happened and Lillemor hadn't received the day's news.

Damn London. She'd arrived there thinking it such a big step from Oslo. One of the world's great cities, full of bohemians and suffragists and adventurers, a place where a woman like Lillemor could make a mark on the world. She'd left her staid parents and her married sister in Oslo without regret, barely remembering to dash off Christmas cards to them, and set herself to join the main current of world events. In London, a youngish woman of modest but independent means could find any new adventure her heart desired, surely?

She'd met many of those famous women, some through Women's Service House, and been there to celebrate the achievement of universal suffrage in 1928. Freda was past her climbing days when they got to know each other, but Lillemor liked her anyway. Though grief had softened Freda's body and hardened her face, Lillemor could see the formidable woman she'd been.

In the aftermath of the Wall Street crash, Lillemor had volunteered to help out in Dr Marie Stopes's Mothers' Clinic to keep herself busy while she waited to see what adventure presented itself. She and Marie had become friends over the last two years. But now she was married and had turned thirty. Life was passing quickly and, with it, her chance to make something of herself.

When Ingrid and her companion returned, the papers would trumpet them as the first women to reach Antarctica and the chance of Lillemor ever being the first herself would be lost. She thought of Robert Falcon Scott, still celebrated as a hero though he'd been second to reach the South Pole. The British mourned him still, with a fervour far greater than the Norwegians showed towards Amundsen. Lillemor herself felt more kinship with Scott and his tragic end. Hjalmar should have borrowed the phrase from Amundsen's telegraph to Scott: 'Beg to inform, heading south', the words that carried, in their unspoken brutality, the death of all Scott's dreams.

When Lillemor finally halted, sweating in the afternoon warmth, she looked around. She was in St John's Gardens in Westminster, near Women's Service House. The sun was slanting downwards, though couples still lay on the lawns in the park and people bared their arms and legs to catch the sun.

She turned away from the park, crossed the road and rounded the corner into Marsham Street. But as she strode into the lobby, she felt her frustration rise. These women thought themselves very fine but they were fools. Chesterfield sofas, whisky, cigars and maids may have been the trappings of power, but they didn't carry any in their own right. If Lillemor had been a man, she'd have had the connections to get herself on an Antarctic expedition. As a woman, the connections were useless.

Lillemor looked around the lounge. Marie was sitting by the fire, nursing a whisky in Freda's usual armchair. Lillemor threw herself down next to her and waved for her own drink.

'That bastard,' she said.

Marie looked across and raised an eyebrow. 'Which one?'

'Exactly,' Lillemor said. 'Captain Riiser-Larsen, who's got no spine to stand up for himself, or Consul Lars Christensen, who wants his own wife to be the first woman on Antarctica and won't let me get in her way.'

'Giving up then?' Marie asked.

'I've rather run out of options.'

They sat in silence. The maid brought Lillemor a double whisky and she took a gulp. It didn't help.

'I know how you feel,' Marie said.

Lillemor felt another rush of frustration. 'You can't possibly know. You've achieved everything.'

'Do you know what I did before I opened the clinics?' Marie put her glass down. 'I worked as a palaeobotanist in Japan and Canada, and travelled all over North America studying geology. I was working to prove Suess's theory that the continents were once joined.'

Lillemor stared at her in astonishment. 'Why did you give it up?'

Marie leaned in close. 'I wanted to go to Antarctica to study the rocks. I asked Scott to take me and he refused. I taught him what rocks to collect, but the rocks that came back from his expedition went to Cambridge, though they should have been mine. I was humiliated.'

She sat back and sipped her drink. 'Oh, and my first husband, Reginald, was impotent,' she added. 'I knew I couldn't be the only woman suffering from sex ignorance, so I decided to research sex and relationships instead. It turned out to be a good choice.'

Lillemor sagged in her chair, feeling the anger run out of her. 'I've got no hope. I'm not even a proper photographer. Freda's right. I've got nothing to offer an expedition.'

'Oh, I wouldn't say that. You're a woman of energy and imagination. Tell me, what's your greatest weapon, do you think?'

Lillemor looked over at her dryly. 'Some would say my vagina. But it's not much help in this case.'

'Proximity,' Marie said.

'What?'

'Things can happen if you put yourself in the path of the action. My one regret is that I stayed home. I should have refused to take no for an answer.'

Lillemor took another gulp and thumped the glass down on the table hard enough to slosh the remains over the side. 'I don't know how that applies in this case.'

Marie smiled. 'I suggest you give it some thought.'

It was dark by the time Lillemor reached home again. Anton was sitting on the front step. He stood up as she approached and pushed herself into his arms. He held her hard, his chin on her head, his arms tight around her.

'I'm sorry,' she murmured, letting her body meld to his.

'Don't even think of it,' he said. 'If I could fund an Antarctic voyage, I'd make you the leader of it.'

She gave a small smile. 'You're sweet. Is there dinner?'

'Warm and waiting,' he said. He opened the door. He'd removed the letter from the bureau, she saw, as she took off her shawl. He took her arm and they started to walk towards the dining room.

'You know that trip you mentioned?' she asked.

'Yes?'

'What about Cape Town?'

He stopped and turned her around to face him. 'What madcap plan are you cooking up now, Mrs Rachlew?'

She shrugged. 'I don't have a plan. But you're a tactician, Anton. You know sometimes you've got to be in the right place at the right time. Will you support me?'

He kissed her. 'You should have been a man, with your brain. But I'm very glad you're not.'

CHAPTER 10

January's antipodean light was dazzling. Table Mountain rose up behind Cape Town with such crisp clarity that Ingrid felt she could have counted each individual tree as they sailed in to the dock. The summer air smelled of sweat and flowers and the drive from the dock to their hotel was a cacophony of light and colour, the streets crowded with coloured minstrels dressed in brilliant silks for the Cape Carnival.

The six months since Lars had agreed to take her had both flown and crawled by. There seemed not enough time to do all that needed to be done, and simultaneously the days seemed to drag as Ingrid waited impatiently for their departure.

She'd come to South Africa with Lars, Mathilde and their new historian, Hans Bogen, in first-class comfort on a passenger liner from chilly London into the heat of a Cape Town summer just after New Year. By the time the taxi disgorged them onto the gravel drive of the Mount Nelson Hotel, Ingrid could feel sweat trickling down her back. Sandefjord in winter, locked at the head of the frozen fjord, with its snug houses and cobbled streets, was a distant memory and the cold of Antarctica was unimaginable in Cape Town's heat.

'Welcome, Consul Christensen. Would you like the post while you're checking in?'

Lars handed the pile of envelopes to Ingrid, who flicked through them. One had been hand delivered. She turned over the perfumed envelope curiously and opened it while Lars arranged their rooms.

It was from Lillemor, and the cheery tone of the note was enough to make Ingrid wish she could have invited Lillemor on their trip instead of Mathilde. On the week-long voyage from Norway via London, Ingrid had tried to draw Mathilde out, but she'd failed to elicit more than monosyllables and eventually she gave up, leaving Mathilde to spend hours at a time in her cabin. Hans Bogen had also tried to engage her, but on the rare occasions she emerged, her silences were near catatonic.

'We have an invitation,' she said to Lars when he turned around from the desk and nodded to a bellboy to pick up their luggage.

'Who on earth do you know in Cape Town?'

'Would you believe Anton and Lillemor Rachlew are here? They've invited us for a private ride on the Table Mountain Aerial Cableway. Lillemor says a Norwegian engineer who is a friend of theirs designed it. We're to go at three.'

Lars looked at her quizzically. 'Seems an odd coincidence. How did they know you're here?'

'You're in the newspaper today, Sir,' the concierge said. 'All of Cape Town knows the whaling king and his wife are here.'

Ingrid smiled at the concierge and took Lars's arm. She moved closer and lowered her voice. 'They're on holiday. Mrs Rachlew is very respectable now, Lars.'

He shrugged. 'Oh, I know. And her husband is important. I just had other things in mind for today. I thought we'd see the carnival.'

'We saw enough of that from the taxi,' Ingrid said. 'I'm certainly not missing a private ride on the cable car. You can see all of Cape Town and miles beyond, I've heard. Mathilde, you'd like to come?'

Mathilde looked at her blankly for a moment. 'Oh. Yes, thanks.'

Ingrid turned back to Lars. 'Good. That's it then.'

He smiled at her and they turned to follow the flock of staff needed to shift their suitcases to their suite.

The Rachlews were waiting in a small pavilion at the base of the cable-car ride. They stepped forward as the taxi drew up and Ingrid looked through the window to pick out Lillemor.

She was as young and glamorous as Ingrid remembered from some years earlier, though she wasn't exactly pretty. Her strong, almost boyish face was set off with a white silk scarf tied casually around her neck and a white hat to keep off the sun. But her face lit up when she smiled, and her enthusiastic rush towards the car was likeable. Ingrid found herself smiling in response as Anton opened the door and gave her a hand out. Lars, Mathilde and Hans followed behind her.

'Mrs Christensen. I hope I can call you Ingrid?' Lillemor stepped forward and kissed her on both cheeks in the French manner, and then turned to Mathilde. 'You must be Mrs Wegger?'

'I'd prefer you call me Mathilde,' Mathilde said. Her tone was flat and Lillemor paused and offered a hand instead of kissing her.

Lars, Anton and Hans were shaking hands with a sudden bonhomie and Ingrid was aware how welcome it was, even after such a short time, to hear Norwegian voices in the midst of Cape Town's unfamiliar accents and languages. Though she only vaguely recalled meeting Lillemor some years ago, she felt she was seeing an old friend.

'Well,' Anton said, gesturing to a butler who popped a chilled bottle of champagne and began to pour. 'Aren't we lucky that a Norwegian designed the cableway? Here's to our countryman's ingenuity.'

'I'm glad you had the connections to bring this about,' Lars said, taking his glass and raising it. 'We are in your debt, Anton.'

'Not at all,' Anton said. 'We're honoured to see you off on such a historic voyage. Now, let's go up, shall we? We'll see if we can spot your ship from the top.'

Lillemor took Ingrid's arm as Mathilde stepped forward into the cabin. 'You're so lucky!' she said. 'Antarctica. What an adventure!'

Ingrid couldn't help smiling back at her. It was such a relief to talk to someone who shared her excitement. 'It's incredible, isn't it?' she said. 'I can hardly believe we're ready to go.'

Inside the cable car Ingrid found a place to stand where she could grip the rail with one hand and her champagne with the other, trying not to stare too obviously at the conductor holding the door open. She had travelled with Lars to England many times and to America once, but this was the first time she'd been to Africa and the city's black and coloured faces were still exotic to her eyes.

The car started with a jolt, slopping everyone's drinks, and lurched up the side of the mountain, the steep slopes falling away beneath their feet and the city spreading out below. Ingrid saw Mathilde clutching the sides of the car as they stared down. Ingrid let go of the railing as soon as she understood the movement of the contraption and could balance. Lillemor stood close by and pointed out Cape Town landmarks as they ascended.

'Oh my God.' Hans moved to the middle of the cabin away from the windows, looking pale. 'I had no idea it was so steep.'

It grew stuffy inside the closed car and Ingrid wished she could fan herself. She glanced over at Mathilde, who was staring fixedly down. Anyone would think she'd been forced to come, the way she acted. It was now getting on for two years since her husband had died; surely enough time for her to have recovered somewhat. But it seemed the friendly wife Ingrid remembered from earlier times had gone. Ingrid wondered why Lars had thought Mathilde such a good choice of companion. She'd thought about suggesting that they send Mathilde back, but when she'd tested him out by referring to Mathilde's strange manner, he waved it off.

The trolley halted at the top of the ascent and the conductor opened the door so they could alight. The air was fresh and cool and Ingrid stepped out into it gladly. She took a deep breath and looked around as the rest of the party filed out. On the edge of one great continent, about to voyage for another. She imagined she could taste the dust of Africa's plains at her back and tried to find any hint of Antarctica in the wind coming off the sea.

'More than one thousand metres up,' Anton said, leading them to the lookout. 'And there lies your ship.'

Ingrid followed the line of his finger and saw, far below, the white oil tanker at the dock. The rest of Lars's whaling fleet had left in November, and the little exploration ship *Norvegia* had gone with them for her first expedition, a circumnavigation of the Antarctic continent. Hjalmar had commitments to the Air Force, so for the first part of the voyage the ship was under the command of Captain Gunnar Isachsen. Leaving three months after the rest of the fleet, *Thorshavn*'s job was to carry down more oil to refuel the factory ship and its catchers, and to bring back the first cargo of whale oil. Hjalmar and his offsider, Nils Larsen, were coming with them to meet up with *Norvegia* and take over her command for a second expedition; dog sledging and mapping continental areas.

But the view to the Southern Ocean lay on the other side of the mountain, not visible from their vantage point. 'Can we go higher?' Ingrid asked.

'Of course,' Anton said. 'After you, ladies.'

Mathilde turned quickly and led the way up the stairs. Ingrid followed. Watching the way Mathilde placed her feet, fast and sure, Ingrid felt a sudden moment of concern. Mathilde hadn't moved so purposefully in weeks. The woman was obviously disturbed and now she was almost galloping towards a cliff edge. Ingrid hurried to keep up on the steep stairway. She was panting by the time they reached the next lookout, and as she topped the stairs Mathilde was already at the edge.

'Mathilde, wait!' Ingrid called.

Mathilde stood still, her shoulders set. Ingrid hurried over and took her by the arm. It was like taking hold of a doll, still and unyielding. She tugged gently until the woman turned to look at her.

'What is it?' Ingrid asked.

Mathilde shook her head and turned away as Lillemor came up behind them.

'The famous tablecloth clouds,' Lillemor said. 'What a pity.'

Ingrid turned to look south, but thick clouds were covering the slopes, blocking the view to the ocean.

'You'll be seeing plenty of the Southern Ocean in the next few weeks,' Lillemor said.

'Yes, plenty,' Mathilde said.

Ingrid felt a moment of irritation and let go of Mathilde's arm. 'It's a pity you're not a little more enthusiastic.'

'I know I'm lucky to be included.'

'Oh, that's so true,' Lillemor said. 'I'm quite envious, Mathilde! We must meet up again in London so I can hear all your stories and see your photos when you come back. You have a camera, of course?'

Mathilde shook her head.

Lillemor looked at them, wide-eyed. 'But this is history being made. You must have a camera!'

Ingrid shrugged. 'I suppose you're right. I don't know how to use one.'

'You can take mine,' Lillemor said. 'I have a new Beau Brownie. You know what Kodak says – *Just press the button and we do the rest.* It's easy. I'll bring it tomorrow to the ship.'

Anton, Lars and Hans reached the lookout and the three women turned to meet them. Ingrid moved away from Mathilde and closer to her husband. She reached for Lars's hand and felt something run between them. It was their dream, at last, she reminded herself.

'You look cold,' Anton said to Lillemor, drawing her close.

'I'm not cold at all,' she said, putting her arm around his waist. 'Goodness, Anton, Ingrid and Mathilde will be facing real cold soon. We mustn't make a fuss about a cool breeze in the face of such courage.'

Hans sidled next to Mathilde but kept a proper distance. She ignored him.

'Ready for your big adventure, ladies?' Anton asked.

'More than ready,' Ingrid said. 'I've been planning this since I was a child.'

'We'd love to come and see you off tomorrow,' Anton said, looking from her to Lars. 'If it wouldn't be an inconvenience. I'd be fascinated to look over your ship. The last time I went to the Arctic was on the *Belgica* Expedition and polar-exploration ships have certainly changed since then.'

Lillemor slapped him playfully on the shoulder. 'Well that was more than twenty years ago, darling; of course things have changed.' She smiled at Lars. 'I'm going to lend the ladies my camera. You simply must have this occasion properly recorded. I could bring it tomorrow.'

'Of course,' Lars said. 'But why don't you join us tonight? We're having dinner with the captains at Kennedy's. You would be very welcome.'

Ingrid looked at him in surprise, but he was beaming and it seemed whatever dislike he'd felt for Lillemor had quite disappeared. Ingrid would have reminded him that Hjalmar was joining them, but there was no opportunity.

'Thank you, Consul,' Anton said. 'Darling, are we free tonight?'

'We'll make ourselves free,' Lillemor said. 'It would be a pleasure.'

They stood in silence for a moment. A filigree trace of wind ran a cold finger over Ingrid's face and was just as quickly gone. She saw Mathilde shiver.

'Let's go down,' she said, feeling suddenly sorry for her. She paused as the others started towards the exit and took Mathilde's hand.

'Don't be afraid, my dear,'

Mathilde looked at her strangely. 'What on earth makes you think I'm afraid?'

Ingrid hesitated and Mathilde pulled her hand free, turned and headed for the steps.

They could almost have been in London or New York, Ingrid thought, as they entered Kennedy's Cigar and Jazz Bar. The big band filled the cavernous room with the irresistible strains of swing jazz. White-gloved, brown-faced waiters weaved gracefully between the tables. The fans circled overhead, swirling the January evening heat and the hum of chatter.

'You wouldn't know we're in a depression,' Ingrid said, looking around at the crisp tuxedos and brightly coloured dresses of the men and women who packed the bar. 'Even London is hardly so merry.'

'London doesn't have gold mines like South Africa,' Lars said. 'Things aren't so desperate here.'

'London is dreary!' Lillemor said. 'It's such a nice change to be somewhere fun.'

The maître d', catching sight of them, hurried forward and greeted Lars with a smile. 'Consul Christensen, such an honour. Your other guests are waiting.'

He led them to a far table where three men stood to greet them. Ingrid was pleased to see Hjalmar, who smiled at her warmly. He looked a little uncomfortable to see the Rachlews, she thought, but quickly adjusted his face and held a hand out to Anton.

Lars shook hands all around. 'Ladies, this is the man who'll be taking us south, Captain Harald Horntvedt,' he said. 'Captain Hjalmar Riiser-Larsen and Captain Nils Larsen are catching a lift south with us to meet up with *Norvegia*.'

Hjalmar bowed his head politely. 'Mrs Christensen, I can see the prospect of Antarctica agrees with you, as you look even more beautiful than when I saw you last in Sandefjord. Mrs Wegger, it's a pleasure to meet you. Mrs Rachlew, a lovely surprise to see you here.'

The waiters drew out their chairs and when they sat down, whisked white napkins into their laps, poured generous glasses of chilled white wine and handed out menus.

'I can hardly believe I'm in such company, having read about you all in the London papers so often,' Lillemor said, smiling at the men.

Nils smiled back. 'Ingrid and Mathilde will soon be more famous than any of us, being the first women to see Antarctica, while Hjalmar and I have only the lowly task of mapping it.'

'If we see it,' grunted Captain Horntvedt. 'You must remember, ladies, there is no guarantee we'll get close enough to see land in a ship as large as *Thorshavn*.'

'I'm sure you'll be able to navigate us successfully,' Ingrid said.

'I cannot promise anything, Mrs Christensen.'

There was an awkward pause and then Hjalmar said, 'No problem, ladies. If the captain cannot get you close to the great continent, then I myself will take you up in *Qarrtsiluni* and you can see the Southern Land from the sky.'

Ingrid felt Lars relax a little by her side. He waved to a waiter and ordered their food.

'*Qarrtsiluni*?' Lillemor asked when the waiter had gone.

'That is Consul Christensen's little joke,' said Hjalmar. 'It means soul of a whale. She's a sweet little seaplane, but unfortunately most of her travel has been on the deck of a ship. How far has she come, Consul?'

Lars spread his hands. 'From Burbank to New York, then across the Atlantic and Northern Seas, then from Sandefjord to Antarctica last year, all without so much as a single ascent. If she indeed has a soul, it would be most ashamed.'

'She is a true explorer then, for humiliation is ever our lot,' Hjalmar said. 'For every great victory, there are a dozen shameful or fatal failures.'

Lillemor leaned forward and rested her chin on her hand. 'How wonderful, flying over Antarctica.'

'I don't think we'll be flying,' Lars said. 'The planes are for Hjalmar and Nils to take on their expedition. I have every faith that Captain Horntvedt will take us through the ice quite safely.'

'With respect, Consul Christensen, safety can never be guaranteed in Antarctica,' said Captain Horntvedt. 'Mrs Christensen, I have expressed my position to your husband. I would not allow my own wife to undertake such a voyage, and especially if I was leaving children at home. Consul, I beg you again to consider carefully. There is still time to change your mind. The ladies can go home on the passenger liner and leave you to come south in peace.'

With exquisite timing, a flurry of waiters arrived with their meals, covering the moment with the precise placement of heavy crockery and the refilling of glasses.

Mathilde looked at Ingrid. 'Lars has not lost a single man from any one of his ships, so I'm told.'

Captain Horntvedt looked up, knife poised. 'You've never been in the fury of a storm on the Southern Ocean, when the waves are higher than the ship's bridge,' he said. 'You have never crept through a field of icebergs in the dark, wondering if at any moment the ship will strike a growler and sink in minutes. Better captains than I have lost their boats, their men and even their own lives. It is tempting fate in the most arrogant manner to take a woman down there as though this is some scenic trip for her own pleasure.'

Lars cleared his throat. 'You've made your position clear, Captain.'

'What's a growler?' Lillemor asked, smiling.

Captain Horntvedt glared at her, then picked up his fork and made a precise slice into the chicken breast.

'A growler is an underwater iceberg that's hard to see,' said Hjalmar. 'Especially dangerous at night.'

'Surely a growler couldn't sink a ship like *Thorshavn*?' Lillemor asked.

There was an awkward silence and then Hjalmar said, 'Don't worry; we keep a sharp lookout for them.'

As they began eating, Ingrid glanced at Mathilde. She was pale and moving her food around her plate.

'Captain, we Norwegians know better than to believe in superstitions about women being bad luck on the sea,' Lillemor said. 'We're descended from Vikings, who believed in the Valkyrie, the handmaidens of war. Mathilde and Ingrid are just like those brave female warriors. Think of the honour they will bring to Norway.'

'I am a Christian. I don't hold with pagan superstitions,' he said.

The musicians finished with a flourish and there was a ripple of applause. Ingrid glanced up to see the singer step back from the microphone. The maître d' stepped up to the stage.

'Ladies and gentlemen, tonight we have the honour of some of Norway's famous polar explorers in the audience,' he said, his voice booming through the microphone.

There was a general shuffling and craning of necks as a spotlight swung around and hit their table, blinding them.

'We welcome Captain Horntvedt, who this year commands the refuelling vessel *Thorshavn*.'

There was a polite ripple of applause.

'Travelling south with him, we have Captain Riiser-Larsen, who flew over the North Pole with Amundsen and just last year met the great Douglas Mawson in Antarctica. He and Captain Larsen will take over command of *Norvegia*, the little ship that's been such a familiar sight at the Cape Town docks and is already down in Antarctica.'

Hjalmar waved and there was a round of enthusiastic applause.

'This year Consul Christensen himself travels south in the hope of seeing Antarctica and perhaps adding some more Norwegian place names to the very blank map of that continent. And that's not all, ladies and gentlemen. Tonight you are witnessing history being made. Hoping to become the first women to land on Antarctica, Mrs Christensen and her companion, Mrs Wegger!'

The musicians played a flourish and a buzz of voices rose around them. Ingrid stared into the spotlight, half blinded until Lars nudged her and she smiled and waved.

'Good luck and godspeed for your voyage. We look forward to welcoming you back to Cape Town,' the maître d' called. The singer stepped back to the microphone and the band began a slow jazz introduction.

'This one's for you, Mrs Christensen, by special request,' the singer said. '"Baby won't you please come home".'

The audience started to clap and Lillemor leaned over to Ingrid. 'They want you to dance. Don't disappoint them. I asked for this song.'

The spotlight was still on Ingrid. She sensed that beyond its brilliance, the whole room was staring. Beside her, Lars rose to his feet, turned to her and held out his hand with a smile. As Ingrid took his hand, the scattered clapping turned into applause.

Lars was smiling as he led her to the centre of the empty dance floor, a space that felt as big as a continent. His enthusiasm for all things modern and American meant they'd learned all the big-band dances and he rather prided himself on his skill, Ingrid knew. He was a good leader, and as long as she could relax and follow him, they were accomplished on the floor.

He took Ingrid in his arms with a confident move that set off another smattering of applause and then they were moving gracefully across the polished floor, in the skipping steps of the foxtrot. Ingrid remembered to tilt her head back and smile.

They came to the end of a diagonal and Lars dipped her low.

'Ingrid,' he said, close to her ear.

'Don't even ask.' She smiled over his shoulder at the audience as he raised her again and they set off across the floor. 'I'm not changing my mind.'

'What about Mathilde?'

'I'm not so sure about her,' Ingrid said.

Lars spun her around. 'I don't want you travelling unaccompanied. If you come, she must come.'

The song ended with a flourish and the diners around them clapped and roared their approval. There was no depression in Cape Town, Ingrid thought, not when a crowd was as happy as this. As she and Lars made their way back towards the table, the next tune started and couples swept past them to the floor. Anton and Lillemor were on their feet and Lillemor winked at Ingrid as she brushed past.

CHAPTER 11

Mathilde had tossed throughout the night, haunted by images of waves that could reach the height of the ship's bridge and invisible icebergs lurking in the water. She rose with terror twisting her stomach and the feeling intensified as she forced down breakfast, packed her bags and travelled by taxi to the docks with the Christensens. It reached a crescendo when she stood on the dock.

Thorshavn towered high above them, white as a bride for its maiden voyage. But the gleaming paint couldn't hide the fact that this was a working ship. Its lines were rude and industrial; its smokestack belched a black cloud into the air. There was nothing to soften its purpose. Mathilde tipped her head back to take it in and realised that even her imaginings had fallen short. She could see the lifeboats hanging along the ship's side, such tiny things. Since *Titanic* had gone down, no ship could be considered invulnerable.

Crowds were gathered to see them off, under a flock of umbrellas to shield them from the sun, and their party had to push through them to reach the gangway. Mathilde heard a volley of howls from somewhere high on the ship – Hjalmar's huskies, outraged at having left solid ground. As she placed her foot on the gangway, something passed through her in a flash; a terror so elemental that it rooted her to the spot, unable to leave the land. Her palm stuck to the metal of the handrail as though frozen.

'Mrs Wegger?' Lars was behind her and she felt that any moment he'd put a fatherly hand in the small of her back to direct her. Her chest had tightened so she could hardly breathe. The roar of the crowd throbbed at her eardrums. The ship was so dazzling against the brilliant blue of the Cape Town sky that it hurt her eyes.

'Mrs Wegger, may I?'

It was Hjalmar, not Lars, and his smile was kindly as he offered his arm. The whole world was waiting and somehow she unclenched her fingers, let go of the railing and gripped him instead, and he was guiding her up the gangway so smoothly that she had reached the deck before she fully realised it. Hjalmar whisked her to the cabin where her bags were waiting, gave her a smile, shut the door and disappeared.

Mathilde knew she was supposed to unpack a few things and settle herself, but she sank onto a chair and stared around her. This would be her prison, this small room with its two bunks and its neat cupboards, and the Christensens just a little further along the corridor. It was one of the nicer cabins on the ship, she knew, but that was little consolation. Antarctica was too far, too dangerous; there was too much wild sea to cross.

There was a knock at the door. Mathilde got to her feet but before she could cross the floor, Ingrid opened the door, smiling fixedly.

'We're casting off soon,' she said. 'Come and wave the crowd goodbye.'

Mathilde felt like she would choke. 'I can't.'

Ingrid stepped over the sill and came into the cabin. 'Oh, you haven't unpacked anything. You'll want a sun hat.'

'You never said it would be so dangerous.' Mathilde's palms were slick with sweat.

Ingrid shrugged. 'Horntvedt exaggerates. It's true Lars has never lost a man, not even from his catchers. You'll be fine.'

Mathilde felt a wave of anger. Back in Sandefjord, when it was first apparent that she had little choice about going, Mathilde had found her pride. She acted as though joining the Christensens on their Antarctic adventure had been her own idea. It seemed Lars and Ingrid were happy to play along and she'd endured several dinners at Ranvik, where they'd talked for hours about their plans to the mousy historian Lars had appointed to come with them. She'd helped Ole and Aase pack to stay with their grandparents and tried to hide how much their excitement hurt. She'd practised a kind of grimace that could pass as a smile and called it up as needed. Her parents-in-law seemed to approve of her better attitude and didn't refer again to the sanatorium. She even continued to open the door to Hans Lund's daily visits. He seemed content to drink her coffee and not press her for anything more.

It was when she said goodbye to the children that the real trouble started. Looking down at them on the dock as the ship pulled away, she was gripped with a premonition that she'd never see them again. She wanted to jump over the boat's side and swim back to them, hold them to her and refuse to be parted from them. How had she let this happen?

She hid herself away during the voyage to Cape Town, trying to regain her self-control. And now, at this impossible stage, it seemed her fear she'd never return to the children wasn't just a foolish notion. Already far from home, the prospect of going countless miles further away from them, into such dangerous territory, was unbearable.

Mathilde's nails dug into her palms. It was no good. Even a sanatorium would be better than this. She turned to Ingrid. 'I won't go. You must let me off.'

Ingrid put out her hand. 'Please, Mathilde. It's just nerves. You'll be fine once we sail.'

Mathilde could feel her muscles quivering with the urge to run. 'You never said a word about the danger. What if we sink?'

'We won't sink,' Ingrid said. 'If, by some remote chance, anything goes wrong, there are twenty-five ships and two aeroplanes in the fleet. One of them will pick us up at once.'

Mathilde stared at her. She was right to distrust Ingrid, who it seemed could leave six children behind without a second thought. She shook her head. 'I'm sorry, Ingrid, my mind is made up. Let me off at once.'

Lillemor stood on the passageway outside the cabins, clutching Anton's hand. The sound of the crowd and the brass band rose up around them, oddly distorted.

'Go on then,' Anton said.

'I can't bear it,' she said. 'So close. What if it doesn't work?'

He gave her a little push. 'Don't lose your nerve now. Your baggage is just down by the gangplank, ready.'

She gave him a quick kiss on the cheek and clip-clipped across the deck to the door of Mathilde's cabin. She glanced back at Anton. He made a V sign with his fingers and then disappeared up the stairs to the bridge. She turned back to the door. Her stomach churned and she wished she'd drunk less champagne the previous night. She raised her hand and knocked.

After a moment Ingrid opened the door, her face grim.

Lillemor made herself smile. 'There you are! I've brought the camera. Why aren't you up on deck? You should see the docks. Half of Cape Town has come to see you off.'

Ingrid rubbed her forehead and Lillemor thought she saw her lip tremble. 'We're having a little problem, I'm afraid.'

'What is it?'

Ingrid moved back to allow Lillemor to step over the sill into the cabin.

Mathilde stood in the centre of the room, clutching her bag, wearing her gloves and hat. 'You can't force me to go.'

Lillemor kept her face sympathetic and concerned. 'What on earth do you mean? You can't lose your nerve. Remember the Valkyrie?'

Mathilde glared at her. 'I don't recall the Valkyrie having children. I had no idea of the risks involved or I'd never have agreed to this. I'm leaving.'

'What about you?' Lillemor asked Ingrid.

Ingrid shook her head. 'Lars won't let me come without another woman.' She turned to Mathilde. 'Please don't do this to me. You agreed.'

'Get me off!' Mathilde's voice rose.

There was a clatter of footsteps outside. Lillemor looked around to see Hjalmar at the door.

'Ladies,' he said, touching his cap. 'We're about to depart. It's time to come on deck.'

Mathilde pushed past Lillemor and grabbed his arm. 'Captain, thank God. Please take me from the ship. Ingrid won't let me go, but my nerve has failed.'

'Mrs Wegger doesn't seem to mind that women won't go to Antarctica this year after all,' Ingrid said.

Lillemor's hands were trembling. Not yet. Not yet. Timing was everything.

Hjalmar glanced at Ingrid, who shrugged helplessly. He turned back to Mathilde. 'Very well,' he said briskly. 'Give me your trunk. Hurry, Mrs Wegger; the gangplank is about to be raised. Come, Mrs Christensen. I'll send a man for your luggage.'

Lillemor heard Ingrid's swiftly indrawn breath. Mathilde pulled her hat down over her eyes and took a step over the doorway.

Lillemor waited a beat. 'One moment,' she said.

The three of them turned to her.

'I have an idea. Mathilde, I could go in your place. My husband can accompany you back to London and put you on a ship to Norway. Ingrid can still go to Antarctica and all isn't lost.'

There was silence in the cabin for a few moments. Hjalmar kept his eyes on Mathilde. Ingrid stared at Lillemor with a pleading look on her face.

'I don't care,' Mathilde said. 'Just let me go and work out the rest yourselves.'

'But Lillemor … you'd need clothing … and your husband?' Ingrid said.

This was the awkward moment. Lillemor raised her chin. 'Anton and I were planning to go mountaineering. I have a trunk of cold-weather clothes with me. It's on the dock.'

At the look of dawning understanding on Mathilde's face, Lillemor felt the heat rising in her cheeks. She fought down her feeling of guilt. What did it matter what Mathilde thought of Lillemor's machinations? She was getting what she wanted – the chance to go home. She should be grateful.

'What a fine solution,' Mathilde said, her voice soft. 'I wish you bon voyage, Mrs Rachlew.' She turned to Hjalmar. 'Please, take me off.'

He looked around at all of them, then appeared to make a decision. He picked up Mathilde's trunk and stepped outside with it.

'Come on,' he said.

Mathilde hurried out behind him. Lillemor and Ingrid looked at each other and then both turned and followed, out of the cabin and down the stairs to the deck. They emerged into the heat and sunshine. Ahead of them, Hjalmar had crossed to the railing. He beckoned to Mathilde, who hesitated. 'Quickly,' he ordered.

The three of them reached the railing at the same moment. Ingrid looked down at the dockyards as a roar rose from the crowd. White faces, shaded by a sea of umbrellas, stared up at them from a spacious area below the ship, smiling and waving. Behind them, fenced off, thousands of brown-faced men and women waved and cheered raucously, many of them still dressed in their minstrel costumes from the carnival. Streamers flew in the air, some reaching the ship, many falling short.

'It is a pity you've changed your mind, Mrs Wegger,' Hjalmar said. 'You and Ingrid have captured the imagination of all of Cape Town. Even the coloureds are your champions.'

Ingrid tried to catch his eye. She'd felt such a wave of relief at the prospect of travelling with Lillemor rather than Mathilde that she wanted to shoo the woman off the ship as fast as possible. 'Don't pressure her, Hjalmar.'

He ignored her. 'Horntvedt is a fine captain. He'll take us safely through the ice. It would be a tragedy if you let his old-fashioned ideas frighten you unnecessarily. You and Ingrid are about to make history. Some last-minute nerves are to be expected.'

A streamer flew up over the railing and fell on the deck beside them. Hjalmar bent down, picked it up and held it out to Mathilde.

She shook her head. 'Give it to them,' she said, gesturing to Ingrid and Lillemor. Ingrid reached out a hand to take it, but Hjalmar didn't look at her.

'If you truly feel you cannot face this adventure, I'll take you from the ship,' he said to Mathilde. 'But everyone who sets off on a voyage into the unknown feels a moment of fear at the start.'

Streamers began to fall all around them. Ingrid turned her head to see Lars and Anton coming towards them along the deck. She smiled at her husband. He'd sort this mess out and they'd be on their way.

'Ladies, there you are,' Lars said. 'Even Captain Horntvedt is happy with this send-off. He's never seen anything like it. I told him we should have taken women down years ago!'

'Exactly right,' Ingrid said, going to his side and tucking her arm into his. 'And I think we should make the most of it. Mrs Rachlew has kindly offered to put aside her plans and join us as the official photographer.'

Anton turned to Lillemor in a move that suddenly struck Ingrid as rehearsed. 'You're full of surprises, my dear,' he said. 'It will break my heart, but I suppose I can spare you.'

Lars looked from Lillemor to Mathilde, confused. 'But –'

'I've changed my mind, Lars,' Mathilde said. 'I can't possibly risk my children becoming orphans. Captain Riiser-Larsen is escorting me from the ship. Mrs Rachlew is generously taking my place so your wife doesn't miss out. Captain, please?'

Hjalmar bent again to pick up Mathilde's trunk.

'That's not possible,' Lars said.

Ingrid turned to him in astonishment. 'What do you mean? We can't force Mathilde.'

Lars shook his head. 'Your father-in-law made it clear he wanted you to stay with us. I'm sorry, Mathilde, but he put you in my care and I must honour that commitment. There's no question of getting off the ship.'

There was silence for a moment. Ingrid looked over at Mathilde. The blank expression she'd worn since they left Sandefjord was gone and Ingrid saw a blaze of anger so vivid that she flinched. She wondered what on earth had caused it.

Lillemor reached out and picked up a streamer from Hjalmar's hand. She raised it high in the air and waved down to the crowd, prompting an answering cheer.

'I think this calls for a photograph,' she said. 'Darling, could you get the camera?'

Anton passed the Beau Brownie to Lillemor. She looked down into the viewfinder and then raised her head.

'Go on then,' she said. 'The first women to go to Antarctica. Smile, ladies.'

'You'd better be in the shot too,' Anton said. 'Here, let me take it.'

'Yes, you come in too,' Ingrid said, dropping Lars's arm.

Lillemor stepped forward and the three of them shuffled till they were standing in a row, their backs to the railing. From the corner of her eye, Ingrid saw a glistening tear fall to the deck in front of Mathilde.

'Smile!' Anton called.

Ingrid looked at Lars, willing him not to make a fuss. She arranged her features into a smile and kept it trained on him.

Anton pressed the lever. 'The first three women to travel to Antarctica. Fabulous! Now I'd best go, or I'll find myself in Antarctica too.' He pulled Lillemor to him. 'Goodbye, my darling. Be good.'

They kissed in a way that suddenly reminded Ingrid of the bargain she'd made with Lars, and then Anton set off at a run. He scrambled down to the dock before the gangplank began to rise with a loud metallic clank and jerk. The horn blasted again.

'This is it,' Lars said, with a slightly stunned air as he watched Anton disembark. 'Mrs Rachlew … er … welcome. Where will you sleep, I wonder.'

'Oh, I see there's another bunk in Mathilde's room,' Lillemor said. 'Perhaps she won't mind us being cabin mates.'

Ingrid turned her head and looked at Mathilde and Lillemor. For a moment the three of them were silent amidst the noise, taking each other's measure. Then Lillemor turned back to the crowd and held her streamer aloft, waving. Ingrid went to stand next to her at the railing. She looked back over her shoulder and gestured. Mathilde came to her side.

Thorshavn started shuddering as the engines moved into gear and it began to ease away from the dock. The streamers stretched and broke and thousands of voices lifted again to call out farewell. Ingrid watched Table Mountain gradually becoming smaller. Whatever bonds she had with home snapped and drifted away as easily as the coloured streamers. The clear southern sunlight was spilling across the water, dazzling her. It was her moment, at last.

CHAPTER 12

Thorshavn steamed into the night, leaving a ribbon of churned water in its wake like a ski trail across the snow. Within three hours of leaving Cape Town the wind had picked up and now it moaned through the struts of the two aeroplanes, beginning to speak of ice and fog. The swells were already starting to lengthen and deepen, and the ship was rolling with their rhythm. There was no land now for two thousand miles ahead and Hjalmar's huskies whimpered and snapped with the knowing of it, feeling the water dropping away beneath them in countless fathoms, turning darker blue as they tipped off the continental shelf and left Africa behind.

Ingrid stood at the stern, sheltered under the wing of *Qarrtsiluni*, alone and unobserved. Now that night had fallen, her elation had worn off and she was shaken at how close she'd come to losing it all. She wanted to let it blow away behind her, all the planning and scheming, all the deals made and agreements broken.

She'd drunk too much through the evening. They all had, to ease the discomfort of their odd departure. Even Mathilde had tipped her head back and swallowed her aquavit with a kind of grim determination. The other guests around the captain's table in the saloon were excited and talkative, and gradually the awkward atmosphere between the three women thawed. Nils and Hjalmar laughed loudly. The first mate, Atle Tang, had an encyclopaedic knowledge of shipping and whaling. Their medical man, Dr Stevensson, fancied himself a teller of jokes and threatened to sing for them, and even shy Hans Bogen loosened up, confiding in Ingrid that he was honoured to share the voyage with the first women to set out for Antarctica.

But it was Lillemor who shone. She was charming, questioning Hjalmar about his explorations, Captain Horntvedt about his shipping and Lars about his whaling activities. As Ingrid watched her enchant them, she gradually understood that Lillemor knew most of the answers to her questions already.

Lars, oblivious, seemed flattered. He'd made a joke, saying his whaling interests were but the tip of the iceberg. He alone had sent his three huge factory ships, fourteen catchers, and of course *Norvegia*.

'It's the largest whaling fleet to ever go south. I calculate at least thirty-seven factory ships are down there this season, perhaps forty in all,' he told Lillemor. 'Each has five, six, sometimes seven catchers. There might be as many as two hundred and fifty vessels down there hunting whales.'

'Surely we couldn't be the only women aboard such a flotilla,' Lillemor had said.

'I haven't heard of any others,' Lars answered. 'You ladies will be the first.'

After dinner everyone had gone up to the bridge. Ingrid had excused herself and slipped away, desperate to be alone. Lillemor would be an interesting companion, Ingrid thought, but after her husband's breezy farewell on the ship and the revelation that Lillemor was prepared in every way for this journey, Ingrid realised the woman had brazenly manipulated them.

As she looked out at the wake spreading behind them, she thought that Lillemor's effort was, in truth, no more manipulative than her own. She had no intention of conceiving a child on this trip, and in that matter she was lying to Lars. There was no getting around it and the deception lay heavy on her.

The wind gusted by, carrying a petrochemical belch from the ship's smokestack and making Ingrid's eyes water. Since she was fifteen she'd dreamed of sailing south on a timber ship like *Fram* or *Polaris*. They were ships constructed of living materials. They lived and breathed, creaked and spoke; their builders could name every wood used in the making of them.

Thorshavn was a new-century steel ship, four times the length of *Polaris* and powered by oil. It was impossible to think of it as 'she'. Every inch of its metallic length was masculine and industrial, from the squat smokestack rising near the cabins to the raised midship catwalk that bisected the deck so that passengers could walk safely between the bridge and the cabins when the sea was rough. The thrust of the engine's pistons would be Ingrid's companion for the next six weeks. She could feel the shudder in her bones and gristle. To this throb she would rise and fall asleep. It would rattle her waking hours and shake her dreams.

It was a top-heavy ship, Ingrid thought, with all human accommodation built above the deck line to leave the hold free for oil tanks. They were full of fuel, not only for their own journey, but to refuel the factory ships and catchers already down south. Those same tanks would be cleaned out and filled with whale oil, siphoned from the factory ships so the fleet could continue hunting.

A crew of eighty-seven manned the huge vessel. Ingrid had met the more senior among them, including the chief steward, the first mate and the bosun, but in some hidden part of the ship, dozens more men laboured at jobs that kept *Thorshavn* running. It was an odd feeling knowing they were there but invisible.

Ingrid pressed herself close to *Qarrtsiluni* and looked around. The empty sea stretched out in all directions, showing no trace of what had sailed before them. As Bjarne had reminded her, the largest whaling fleet in history had gone south this season.

She had kept one more secret from Lars and it wasn't one she'd planned. Bjarne had come to see them off in London, clearly offended that Lars had chosen to take the younger historian Hans Bogen instead. He'd been cool with Lars, shaking his hand formally. He'd waited till Lars was engaged in conversation to take Ingrid's hand and lean in close to speak to her privately.

'Observe carefully, Mrs Christensen,' he said. 'For I'll want to talk to you when you return. Tell me truthfully, once you've witnessed it, if you think the whales down there can withstand this kind of hunting. I don't want to hear what your husband thinks. I want your own response.'

She'd tried to draw her hand out of his but he resisted, clinging to her fingers. 'I'll give you my honest opinion,' she said at last.

He loosened his grip and met her eyes steadily. 'I believe you will. I know you're a woman of honour.'

Ingrid hadn't mentioned it to Lars in the flurry of leaving and now she thought she might not raise it at all. She shook her head to clear the unease of the idea. She was here at last, her feet planted firmly on the metal deck, the railing cold under her hands. No matter what ship it was she travelled on, Antarctica lay ahead of them and no one could stop her trying for it now. She felt the flutter of excitement in her belly return at the thought.

A call came on the wind and she lifted her head. It was Lars. She stepped away from *Qarrtsiluni* and climbed the stairs up to the cabin deck before calling out an answer, not ready yet to reveal her private place.

'There you are,' he said, gripping the railing as the boat moved beneath him. 'I thought you were coming up on the bridge.'

'I just needed some fresh air.'

He came closer and put out a hand. 'Are you all right? I hope you're not seasick already.'

'I'm fine.' She came close to his side. 'Do we need to see our guests to their cabin?'

'Lillemor is staying on the bridge a while longer. Mathilde has already gone to bed.'

'That was rather strange with Mathilde,' Ingrid said. 'Why didn't you let her go home? She obviously doesn't want to come.'

He pulled her in to his body, sheltering her from the wind. 'Ole asked me to take her as a favour,' he said. 'He and Gerd want to give their grandchildren a break from Mathilde's misery. I couldn't very well send her back. Think of those poor little ones.'

'I suppose not,' Ingrid said thoughtfully. She'd presumed Mathilde had freely decided to come with them. It seemed there was more to the arrangement than she realised.

'Ready for bed?' Lars asked, tightening his arms around her.

She nodded. Their cabin was just a few steps away and they were inside in moments. A double bunk had been specially built for them on this maiden voyage, but it was a snug fit. Ingrid undressed and cleaned her teeth in the small bathroom off their sleeping quarters, bumping into Lars as he did the same. The ship lurched as she was getting into bed and she fell against him, sending the two of them tumbling to the bunk. She tucked herself into his arms.

'Listen,' Lars said, raising his head.

The wind was rattling the door in its frame and the whistle of it in the stays was getting louder. Below them, *Thorshavn*'s pitch altered slightly and Ingrid felt a sideways roll.

'Dr Stevensson has the latest drugs if you feel unwell,' Lars said.

'I don't need them,' she said. 'Turn off the light.'

He pulled the blankets up making a cave around them, and shifted his body alongside hers. It was no closer than they'd slept on a thousand nights, but somehow different. She'd missed him, Ingrid realised. Not just over the past months when she stopped him from touching her, but before that, in the quietening of their marriage's fire. She'd missed the easy way passion rose when they were young. Perhaps on this unknown sea, with the waves beginning to rise around them, they could leave their staid, long-married lives behind.

But she'd have to be careful. Ingrid had studied her cycle in the months before leaving. She didn't have the option of using a dutch cap, as recommended by Dr Stopes to prevent pregnancy, so timing was everything. It would take careful management to ensure Lars didn't realise she was avoiding making love at her fertile time. Ingrid had been relieved when her calculations showed the start of the trip to be safe. Perhaps she could wear Lars out a little, she thought. She wished she could come to him without this duplicity.

She pressed her palm on his chest and felt his heart thudding under the blond trace of curls, steady as *Thorshavn*'s engine. They were both breathing heavily, full of expectation. Her hand slid lower, crossing the softened plain of his belly, and then down until she had him in her grasp and he began to move. It had been such a long time that Ingrid felt an answering urgency and when he reached between her legs, she was already slick. His fingers stroked her and she remembered how well he knew her body. It wasn't long till she was ready for him and then he rolled on top, pinning her.

She gripped him with her thighs and strained towards him. He held back a moment until her breath came out in a gasp and her fingers raked his back and then he moved into her and they rocked together, the full length of *Thorshavn* rising and pitching beneath them, its roar loud in her ears.

Afterwards Ingrid lay next to him, her leg draped over his hip. Their breathing slowed and she felt Lars twitch as he began to fall into sleep's abyss.

'I think you were right.' His voice was sated. 'We'll make a child on this trip.'

At his words she felt a tightening in her body, a drawing away deep inside, as if her womb recoiled from him. It was true that if ever a child would be conceived to run a shipping empire it would be here, formed in the growl of *Thorshavn*'s belly. But Ingrid realised she'd already put her children to one side. She hadn't given them a thought since she boarded.

The truth was, deep down she didn't like being a mother. Being a woman of wealth, she could employ any number of servants and helpers to look after them and she'd done exactly that since they were young, sparing herself from their demands. She'd have been happy having just two, she thought. Her eldest daughter, Motte, and a boy who was like Lars to take over his business empire. That would have been plenty.

Lars gave a gentle snore and Ingrid eased herself away from him. She sat up, pulled the curtain open a crack and pressed her face close to the glass. It was too dark to see anything much, but the roll of the ship was starting to make her feel disoriented.

Lars, a modern man in almost everything, was old fashioned in this. He was like her own father, believing that a large brood of children guaranteed the survival of his own line.

Perhaps that was why Alfhild had gone mad, she thought. Perhaps her mother hadn't wanted more children either, and her only escape from Thor had been to lose herself in the snow.

CHAPTER 13

Mathilde tried to settle her body in the narrow bunk. To roll from her back to her side required planning, shifting with care, realigning herself. The only saving grace of the trip had been the possibility of solitude, the chance to go deep into her grief without the need to function, at least nominally, for the children. But the weight of their absence, loaded on top of her grief, threatened to crush her. Alone, she could have made the cabin a sanctuary, a grieving place where she could come all undone. But that damned woman would be here with her, and there was no choice but to breathe each other's air and smell each other's sour breath and broken wind.

Mathilde had put thought into avoiding Lillemor. Over dinner, watching her down her wine with enthusiasm, Mathilde surmised that the woman was likely to keep late hours, and decided she'd keep early ones. If she took herself to bed well before Lillemor, and rose before her, she could avoid conversation altogether. It was important not to let any notion develop of friendly chatter or schoolgirl confidences after lights out.

It was much later when Lillemor came in, though Mathilde was still trying to get comfortable. Hearing the rattle of the door handle, she shifted so she was facing the wall. Lillemor flipped on the light, sending a blaze through the cabin. In the moment of silence that followed, Mathilde held herself ferociously still. She heard Lillemor begin to undress and could follow the sequence of it with awful clarity: the fur coat, the dress, the shoes, the stockings, the silk slip, the underpants. She squeezed her eyes more tightly shut. Six weeks of this ahead of her. The whisper, slip, scuffle went on and on, how many layers was she wearing? And then there was the putting away, the opening of drawers, the clatter of hangers.

Mathilde had seen Lillemor's luggage carried up to the cabin by a couple of muscular, jovial Norwegians. She had a big wardrobe suitcase and a number of smaller bags. Mathilde suspected she'd never planned to go mountaineering. She'd come to Cape Town in the height of summer with trunks of furs and mufflers, intending from the outset to take Mathilde's place.

Mathilde could have groaned aloud with frustration. She'd have gladly given it to her, but once again she was under someone else's power. Some man always had a say over her, without the softening effect of a marriage where she could convince, cajole or negotiate.

These wealthy women and their indulging husbands! Anton looked at his younger, glamorous wife the way a dog would – hungry, adoring, deferential. Lars and Ingrid were a well-oiled unit, running an empire of shipping and whaling and God knows what else. Lars was more powerful than her father-in-law, Ole, and of a newer generation, one not so afraid of women. Ingrid seemed more like his equal. But Mathilde was at the mercy of them all.

At last Lillemor finished her fussing around, switched off the light and settled herself in her bunk with a sigh. Mathilde slowly unclenched her tense muscles in the glorious dark, her only safety. The door rattled, startling her, but it was just the wind. Lillemor twisted and turned for a few minutes, finding the shape and heft of the bunk as Mathilde had, and then her breathing deepened, horribly close by. She exclaimed once, a kind of sleepy whimper, and then was silent.

The ship lifted beneath them, rising higher and higher, then peaking and pitching forward. Mathilde had never been on an ocean-going ship before the passenger liner that carried them to Cape Town and now they were heading into much wilder waters.

She thought of the children, concentrating on forming their image in her mind, recreating their features until she could almost see them standing in the cabin in front of her. She'd been unable to recall Jakob's face and his voice within just a few weeks of him going to Venezuela and she'd wondered if this failure to keep him alive in her heart had contributed in some way to his death. She vowed she wouldn't forget the children's faces or the sounds of their voices. She'd recall them every hour of every day, imprint them upon herself.

Mathilde decided to imagine she was sailing in their direction, as if the children had cast a silver fishing line into the sea and were reeling her in. There would be no north and south. She would set her journey instead to the pole point of her children and sail to her own compass, her path laid down clear and straight across the sea, simply a distance to be travelled until she was with them again.

She'd have to be careful now and not show weakness. Lars acted for her parents-in-law and if they dreamed of taking her children, he'd help them. Mathilde had wanted nothing more than to hide herself away but she saw now it wouldn't do. Her children may already have been taken from her. She had to start thinking in terms of winning them back, even before fully understanding she'd lost them.

She hadn't missed the look of irritation that had crossed Ingrid's face at the Cape Town dock when Lars refused to let Mathilde disembark. It had hurt, but more than that, it showed there was no past loyalty that Mathilde could rely on. She was alone in this battle. Her casual friendship with Ingrid from past years meant nothing, and Lillemor was a woman willing to do anything to get her way. The only person who'd shown her real kindness so far was Hjalmar.

The ship rose and fell slowly, tracing the arc of a swell, and Mathilde realised the movement was somehow reassuring. Rocked in the cradle of her bunk, heading home. She moved her feet until they were pressing up against the bunk's end, braced herself and then surrendered to the ship's motion. She gave up all resistance, letting it carry her. The feeling was somehow familiar, but she couldn't place it. It wasn't until she was on the lip of sleep, dropping down the face of it, that she remembered. Like sex, bracing herself on Jakob's body, letting the movement carry her, recognising it as a bigger force than herself. She'd forgotten what it was like.

CHAPTER 14

Lillemor woke with a start in the thick, moving darkness. The world was shifting around her. She felt herself sliding and flailed till she caught the edge of her bunk and wrapped her fingers around it, trying to orient herself. The ship knifed down into the sea and she could hear the waves parting beneath them. When she raised her head, she felt a sickening nausea and lowered it again with a moan.

The ship rose again, higher this time, and Lillemor panicked as it tipped over the top of the wave and started down, nose first. *Thorshavn* had looked as substantial as a building in Cape Town. The small waves had lapped against her solid sides, giving no suggestion that the sea could throw her around like this, let alone on their first night out.

The ship crashed into the trough with a shudder. Lillemor clenched her teeth as her stomach lurched in sympathy. She tensed, ready for the next wave.

She hadn't counted on the adventure being painful. She'd expected to stand at *Thorshavn*'s bow in the wind looking towards Antarctica, but instead she couldn't raise her head from the pillow.

It was shocking how quickly and thoroughly seasickness changed a person's outlook on the world, she thought dimly. It turned the greatest adventure into a nightmare, took a personality and wrung it out, leaving only the sorry dregs. If she'd had the chance to be magically transported from the ship and returned to land, at that moment she'd have taken it. Even the great Mawson had been dreadfully seasick, she remembered. She wondered how he'd had the courage to voyage south more than once.

Somehow she managed to doze. When she woke again, Mathilde was out of her bed, pulling aside the curtain that covered the porthole and sending in a blaze of daylight. Lillemor tried to sit up but the movement caused her stomach to lurch again and she fell back to the pillow. She heard Mathilde cross the cabin to her side.

'A bit rough, eh?' Her voice was matter-of-fact, hard. 'Are you all right?'

Clenching her teeth, Lillemor made a small shake of her head.

'Need a bucket?'

She managed a nod and closed her eyes. The trick seemed to be not to move and not to look at anything. She heard Mathilde return and felt the cool of the tin pail on her fingertips.

'I'll hook it here for you next to the bed. Do you want something to eat?'

Lillemor retched then, somehow lurching across to the bucket to bring up a remnant of last night's dinner. She hung over it, wanting to move away from the acrid stench, but afraid that any movement would set her off again. She felt a firm hand on her hairline.

'I'll get the doctor,' Mathilde said.

Lillemor vaguely recalled the doctor talking at dinner about a new medicine for seasickness and felt a glimmer of hope. But Mathilde started to move her hand away, and with it went any sense of stability.

'Wait,' Lillemor croaked. The hand halted. Lillemor felt Mathilde tilt her head back slightly and wipe her mouth with something – a handkerchief, she thought. She kept her eyes tightly shut, though she could feel tears escaping from them anyway. 'Please, stay with me,' she said. Mathilde's hand was the only thing between her and the abyss.

'Lie still,' Mathilde said. 'I'll ring for the steward and he can get the doctor.'

Mathilde's cool hands guided her back towards the pillow. Lillemor kept her eyes closed, sunken in misery. There was no world outside the tiny cabin, which shook as though some god had picked them up in a box and decided to rattle them like dice. There was no London, no Cape Town, no Antarctica even.

If it were easy, everyone would do it. That sounded like Freda's voice echoing around in her head. It was true, Lillemor supposed. Why hadn't she taken up something on firm ground – mountain climbing, perhaps? Freda could have trained her and she wouldn't have had to cross half the world in a ship in order to be the first woman to do something.

'Dr Stevensson's here,' Mathilde said.

'Mrs Rachlew, I hear you're not too well.' His voice boomed through the cabin, bouncing off the inside of her head. She winced.

'I've got a little injection here that should be just the trick,' he said. 'I'll just need your haunch if you don't mind.'

She felt Mathilde roll her onto her side and pull back the covers. A rush of cold air on her skin, a quick sting, and she was lying on her back again, covered.

'Good girl,' he said. 'You'll start to feel better in half an hour. In a day or two you'll have your sea legs.'

Half an hour. Eternity. She couldn't imagine surviving that long. Mathilde and the doctor talked in low voices but Lillemor couldn't hear them and didn't care.

Then Mathilde was back at her side. 'Doctor says to try and eat a few soda biscuits. Can you manage one? Come up on your elbow so you don't choke.'

With Mathilde's help Lillemor raised herself. The salty biscuit seemed to dry out and swell in her mouth. It took her an age to chew and swallow and her belly cramped dangerously when the first mouthful landed, but it seemed she might be able to hold it down. She finished the biscuit, took a few sips of water, and lay down again.

She looked up at Mathilde. 'Could you stay?'

Mathilde sighed but kept her hand on Lillemor's forehead. Lillemor closed her eyes. The ship continued to rise and fall, but gradually she realised she cared less about it. She felt a heaviness come over her, pinning her to the bed. She wanted to say something to Mathilde, but what?

'I'm sorry,' she said, or dreamed she said. There was no answer.

CHAPTER 15

Ingrid felt a tendril of wakefulness steal into her dream. She pulled back, resisting. She was aware of motion and for a moment, in her half-waking state, she thought it was the fishlike movement of a child inside her. Her hands went to her belly. Finding flatness, she jolted fully awake.

She was being rocked in the ship, that was all. She sighed with relief, hoping the thought of a child wasn't some kind of prescience, and sat up. Lars had gone. His side of the bunk was empty, his pyjamas neatly folded. He hadn't been seasick a day in his life.

Ingrid rose and pulled back the curtains from the porthole. She could see swells washing past, tipped with spray, and some small birds flashed by. She hugged herself and began pulling out her clothing, desperate to get out of the cabin and see their surroundings. Woollen stockings, a warm woollen dress, a heavy coat with a mink collar and lapels, and her black woollen beret. She wedged herself in front of the mirror, drew on her eyebrows, rinsed her mouth and added a little lipstick. Her cheeks were pale, she noticed. She didn't feel ill, exactly, but the ship's rise and fall left her queasy. A bread roll and some coffee would help.

The wind slapped her as she stepped out of the cabin. The sky was a dull, glaring grey and the steely blue swells rose in jagged, messy peaks. Overnight, it seemed, they'd passed from seas softened by their proximity to the African continent to those wild and remote. They were crossing the Roaring Forties, she knew, and their passage was likely to get rougher as they moved into the Furious Fifties and then into – what did they call them? Ah yes, the Screaming Sixties.

Ingrid pulled her beret down hard and stepped out on the catwalk that ran from fore to aft. It had seemed such a practical structure back in Cape Town, raised above the flat deck below. But as she moved along it, Ingrid realised it was a precarious thing. She gripped the metal railing, feeling its slipperiness under her fingers. It wouldn't take much to slither through the gaps in the railings and fall to the deck a good dozen feet below. As it tilted, she could see that a person conceivably could be washed from the deck into the sea. She wasn't someone who worried about such dangers normally but she suspected Mathilde would find the reality of the ship terrifying.

'Mrs Christensen?'

She turned to see one of the mess boys standing behind her, holding a tray.

'Your husband told me to bring you breakfast.'

'Ah,' she said. 'Thank you. What's your name?'

'Tobias.'

'Where is my husband taking breakfast?'

'He's done, ma'am. He's on the bridge.'

'Then I'll have mine there,' she said. 'You go first; I'll follow.'

He flung her a nervous look, then stepped around her with the tray, swaying with bent knees to stay upright. Ingrid followed more slowly, gripping the rails. The ship was both pitching up and down and rolling from side to side as it climbed over the swells. It was nothing like the motion of sailing on the fjord at home.

She followed the boy through a confusing maze of corridors and stairs and then they halted outside a heavy door.

'After you, ma'am,' he said.

She stepped past him, pushed the door open and stepped over the sill into the bridge. At first all she could see was the panorama through the bank of windows, revealing the waves in their full size and scope, marching shoulder to shoulder towards them in ranks that stretched to the horizon. As her eyes adjusted, Ingrid saw Horntvedt was glaring at her from behind a console.

Lars came hurrying across to cut her off. 'My dear, it's best if you take your breakfast in the saloon. This is the captain's workplace.'

Tobias immediately began backing out the door. Ingrid looked around. The bridge even smelled masculine, of tobacco and some kind of hair oil. Her belly growled; she was in dire need of sustenance and it was fast disappearing.

She lifted her chin. 'I see. I'll come back shortly.'

She held the door for the boy, stepped out behind him and let it fall shut, feeling the heat rising in her cheeks. As if she were a child and might spill her food!

'Will you go to the saloon?' Tobias hunched his shoulders as if he was afraid of being whipped.

His posture reminded Ingrid of Lars Junior and she had to stop herself from telling him to straighten up. She forced a smile. 'Good idea, young man.'

But the heat in her cheeks was still there as she finished her breakfast and drained her second cup of coffee. It would take courage to turn around and go back there again without being cowed. The bridge was the domain of the ship's captain and although Horntvedt couldn't actually prevent her from visiting – not with Lars on board – he could certainly make it uncomfortable. Ingrid needed to stake her claim early, but she was still disoriented. The ship was unfamiliar and after breakfast her stomach had become unsteady. She was afraid she might get seasick up on the bridge, where the roll and pitch was greater than on deck level, closer to the ship's centre of gravity.

Ingrid wiped her mouth and hands, laid down her napkin and decided she'd explore instead. Make a territorial reconnaissance and then a second foray into enemy territory when she felt more secure. She wondered if Mathilde and Lillemor were awake. She sighed, wondering if the three of them could be friends on this trip. Hopefully their strange start wouldn't taint the whole voyage.

She pulled her heavy coat back on and stepped outside. The forecastle deck at the front of the ship, in full view of the bridge, felt too exposed so she climbed down a stairwell to the central deck. Hjalmar's team of huskies were tied up there in a section with high edges to keep them safe. They all lay on their sides. Ingrid called out in a friendly voice, but though one or two raised a head, most ignored her. She wondered if they were dangerous. They were working dogs, but she'd seen Hjalmar handling them and they didn't look vicious. She moved closer, reached a hand out to fondle one. Its tail thumped weakly. Then it retched and she realised they were seasick. She drew her hand back and continued on her way.

Ingrid skirted around the cabins and came to the boat's stern where the two planes were lashed to the deck, flightless *Qarrtsiluni* and the pragmatic *F18*, ready for use in finding and mapping new areas that the ships couldn't reach. She stationed herself behind *Qarrtsiluni*. Sheltered under its wing she was invisible from any vantage point on the ship.

This was her world for the next six weeks. There was little of it, and no place exclusively her own. There was a very long way to go, Ingrid realised, before the scenery changed and she could finally see the ice she longed for. For the first time it occurred to her that she might become bored.

She heard voices approaching and felt a flash of irritation at the disturbance. Hjalmar appeared around the side of the planes, and, behind him, Mathilde.

'Oh. Ingrid.' Mathilde stopped. 'I didn't know you were here.'

'Mrs Christensen, I trust you were able to eat your breakfast in comfort?' Hjalmar said.

'No thanks to our captain,' Ingrid replied, her voice sharper than she intended. 'It seems the bridge is too sacred for someone to eat there.'

Hjalmar propped himself beside her, leaning against the railing for balance. 'Have you spotted the albatross?'

'Where?' Ingrid asked.

'Let us try to find it,' Mathilde said. She came and stood by Ingrid at the railing and they both gazed out at the horizon. Mathilde leaned forward and put her hand to her brow to shield her eyes from the glare. The ship rose to crest a wave.

'There!' she exclaimed and lifted her arm to point.

'A wanderer, by the looks of it,' Hjalmar said.

By the time Ingrid could make out a distant moving blob, she felt sour and annoyed. She pulled her beret down around her ears and tucked the fur collar of her coat around her face. Mathilde moved around the railing, following the bird's path.

Hjalmar glanced at Ingrid after Mathilde was out of earshot. 'Horntvedt is old fashioned, and passengers have to respect a captain on his ship. It's not personal.'

The wind whistled behind them through the struts of the aeroplanes. 'That almost makes it worse,' Ingrid said. 'I already feel like a piece of baggage, just like *Qarrtsiluni* there, carried on the deck all that way and good for nothing.'

Hjalmar turned his head to take in the aircraft's sturdy lines. 'Poor old thing. Your husband is a romantic. You can't name a plane after the soul of a whale and then expect it will rise up and find its brethren for the slaughter. We always called her *Grey* to stop such superstitions, but I think they've clung to her anyway.'

He watched the albatross for some time. 'This first part of the trip is hard, rolling and pitching for days with nothing much to see and no one having their sea legs,' he said at last. 'Even the best sailors are cranky. When we get to the ice, it's another world.'

'Let's hope so.' Ingrid turned back to the railing. The wandering albatross swooped into view again, closer this time, and she could make out the extraordinary width of its wingspan. It hung in the slipstream behind the ship, effortlessly keeping aloft. She'd read that such birds lived at sea for years, taking sustenance from the fish they caught and only landing to carry out their biological duty to breed. At the thought of it she felt a dull ache in her abdomen.

Hjalmar called out to Mathilde. 'Mrs Wegger, would you like a coffee?' When Mathilde reappeared around the side of the plane, he looked at Ingrid. 'Do you want to come too?'

Ingrid shook her head. Staring at the albatross had disoriented her even more. The ship's movement was making her queasy and the thought of succumbing in front of them was unbearable.

'No, thank you,' she said.

They seemed to hesitate and her mouth flooded with saliva. She couldn't remember when she last vomited, but there was no mistaking the warning signs.

'Leave me alone please,' she said through gritted teeth.

They stepped away and up the stairs and Ingrid tried to fight off the sensation. Then the ship rolled and her stomach did the same. It was an awful feeling, as though her body had suddenly become her enemy. A second rise and fall was all it took. The spasm gripped her and she bent double over the railing. Her stomach emptied, its contents shooting out into the wind and falling into the ship's wake.

She hung, suspended, drooling, gripping the railing, despising her own weakness. In her excitement about Antarctica she'd somehow forgotten the long, rough voyage to get there. She had no function in the smooth running of the ship, no reason for existing in this streamlined, industrial factory. Perhaps Horntvedt was right that there was no place for women here.

CHAPTER 16

Mathilde walked across the catwalk, feeling Hjalmar close behind. Unaccountably she was the only one of the three women who wasn't seasick and she felt a moment of grim satisfaction. Ingrid had been a pale shade of green when she ordered them away from her, and back in Mathilde's cabin, Lillemor had fallen back asleep after the doctor's injection. Unguarded, clammy-skinned and pale, her face was quite severe in its lines. Without the electrifying effect of her personality, Lillemor's was a plain enough countenance after all.

After the stuffy air of the cabin, the wind was fresh and cool on Mathilde's skin. It smelled simple, of salt and sea. She blinked and inhaled deeply a few times, then looked around as they walked above the mid deck of the ship. She'd not really absorbed the ship's layout the day before. They were on the raised catwalk that joined the rear superstructure where the cabins were located and the front, housing the bridge and the saloon. Ocean and sky spread out in every direction.

But the way Ingrid told them to leave her alone reminded Mathilde of how powerless she was on the ship, no matter how strong her stomach, and it was a depressing thought. It hung over her as Hjalmar guided her down the stairs to the mid deck.

'Mrs Wegger, look in here,' he said, bringing her to the side of a wide wooden box lashed to the deck.

She peered in and six sets of eyes peered up at her, wreathed in the thick smell of wet dog. The surprise of it jolted her from her thoughts. 'Puppies?'

'Too young to leave their mother and she's my best team leader, so they had to come along. Want to pat one?'

At her nod he reached in and hefted one out by the scruff of its neck. The adult huskies, with their snub noses and thickset features, weren't especially attractive animals, but the pups were clown-faced and charming. The creature hung limply in Hjalmar's grasp, staring at Mathilde. He brought it closer and the pup suddenly flipped out a pink tongue, catching her nose. It made her laugh unexpectedly. A quick laugh, just a pulse beat long, but a real one. She held out her arms.

Hjalmar deposited the pup into them. It squirmed, trying to turn around and lick her. One of the dogs growled, but a stern word from Hjalmar silenced it.

Mathilde felt the pup's warmth in her arms as it wriggled to get in closer to her, and she hoped her pang of longing didn't show. Aase was reasonably amenable to being held, but not for too long, and Ole would endure the confines of her arms for less than a minute, as if they both sensed the vortex of grief in such hugs and instinctively avoided it. But the pup was either oblivious to such things or knew itself immune to human sorrow. It rested its muzzle on her arm, wriggled around to get comfortable, and fell asleep.

'He likes you,' Hjalmar said. 'His name is Babyen. The runt.'

Mathilde kept her eyes on the top of the pup's head. This was too dangerous; she was too exposed. After a moment she thrust out her arms and shoved the puppy towards Hjalmar. 'He's heavy,' she said.

The pup whimpered at the sudden awakening, a sound that could have come from her own throat. She turned away.

'Would you like to see the forecastle?' Hjalmar asked. 'You may get a little wet.'

She turned to him. With both Ingrid and Lillemor out of action, she had a chance to assert herself. 'I'd like to see the bridge.'

He smiled. 'Very well, why not? There's a few rules – no touching the instruments, no distracting the captain, no loud talking. Just common sense.'

'I've plenty of that,' she said. 'Lead the way. It's easier for me to follow you.'

As she walked behind him, it occurred to her that here she could be anyone. Lars and Ingrid only knew her superficially from home. Lillemor didn't know her at all, and neither did Hjalmar or Nils or anyone else on the ship.

She wondered if she really knew herself. Away from her ordinary life, out of her marriage, perhaps she was braver and more adventurous than she'd imagined. Perhaps she could stand up to these people with the same kind of effortless power that Ingrid seemed to have and simply demand to get her way.

Hjalmar opened the heavy door and waved her inside. 'Captain Horntvedt, Mrs Wegger would like to see the bridge,' he announced.

She stepped out of the wind. It was warm and a little fuggy inside, with a commanding view of the ship and the immensity of the ocean ahead of them. Mathilde looked around and saw Horntvedt at the wheel. His animosity was palpable, strong enough to drive her straight back out the door again if she allowed it.

She forced herself to walk towards him. 'Thank you, Captain; it's kind of you to allow us in here. You can be sure I won't disturb your concentration.'

She'd taken him by surprise, she saw, as he wrinkled his brow, but she'd surprised herself even more. She crossed the bridge with calm, measured steps, bending her knees to accommodate the ship's motion and hoping she wouldn't miscalculate and careen into a window or wall. But she made it without incident to the far side.

'Mrs Wegger, good morning.' Lars was standing by the window with a proprietorial air.

'Good morning, Consul,' she said.

'I thought my wife would be with you.' He looked questioningly over at Hjalmar.

'Your wife preferred some time alone for bird watching,' Hjalmar said. 'And Mrs Rachlew is a little poorly this morning.'

Mathilde walked across to the windows. From this vantage point she could see down onto the forecastle and ahead to the expanse of ocean. Sandefjord, like most of Norway, was a small and complicated place, with a multitude of rocky bays and inlets fringing the coast, knolls and boulders cropping up in back gardens and between houses. But here the open ocean was space and simplicity; here was nothing but wind blowing across emptiness and the ship making its steady way forward. She liked its rise and pitch; it felt like a living creature, bearing them south in safety. Here, there was nothing she could do, no decision to make, no responsibility for anything.

The albatross made a graceful arc across the front of the ship. Lars took up a pair of binoculars to follow it, and then handed them to her. She raised them to her eyes, taking a moment to adjust her vision.

The bird wheeled, barely moving its expanse of wing, and then dipped down. She was sure it would be caught by a moving swell. It disappeared and she stood on her toes to try and see it again, moving the glasses. Yes, there it was, skimming so low that surely its wings were brushing the water. She wondered if they ever misjudged, dropped a wingtip too low and catapulted into the sea. Or were they born with the knowledge of how to move through the world? There was nothing flustered or ungainly about them. She'd be like that if she could, Mathilde thought. Riding the cross currents of the voyage with supreme calm.

A waft of tobacco smoke drifted past her nostrils. Mathilde recognised it as the same type Jakob smoked and the scent brought his presence back with a wallop. For a second she could see him before her, puffing on his pipe and regarding her. It was the first clear image she'd had of him in a year, and she gasped.

'I'm sorry, Mrs Wegger. Does the smoke trouble you?'

She turned her head to see Nils still holding a match. He'd taken his pipe out of his mouth to speak to her and she could see it was in danger of going out.

'It's fine,' she muttered, and turned away from him. But Jakob was gone after just one tantalising glimpse. She could have cried out with the pain of it, and she bit down hard on the inside of her cheek to control herself.

She'd forgotten him, and the children, for a few minutes. She couldn't afford such a thing. She had to keep the children alive with the strength of her memories, of them and their father. She breathed in as deeply as she could, drawing the whiff of tobacco to the bottom of her lungs, trying to call her husband back.

CHAPTER 17

The bout of seasickness passed, leaving Ingrid quivering. She leaned on the railing again, training her eyes on the horizon till her belly calmed down. Her head ached and she pressed her fingers to her temples, bracing her ankle against the stanchion to keep her balance. Perhaps it was just as well they'd not gone to Antarctica in *Polaris* all those years earlier, she thought. It was much smaller than mighty *Thorshavn* and would have tossed more violently.

She'd watched *Polaris* being built during her engagement, visiting the yards weekly with Lars to see how she progressed. The shipbuilder showed them the precious bow timbers, cut from a single oak tree selected for its curve, and the Norwegian fir and greenheart that sheathed it, with every joint and fitting cross-braced. As well as three masts for sails, *Polaris* had a powerful coal-fired steam engine.

'The only living ship stronger than this is *Fram*,' the builder had declared.

But it turned out that their journey to Antarctica was a young man's promise, made by Lars when the century was still new and Norway was freshly independent from Sweden, and no one knew what it meant to be rocked by a world war. Ingrid had fallen pregnant in the first winter of marriage and Motte was born around the time Lars's business partner, the explorer Adrien de Gerlache, ran into financial difficulties and pulled out of *Polaris*.

The conversation they'd had that night marked the first branch in their paths.

'Can't you find another partner?' she'd asked him. 'Perhaps my father?'

Lars had shaken his head. 'De Gerlache is an explorer. I needed that experience as much as his money.'

'You're not giving it up?' Ingrid asked, her heart sinking.

'It's not a good time right now,' he said. 'Setting up the stock exchange is a big job, and there's the steamship company, and your father thinks we should get involved in hydroelectricity.'

'But when will we go to Antarctica?'

Lars waved his hand. 'We can't go now, not with a baby. And *Polaris* would need to take tourists to Svalbard to shoot bears for a few years before I could afford to send her to Antarctica, even with another partner.'

'Shoot bears?' Ingrid asked, her belly sinking. In her arms, Motte squirmed.

'The ship has to pay herself off,' he said. 'That was always the plan.'

Motte set up a wail that matched the surprise Ingrid felt. 'You never mentioned this.'

Lars got up and put his arms around Ingrid and the baby. Cuddled between them, Motte stopped crying and hiccupped.

'My love, if I told you everything going on in my business, you'd be bored stiff,' he said. 'I've got my fingers in a dozen pies. I want a break from all that when I come home.'

Without a partner the building took longer, but *Polaris* was eventually finished and launched at Sandefjord with great celebration in 1912. Given that Bolle was born nine months later, Ingrid thought she was probably conceived the very night of the launch. There was no question of going anywhere with two baby girls, and in the middle of 1914 Lars told her that he was selling *Polaris* to Ernest Shackleton.

'I don't like the look of what's going on with the Serbian war,' he'd said. 'It's time to call in some investments. Shackleton's getting a bargain, but it won't hurt my reputation to sell her to an explorer of his fame.'

'What's he doing with her?' Ingrid asked.

'He's planning to cross the Antarctic continent from sea to sea,' Lars said. 'He's missed his chance at the Pole, but an explorer can always find another first.'

Ingrid felt she was seeing Lars through new eyes. His spirit was entrepreneurial in essence, she finally understood. He didn't adventure for the simple pleasure of it. She felt a deep sadness come over her.

'Bed?' she asked him, standing up.

'You go,' he said. 'I'll be up shortly.'

Ingrid kissed him on the cheek and slid her hand down his chest, nuzzling her face into his neck. 'Can't it wait?'

He chuckled. 'I have to finalise the paperwork for *Polaris*. Shackleton wants her as soon as possible.'

Ingrid straightened. 'Don't be long,' she said, trying to keep the disappointment from her voice.

'I'll be right up. Oh, and Shackleton's changing her name. He wants to call her *Endurance*.'

'Isn't it bad luck to change a ship's name?'

Lars had shrugged. 'I don't believe in those old superstitions.'

But Ingrid wasn't surprised when, in 1915, as Europe exploded into war, the Antarctic pack ice took *Endurance* in its fist and slowly crushed her to pieces. Those hand-carved timbers still lay in the deep, drowned in some ice-covered ocean in the south.

Now, all these years later, she was sailing to Antarctica in a motor tanker as the middle-aged wife of the fleet's owner.

The two planes rattled above her head, and she glanced up at *Qarrtsiluni.* The enclosed cockpit looked warm and sheltered. Ingrid ducked under the wing and reached up to the handle of the rear door. Her gloved hands closed around the metal – she could feel the cold of it even through the leather – and she pulled the handle down. The door creaked open. Ingrid glanced around to make sure no one could see her, and reached inside. The small set of steps folded up into the plane itself. They were stiff and it took her a while to work them free.

Ingrid placed her foot on the first step. It felt different from being on the ship; less solid. She reached up, grasped either side of the door and pulled. Her feet began to slide and she threw herself forward and landed half inside the plane. It rocked as she pulled herself into the passenger compartment. She tucked her legs in, pulled the lever that brought the steps folding upwards and shut the door.

In the passenger seat she sat low so her head was less visible from the outside. The wind whistled past the shrouds. She felt at home in *Qarrtsiluni*'s cockpit, safe and enclosed. Her stomach settled immediately without the confusion of sky and sea and ship moving in different directions. Ingrid looked down at the instrument panel and wished she knew how to fly. Imagine if she could pilot the plane to the continent, land on the ice, switch off the engine and revel in the silence.

A gust of wind rocked the plane. It was easy to be romantic about flying when on the ground, she thought. She rested her hands on the yoke and peered out through the windscreen, wondering what it felt like to crash. She wanted to think that in the heavy fog Amundsen and his crew had not known a thing until the moment of impact obliterated them.

Ingrid heard a voice somewhere outside and recognised it as Hjalmar's, calling her name. She didn't want him finding her in his plane. She checked to make sure he wasn't on the rear deck, then flipped open the door, scrambled out of the plane and managed to fold the steps back into place. She had straightened herself and was standing innocently under the wing when he came down the steps.

'There you are! There's a whale nearby. Hurry!'

Ingrid felt a rush of excitement and followed him to the port-side railing. The wind had dropped a little and the sea was smoother. She stared out expectantly, but could only see the long white lines the breeze made on the surface of the waves. Then, not fifty feet from the ship, a plume of vapour rose and the dark, shining shape of a whale broke the surface. The blowhole flared and then closed and dipped beneath the water. Its back arched till the ridiculously tiny dorsal appeared and then the whale lifted its tail flukes noiselessly and disappeared into a deep dive.

Ingrid realised she'd been holding her breath and let it out. She had expected an Antarctic leviathan, not some small creature like the ones easily seen near Norway.

'What sort was it?' she asked.

'A little minke, most likely, and one that hasn't been hunted,' Hjalmar said. 'Once we're on the whaling grounds, no creature can rise for an innocent breath near a ship, even a minke.'

Ingrid thought of Bjarne. 'Do you think they're being overhunted?'

A shadow crossed Hjalmar's face. 'I'm not qualified to say.'

'But no one has spent more time sailing Antarctic waters than you. You must have an idea.'

'I really don't know, Ingrid.' He stepped back from the railing and looked up at the sky. 'I think there's a change of weather coming.'

And he was gone, striding up the deck at a fast clip. Ingrid stared after him. She heard a whoosh again and swung back to face the sea. The whale had moved further away, its dorsal disappearing as she watched.

Lars had told her often enough that the main principle of business was not to deplete your capital. Ingrid couldn't believe he'd be investing in whaling if there was a chance of the creatures being fished out. A fool could see that wouldn't work, and he was no fool.

But all explorations were funded by something, Lars had told her more than once.

Ingrid waited until the day was over, until she'd spent time on the bridge with Lars, until they'd eaten another few hearty meals in the saloon, until she'd inquired after Lillemor's health and heard she was still bedridden, until she'd made some superficial conversation with Mathilde and was relieved to find the woman less depressed. She watched the sun set into the jagged horizon, staining the tips of the waves red for a few moments.

'I'm sorry I couldn't spend more time with you, but there's a lot for me to understand before we get to the factories,' Lars said, when she finished getting ready for bed and slid into the bunk beside him. 'Have you enjoyed the day?'

'I did enjoy myself,' she said, laying her head in the crook of his arm. 'Though Horntvedt is a bad-tempered fellow. He doesn't like women around, does he?'

'Just give him a captain's respect, that's all.'

'That's what I tried. Oh, and guess what? Hjalmar and I saw a whale!

Lars sat up quickly. 'Really? When?'

'This morning some time. It was gone in a minute. Just a minke.'

He settled back down. 'That augurs well for the season.'

'Not according to Aagaard,' Ingrid said.

Lars sighed. 'He's become fixated on the whale hunt. Unfortunately he only sees what he wants to see. Bogen is still an objective historian; he'll do the right thing in recording our travels.'

Ingrid stroked Lars's chest. 'What if Aagaard's right?'

'Aagaard ignores that Norway is the only whaling nation with laws limiting our catches,' he said. 'No mothers with calves, no blue whales under seventy feet, and the rest. No one is stricter about them than I. These have been worked out by scientists, Ingrid, who know much better than Aagaard the level of harvest that the population can bear.'

'I'm pleased to hear that.' Ingrid felt the tension leave her belly.

Lars shifted his weight and pulled her close. 'I think Aagaard has become emotionally involved with the whales. Perhaps I should have brought him along and he could have seen for himself. We use the most humane methods known. We're trialling an electric harpoon, which delivers a shock to the whale and kills it immediately. I'm very keen to see how that works. Really, we've minimised the suffering of the animals as much as possible.'

'I think his concern is for the men working in the industry, and what will happen to them if it collapses,' Ingrid said.

'If we were to cut back on the hunt, they'd be out of work right now. He can't have it both ways.'

Tired of the conversation, Ingrid put her face to his neck. He murmured appreciatively and she kissed him, tasting salt on his skin.

'You know, I think perhaps you ladies might be better off away from the factory ships,' he said. 'It's meant to be a pleasure cruise for the three of you, and those factories are quite disgusting. You can smell them from miles away, I've heard.

I'll get on the radio tomorrow and find out where *Norvegia* is. Perhaps we can organise the rendezvous so you can spend a week or two on the small boat while we refuel the factories, and then we can pick you up again.'

Ingrid lay still, feeling the disquiet come back again. 'I'd like to see the factory ships. This is our livelihood, Lars. This is what you want your sons to do. I don't want to shy away from it.'

'That's all very well but what about your friends? Mathilde isn't quite of sound mind, and as for Mrs Rachlew, she'll get out her camera and who knows what will happen to the photographs? We could end up with pictures of dead whales in the newspapers, offending somebody and attracting too much attention.'

He rolled on his side so they were face to face. 'You could use the opportunity to scout out landing places for us,' he continued.

Perhaps he was right, Ingrid thought. *Norvegia* wasn't *Polaris*, but she was at least an exploration ship, made from wood. And if she was away from Lars, there was less risk of conceiving.

As if reading her thoughts, he moved closer so their bodies were touching. 'It's like being on our honeymoon again, without the children,' he murmured. 'I like it, Ingrid.'

Ingrid closed her eyes as their lips touched. In truth, she didn't feel like making love again so soon, but she couldn't appear reluctant. She let Lars draw her on top of him. She would have preferred to lie back herself but she straddled him with the appearance of desire and moved with the motion of the ship, until he stiffened and groaned and fell asleep almost at once.

She lay for a long time beside him, imagining the little whale diving deep down under the water. Was there something particular, she wondered, that Lars didn't want her to see? Perhaps she wasn't the only one with something to hide.

CHAPTER 18

Lillemor felt she was sinking underwater. The light shifted from grey to black and back again in surreal intervals. She clung to her bunk, the only place of comfort in a shifting world, and drifted in and out of consciousness.

She dreamed she was riding in the belly of a whale, or did she wake and imagine it? She thought she had nibbled at the crackers by her bunk, but the pile seemed undiminished when next she forced open an eyelid and looked. She felt the prick of the needle through a fog and surmised that Stevensson had given her another injection. Once she thought Mathilde was stroking her head and murmuring, but when she opened her eyes no one was there. Nonsense sentences formed in her head, every word unrelated to the last, the flow of them seemingly unstoppable until Lillemor felt she would go mad.

She couldn't have said if a few hours or a day had passed by the time she woke properly. She lay with her eyes closed for some time, feeling the motion of the boat and trying to orient herself. She felt childlike and alone, as if waking from a nightmarish sleep and wanting her mother. After a while she opened her eyes. Mathilde was sitting across the cabin on the other bunk, watching her. It was unnerving.

'Better?' Mathilde asked.

'I think so.' Lillemor slid up into a sitting position and rubbed her face. Her belly growled, but with hunger, not nausea. The seasickness seemed to have passed. But the dim memory she had of Mathilde stroking her hair was at odds with the stern-faced woman before her, and she tried to gather her thoughts.

'What on earth did that man give me? I feel like I've been asleep all day.'

'Nearly three days,' Mathilde said. 'Some kind of new sedative, he said. He dropped by to top you up a few times.'

Lillemor shook her head to clear the muddle. '*Three* days? My God. What have I missed?'

Mathilde shrugged. 'Not much. Waves. Wind. A few birds and a whale or two. Plenty of meals. They're all waiting for you. The scenery hasn't changed.'

Lillemor swung her legs around to the side of the bunk, put her feet on the floor and stood up slowly. The ship rolled and she put a hand against the wall to steady herself. She found her knees shifted of their own accord to keep her upright and her stomach seemed stable. She wondered what Mathilde had told everyone, and felt a stab of shame. So much for impressing the men of the ship with her adventurous spirit. It wasn't a good start.

'Looks like you've got your sea legs,' Mathilde observed.

'Well, I don't intend to spend the trip in bed,' Lillemor said. 'What time is it?'

'Almost lunch.'

'Excellent. I'll get dressed and you can help me find the saloon. How's the food been?'

'Not bad,' Mathilde said. 'But I'm sure you can find the saloon yourself. I've done you enough favours, I think.'

Perhaps there was more to mousy Mathilde than Lillemor had thought. It looked like she could be tough enough when she wanted.

'I don't know what you mean,' she said.

'Of course you do,' Mathilde said. 'I think, Mrs Rachlew, we could say you're in my debt.'

Lillemor made her way across the cabin to her luggage while she considered her response. Keeping her back to Mathilde, she opened the door. 'How cold is it outside? Will I need my woollen underwear?'

'It's not that cold. I'm sure you'll stand it if you wear a coat.'

Lillemor chose a dress and turned around. 'I think we could help each other considerably on this trip, Mrs Wegger. If there's anything I can do for you, I'd be more than happy to help.'

'Good,' Mathilde said. 'I'll be sure to let you know. And I prefer Mathilde.'

'I prefer Lillemor. Glad we've got that straight.'

'I'll wait for you outside,' Mathilde said. 'I won't be going to the saloon for a few minutes yet, so if you hurry you can come with me.'

She left the cabin and Lillemor made a rude face at her departing back. '*If you hurry …*' she mimicked under her breath. She stripped off her nightwear and started pulling on her clothes, struggling to keep her footing as the ship rolled. She laced her boots, pulled on her woollen hat and hurried to the door. She kicked her toe misjudging the height of the sill and stumbled out. Mathilde looked at her without putting out a hand to help.

Lillemor regained her balance. 'Lead on,' she said. Mathilde turned away from her without another word.

By lunchtime's end, Lillemor realised just how much she had missed while sleeping. Mathilde knew the names of the dogs and when she called down to them from the catwalk, they jumped and barked at her voice. Mathilde had engineered a seat between Hjalmar and Nils at the captain's table, leaving Lillemor between Horntvedt, who was perpetually grouchy, and

Hans Bogen, the historian, who was fussy and dull. She was far away from Lars and Ingrid and their end of the table seemed to sparkle with interesting conversation, while the men either side of her ate silently.

Lillemor, with brief glances, watched Mathilde. She and Hjalmar conversed with a warmth that seemed more than warranted by mealtime proximity and they were often talking privately rather than to their companions at large. Mathilde had seemed a plain woman when they'd first met in Cape Town and at their dinner at Kennedy's, Lillemor had seen how easily she became terrified. It was only then Lillemor had had the idea of taking Mathilde's place. The plan had worked, in the main – here she was, on board, on the way to Antarctica and it was clear Mathilde had little interest in being the first to land. But it was disconcerting that she'd seen through Lillemor's machinations so clearly.

Mathilde was smiling at Hjalmar as they talked, and her face looked years younger. Not pretty, she wasn't pretty, but she had dimples that appeared when she smiled, and they were an asset of which she could make much, if she chose. Lillemor strained her ears to hear their conversation. He was talking about Amundsen and his explorations of the North Pole. Lillemor wished she was close enough to join in. It would be wasted on Mathilde, who in all likelihood knew nothing of polar exploration history, while she, Lillemor, who'd studied it, could possibly tell Hjalmar a thing or two he didn't know.

Lillemor turned her attention to Ingrid, who'd given her a friendly enough smile and a kiss on the cheek when she arrived in the saloon, together with queries about Lillemor's health, but now seemed rather distracted. Lillemor wondered what brought her to Antarctica. She certainly wasn't the kind of woman who came because she couldn't be apart from her husband. Was she really just enjoying the latest holiday, or was she, like Lillemor, driven to be the first woman there?

If she did want to be the first, there'd be no question of whose name was attached to any discoveries or landings. But there were sometimes ways around expedition leaders. The very first landing on Antarctica was still being disputed. The expedition was under the leadership of Henryk Bull, but when the time came for a landing at Cape Adare in 1895, three men claimed to have leaped from the boat first, including a junior seaman. The matter of who had set foot first on the mainland had never been resolved. In such moments and by such slender margins were reputations made and histories written, Lillemor knew.

Ingrid would be the priority in any Antarctic landing and hers the name bestowed on any piece of landscape that needed it. Mathilde was inconsequential and Lillemor knew her own part in the trip might go either way. She was the youngest of the three – thirty years old – while Ingrid and Mathilde must both be closer to forty. She was the strongest and the fittest, but she'd lost ground in the embarrassing three days of seasickness. She needed to work her way up to the interesting end of the table, ingratiate herself with those who mattered, demonstrate her capability and make sure that if opportunities arose she was ready to take them.

Lillemor turned her attention to the men. The biggest fish to fry here on the boat were Lars, Hjalmar and Horntvedt, and she judged them the way she usually did, by speculating on what they'd be like in bed. Would Lars bring his power with him, treating a woman's body like something to be conquered? Or was he one of those powerful men who liked to become little boys in bed, wanting one place in their lives where they could surrender?

Hjalmar was handsome and confident, a man who liked discovering new things. He was the latest of Norway's dashing explorers, the one who could never settle with a woman, even if he married her. Lillemor thought she had lost Hjalmar's sympathy after he saw her manipulations get her own berth on the ship. It was annoying – she'd been doing all of them a favour after all, and she'd have to work to bring him back on side. She'd remind him of his friendship with Anton.

Horntvedt was an interesting proposition, with his unrelenting sternness and his professed wish that women stay in their rightful place. It could be fun to surprise a man like that, to show him he wasn't in charge. Or he might be thoroughly unpleasant, the same in bed as he was out, or worse.

Nils: too nice. There'd be no challenge in bedding him; it would be sweet upon sweet with no spice in it.

She turned her gaze on Hans, every inch the historian, bespectacled and quiet, easily overlooked when they were all together. He was gazing at Ingrid and Lillemor caught something in his expression. Behind his glasses there was longing on his face. Lillemor stored the information away for later consideration.

The men were important, but she needed to befriend Ingrid, and quickly, in case favours were on offer. She'd seen Ingrid's relief at the prospect of getting rid of Mathilde and taking Lillemor instead. It would be better to align herself with Ingrid rather than Mathilde, she thought.

Photography was her unique skill and she needed to use it to her advantage. They'd all want a record of this voyage once it was over, especially Lars, Ingrid and Hjalmar. Perhaps she might yet travel with Hjalmar on the smaller ship, on the pretext of photographing his explorations. A photographer might be included in things that she would otherwise miss.

It was time to get out her camera, and to start recording the voyage in her journal too. Smart expeditioners laid depots along the way, and that's what she was doing now. Emotional depots that she could draw on as the final stages approached.

'I'm going up to the bridge,' Lars said, finishing the last of his drink. 'Hjalmar, could you look after the ladies, please?'

Hjalmar, still eating, smiled. 'Always a pleasure. I won't be a minute, ladies, if you don't mind waiting a little.'

'Not at all,' Lillemor said, raising her voice to be heard from the other end of the table. 'Ingrid, Mathilde, let's wait for Hjalmar outside.'

She pushed her chair back and stood, and Mathilde and Ingrid followed. The three of them pulled on their heavy coats in the saloon's vestibule and stepped outside.

It was a shock, moving from the cosy interior of the saloon to the external reality of a ship surging through the wind and waves of the Southern Ocean. Even in the darkness it was possible to sense the horizon stretching out in every direction and the ship moving further away from civilisation every hour. They went down the steps to the mid deck and crossed to the railing. Lillemor blinked in the wind as she positioned herself in between Ingrid and Mathilde.

'When will we start seeing icebergs, do you think?' she asked.

'Lars says by tomorrow, in all likelihood,' Ingrid said. 'I can't wait.'

'Me neither,' Lillemor said, glancing behind to see if Hjalmar was coming. She couldn't resist a little investigation. 'I bet Captain Riiser-Larsen has left some broken hearts behind when he's gone off exploring,' she said, lowering her voice.

'I expect so,' Ingrid said.

Lillemor turned to Mathilde. 'Did I hear you and Hjalmar talking about Amundsen?'

Mathilde nodded. 'He was telling me about one of his rescue missions. Do you know, if Hjalmar hadn't got all the men squeezed on one plane and into the air, they would have died after their other plane was damaged.'

'Well, it's true enough, Mathilde; he was a hero,' Lillemor said. 'But not an infallible one. They spent weeks carrying snow to try and make a runway before someone worked out they just had to stamp on it to flatten it. That lost time nearly killed them all.'

There was a laugh from above them. 'Sadly you're right, Mrs Rachlew.' Hjalmar's voice came from the stairs. Mathilde frowned at Lillemor.

Lillemor smiled. It looked like she was accurate about Mathilde's weakness. 'Ah, Hjalmar, here I am blackening your name,' she said. 'How frightful of me.'

The three of them turned to meet him as he came down onto the deck.

'It's true; we were so cold and frightened we lost our judgment,' he said. 'If we'd had women with us I doubt we'd have been such idiots.'

'I don't like you making fun of us.' There was no laughter in Ingrid's voice.

Hjalmar became serious. 'I'm not at all. Women bring out the best in men, I believe.'

'Funny then that you're not taking any women with you,' Lillemor said, to see how he'd respond. 'No explorer seems to want women along, no matter how nicely we ask.'

'Unlike Mawson, I wasn't inundated with requests from women to come on my expedition,' Hjalmar said. 'But then, I'm not nearly so handsome as he is.'

Lillemor laughed. 'Oh, you're not so ugly, Hjalmar.'

'Just let me light my pipe, ladies,' Hjalmar said. 'Then I'll show you inside the planes, shall I?' He began packing tobacco into the bowl, standing with his back to the wind to shelter it.

'It's rather a pity we're not coming with you,' Lillemor said. 'Mathilde and I think exploration sounds much more romantic than whaling.' She glanced at Ingrid and smiled. 'Although of course we're very pleased to be guests on *Thorshavn*.'

Hjalmar lit the pipe, puffing rapidly. 'It's not romantic. Just you wait till we're in bad weather. When the boat's iced from stern to aft and the wind's strong enough to sweep you off the deck, you'll be grateful to be safe in *Thorshavn*'s big steel hold and not shivering on little *Norvegia* and praying she won't be splintered on a growler.'

'Are you ever afraid?' Mathilde asked.

'All the time,' he said. 'Exploration means heading into the unknown, in a boat small enough to move easily through the ice. We could be caught and crushed, or sunk or lost at any time. If someone as experienced as Amundsen can die, any of us can.'

He glanced at Mathilde and cleared his throat. 'Of course, it's a different matter on *Thorshavn*.'

'Why do you do it?' Mathilde asked.

'The question explorers always get asked,' he said. 'It's so expensive and so dangerous, why do we keep going?' He leaned against the railing and rubbed his chin. 'The Poles have a pull on you. Once you've visited, you always want to come back.'

'Really?' Lillemor asked.

'I'm like a fool in love,' he said. 'The North Pole is my first love, but now I've been south I have a secret mistress and I can't stay away from her.'

Lillemor saw the colour rise in Mathilde's cheeks and sensed Hjalmar's sudden embarrassment. It was banter he might have made with a woman like Lillemor, but not with the three of them.

'I think this is such a fascinating question, with so many answers,' she said. 'Ingrid, I'd love to know – what is it that brings you south?'

Ingrid was looking out at the ocean. 'My husband's business interests are here. He very much wanted to see them first hand.'

'But what about you?' Lillemor persisted.

'When I was a child I wanted to go to the South Pole, especially after I met Amundsen. He promised I could go with him, but when the time came, he made the decision to go south after he'd already left Norway, so I missed out. It looks like this is the closest I'll get.'

Interesting, Lillemor thought. She turned to Mathilde with an eyebrow raised.

'I'm here to rest my nerves,' Mathilde said. 'My family thought an expedition to Antarctica would be a nice way for me to relax.'

There was an awkward pause. 'And what about you, Mrs Rachlew? Why did you want to come with us?' Hjalmar asked.

'I met Amelia Earhart a few months ago and I was inspired,' Lillemor said. 'I think it's time women did courageous and wonderful things. I'm very grateful to have this chance.' She was looking at Ingrid as she spoke, hoping the woman would feel her sincerity.

'Let's go and have a look at the planes,' Hjalmar said. 'Did you know, ladies, *Qarrtsiluni* is a Lockheed Vega, the same type of plane Amelia Earhart flew across the Atlantic?'

As they followed Hjalmar towards the back of the boat, Lillemor thought of Amelia. No woman had yet flown over Antarctica, she remembered.

CHAPTER 19

'Look up!'

Mathilde squinted obediently into the sun, blinking. Above them, Lillemor was silhouetted, bending her head to look into the viewfinder of the camera. Next to her, Ingrid patted her hair and adjusted her beret.

The ship began to tilt to the side and Mathilde took a tighter grip on the railing. Lillemor had already spent considerable time setting up the shot, posing them so that the mid deck stretched out behind them and she could get the ocean into the background.

'The wave's coming,' Lillemor called down. 'Hold on and smile.'

'This feels so silly,' Ingrid said.

Mathilde looked up at the bridge, looming above Lillemor, and was grateful that at least they were posing behind it rather than in view of the captain. A wash of spray flew across the deck, splashing them as the ship rocked. Mathilde shivered. They were well into the fifties latitudes now and the air temperature was close to freezing. *Thorshavn* ploughed south, so heavy and unswerving it seemed nothing could knock it from its course. Against the resistance of the ocean and wind it seemed unstoppable.

'Are you done yet?' Ingrid called up.

Lillemor raised her head. 'There's one more wave coming. Just stay there another minute.'

Ingrid's hair was blowing loose and Mathilde watched her try to tuck it back out of the wind's way. The ship started to ride over the next swell and they smiled at Lillemor with fixed grimaces as the spray showered them from behind.

'Done!' Lillemor called. 'You look fabulous. Very adventurous. What about a round of rummy to warm up?'

'Good idea,' Ingrid said. 'Coming, Mathilde?'

'I'll just say hello to the dogs,' Mathilde said. 'I'll be up soon.'

She waited until Ingrid had climbed the stairs and the two women had passed out of sight before she turned to the huskies.

For the past days the scenery had been unchanging; grey and rough. The winds blew and the waves swelled under them, pummelling the ship and tossing it as if from hand to hand. In bed Mathilde slid from one end of her bunk to the other, gripping the edges till her knuckles whitened. In the saloon they clung to their plates and cups, and the mess boys dampened the tablecloths to stop the crockery from crashing off.

Time was starting to hang heavily on all of them and playing cards, with Nils or Hjalmar or Hans making up a fourth, helped it pass. But Mathilde was lonely. She and Lillemor, by unspoken agreement, left each other largely alone. Lillemor would sit up late talking to Lars and Ingrid, or flirting with whatever men were around – Hjalmar by preference, Mathilde thought, but it seemed any of them would do. Mathilde watched, sometimes amazed. Didn't men realise they were being played for fools? But Hjalmar became animated in Lillemor's presence, laughing and joking, matching her move for move, quip for quip. Nils tried to compete with him, cutting in with poorly planned jokes that fell flat, but he was such a nice man that everyone laughed anyway and Mathilde hoped he didn't hear the edge of pity in their voices. With Lars, Lillemor was serious, discussing business and economics with a surprising grasp of details. Hans Bogen developed a stammer whenever he was with her, and picked at the skin around his nails until they bled. She'd even succeeded in prising a smile or two from Horntvedt, in itself a miracle.

Mathilde watched Ingrid and Lillemor together, and thought that any observer would conclude that theirs was a long and established friendship. It threw her own isolation into sharp relief. She didn't know how to make normal womanly chit-chat any more, she thought.

If it weren't for Hjalmar, Mathilde would have made no impact upon the life of the ship. She was resigned to it, would have tolerated it, but then he'd pass her on the catwalk, or stop and talk to her when she'd crept away to play with the puppies, and she couldn't recall when she'd last had conversations like those, not since Jakob had died of course, but perhaps not before then either. Hjalmar talked to her easily, without any suggestion of the flirtatious tone he took with Lillemor. They might have been friends, in fact, the way they conversed, about dogs and music and the sea.

When she could be sure no one was looking, Mathilde spent her time with the huskies, which had been moved to a corner of the forecastle below the line of sight from the bridge. The dogs were uncomplicated: happy to see her, glad of attention, philosophical when she left. The puppies were a different matter, with their intense feelings and wants. Catching sight of her approach they'd cry out for her to hurry up, wagging their tails so hard their whole bodies wriggled. In her arms they'd squirm with pleasure, and if she left them, they'd cry out in sorrow.

She had a favourite. Babyen, the smallest of the litter, the one Hjalmar had let her hold on the first day. A little male marked in black and white, his tail already curling up over his back. Unlike the bigger pups, he'd lie in her arms for hours, drowsing while she stroked him. She always made sure she was alone with them; such tenderness was a vulnerability she didn't want to show. Lillemor seemed to have an unerring instinct for spotting weaknesses and storing them away with a knowing smile, and the thought of what she might do with them later was frightening.

But Mathilde was sleepy after a rough night of sliding around the bunk, and the sun was warm in the corner of the forecastle where she'd tucked herself with the weight of the pup on her lap and she let herself drift, her back pressed against the ship's metal side, her body vibrating pleasantly with the engine. Her eyes were closed; she could feel herself slipping into a doze, a delicious dropping down, her muscles loosening, relaxing.

The sounds of the ship took on a musical quality. *Thorshavn* creaked and groaned around her as it moved through the sea, every joint and seam, every piece of the ship that touched another piece making a musical connection, with the underscore played by the ocean, a steady swishing as the ship's prow carved through the waves.

'Mathilde?' The voice was soft and deep, almost a part of the sleep she was sliding into. She was dreaming it, surely. Was it Jakob's voice?

'Mrs Wegger?'

Her eyes flew open. Hjalmar was standing there, leaning against the railing looking down at her. She sat up, jolting Babyen, who woke and stretched, his paws extended, his tongue curling, finishing with a doggy squeak before shaking his head.

'You startled me,' she said, hoisting the pup into her arms and scrambling to her feet so quickly that her head swam.

'I'm sorry, I didn't mean to,' he said. 'You're wanted for cards. But first I have something to show you.'

She looked at him inquiringly but he put his finger to his lips and shook his head. He took the pup from her, deposited him on the deck and gave him a little shove to send him back to his kennel mates. He took her around underneath the bridge to the other side of the ship and stationed them in the lee of the wheelhouse, a spot that Mathilde already knew was invisible from above.

'Can you see it?' he asked.

She stared out at the horizon, squinting. The temperature difference between her sheltered spot out of the wind and facing straight into it was extreme, and her eyes watered. The boat rose and fell, the horizon was jagged, there were deep troughs between the swells. At first she couldn't see what he meant. Then she glimpsed something at the far range of her vision, pale, almost ethereal in the distance.

'The first iceberg,' he said. 'It's good luck to spot it.'

'But you saw it first,' she said.

'I don't count,' he said. 'I want you to have that bit of luck.'

She kept her eyes trained on the horizon. 'Don't give it away so easily, Captain. You might need your luck when the ship's iced from stern to aft and the wind's strong enough to sweep you off the deck and there are growlers everywhere.'

He chuckled and she smiled to hear it. He had a nice laugh, open and warm. Lillemor's laugh made her shiver, as though she were executing some exquisite cruelty.

'You could do with some luck, Mathilde,' he said. He only called her that when they were alone, but she wished he wouldn't. You couldn't ever be sure, on this ship, that no one was listening.

'I don't know what you mean,' she said lightly.

He stepped a little closer to her until their sleeves were almost touching and she fancied she could feel the warmth of his body.

'Mrs Rachlew is ruthless,' he said softly, turning his head to speak close to her ear, but not too close. 'Be careful of her.'

Mathilde felt cold fingers of wind find a crack between her

scarf and her coat and work their way inside. She shivered. 'I'm of no significance to her.'

'She's very ambitious.'

She shrugged. 'She can achieve whatever she likes. I don't care to stop her.'

'You've spotted the first iceberg. Discoveries can happen as easily as that. The right place at the right time, a bit of luck and there you go.'

'Then don't do me any more favours,' she said. 'Just ignore me.'

'Is that what you'd like?'

She should have answered at once, without hesitation, but she paused and he saw it.

'You need a friend on board,' he said. 'I'd like to be that friend.'

'Why?'

It was his turn to pause. 'Mrs Rachlew will probably get her wish and land first,' he said at last. 'Ingrid will get her name on something, no matter who sees it. There seems to be no one looking out for you.'

'That's kind of you, Captain, but I don't need your pity,' she said.

He didn't answer and she regretted it then, but his open favour would only cause trouble and she was better to discourage him.

They heard a shout from up on the bridge and both turned towards the sound.

'They've seen it now,' he said. 'We'll keep it our secret, who really saw it first.'

'I just want to get home safely to my children.'

'You're making history. Don't you care?'

She laughed then, but it was bitter. 'I'm not the kind of woman whose name will appear on maps.'

'I'd like to name something after you,' he said. 'Some strong little headland or promontory.'

Mathilde didn't trust herself to look at him. How should she respond to such a thing? 'You could name one of the pups after me,' she said, and risked a glance.

She'd been joking, but he wasn't smiling. He looked at her and in his expressive face she saw concern and regard. She knew him capable of acting with Lillemor's skill, having watched him banter with her. Could she ever trust him?

'I'm going up,' he said. 'It looks like a good one, that iceberg, and we may pass it closely. Enjoy it.'

She didn't watch him go, but she could hear his footsteps quite clearly clanking across the deck and echoing up her legs, the way she could feel everything on the ship as a vibration through metal. She'd wait, she decided, down there. It was only a piece of ice after all. What was the fuss? There'd be plenty more coming and she'd seen enough white frozen stuff in Norway to last her a lifetime.

CHAPTER 20

Ingrid awoke, dry mouthed, alone in the bunk, her head aching. A soft grey light glowed through the porthole. In a strange reversal of rhythm, as the days grew longer the weather grew steadily colder. Her blood still moved to the seasons of Norway and knowing the long dark days and the cold that hung over the country at that moment, the shifting hours of light and time left her disoriented. But the main culprit, she knew, was the extra aquavit she'd drunk the night before, ostensibly to celebrate the first iceberg, but in reality to drown the disappointment of seeing nothing more than a white blob in the distance.

A week into the voyage, she was sick of heaving seas and endless horizons. It was another day and another day and nothing to mark the passing. The trade winds blew without a pause, the ocean rolled towards them, *Thorshavn* ploughed south, unswerving. The light was flat and featureless as they sailed beneath what seemed a permanent grey cloud cover.

But something felt different and Ingrid lay still, trying to work out what it was. After a few long moments her sluggish brain finally made the connection. For the first time since they'd left Cape Town, the ship was moving forward without pitching or rolling.

Ingrid resisted the urge to slide back into a doze and pushed herself out of bed, wondering how long she'd slept. She splashed her face and pulled on her clothes from the previous day, buttoning her heavy coat over the top before she pushed open the door, stepped outside and walked out onto the catwalk.

And into a still, white-on-white world. Thick fog hung close. Instead of ceaseless wind, all Ingrid could hear was the low throb of the engines as *Thorshavn* slid slowly through water as dark and smooth as black glass.

The air was much colder and she took a deep breath, feeling its chill pour down into her chest. Some knot inside her began to loosen. After the harsh light and rough seas, the soft glow of the fog blanketed them. They were slipping through the water instead of ramming through it, as if the ocean had ceased to be indifferent to them and was allowing their passage.

Wonderingly, Ingrid turned for the back of the ship, wanting to be alone in the precious quiet. She climbed down the stairs to the rear deck and took up her place underneath *Qarrtsiluni*'s wings. The engine was ticking so softly she could hear the gentle swish of small waves spreading out in the ship's wake, and with it felt the possibility of peacefulness.

She watched her breath forming clouds over the edge of the railing. A flock of small white birds gathered at the back of the ship and hung in the slipstream, hardly visible in the mist except for their black eyes. They must be snow petrels, she thought. The continent couldn't be too far off.

A shape caught Ingrid's eye and she turned her head in the direction of the ship's motion. Something was gradually emerging from the fog, separating and taking shape, something made of the same substance, but different. The fog lifted slightly and then it was close enough for her to see clearly. Her breath caught in her chest as she realised what it was.

The iceberg – was ever a word so inadequate? – floated towards her, tall and faceted in pure, opaque white. From every crack and gouge shone a blue so intense that it hurt her eyes; a blue that made her throat catch. Hjalmar had tried to describe it to her once but she saw now how he'd utterly failed to convey it. The centre of the berg had melted out to form a cavern – a transparent pool of aquamarine surrounded by fringes of long, clear icicles. Cracks of that turquoise blue ran like veins down its side. It was like staring into a piece of sky, trapped and glowing from within the iceberg with unearthly light.

The water was so still that Ingrid could clearly see the underside of the berg extending far into the depths, the same fantastic caverns and tunnels filled with water instead of air.

She had hoped for something unnameable from the ice, hoped that some magical place was waiting for her down at the bottom of the earth. And here, already, it was. She clung to the railing and lost herself in the blue caverns until the colour seemed to run before her eyes.

Thorshavn slipped through the water past the iceberg and Ingrid watched it, feeling a lump in her throat as it disappeared into the mist. Before long, another appeared from the fog, and another, each as individual as a human face, each with its own shape carved by sea water and wind, each with its own variation of blue, hidden or revealed.

The fog gradually lifted, revealing a field of icebergs surrounding them. The wash from the ship broke on their edges and Ingrid fancied the sound whispered secrets of the world that spawned such majesty. She clutched the railing, unable to leave them.

When Ingrid opened the door to the saloon a blast of jazz from the gramophone and the rich smell of roast pork jerked her into the ordinary world. She'd spent most of the day at the back of the ship and the transition to human company was abrupt.

'My dear, you're frozen.' Lars stood and gestured for her to join the table. 'Where have you been?'

'Looking at the bergs!' Ingrid felt a smile spreading across her face of its own accord. 'Aren't they incredible?'

She wasn't the only one moved. Faces that had been grim for the past few days smiled back at her and the feel of the room was different. It wasn't only that the ship was travelling steadily. There was a new lightness among her fellow travellers as they nodded and murmured agreement.

'Quickly, take an aquavit and warm yourself,' Lars said. 'Dinner will only be a few minutes. Mrs Rachlew is going to read to us from her diary.'

Ingrid sat between Lars and Hans Bogen and sipped the fiery drink, feeling its warmth slide down through her chest and into her belly like joy. Yes, it was joy. She couldn't recall when she'd last felt such a simple sense of it. Even Hans had a dazed kind of smile on his face, as if he couldn't believe what he'd seen outside.

Lillemor flipped through her diary and stopped. 'Shall I?'

'Please, go ahead,' Lars said.

'Very well.' Lillemor began to read. 'At one time during the morning it became a little calmer and I made my way along to the veranda – as we called the built-in deck beneath the captain's bridge – with my cine camera under my arm, to see if I could get any snaps of what could be seen of the after-deck between the waves. Suddenly the ship lurched violently and I fell and rolled in snow slush right across the veranda, coming to anchor with a crash on the port side, in the midst of some chairs and tables that were lashed securely there. Once there, I made use of the opportunity to take some snaps, and I very much hope they will be good – I'm sure I deserve it after all I went through!'

'Very nice description,' Lars said. 'I may have to borrow some of your words when it comes to writing my book, Mrs Rachlew. I do hope your photographs come out well.'

Lillemor smiled and inclined her head.

'Now that Ingrid's here, I'll make a toast,' Lars went on. 'I've had wireless reports from all three factories today, and icebergs are not the only things in abundance. There are whales by the thousand, plenty of blues and fins, some humpbacks and even a few sperm. *Solglimt* is already almost full of oil and desperate to rendezvous with us so she can clear her tanks, and the others aren't far behind. It looks to be a record year, and what better season for it than when we have a contracted buyer. *Skaal*!'

Ingrid raised her glass with the rest of them. She knew well the deep pleasure Lars took in the heart of business. This propitious coincidence of the whales, the means to harvest them efficiently and the contracted buyer, all in the midst of a worldwide depression, was thrilling for him.

She glanced at Hjalmar as she set down her glass on the tablecloth and caught an expression on his face that she couldn't quite read. Mathilde was seated close to him and she leaned in to ask him something. As he turned to answer, Ingrid watched the two of them. In the lamplight Mathilde looked much younger than when they'd left Sandefjord. Her eyes were shining.

Ingrid blinked. The tilt of Hjalmar's head seemed so intimate that she felt she was spying on them and she was shocked at what she could suddenly see. How had this crept up on her? The proximity of Hjalmar's body suggested some new physicality between them. Mathilde looked nothing like a widow and very much like a woman being courted.

Confused, Ingrid looked away and picked up her glass again. She glanced across the table. Lillemor was watching her and, as their eyes met, the woman raised an eyebrow in Mathilde's direction and winked.

Such confirmation was even more shocking and Ingrid trained her eyes on her husband's animated face as he talked to Horntvedt about their plans for the next few days. But she couldn't concentrate on the words, and from time to time she glanced back surreptitiously at Mathilde and Hjalmar, who continued their private conversation, seemingly oblivious to anyone else. Ingrid made sure she didn't look at Lillemor again, though a few times she could feel the woman observing her. It felt as though Lillemor could see right through Ingrid's own confusion and in her terribly knowing way had judged and categorised it already, as if Ingrid were jealous.

Which was true. There was no real reason why Hjalmar and Mathilde shouldn't be friends, or even more than friends if they wished. He was divorced and she was a widow. But the thought of them being together made Ingrid want to clench her fists and order them apart as if they were children. Hjalmar was hers – and her last link to Amundsen. Their friendship was special, in some way she'd never put a name to. She hated the feeling that Mathilde was usurping her place.

'Ingrid?' It was Lars, and by the way he was looking at her, she'd not heard him.

She gave herself a mental shake. 'I'm sorry, what did you say?'

'Come up to the bridge.' He was smiling at her, all uncomplicated fondness, oblivious to the undercurrents around the table. 'There's a fabulous view of the icebergs. The captain prefers only one or two passengers at a time, so he can concentrate.'

Ingrid was reluctant to leave Mathilde and Hjalmar alone together. 'I'll come up a bit later.'

Lars looked disappointed and she realised they hadn't spent much time together yet. Lars was nearly always on the bridge. He often asked Hjalmar and Nils to stay with the women, and as they were only passengers until meeting up with *Norvegia* they always seemed happy to oblige. She should make the effort to go on the bridge more, Ingrid thought. She gave him a smile and a small nod.

Lars rose to his feet. 'I'll see you soon.'

'Let's have an iceberg competition,' Lillemor said to the table at large after he'd left. 'Who can find the one that looks most like something real? Come on. We can all stand on the catwalk.'

The woman could certainly get something going – everyone got to their feet obediently, shuffled into their coats and pulled on their hats. Ingrid tried to hang back close to Mathilde and Hjalmar, but Lillemor took her by the arm and she was forced to be the first to step out of the warmth.

The mist had lifted, the visibility was good and the ocean was thick with bergs. Lillemor stationed them at one end of the catwalk. To Ingrid's frustration, Mathilde and Hjalmar moved to the other end. She tried to shake off her annoyance and focus on the icebergs, but it was as if the magic had been stripped from them.

'It seems we have a romance budding,' Lillemor said in a half-whisper. 'Goodness me, I wouldn't have thought it. Our Captain Riiser-Larsen could have his pick of women. Why would he choose funny little Mathilde?'

'I think he's just being friendly,' Ingrid said. 'I'm sure there's nothing more to it.'

'I wouldn't be so sure,' Lillemor said with a smile.

Ingrid turned away, irritated by Lillemor's worldly wise air, and pointed to a nearby berg to change the subject. 'Look at that one.'

'I suppose Mathilde thinks it doesn't matter what happens on the ship,' Lillemor said. 'I hope she knows how to not get in trouble.'

Ingrid turned to her, shocked. 'Surely you don't think it's gone that far?'

Lillemor shrugged and looked out to sea. 'That one at three o'clock looks exactly like a car,' she said loudly, and pointed. 'What do you think, Nils?'

'Lars and I are responsible for her,' Ingrid said, her voice low but sharp. 'If there's something I should know, tell me.'

'You saw it yourself,' Lillemor said. 'If you don't like it, you'd best do something quickly.'

Ingrid glanced down the catwalk. The two of them were standing too close together. She felt another rush of resentment.

'My God, look at that one.' Lillemor interrupted her thoughts.

Among its smaller cousins, one massive berg had moved closer to them, its motion at odds with the direction of the air and water. It rose far above them in height and the waves broke upon its base as if on solid land.

'It's hard to think of something so lovely as dangerous,' Lillemor said.

'Indeed,' Ingrid replied.

Small grey whale birds flew around the ship, their chattering loud on the evening air. The engines throbbed through the soles of Ingrid's feet. Suddenly she felt exhausted. The effort of going to the bridge seemed too much.

'I think it's time we ladies retired,' she said, loud enough for her voice to carry the length of the catwalk.

Mathilde looked away from Hjalmar, her smile fading as she met Ingrid's eyes.

'What a good idea,' Lillemor said, linking her arm through Ingrid's. 'The three of us can have a nightcap and leave the men to their business.' She bustled Ingrid down the catwalk until they reached Mathilde. 'Come on.' Mathilde nodded goodbye to Hjalmar, turned obediently and followed them.

When they reached the cabin Ingrid disengaged herself from Lillemor. Now Mathilde was away from Hjalmar, she felt relieved. 'Actually, I'm exhausted. I think I'll just go to bed. We have a big day tomorrow – Lars thinks we'll arrive at the first factory ship and everyone on board will be very busy.'

Lillemor shrugged. 'That's a pity. Mathilde and I will have to drink by ourselves.'

Mathilde hesitated, then nodded. 'Goodnight, Ingrid.'

'Goodnight.' Ingrid went into her cabin and shut the door. She leaned on the wall for a few moments before undressing then rolling herself into the bunk and squeezing her eyes shut. Outside, the icebergs were passing the ship, their green undersides glowing in their silent subterranean world. What creatures swam in those caverns? She tried to lose herself in imagining it, but her anger at Mathilde kept intruding.

It was a jealousy that a married woman had no right to feel in relation to a man not her husband. Ingrid had never realised her regard for Hjalmar had a dangerous element within it.

If only Lars had let her come alone. Without Mathilde, Ingrid wouldn't have to face that uncomfortable knowledge.

Ingrid turned over, dragging the blankets with her. She wanted Lars's simple warmth to take her away from all this. She relied on his regard for her. It was a precious thing, and she'd taken it for granted lately, she realised. What if she lost him suddenly, like Mathilde had lost her own husband?

CHAPTER 21

As soon as they were inside the cabin, Mathilde turned her back on Lillemor and began undressing for bed.

'What about that nightcap?' Lillemor asked, peeling off her coat.

'I'm not thirsty.' Mathilde finished her preparations, got into the bunk, pulled the covers up and rolled over without another word.

Lillemor stood still, considering. She wasn't the slightest bit tired and some male company would be pleasant. She put her coat back on, tucked her journal and pen into the pocket, slung her camera over her shoulder and went back out onto the catwalk. She crept along it, feeling the whistle of icy wind on her face. It had been quite still only minutes before, but the water's black surface was ruffled with wind and the scent of coming snow was sharp in her nostrils. She stopped and looked up. A few light flakes were falling, drifting down in the Antarctic twilight.

Lillemor made her way to the bridge. It was dim, with just a soft, shaded lamp over the charts, presumably to not affect the captain's view outside. Horntvedt and Hjalmar were talking in murmurs. Lars wasn't there.

'Looks like the weather's changing,' she said, by way of greeting.

Horntvedt shrugged. 'Likely to be a blizzard coming. You had a treat, Mrs Rachlew, for the last ten days. That was an aberration. Expect some real Antarctic weather now.'

Lillemor went to stand near him at the chart table. 'Excellent news. If we get off too lightly on this voyage you'll keep thinking women aren't up to it. Bring on the blizzards, I say.'

'Don't wish that on me,' Hjalmar said. 'I can't fly in a blizzard.'

'So where are we?' Lillemor asked.

Hjalmar came to her side and pointed a finger to indicate their location. According to the chart they were sailing through open sea. But ahead in the gloomy light, the bergs stood shoulder to shoulder in their path.

'How do you know which way they're going? That one looks like it's heading for us.'

'They're driven by the currents, not the wind,' Captain Horntvedt said.

'And ghosts,' Hjalmar added. 'I've been at anchorage when I swear an iceberg was pursuing us, and even though we moved the ship three times, it kept following.'

'Intriguing,' Lillemor said.

'Rubbish,' Horntvedt said. 'Antarctica's full of strange ideas. The weather and the ice play on men's minds. There are always a few of the whaling crew who go home in restraints at the season's end.'

'I think that can be attributed to exhaustion and months of working like slaves in bitter conditions, don't you think, Captain?' Hjalmar said.

Horntvedt looked uncomfortable and glanced at Lillemor. 'That's enough.'

There was a tense silence for a few moments and Lillemor wondered if Lars knew the men on his ships were dissatisfied. It was time for a change of subject. 'How long till we arrive?'

'We should meet *Solglimt* by the morning, if all goes well,' Horntvedt said. 'I'm sorry if you were hoping to go on *Norvegia* and miss the factory ships, but she's nowhere to be found.'

'Excellent,' Lillemor straightened up. 'I'm keen to see the business side of the voyage. I've heard such things about the floating factories.'

Horntvedt turned to her. 'I doubt you'll find it to your liking, Mrs Rachlew. You'll need a strong stomach.'

'Don't worry on that score, Captain. Now I've got my sea legs, my stomach is as strong as any man's. Though of course I'd love to have a stint on *Norvegia* too.'

'It's possible,' Hjalmar said, and Lillemor thought he was avoiding her eyes. 'But we don't know where she is yet, so it depends on her course.'

Lillemor walked away and found herself a chair by the windows. The jostling icebergs surrounded the ship and she could see snow blowing horizontally across them, as if flung from the ice continent itself. It was too dark for photographs, so she opened her diary and jotted down the day's activities. As she finished, she found herself doodling.

A chance to go on *Norvegia* was a chance to look for the mainland. The smaller ship would have a much better chance of getting close to it. Close enough to make a landing perhaps, and without Lars on board to make sure Ingrid stepped ashore first.

The snowstorm blew itself out as the short Antarctic night ended and dawn came, but the light was still gloomy as people began to gather on the bridge for their approach to the first factory ship. Coffee was served as *Thorshavn* nosed slowly through the ice, leaving a twisting wake of broken ice stretching out for miles behind them.

Lillemor scanned the dim sea for the first glimpse of *Solglimt*. Ahead, a pale glimmer reflected from the underside of the clouds, an indication, according to Horntvedt, that the Antarctic pack ice was close. The wireless crackled and the distinctive sound of Vestfold Norwegian rang out across the bridge. Though they couldn't see a ship ahead, the conversations buzzing on the wireless left no doubt that they'd entered the whaling grounds.

Restless with excitement, she stationed herself next to Mathilde and Ingrid. Lillemor was sure Mathilde would have preferred to stay in her cabin; she was emanating distaste already and they hadn't even seen a ship.

'Mast light,' the first mate said, pointing.

Horntvedt followed his stare, nodded and adjusted his course slightly. Lillemor peered until she could make out what looked like a low-lying star, twinkling. It brightened and grew until she saw the outline of a ship in the distance illuminated by powerful searchlights. As they chugged closer she understood the perspective and realised the factory ship was huge, bigger even than *Thorshavn*. Dark, oily smoke was rising from a funnel on its deck. Lillemor heard the distant clanking of winches above the throb of the engine. A stench filled the bridge, in which she could pick out blood, rancid oil and a powerful fishy smell. The overall effect was like a punch. Down on the forecastle the huskies barked furiously.

Ingrid pressed her face close to the glass. 'What's that?'

No one answered. The shape of the factory ship was clear now and Lillemor could see men moving about. The searchlights glistened off a huge red shape hanging high above the deck. She squinted and then realised what they were seeing. It was the carcass of a whale, pulled up with giant winches and half stripped of its blubber. The flensing deck was dark crimson with blood, heaped with entrails and flesh.

Lillemor heard Mathilde swallow hard beside her and felt her sway. Good God, surely she wasn't a fainter? She turned and saw that Mathilde's face was pale and her top lip beaded with sweat. An expression of horror was spreading over her face. Lillemor remembered Mathilde's hands on her forehead the first night on the ship and felt sorry for her.

'Your first whale, ladies,' Horntvedt said. Lillemor reached out and took hold of Mathilde's hand behind her back, where Horntvedt couldn't see. Mathilde started at the contact.

'Quite a sight, Captain,' Lillemor said lightly. *Don't faint*, she urged Mathilde silently.

'Fenders ahead,' Nils called.

Horntvedt drew back on the throttle, slowing *Thorshavn* so it could draw alongside the factory. He turned on the searchlights, throwing huge black shapes in the water into silhouette. Lillemor saw the bulging bellies of three inflated whales floating upside down between them and *Solglimt*.

The wireless hissed and the voice of *Solglimt*'s captain blared out. 'Welcome, *Thorshavn* and crew; welcome, Consul Christensen and guests.'

Lars picked up the handset. 'Thank you, Captain Bull. Captain Horntvedt advises me that your men can start coupling the pipes for the oil transfer as soon as we've made fast to you. And we have the mailbags standing by.'

'Excellent,' Bull replied. 'One of our catchers is on its way back with a couple of blue whales, so if you'd like to come across, Consul, you can soon see us in action.'

Horntvedt blew the ship's siren in three short deep blasts that shook the decks beneath their feet. On the factory, a crowd of men gathered, waving at them. Lillemor lifted a hand and waved in return.

The men were grinning furiously, their faces streaked dark with blood and oil as they raised their tools in the air, the searchlights glinting off the blades. Lillemor felt a surge of adrenalin in her body. She hadn't felt it since she and Anton had gone hunting in Africa and she'd almost forgotten the thrill of the chase. Shooting a rhino was something, but these ships hunted the biggest creatures on earth.

CHAPTER 22

Ingrid watched Captain Horntvedt in action as the two ships came together and the men began the complex process of making them fast. He glanced in their direction and she hated the triumphant curl of his lip as he looked at Mathilde. The sight of the factory was repulsive, but she was determined not to prove him right.

'Coming over, ladies?' Lars asked.

'We wouldn't miss it,' Ingrid said.

'Excellent. Can you cross the way the men do, or do you need to wait till we have something more civilised set up?'

'We'll cross like the men,' Lillemor said.

By unspoken agreement, Ingrid and Lillemor bustled Mathilde out of the bridge between them. The stench was stronger outside and Ingrid began to breathe through her mouth as they went single file down the catwalk. At the cabin door, Mathilde turned to her.

'Please don't make me go there,' she said. 'I can't bear it. I'll vomit. Or faint.'

Ingrid looked at Mathilde's sweaty, pale face and thought she could easily make good on that promise. What would be more satisfying to Horntvedt, she wondered – for one of them to swoon at the sight of the whales, or for them not to go at all?

'We've a duty not to be weak, Mathilde,' she said. 'Don't give Horntvedt the satisfaction.'

Mathilde's skin glistened with a greenish pallor. 'Do you really think it right for a woman to go on that ship and watch what they do there? Can you do it without feeling ill?'

Ingrid drew herself up and set her face. 'Of course.'

Mathilde looked to Lillemor. 'And you? You've got a weak stomach, I seem to remember.'

'My stomach's fine,' Lillemor said. 'For God's sake, Mathilde, don't tell me you've never killed something.'

Mathilde shook her head. 'Never.'

Ingrid was surprised. 'What, no fish? No rabbit?'

'Jakob always did that.'

Ingrid looked at Lillemor, who shrugged. Ingrid always hunted with Lars and was nearly his equal in skill, if not enthusiasm. She'd never shied away from the reality of it, though for many years she'd had servants to do the bloody work of butchering once the beast was shot.

'Myself, I adore hunting,' Lillemor said. 'I'm hoping to shoot a whale. What a trophy!'

Mathilde clasped the door handle as though it were the only thing holding her up. 'Don't you feel sorry for the whales?'

Lillemor laughed. 'Why should I be any sorrier for them than for the cattle and chickens we slaughter every day? I notice you're happy enough to eat them.'

'That's enough,' Ingrid said. 'Mathilde, the smell is disgusting, I know. But in a day or two you'll scarcely notice it.'

Mathilde shook her head. 'I don't want to get used to it.'

Ingrid felt a rush of irritation. 'This is how the men of Sandefjord make their living, and their wives and children eat. Lots of industries aren't so lucky.'

Mathilde raised her head. 'I still don't have to like it. Now if you don't mind, I'd like to go inside.'

Ingrid spread her hands. 'I can't force you to come with us.'

'That makes a nice change.' Mathilde wrenched the door open and stumbled into her cabin.

Lillemor rolled her eyes, then reached over and linked her arm in Ingrid's. 'Come on. Unlike Madam Squeamish, I can't wait to see the factory.'

Ingrid dressed in her heavy coat, laced on her stoutest boots and pinched her cheeks hard to cover any pallor of her own before she gathered Lillemor and went to meet Lars. She was determined to be strong when she stepped up to see the workings of her husband's enterprise, born from his intelligence, resources and courage. She didn't want to flinch from it.

As she came back up on deck, she could see the whale catcher returning, towing two upended whale carcasses through the water by their tails. Ingrid had never seen a living blue whale, but the size of these dead ones, distorted by their inflated bellies, was hard to comprehend. They were almost as long as the catcher dragging them.

The effect of the mailbag on *Solglimt*'s crew had been electrifying, and as the catcher drew close, the flensers leaned over *Solglimt*'s tall sides, shouting down news from home to their mates.

'Listen to that,' Lillemor said. 'Fatty's wife has had twins. It'll be a while until he sees them, poor man.'

Lars offered Ingrid his arm and though his face was solemn, she could see a small smile beneath his moustache. 'At least it's good news,' he said. 'Nothing worse than bad news arriving down here by mail. It can ruin a man's whole season. Are we ready?'

He led Ingrid to the railing. Lillemor was close behind and the three of them looked down to see a whale carcass floating upside down, wedged between the two ships. A line of men stood on it with their flensing hooks.

'So that's how we get across?' Lillemor said. 'Excellent. What an adventure.'

Lars turned to them both. 'Are you sure you can manage? We can have you lifted over in a basket if you like, but we'll lose time getting the crane ready and we might miss seeing them bring those whales in.'

'I'll walk,' Lillemor said eagerly.

Alone, Ingrid might have opted for the basket, but Lillemor's determination pushed her on. 'Of course we'll walk.'

'You first then, my dear,' Lars said, gesturing.

Ingrid climbed down the ladder slung over the side of the boat, with Nils reassuring her from a few steps below and Lars encouraging her from above. She landed on the floating whale carcass with a thud. The flensers were waiting on either side of her, having cut a series of footholds with their long-handled blades. Ingrid breathed through her mouth while Lars and then Lillemor came down the ladder. The smell seemed almost enough to carry them across to the factory ship without human agency. But, in fact, she had to balance and walk several steps across the body of the whale, then climb another ladder up *Solglimt*'s side.

Ingrid stood still for a moment. She was standing on a whale's belly in the Antarctic. Disgusting as it was, the smell made the experience real.

She could hear Lars climbing down the ladder, and bizarrely she had a vivid memory of their wedding, the moment after they had made their vows and turned to walk out of the church together, husband and wife for the first time, the long aisle lined with expectant faces.

Here, the crewmen lined the railing of the factory ship and blood-spattered men hovered alongside, poised should one of them slip. The pathway was laid out before them across once-living flesh, each foothold oozing blood and oil, freezing as it met the cold air. As he had twenty years earlier, Lars stood by her side, steady and rock-like.

She reached out, took his hand and then stepped into the first hole, her boots crunching through the frozen surface into the squelching blubber below. The watching men began to cheer. Their voices rose as Ingrid and Lars crossed the whale, step by greasy step, Ingrid's smile fixed on her face as surely as it had been on her wedding day, her misgivings buried hard and deep. Lars Christensen was the right man for her, she'd repeated to herself with every step. Amundsen had never been a contender for marriage. So why had his face haunted her as she walked down the aisle?

She reached the ladder and stopped, her boots standing in pools of oily blood as she reached up and clasped a rung. She had boarded *Solglimt* before, when the ship lay at dock in Sandefjord, scrubbed down and gleaming in the summer sun. It felt a world away.

Ingrid started to climb. She looked quickly over her shoulder to see Lars behind her and then Lillemor, Horntvedt, Nils and some of the other officers following their tracks across the whale. Hjalmar, she noticed, wasn't among them.

Captain Bull was waiting at the top of the ladder to help her up and onto the deck. Ingrid skidded slightly as her boots hit the oily metal and he put out a hand to steady her as Lars clambered up behind. When they were standing together, he gave a little bow.

'An honour to have you on board, Consul,' he said. 'And a double honour to have you, Mrs Christensen.'

Lars regarded the gleaming remains of the whale hanging high above their heads in the searchlights, and laughed.

'Captain,' he said, 'I tell you, it's one thing to know what the factory ships are doing, but another altogether to see it myself. I wish my father could have seen this too.'

'He'd be very proud,' Captain Bull said, stepping forward to help Lillemor, who'd reached the top of the ladder and was fumbling with the strap of her camera. The men clambered up behind her until they all stood in a small group.

'I'll show you how we deal with a whale right from the start,' Captain Bull said. He led their group over the bloody deck to the rear of the ship where they could see down the slipway to the water. The little catcher ship chugged up to the factory, dragging two whales, their pleated bellies distended so they floated high in the water. It cast off the whales at the edge of the slipway and steamed away.

Men scrambled down the slipway and attached a cable around the tail of the first whale. With a metallic groan the electric winches started up. The cables straightened and rose from the deck, and Ingrid could feel the moment when the winches took the dead whale's weight. The chains went taut and droplets sprayed onto the deck. Tail first, the whale started to slide up towards them.

'The slipway is a major breakthrough,' Captain Bull said. 'It wasn't a decade ago that men still got down on the whale in the water to do the flensing, and you can't imagine a colder and more miserable job. Follow me.'

As they walked, the captain explained how the whales were processed. After each was winched up the slipway, the flensers descended with their long-handled, razor-sharp knives and stripped away the blubber as if peeling a thick-skinned banana. They used a hoist to lift the carcasses in the air and enlisted gravity's help, pulling the blubber off with hooks and winches. They sliced the strips of blubber into chunks and pushed them through holes in the flensing deck so that the pieces fell into the trying pots below. There they were boiled until the oil separated from the blubber and rose to the surface, where it was skimmed off.

Meanwhile, the carcasses still had plenty to offer. They were dragged with pulleys and winches to the boning deck, where the crewmen handled the massive saws as though they were toys, cutting the whales into chunks for the boiling pots. Whatever remained went into the meat meal cookers, where it was minced, cooked and dried for pet food.

'Every part of the whale is used,' Captain Bull finished proudly as they completed the tour. 'The new factories are the most efficient method of whaling known to man. From an average blue whale we can extract more than one hundred barrels of oil, not to mention the meat meal. It's a revolution, Consul.'

The colour of the blood on the deck was vivid under the slowly lightening grey sky. Ingrid could feel Lars's satisfaction. His vision of a modern efficient fleet, devised so far away in Norway, was a reality.

Ingrid saw a small grey mass lying on the flensing deck as the last chunks of blubber were being hooked and thrown down into the trying pots. She squinted but couldn't make it out.

'Captain, what's that?'

'Come and look,' he said. 'Walk carefully; the deck's very slippery here.'

They all followed, stepping flat-footed. Lars was holding her arm hard and Ingrid sensed his hesitation.

'This,' Bull said with a flourish, 'is a blue whale in miniature.' He called out an order and the searchlight swung around. Ingrid stared, uncomprehending, at the tiny whale lying on the deck.

'We often find foetuses during processing,' Bull said. 'It's excellent news. Pregnant females hold the most oil. We can get one hundred and twenty barrels or more from them.'

'I must take a photograph,' Lillemor said, reaching for her camera. 'How extraordinary.'

Ingrid had watched all the stages of processing the whale with a fixed smile, but she felt a lurch in her stomach looking at the lines of the little creature. Its mother had been reduced to blood, bone and blubber, boiled in the vats beneath their feet.

'What do you do with them?' Lillemor was staring down into the viewfinder.

'There's not much blubber on the young, so we just slice them up and put them into the meat boilers. The real value is in their mothers.'

Beside her Ingrid could feel Lars silently begging her to be all right, to approve, to not undermine him. She felt it through the pressure of his fingers on her arm, the silent language of marriage. She took a last quick glimpse of the baby whale, swallowed, and faced the captain.

'You've done better than either of us could have imagined. What a feat of modern production.'

Beside her she felt Lars relax. 'You've achieved much,' he agreed.

Captain Bull smiled. 'Thank you, Consul.' He glanced at Lillemor. 'Since you have a camera, and we have another blue whale on deck, why don't you come over for a photograph? You can fit six men in the mouth.'

'That will show the size beautifully,' Lillemor said. 'Shall we?'

Lars was still holding Ingrid's arm as they approached the whale, and she halted, automatically baulking.

'Don't you get in,' he said. 'It will ruin your clothes.'

Ingrid waited while Lars, Captain Bull and four of the flensers climbed into the yawing mouth of the whale. Lillemor lined up the shot and pressed the lever on the camera.

Lars clambered out, smiling. 'You must come and join us for dinner,' he said to Captain Bull. He glanced at the sky. 'Or perhaps breakfast. I want to go through a few more details with you and look at the American meat boilers, but for now a little celebration is in order. A full load of oil by February is an extraordinary achievement.'

Captain Bull nodded, pleased. 'Give me a few minutes to change my clothes and I'll follow you across. One thing that hasn't changed over the centuries is the smell.'

He walked them to the railing and the bloody-faced crewmen helped Ingrid down the ladder and onto the bridge of whale flesh again. Lars was right behind her. While Lillemor and the men climbed down, Lars clasped her hand and released it. I'm proud of you, his gesture indicated.

Ingrid nodded, raised her chin and smiled. I'm proud of you, she said silently back.

She was becoming far too accustomed to lying to him.

CHAPTER 23

Mathilde hunched over on her bunk and concentrated on not vomiting. Her stomach had been rock-steady through the wildest tossing of the ship, but she felt now if she made a sudden move, she wouldn't be able to hold its contents down. Every time she closed her eyes she could see, with hideous clarity, the image of the hanging whale carcass. As they'd returned to the cabin, she'd made the mistake of glancing at the factory ship when a high-pitched noise started up. She saw a long saw on a hinge descending and a spray of red liquid. It was flesh and bone under that saw, she understood, and the knowledge nearly finished her off.

She could have stood this journey, she thought, if it hadn't been for this. But she knew now that Sandefjord, the place she'd thought of as home – those men and women who lived there, even her children – all survived because of this.

She'd heard that soldiers who made it home from the war rarely spoke of what they'd seen. Did Sandefjord's whaling men deal with this horror in the same way – coming back and talking only of icebergs and penguins and snowfalls? Or were they truly unaffected by this, seeing it as a day's work, the blood and guts just something to be washed off like soil on a farmer's hands?

Their porthole looked straight across to the factory ship so Mathilde drew the curtain across it. She paced around the cabin, past Lillemor's bed, around her wardrobe luggage. The motion of walking seemed to help her stomach and she kept it up, back and forth, like one of Hjalmar's huskies on a chain.

The tap at the door was so soft Mathilde thought she'd imagined it. When it came a second time, she hoped it wasn't Lillemor returning for another try at convincing her to come across. Though a soft knock wasn't really Lillemor's style.

'Yes?' she called.

'Mrs Wegger? It's Hjalmar.'

Why wasn't he touring the whaler with the rest of them? She crossed the cabin and opened the door. The smell hit her afresh.

'I just wanted to see if you were all right,' he said.

It took all her self-control not to break down. 'How can they stand it?'

'I don't know.' He glanced around. 'Do you want to come up to the bridge? There's no one else there, and a pot of coffee is waiting.'

Mathilde was so grateful for his kindness she wanted to weep. It meant having to cross the catwalk while keeping her eyes averted from the factory ship, but the promise of sympathetic company was enough.

'I'll get my things.' She wound her scarf over her mouth and nose, pulled on her coat and went outside. The smell seemed like a solid presence in the still air and the sound of industry echoed around them as the crews called to each other across the gap between the two ships. The huskies were still howling, driven wild by the smell of flesh, she surmised, and the sound added to the nightmarish quality of the scene.

'Why aren't you over there?' she asked, as they neared the bridge.

'Horntvedt wanted to go, so I'm standing in while he's away.' He leaned close. 'I can't think of anything more unpleasant, personally, so I don't mind putting it off for a while.'

She moved to keep a distance from him, conscious of invisible eyes. 'Ingrid and Lillemor are actually looking forward to it. They told me not to be weak like a woman.'

Hjalmar opened the bridge door and she stepped inside ahead of him. A faint aroma of coffee lingered there, taking the edge off the stink. 'I don't think it's female weakness not to want to see that,' he said and started pouring her a coffee.

Mathilde felt herself relaxing a little. She took the proffered mug and sipped. 'How long will we be here?'

'A few days,' Hjalmar said. 'I hoped we might rendezvous with *Norvegia* before the factories, and I could have missed out on this, but no such luck. She's still far away, unfortunately.'

The coffee, strong and bitter, calmed her rolling belly a little. The huskies whined and complained below, lunging against their collars to get closer to the blood and meat they craved. The whine of the bone saw cut the air, and Mathilde and Hjalmar stood in silence, sipping, with their backs to *Solglimt*. She tried to distract herself by thinking of Jakob and the way he slurped hot coffee into his mouth to cool it. It was a habit she'd disliked, but she was accustomed to it and she realised Hjalmar blew on his and then sipped it silently.

Mathilde had assumed all men were much like Jakob, in bearing and manner and style. But how did she know? Hjalmar might be different in every way to Jakob. She sneaked a sideways glance and found he was regarding her. She turned away at once, mortified.

'I won't bite you, Mathilde,' he said.

'I know.' She studied her coffee mug.

'Do you wish to marry again?'

'I've no idea.' Her voice was sharper than she intended. 'I must consider my children, Captain.'

'Of course. Forgive me for prying.'

He fell silent and she regretted rebuking him. She searched for a way to continue the conversation. Lillemor had told her he was divorced and she wondered if he was one of those men on the sea who kept a woman in every port, as the old joke ran. He had a way of making her feel she was the only woman of interest to him when he was talking to her, but perhaps all charming men could do that.

'The dogs seem upset,' she said at last.

'They'll be quiet when the crew brings over some whale meat for them. It seems a waste to feed those creatures to dogs, but I suppose it's no worse than using them for soap and margarine.'

'At least we don't use them for corsets any more.'

'I'll be glad to get off this ship and away from it all,' he said. 'Aagaard is right. It's like watching the fur sealers at work all over again. The fleets will hunt till every whale is gone.'

She'd been able to block the image of the whale carcass, but at his words it came back to her and she felt nauseous. How could she bear it?

He turned away from her and crossed to the side of the bridge closest to the factory ship. 'They're on the way back.'

Mathilde didn't answer. Hjalmar could escape from this, on his little wooden boat, while she had no choice about the matter. It seemed unfair. He had been her only friend on board, the only one willing to help her. It would be lonely without him.

She heard the bone saw scream again and even on the bridge with the door shut to muffle it, the sound made her flinch.

At Cape Town she'd capitulated when Lars had said she couldn't leave the ship, but since then Mathilde had seen how women like Lillemor and Ingrid got their way. She could be as determined as Lillemor, and simply insist on going with Hjalmar. He would take her, she was sure of it, and once away from this nightmare she'd have some chance of holding on to her sanity.

They gathered in the mess for an early hot breakfast with the factory ship's captain and this time Mathilde had to attend. She heard that the calm conditions meant the crew had been able to couple the oil lines between the two ships and begin the transfers. *Solglimt*'s full tanks of whale oil were emptying into *Thorshavn*'s maw, while through another line, fuel oil ran across into the factory's tank.

The thought of the space beneath them filling with whale oil made Mathilde's appetite disappear. She sat quietly amidst the toasts and conversation. Hjalmar joined in the good cheer with the rest of them, but she was glad of his warm presence beside her, an invisible comfort.

Ingrid rose before the end of the meal to excuse herself. Mathilde saw that Lillemor was still absorbed in conversation; it was a chance to escape her. 'May I walk to the cabin with you?' she asked Ingrid.

'Of course.' Ingrid's voice was relatively friendly and she was even smiling.

Mathilde followed Ingrid outside. On the deck she clapped her hand to her mouth, wondering if she'd ever get used to the smell. The men from *Solglimt* showed no sign of noticing it.

'Can we hurry?' she asked Ingrid.

Ingrid took her arm and they scurried along the catwalk to the cabin. Mathilde fumbled with the latch of her door.

'You've gone a bit pale,' Ingrid said. 'Are you all right?'

Mathilde shook her head and stood back while Ingrid opened the door and ushered her inside. She went straight to the bunk and lay down on it with a moan, fighting not to be ill.

Ingrid sat on the other bed. 'It's probably like seasickness. I'm sure you'll get used to it in a day or two.'

Mathilde turned her face to the wall. 'Horntvedt was right. This is no place for a woman.'

Ingrid stood up. 'Why shouldn't a woman be here? Don't be so squeamish. It makes us all look bad.' The note of impatience she often seemed to have when speaking to Mathilde had returned.

It occurred to Mathilde this was the first time she and Ingrid had been alone together since leaving Cape Town. It was a chance to talk to her without Lillemor hearing.

'I could go on *Norvegia*,' she said softly.

Ingrid shrugged. 'I'm sure we'll all be looking forward to a cruise on *Norvegia* if we meet her in time.'

The idea was forming as Mathilde spoke. 'I don't mean a cruise. I could change ships and go back to Norway with Hjalmar.'

Ingrid's voice hardened. 'What are you talking about?'

Mathilde pushed herself up to sitting. 'He doesn't care for this business either. He says the factories will clear all the whales from the Antarctic in a few seasons, just as the fur sealers decimated the seals, and then you'll see that this is wrong.'

'Did he invite you to come on *Norvegia*?'

Mathilde didn't answer.

'Tell me the truth. Did he?'

'He would take me if I asked.'

Ingrid was silent for a few moments. 'Mathilde, you're a guest of Lars, and my companion,' she said at last. 'But it's not a pleasure cruise. Neither you nor I, or even Lars can control where we go and we certainly can't change ships as it pleases us.'

Mathilde glared at her. Was she serious? 'Lars has a great deal of control, it seems to me.'

'We all have to make the best of it.'

Mathilde felt a rush of rage, not impotent this time, but explosive. 'Since when do you force a guest against her will? I'm not your servant. If I want to leave with *Norvegia*, I will.'

'You can't just go on a boat without permission of the captain!'

Mathilde got to her feet and stood facing Ingrid. 'And that I'll have. You wait and see.'

Ingrid reached for her hand, but Mathilde pulled away.

'You're a widow. What would people say?'

'I'm past caring,' Mathilde said.

CHAPTER 24

Heavy cloud hung over a steel-grey sea. *Thorshavn* nestled up to the mother ship, as Lars called the factory, sucking *Solglimt*'s tanks empty like a nursing babe, and the wind carried the promise of a chill deeper and more dangerous than they'd known.

Leaning against the rail, Ingrid saw *Solglimt*'s crew waiting, hooks up, for the next whale to come in. They watched her openly, perhaps enjoying the novelty of a woman. She smiled and raised her hand in a wave and they waved back, pulling their pipes out of their mouths, their filthy faces splitting into wide grins.

The factory's winches started up again. Another catcher must have arrived with a load of whales and the men turned away to begin their work. Ingrid made her way to where *Qarrtsiluni* and *F18* were moored and dodged out of sight, to a spot where she could see open water on the other side of the ship. A squall was coming, blotting out the faint distinction between sky and sea. Ingrid wanted it to blanket the ship, cut off her line of sight to *Solglimt* and blow away the stench that hung over them.

Ingrid was a hunter and she didn't flinch from killing. But there was something about the mechanised harvest of the whales that took this out of the realm of hunting. She'd been fine until she saw the whale foetus slumped on the deck. She couldn't stop wondering what it felt when its mother was harpooned. Did the aftershock of the harpoon's head exploding in its mother's flesh ripple through to the womb? Did the foetus sense its mother's death throes? She shook her head and pressed her eyes with her gloved hands to dispel the image.

Lars had told her she would need courage for this trip and she'd thought it would be the courage to face the unknown, to endure the ship's tossing and the cold and the ferocious Antarctic storms. But that was the least of it. She hadn't expected squeamishness and jealousy to be her challenges.

She gripped the rail hard. The prospect of Mathilde boarding *Norvegia* with Hjalmar and joining his expedition enraged her, though she hoped she'd been able to hide it. If she had to face the reality of whaling without showing disgust, she didn't see why Mathilde should be let off so easily. Nor why she should be the only woman on *Norvegia* when Ingrid herself hadn't been permitted to travel without a female companion.

The squall was coming closer and Ingrid pulled her collar up around her ears. The cold wind cut through her attempt at self-deceit. In truth, she wanted to go on *Norvegia* herself, but could never abandon Lars and her duty to him. So the thought of Mathilde blithely going where Ingrid longed to was insufferable.

Sleet began to slice into her face and she turned away and went back to the cabin. Lars was sitting up in the bunk writing in his diary when she came in, pushing the door shut behind her against the wind.

'I thought you'd be asleep,' she said.

'I can't.' He rubbed his hands through his hair. 'It's too light and too exciting. We're going to take one of *Solglimt*'s catchers and look for land.'

'Not with a storm coming, surely.'

'After the storm.'

Ingrid smiled. 'Then we might catch some lost sleep?'

He nodded, closing his diary. 'Yes, please. I always sleep better with you.'

She began to undress. The wind was moaning through the ship. She closed the curtain so the room became semi-dark and clambered into the narrow bed beside him, pressing her body against his welcome warmth.

'You did well today,' he murmured, tucking her head under his chin.

'We may have a problem,' Ingrid said. 'Mathilde is revolted by the whole business. She says she will change ships and go home with *Norvegia* to get away from it.'

'Unfortunately, *Norvegia* has been delayed by ice. We won't be meeting her until after the factory ships, so there's no point in Mathilde going with her.'

'I think there's something else going on,' Ingrid said. 'She wants to get away from us.'

Lars shrugged. 'Perhaps it wouldn't be a bad thing.'

Ingrid rolled apart from him. The wind howled and whirled and the running of the oil pumps vibrated through ship and bed and body.

'You couldn't seriously allow her to travel unchaperoned on Hjalmar's boat, even if it were safe,' she said.

'Of course not,' he said. 'I just thought –'

'You must make sure she knows it's impossible.'

'Well, just tell her.'

'I did, but I have no authority here. She says she'll throw herself on Hjalmar's mercy and beg him to take her.'

He rolled his eyes. 'Don't worry; she won't do any such thing. Once she sets eyes on *Norvegia* and sees her bobbing like a cork on the ocean, she'll stay.'

'Can you at least speak to Hjalmar?'

'I'm sure it won't be necessary,' he said. 'Mathilde just wants to get home, and *Thorshavn* is the most direct route.'

Ingrid didn't want to press any further, lest Lars see her

jealousy. She curled in closer to him as the wind screamed around the porthole. 'Do you think we're close to land?'

'One of the catchers has done depth soundings not too far away and the water was unexpectedly shallow,' he said. 'Hjalmar tells me that's as good an indication as any. But there are lots of icebergs around this season, so conditions are treacherous.'

'When are we going?'

Ingrid felt his body draw back from hers, a subtle tightening across the surface of his skin.

'I'll have no argument on this,' he said. 'I agreed to bring you on the tanker, but I'll not let you travel on a catcher into unknown waters.'

She sat up. 'You can't be serious? Leaving me here covered in the stink of whale while you go looking for land?'

'The catcher is a more dangerous proposition. It would be unfair to our children to put us both together on one.'

Ingrid took a deep breath lest her rage become white hot and blast out of her. 'Surely you don't think that's fair.'

'The catcher stinks as much as any factory, and it's small, wet, cold and uncomfortable. It won't be an easy trip. I won't discuss it further.'

Ingrid slid out of bed and began to fumble for her clothes.

'Where are you going?'

Where indeed? Ingrid stood shivering in her half-dressed state. A blizzard was howling across the ship and she couldn't think of any place she'd be welcome.

Lars propped himself up on one elbow. 'Don't let's fight over this. You won your victory. I brought you with me.'

'But I came to see Antarctica.'

He held out his hand. 'And you will. When Hjalmar and I have done our reconnaissance in the catcher, I'll have Horntvedt bring the ship to land if we find it. You won't miss out.'

Ingrid fought down her anger for another moment and then walked back to the bed. She got in and rolled away from him. He curled around her back and she forced herself to relax against him, leaning back in the familiar position that inevitably led them both into sleep. His breathing slowed and Ingrid slowed her own to match it.

The wind sped up outside and she heard the scream of the saw descending on a whale carcass. She pressed her eyes closed and tried to remember the icebergs, but the insides of her eyelids were red.

Ingrid felt Lars kiss her cheek. She pretended she was still asleep as he climbed out of bed and dressed. She heard him pause at the door but she kept still, facing away from him and after a time she heard the cabin door close. She lay in bed listening to the thumps and clanks as *Thorshavn* rose and fell, coupled to *Solglimt*. She couldn't bear to watch Lars and Hjalmar preparing for their adventure, but lying in bed left her free to dwell on Mathilde.

It occurred to Ingrid that she could speak to Hjalmar herself, making it sound like Lars had asked her to deal with the matter of Mathilde discreetly. She checked the clock. There may still be time to catch him alone before he departed with Lars. She got out of bed and struggled into her outdoor clothes, clumsy with haste, her bootlaces in a tangle. In the end she groaned with exasperation, wrenched the door open and rushed out. As she stepped on the icy deck her feet skidded, the laces tangled around her ankles and she went down, arms and legs flailing, hip and elbow connecting with the steel in a sharp jolt of pain.

She came to rest staring up at the sky, and as she waited for the pain to subside and her thudding heart to return to normal, she saw it was blue for the first time in at least a week.

'Mrs Christensen? Are you all right?' Tobias, the mess boy, was holding a tray and staring down at her in concern.

Ingrid sat up. 'I'm fine. I just slipped.'

He helped her to her feet. 'Thank you,' Ingrid said. 'Do you know where Captain Riiser-Larsen is?'

Tobias grinned. 'Flying!' At her perplexed look he pointed towards the rear deck. *F18* and *Qarrtsiluni* were strapped in their usual places. Ingrid peered more closely. She could see the outline of a head in the pilot's seat. *Qarrtsiluni* wasn't just her private refuge, it seemed.

'His favourite hidey spot,' Tobias said.

Ingrid took a coffee from Tobias, descended the steps and crossed the deck, her soles clanking on the metal and making the two planes quiver. She stopped at *Qarrtsiluni*, the coffee cradled in her hands. With a creak the door opened. Ingrid saw Hjalmar pull the lever, and the steps folded out, coming to rest on the deck beside her. She gripped the handrail, stepped up, ducked her head, and entered.

Hjalmar took the proffered coffee without a word. Ingrid lowered herself into the rear seat while he drew up the steps and shut the door. It was only a little warmer inside the cockpit than out, but its snugness felt comforting. As Hjalmar gulped the coffee Ingrid looked across his shoulder. Through the tiny windscreen the vast landscape around them shrank. Through that portal she could see nothing of *Thorshavn* or the factory ship, just sea, sky and icebergs, neatly framed.

'I can't help thinking of Amundsen in here,' she said. 'Do you think they died quickly?'

Hjalmar sighed. 'No, I don't. I saw the wing float that was found. It had been interfered with after the crash. Someone was still alive.'

Ingrid felt a pain in her chest. 'You never told me that.'

He shrugged. 'Did you really want to know?'

She watched his profile. His face was naturally cheerful but at the mention of Amundsen it creased with grief.

'You must miss him,' she said. 'Although I know you had some differences.'

Hjalmar glanced back at her. 'He never forgave me for supporting the Italians in going to the North Pole. He refused to speak to me for the last two years of his life.'

Ingrid was silent as Hjalmar took a puff on his pipe. There was no one else who shared this understanding, no one who'd known and loved Amundsen like they both had. The man had wounded them both, she realised.

Smoke drifted back towards her, strong and earthy, and the stench of the factory ship seemed to recede. At home she didn't like the smell of tobacco, but here, with a need to inhale something that didn't stink of viscera, it seemed appealing.

'May I?' she asked, reaching out her hand.

He passed it back and she grasped its stem. Suddenly the request seemed terribly intimate, to put her own lips where his had been moments ago.

'Don't draw the smoke in,' he said.

Ingrid puffed and felt an illicit thrill travel down her body. The long, dark pipe tasted undeniably of him. She could feel herself blushing and was glad he hadn't turned to watch. She took a couple more puffs. Her head spun and she closed her eyes. The tobacco crackled and glowed in the pipe bowl. Ingrid cupped her hand around it to extract the heat before returning it.

'I could come to like that,' she said.

He put his lips to the stem and suddenly Ingrid wished she had wiped it. The cabin, with two bodies in its confined space, was beginning to warm up.

She sensed that Hjalmar regretted speaking of Amundsen, and changed the subject. 'You must be looking forward to joining *Norvegia*.'

He nodded.

'You don't care much for this business.'

The silence was so long Ingrid thought he wasn't going to answer. She had just opened her mouth to speak again when he did.

'My business is going places no one else has been. When I came here four years ago, the Antarctic was full of whales and empty of men. Now there are two hundred and fifty ships and ten thousand men hunting whales.'

The windscreen was fogging from their breath and Hjalmar reached forward with a gloved hand to wipe it clear.

'Mathilde says you think whaling is wrong,' Ingrid said.

'I don't think any creature can survive such an onslaught for long. I fear the whales will go the way of the fur seals.'

'But Lars operates under the strictest guidelines.'

He swivelled. 'I'm not criticising your husband. I know he instructs his crews to work under those regulations. But he's just one fleet owner. There are ships from half a dozen nations whaling here. We're a very long way from where regulations are made, and Antarctica is not a place where regulations stick.'

'No,' Ingrid said slowly. 'I'm beginning to see that.'

'Every whaling industry in the past hundred years has fished its grounds until there were no whales left.'

The wind whistled through the plane's stays and in the distance, muffled through the cockpit, Ingrid could hear the scream of *Solglimt*'s bone saw. 'I need to speak with you about Mathilde. She has some foolish idea of going home on *Norvegia*.'

'And that would be quite impossible?'

Something in his voice made her pause. Perhaps he did want to take Mathilde with him. 'Completely impossible. You mustn't let her think otherwise.'

'I'm surprised you're so old fashioned,' he said. 'The world's changing, as I told Lars when he first refused to take you. A woman on a ship isn't the scandal it would have been once, as you know.'

Ingrid tried to think of another approach. Lillemor, she thought, would have no trouble convincing him. What would she have said?

'You're only just divorced, Captain. Are you looking for another wife?'

'I beg your pardon?' He swung around.

Ingrid mustered all her nerve to meet his eyes. 'Mathilde is a widow with children. Do you intend to marry her? Or just leave her alone back in Sandefjord after your jaunt on *Norvegia*? It's easy for you to think there's no scandal, being a man. For Mathilde it would be a scandal by any count back in Norway, and would ruin her chances of finding another husband. She's probably not thinking of that clearly, as she seems to still be grieving. Her judgment's poor.'

He eyed her in silence, until the moment became uncomfortable. *Qarrtsiluni* rocked in the wind.

'Are you giving me an order?' he asked.

Ingrid slid forward in her seat. 'Could you let me out, please?'

Hjalmar cracked the door and icy air streamed in, metallic with the smell of freshly flensed whale. He pulled the lever to unfold the steps. Ingrid climbed down.

'I'm sure we don't have to make it an order.'

'On *Norvegia* I'm the captain,' he said.

'Lars makes the ultimate orders on all his ships.'

'I won't forget that.' He pulled the lever to raise the staircase. He reached across and took the door handle. 'Thanks for our little chat, Mrs Christensen,' he said, and pulled it shut with just enough force to qualify as a slam.

She'd lost him, she realised, with a sinking heart.

CHAPTER 25

The safety rope tightened around Lillemor's waist as her foot scrabbled against the wall. For a moment she thought she was falling and the fright jolted her, until she realised it was just the oil sliding under her soles. She turned so her headlamp sent its beam down into the depths of the fuel tank. She saw headlamps flashing below and several turned up towards her. Four men were working on the tank floor with brooms, buckets and shovels.

'Hello!' she called. 'How's it going down there?'

'Couldn't be better, missus,' one of them called up.

The first mate, Atle, was coming down beside her on a rope, his face drawing level with hers. 'Are you all right?'

The glare of his headlamp blinded her for a few seconds. 'I thought the factory ship stank,' Lillemor said. 'But this is lethal.'

'Gives you a hell of a hangover.' Atle drew level with her and let out a yell to the men lowering him down.

Lillemor jumped as the sound echoed around the tank. His descent halted and they hung at the same height, each clipped to the heavy rope, one foot jammed into a loop at the bottom.

'Can we go to the bottom?' Lillemor asked.

He shook his head. 'There's six inches of fuel sludge down there. The fumes are terrible and you'll never get it off your shoes.'

He called up to the top: 'Is Mrs Christensen on the way down?'

Shouts came in reply and Lillemor could see a large basket descending. Ingrid had refused to get into the tank on a rope, but Lillemor convinced her to be lowered down. In a few more moments she drew level with them and the winch stopped. She was gripping the edges of the basket, but she smiled at Lillemor.

'Isn't this something?' Lillemor asked.

Ingrid nodded. 'So how does it work, Mr Tang?'

'It has to be spotless before we can put whale oil into it,' he said, his voice booming off the walls. 'There's not much time after getting the fuel out, so we do shifts round the clock. It takes a dozen of us about three days with a steam hose and scrapers to get the fuel off the ceiling and walls of the tank. Those chaps down the bottom are cleaning up what's left with shovels and buckets, and then we'll give it a final steam and hose out.'

'So a cigarette is out of the question?' Lillemor laughed.

He didn't join in. 'Not a good idea.'

'I'd like to go up now,' Ingrid said. 'I'm getting a headache.'

He called to the men above and Ingrid's basket started to rise.

'When will you be finished with this one?' Lillemor asked. 'I'd love to walk around the bottom.'

'You're a funny one, Mrs Rachlew. Most men don't even like that. Should be done by tonight if all goes well.'

'Excellent.' She could see he was nervous having them in the tank. 'I suppose we'd best go up then.'

As she neared the surface of the tank and sunlight flooded down on her, Lillemor thought she'd talk to Ingrid about encouraging Mathilde outdoors. She had declared that morning she wouldn't come out of the cabin while they were at the factory ship.

They emerged from the tank into a clear, sunny day, with almost no wind. When the two of them thanked their helpers, they crossed to the railing, away from the factory ship. The clear weather had made the water sparkle in the sunshine and the icebergs looked even more imposing with their deep blue hearts. But the smooth weather was infuriating.

'You couldn't have ordered better conditions for exploring,' Lillemor said. 'We'd have been more safe than on the ferry at home.'

'Well, at least we've had our little adventure,' Ingrid said. 'I don't think Lars has ever been inside a tank.'

Lillemor didn't reply. She'd been bitterly disappointed when she'd found they weren't allowed on the catcher, and her idea of being lowered into a fuel tank, while fascinating, didn't come close to making up for it.

'We'll have to talk them into taking us next time,' she mused.

'I tried talking Lars into it this time and got nowhere.'

Lillemor could see by the set of Ingrid's mouth that she was still angry about it. 'Perhaps you're going about it wrongly. I don't have many talents, Ingrid, but I'm good at convincing men to let me have my way.'

'I can see that.' Ingrid was watching the icebergs surrounding them and she peered more closely. 'Is that them coming back already?'

Lillemor saw a ship in the distance. 'The shape isn't right for a catcher.' She called one of the men over. 'What's that?'

He shaded his eyes with his hand to see better. 'Not one of ours.'

'Let's go up to the bridge,' Lillemor said. 'Horntvedt will know.'

When they reached the bridge, the radio was crackling. Instead of familiar Norwegian, a different language blared forth.

'Any word from my husband?' Ingrid asked.

'They radioed in two hours ago that they were doing depth soundings, but nothing to report,' Horntvedt said.

The radio blared again, the sound harsh. It was familiar to Lillemor but she couldn't place it.

'What's that?' Ingrid asked.

Nils gave her a smile. 'English of course.'

'But I didn't get a word of it!'

'Even the English have a hard time understanding Australians. Listen.'

When the voice came again, Lillemor concentrated. She heard 'Whalers … Re-coaling …' It was Freda's accent, she suddenly realised, the vowels long and flat.

'I didn't know the Australians were whaling down here too.' Horntvedt and Nils were both staring intently out the window at the ship, which was coming closer.

'That's not a whaler,' Nils said. 'It's *Discovery*.'

Lillemor and Ingrid both hurried to the window and Lillemor pressed her hands to the glass. If Mawson had accepted her application, she would have been on that very ship.

'Are they coming here?' Lillemor asked.

'They've sent no message,' Horntvedt said.

'Send them one!' Ingrid demanded. 'Lars has always wanted to meet Sir Mawson.'

'Your husband is hours away,' Horntvedt said.

'I insist you send a message. I'll meet Mawson myself on my husband's behalf.'

'I can't do that, Mrs Christensen. I can only take orders from your husband and he's not here. Perhaps you're not aware that there's animosity between Norway and Australia over this territory?'

Lillemor saw an angry line settle around Ingrid's mouth. She turned back to Horntvedt and put on her most winning smile. 'Captain, this is a historic occasion,' she said. 'Could you at least get Lars on the radio?'

Horntvedt refused to look at her. 'The catcher is out of radio range.'

'For God's sake, Captain Riiser-Larsen went on board *Discovery* last year and spent two hours with Sir Mawson!' Ingrid snapped. 'This is madness.'

'He went on board and shook hands, and then Mawson went ahead with charting the land he agreed to leave to Riiser-Larsen,' Horntvedt said, his face hard. 'He's no friend to Norway.'

Ingrid banged her fist on the window ledge and let out a groan of frustration. Lillemor saw Horntvedt look at her disapprovingly. In another moment he'd throw them off the bridge, she thought. Ingrid, in her usual manner, seemed inclined to keep arguing the point.

Nils came close, his face concerned. 'Perhaps you'd be more comfortable in the saloon, Mrs Christensen. Can I accompany you?'

Lillemor stepped forward. 'What a good idea.' She took Ingrid's hand. 'Come on.'

'I'm perfectly capable of finding my way,' Ingrid said sharply to Nils. He stepped back at once.

Lillemor pulled on Ingrid's hand, till it felt like she was half dragging her across the bridge. She managed to get the two of them out and the door closed before Ingrid could say anything else.

'That man,' Ingrid exclaimed, when they were out of earshot. 'I could kill him.'

'He's an old fool, but don't get us banned from the bridge,' Lillemor said.

'He wouldn't dare!'

'Oh yes he would. A captain is king on his own boat.'

Lillemor picked out the ship among the icebergs again. Its

tall masts were coming in to clearer view, though it was still some way off.

'I have an idea,' Lillemor said slowly. Ingrid turned to her, and Lillemor couldn't help but laugh. 'He'll wish he'd let us stay on the bridge when he sees it. But we need Mathilde. Come on!'

Lillemor started running along the catwalk to the cabins. She could hear Ingrid hurrying to keep up behind her as she reached the door of their cabin and grabbed the handle. It was locked.

Lillemor pounded on the wood. 'Mathilde, quick.' She leaned close to the crack of the door. 'Mawson's ship is about to pass. It might be our only chance to see him.'

Ingrid came to a stop next to her and Lillemor heard Mathilde's footsteps in the cabin. 'Who's Mawson?'

'Only the famous Australian polar explorer!' Lillemor said. 'Captain Riiser-Larsen's great friend and rival. But that damned fool Horntvedt refuses to send a message and so there's no reason for him to stop.'

'What do you want from me?' Mathilde asked.

Lillemor smiled. 'The three of us are going to put on our brightest dresses and hats and go on the catwalk and wave like mad. Then he'll see us and perhaps come alongside.'

'You go,' Mathilde said. 'I don't care.'

'Oh, come on, Mathilde,' Ingrid said.

There was silence behind the door.

'Hjalmar will be so disappointed.' Lillemor winked at Ingrid. 'You know he met Mawson last year in the ice and went on board? He says it was one of the highlights of his life.'

The lock turned and Mathilde opened the door.

'You need some fun,' Lillemor said. 'Come on; let's show Horntvedt a thing or two.' She stepped forward into the cabin before Mathilde could change her mind, glancing over her shoulder. The ship was close. 'We only have a minute.'

'What shall we wear?' Mathilde asked.

Lillemor smiled and clapped her on the shoulder. 'That's the spirit. Hats! Something with feathers. Scarves to wave. Dresses!'

She crossed the cabin, flung open the door of her wardrobe trunk and started rifling through her clothes.

'We'll freeze!' Mathilde said

'It won't be for long,' Lillemor said. 'Quick!'

Mathilde started pulling off her heavy clothes and Ingrid did the same. Lillemor threw her most brightly coloured dress over her shoulder. Ingrid was a little stouter than she, but could squeeze into it if she tried. The three of them started pulling on clothes, a garish mix of colours that had looked fashionable in Cape Town, but were shocking here.

'Lipstick!' Lillemor said, brandishing the tube.

'They won't see lipstick from so far away,' Ingrid said.

'Oh yes they will.' Lillemor applied the tube expertly and handed it to Mathilde, who followed suit more slowly, then passed it to Ingrid.

They stood for a moment staring at each other and Lillemor laughed aloud. Ingrid followed suit and a moment later even Mathilde joined in, if a little hysterically.

They headed to the door and out, ignoring the rush of cold on their bare arms. As they ran out on the catwalk, Lillemor could see *Discovery*'s three tall masts clearly. The ship was only a few hundred yards away.

The three of them halted and Lillemor waved her hands over her head. 'Hello! Sir Mawson! Hello!' She nudged the other two. 'Come on!'

'Hello!' Mathilde and Ingrid called together.

'Louder! Wave your scarves!' Lillemor said.

They made an incongruous sight, Lillemor could see from the expressions of the crewmen below them on the deck who were staring up in disbelief. Lillemor trailed her scarf through the air, a slash of colour against *Thorshavn*'s industrial deck.

Discovery drew closer, her sails aloft. She looked like something from an older world, Lillemor thought. *Thorshavn*'s purpose was evident in its long streamlined shape, industry stamped into every rivet that held its metal construction together. *Discovery* wore her exploration lineage like a cape of royalty.

'You know that's the ship that carried Captain Scott to Antarctica?' Lillemor said.

'Really?' Mathilde asked.

'The first time, when he went with Shackleton,' Lillemor said. 'The next time he took the *Terra Nova* and never came back.'

'The next time Shackleton went, he took my husband's ship *Polaris*,' Ingrid said.

Lillemor stared at Ingrid. That was something she didn't know. 'Don't you mean *Endurance*?'

'Shackleton changed the name of *Polaris* when he bought her,' Ingrid said. 'I always thought I'd go to Antarctica on that ship.'

'Lucky you didn't,' Lillemor said.

'They're looking!' Mathilde cried. 'They're all coming to the rails.'

Lillemor turned her attention back to *Discovery*. They were close enough to make out the faces of the men on board. 'Blow them a kiss!'

'What will they think?' Mathilde said.

'Who cares?' Lillemor waved again and made a theatrical pucker.

A ragged cheer rose from the ship and Lillemor could hear the sound of clapping.

'Can you see Mawson?' Ingrid asked.

Lillemor looked more closely. 'They're standing back to let someone through. I think it must be him.'

Discovery turned so that it faced into the breeze as it came within twenty-five yards of *Thorshavn*. The sails flapped and billowed and *Thorshavn*'s foghorn suddenly blasted out across the water, making all of them jump. Lillemor glanced up but all she could make out of Horntvedt through the window of the bridge was a blurry profile.

She turned back to *Discovery*. The man who was obviously Mawson stared at them, unmoving, while around him the men cheered and clapped and let out a few wolf whistles. Lillemor could feel his authority even at a distance. Not a heavy-handed one, like Horntvedt's, but a palpable air of strength. She waved and blew another kiss. Mathilde and Ingrid were both more ladylike now the ship was so close, but they waved.

Mawson tipped his cap at them. *Discovery* turned. Her sails filled and she began to slide away. Lillemor was aware of the freezing air on her exposed arms and shoulders. Many of *Thorshavn*'s crew had come out on the deck, attracted by their cries or the blast of the horn, and were staring up at them curiously.

'You're shivering,' Ingrid said to Mathilde.

Mathilde was staring after *Discovery* wistfully. 'She looks so graceful.'

'She doesn't have hot baths or roast pork,' Ingrid said. 'Can you imagine how she rolls in heavy seas?'

'At least she wouldn't stink.'

'I wouldn't be so sure of that! How often do you think they wash?' Ingrid said.

They laughed but Lillemor felt a pang of loss. If the world had been different she might have been exploring on *Discovery*, not capering on *Thorshavn*'s deck. She caught sight of the mess boy on the deck below them and waved to get his attention. She leaned over the railing. 'Could you bring coffee to my cabin?'

She turned to the two women, both still staring after the ship. 'We'd better keep out of Horntvedt's way for a while. Come on.'

The three of them scuttled back along the catwalk. The cabin was warm compared to the air outside and they stripped out of their dresses and back into their ship clothes. Tobias arrived in minutes with a tray of coffee and once he'd left, Lillemor opened a drawer and withdrew a bottle of aquavit.

'That was fun.' Ingrid sat on the bunk and threw back a shot without blinking.

'Well, we showed that stupid captain at least,' Mathilde said.

Lillemor decided not to draw attention to Mathilde's improved mood. She opened another drawer and took out a packet of cigarettes and a lighter. She put one between her lips and held out the packet to Mathilde.

Her eyes were wide. 'I don't smoke.'

'Come on,' Lillemor said. 'You won't believe how it takes away the smell. Ingrid?'

'Oh, why not?' Ingrid reached for the pack. She took a cigarette and made a clumsy attempt to flick the lighter. Lillemor took it from her, clicked it into life and lit the three cigarettes with a practised air. Mathilde and Ingrid both inhaled, coughed, and puffed again.

'Actually, it's not too bad,' Mathilde said. 'I could get to like it.'

'Me too,' Ingrid said.

By the second drink and cigarette the cabin was warm, filled with a comfortable fug of smoke, and they were sitting on the bunk, in a semblance of camaraderie.

'That's better,' Ingrid said. 'Once we're away from the factories, there won't be any smell.'

Mathilde sniffed at her coat and wrinkled her nose. 'Everything stinks. I'll have to burn my clothes when I get back.'

She inhaled and blew out an elegant stream of smoke as though she'd been doing it half a lifetime. 'Norway feels so far away.'

She reached her glass out to Lillemor for a second refill. Lillemor hesitated for a second, and then filled it. Mathilde wasn't a drinker; three glasses would finish her off. But really, what did it matter? She needed to loosen up.

'Be careful,' Ingrid said. 'We'll be back in Norway soon.'

Mathilde blew smoke in her direction. 'Be careful of what?'

Ingrid looked uncomfortable. 'You know what I mean.'

Lillemor laughed. Ingrid was such a prude. 'What, Mrs Christensen? What are you saying to poor Mathilde?'

Ingrid hesitated. 'Things that happen here – well – it's different from home. People would see them differently.'

'You know what? I liked having those men cheering,' Lillemor said. 'I liked the idea of a ship full of men all hungering for a woman. I think Mathilde liked it too. Didn't you, Ingrid?'

Ingrid was twisting her fingers together. She put her hands down in her lap. 'I don't know.'

'It's all right for us married women, but Mathilde is a widow. She needs a little male attention, or she'll shrivel up and die.'

Mathilde giggled. 'I think I'm getting drunk.'

Lillemor could see Mathilde was already drunk and she couldn't resist the prospect of inflaming her crush on Hjalmar, and the vicarious entertainment that might ensue. 'I suppose your husband was your first lover. Don't you ever wonder what another man would be like?'

Mathilde blushed and dropped her head.

Ingrid gave Lillemor a warning glance but she ignored it.

'Have you been wondering about someone we all know, by any chance? I think you rather like one of our captains, Mathilde?'

Mathilde didn't answer.

'I don't blame you.' Lillemor took a deep drag on the cigarette. 'He's a very handsome man, Mathilde, and he obviously likes you.'

'Do you think so?' Mathilde asked.

Lillemor could see Mathilde was having trouble focusing her eyes. It hadn't taken long for the alcohol to affect her. 'Oh yes. Wouldn't you say, Ingrid?'

'He's a very kind man,' Ingrid said.

'It's not just kindness. I've seen how he looks at her. Isn't that right, Mathilde?'

Mathilde put out her cigarette. 'I don't know. How could I tell?'

'I can tell, I assure you,' Lillemor said. 'But what are you going to do about it, that's the question?'

Mathilde blushed again. Lillemor wondered if she herself had ever been so naïve. She doubted it. She had been aware of men and how to get their attention for as long as she could remember.

'I'd like to go with him on *Norvegia*,' Mathilde said at last. 'I hate the factory ships.'

Ingrid swung her legs around and stood up, and then staggered and gripped the side of the bunk. 'Don't be fooled, Mathilde. I've known Hjalmar a long time. He's very charming, but don't think for a moment he'd give up his freedom for a woman. You try to hold on to a man like him and he disappears like a handful of snow. His first wife could tell you that.'

'Why do you care?' Mathilde said. 'I'm not looking for a husband, Ingrid.'

'Ladies, ladies!' Lillemor broke in. 'Enough. Why shouldn't she go on *Norvegia*, Ingrid?'

Ingrid stared at her. 'Are you mad? Don't you think there'd be a scandal when she got home?'

Lillemor shrugged. 'I've had my share of scandals. You get through them.'

Ingrid shook her head. 'You're not living in Sandefjord, Lillemor.' She reached out and took Mathilde's shoulder. 'No, Mathilde! That's the final word. There's no way you're going on *Norvegia*. Forget it.'

Mathilde's face slowly crumpled and she began to cry. She wriggled her shoulders until Ingrid let go. She covered her face with her hands, her shoulders shaking. 'I hate this fucking place.'

Ingrid visibly flinched at the word. She looked over at Lillemor, shaking her head as Mathilde's sobs intensified.

Lillemor returned the gaze steadily. 'Mathilde should have an affair with him. She needs something good from this trip, Ingrid. Why not let her have that? The three of us can keep it secret. It's only for a week or so until he meets his ship. What's the harm in it?'

Ingrid spluttered and stepped back. 'She could get pregnant for a start.'

Mathilde stopped sobbing and lifted her face.

Lillemor couldn't help smiling. 'Oh, that's nothing. England's behind in many things but it's quite good at birth control. The dutch cap is virtually infallible, and I always carry spares.'

'She'll fall in love with him, and expect him to marry her,' Ingrid argued.

'I will not,' Mathilde said, her voice slurring a little.

Lillemor was enjoying the sparring. Mathilde was too drunk already to realise what any fool could see – that Ingrid wanted Hjalmar for herself. With enough prodding in the right direction, Mathilde could be convinced to have an affair with him. Jealousy might take Ingrid's mind off the main game – landing on Antarctica.

'Don't expect anything from him, Mathilde, and you'll be

fine,' Lillemor said. 'We'll keep your secret. No one will know from me if you don't sleep here.'

'I can't believe this,' Ingrid said, her voice tight.

'No telling your husband,' Lillemor warned her. 'This is between the females only.'

Ingrid shook her head. 'It looks like I can't prevent you. I'm going to bed.'

She let go of the bunk and started weaving towards the door. Worried that Ingrid might fall, Lillemor jumped up, took her arm and guided her.

'Will you be all right?' she asked, as Ingrid opened the door and the cold air rushed in.

Ingrid was pale. 'It strikes me you always get your way, Lillemor.'

Lillemor laughed to try and lighten the mood. 'I do my best. But neither of us were on that catcher today, Ingrid. Sometimes you've got to take devious routes to get your way.'

She felt in her pocket and brought out a half-empty packet of cigarettes. 'You might need these,' she said, pressing them into Ingrid's hand.

Ingrid pocketed them. 'Good evening, Mrs Rachlew.'

Lillemor shut the door behind her, feeling suddenly uneasy. What had she set in motion here?

She turned back to the bed. Mathilde had passed out. She'd slid down into the bunk and her eyes were closed. Lillemor unlaced Mathilde's boots and drew them off, then pulled the covers over her. She gently lifted Mathilde's head and put the pillow under it. From the way her head lolled, she was deeply asleep.

Neither of them could take their alcohol, she thought. She stroked a damp tendril of hair from Mathilde's pale forehead, remembering when Mathilde had done the same for her. Perhaps

Hjalmar did want her. Lillemor had no idea what he thought, and not much interest. It was something to occupy Mathilde, and possibly bring her some joy, though more likely heartbreak. But she found herself hoping he didn't hurt her too much.

CHAPTER 26

Ingrid stepped out of the cabin, shaken. The sun had dropped just below the horizon and the sky was a palette of hues, deep violet, through blue, to the palest pink. The icebergs picked up the colours and glowed with them. She was drunk, she knew. She weaved along the catwalk where they had waved at *Discovery* a few hours earlier, and halted, leaning on the railing, to fumble with the cigarette packet. A book of matches was tucked inside, and she struck one on the third attempt, lit a cigarette and put it in her mouth.

It was a relief to be away from Lillemor's knowing smile. That woman had the unnerving ability to home in on uncomfortable thoughts and drag them out for scrutiny. Ingrid hated to think what Lillemor read into her protestations about Mathilde and Hjalmar. But she almost certainly understood the truth – that Ingrid didn't want another woman to have him.

It was something hard enough to admit to herself, and she certainly didn't want Lars to know. She leaned on the rail and blew smoke out over the edge, trying to calm herself before heading back to the cabin. Her head spun, from the smoke and the alcohol, and she wanted to steady herself.

Ingrid looked up. The sky seemed enormous, as if she had never appreciated how much of the world it took up. For once the ship's engine wasn't running and she could hear the silence. She fancied she could hear the hiss of the Primus stove in the galley, the soft click of a game of dominoes being played on the bridge.

She could hear a conversation on the deck of *Solglimt*, scattered laughter across the water. Was it because she was drunk, she wondered?

She closed her eyes against the massiveness of the sky, feeling her head spin. She could hear her own heart beating, even the sound of her own blood washing around her veins. She felt that if she tried she could hear the very sound of Antarctica itself, an unimaginable song. She inhaled again and the tobacco crackled. Far off, she heard the surface of the water break and a whale rise up from its element to penetrate the harsh world of air. There was an explosive whoosh as it opened its blowhole, expelled a briny breath, and drew in fresh air. She heard its blowhole close as it rounded its back and sank into the water again.

Ingrid opened her eyes, but could see nothing on the dark, silky surface of the water. '*Blaast*,' she whispered, and blew out a stream of smoke.

'Coffee, Mrs Christensen?' Tobias was at the other end of the catwalk.

Ingrid jumped and put her hand on her heart. 'Tobias! You startled me.'

As he walked towards her she turned so he didn't see the direction she'd been staring. Whales near the mother ship were easy prey, taking only a few minutes to be shot and towed to the slipway. Lars had told her that the men and boys on the tanker were alert for any whales that came near *Thorshavn*, hoping for a few coins from a grateful gunner later on.

'It's nice to have the engine off,' Ingrid said loudly as she took the cup from his hands.

'It is,' he said. 'You can hear the whales sing.'

'What?'

He put his finger to his lips and leaned close. 'Down in the tank. Press your ear against the hull. You can hear them.'

'Now you're teasing me,' Ingrid said.

He reached out and touched her sleeve timidly. 'I swear, Mrs Christensen, it's true. I've been down there just now. You can only do it when there's no engine running and no catchers nearby.'

'What do they sound like?'

He shook his head. 'I don't know how to say. Sort of sad.'

Ingrid stared up at the sky again. Earlier that day the tank had felt frightening and poisonous, but now, emboldened by alcohol, the prospect of hearing the whales felt irresistible. She took the cigarette from her lips and ground it out on the railing. 'Take me down.'

He drew back, looking nervous. 'I can't winch the basket down by myself.'

'Well, get a few of the men.'

He shook his head. 'If they know there's whales around ...'

'Oh.' Ingrid paused. 'How did you get down there?'

'The ladder.'

'We'll go down the ladder then,' she said.

He was afraid, she could tell. He hesitated.

'I promise you won't get into trouble.'

He glanced around to make sure no one was watching and started walking. She followed him to the catwalk's end and down onto the deck. He lifted up a heavy hatch and laid it back.

'Cleaning's just finished, ready for the whale oil,' he said. 'Won't smell as bad. I'll go first.'

He clambered over the side and started down the ladder into the dark. Ingrid took a deep breath and followed. He was right; the fuel fumes from the morning were nearly gone. As her eyes adjusted, the evening light coming through the hatch softly illuminated the tank so she could make out its size. She concentrated on one step at a time, feeling her way, hearing

Tobias's breath below her echoing strangely. Then she heard a groan that made her jump with fear.

'Tobias?'

'That's them!' he said.

Ingrid stopped. The dark space yawned beneath them.

'Come on. You can hear them better at the bottom.'

She continued down the ladder, wishing she'd worn her gloves. Her fingers were chilling quickly against the cold metal and she was starting to shiver. Tobias grunted below and she realised he'd reached the floor. Another few rungs and she was there too.

'Here, put your ear against it,' he said.

The hull was cold against her ear. For a long time, silence. Then, at the edge of Ingrid's hearing, a moan. She pulled back and as she broke contact with the hull, the sound almost disappeared. She shook her head slightly, and then pressed her ear back to the metal. The sound was distinct, somehow transmitted through the water and into the ship itself. It was a high wail, haunting and oddly melodic, finishing on a rising note, followed by a deep rumbling.

Ingrid thought she heard whining, then a plaintive lowing. An unexpected bellow, like a man standing in a field, his voice raised to summon someone. An unearthly whistle, sliding up the scale like a child's tin flute.

'No animal could make those sounds,' she said, moving her ear from the wall.

'I swear it's them,' Tobias said.

'How far away are they?'

He shrugged. 'The sound travels a long way, the whalemen say.'

They both pressed their ears to the hull again. Ingrid heard a groan of ancient weariness. In her intoxicated state, it sounded as if some great leviathan of the sea waited below them, planning its revenge. She drew back, suddenly afraid.

'Take me up,' she said, her heart pounding.

'You go first,' he said. 'I'll be right behind.'

She found the ladder and realised that her hands were shaking. It was foolish, she told herself. She was inside the hull and whatever made that sound was outside. But the fear was primeval. She wiped her aching, cold hands on her coat, reached up for the ladder and began to climb.

'Ingrid?'

She opened her eyes to a slash of light that cut into the numbing comfort of sleep. Nausea rushed over her and she groaned softly. *Thorshavn*'s engines were running and their thrum penetrated her skull.

Lars sat down on the bunk beside her. 'I'm back. We're on the way to the next factory. Do you want some coffee?'

Ingrid rolled towards him. 'What time is it?'

'Early, around four, I think,' he said, finding her hand and wrapping her fingers around the mug.

Ingrid pushed herself up onto one elbow. Her mouth tasted foul and she was glad he hadn't kissed her. She took a sip of coffee. Lars was looking at her expectantly. She lowered the mug and tried to collect her groggy thoughts. 'Did you find land?'

'The pack ice was so thick we couldn't get far into it,' he said. 'But we're heading for *Thorshammer* now and the captain says he thinks they might be closer to land over there. And I hear you had some excitement?'

Ingrid blinked.

'*Discovery* passed by, Horntvedt told me.'

'Ah, yes.' She rubbed her eyes and at the memory of Horntvedt's intransigence she pushed herself up into a sitting position. 'Did he tell you he refused to make contact?'

'He told me you ladies cavorted on the deck like mad women to get Mawson's attention.'

'I had no choice,' Ingrid said, as the coffee started to do its work and she felt herself coming properly awake. 'That man is a stubborn ass! It might have been our only chance to see Mawson.'

'He's the authority on the ship when I'm away,' he said. 'But did you see Mawson?'

'Yes.' Ingrid pushed the hair out of her eyes. 'Yes, we did. We made such a carry-on to get his attention that every man on his ship saw us. He probably thinks *Thorshavn* is carrying some loose women.'

'That's not exactly helpful to your cause,' Lars said, and there was an edge of anger in his voice.

'What else should I have done? Just let Mawson go by?'

'It's too late now at any rate. But try and remember you're the first women down here. You're on show.' He stood up. 'Let's have breakfast. I'm ravenous. Food on the catcher is very basic.'

'You go up,' Ingrid said. 'I'll be there shortly.'

'Yes, you'd best make yourself presentable. You've some respect to win back.'

Ingrid said nothing as he left the cabin. When he was gone she got out of bed shakily. She splashed some water on her face and looked at her pallid complexion in the mirror. How long, she wondered, until she could feel the simplicity of ice and snow and nothing more?

She pinched her cheeks hard until some colour came up, drew on her eyebrows, gulped down three aspirin tablets, pulled on some clothes and followed the sickly smell of frying towards the saloon.

CHAPTER 27

The gloom of the past days had disappeared. Antarctica felt almost friendly, Mathilde thought, as they weaved through the icebergs. Reflecting the sky and the ice, the water was benign blue and white instead of the inky black it had been near the factory ships. The air was so warm that the passengers had gathered on the catwalk in the morning sunshine instead of on the bridge to look out for the second factory ship, *Thorshammer*.

Mathilde stationed herself upwind from Hjalmar and closed her eyes. The smell of his pipe had made her want to gag. She'd never heard that cigarettes could make one ill the way alcohol did, but she felt as if poison was running through her veins. Ingrid looked pale too, while Mathilde could swear that Lillemor looked better than usual, as though she thrived on the things.

The men bantered with each other cheerfully, shielding their eyes and looking ahead, trying to be the first to spot their destination. Mathilde squinted at the brightness around her and glanced over at Hjalmar. He seemed a different person away from the miasma of the factory ship, standing bareheaded in the sun, puffing on his pipe and looking around in pleasure. He had a strong jaw, just right for holding a pipe in his mouth, and his hat was on a jaunty angle.

Mathilde half thought she had dreamed the previous night's conversation. If she remembered correctly, thanks to Lillemor's pushing, her half-formed thought of an affair with Hjalmar had been discussed as though it was a real possibility. But the idea now felt distant with the advent of morning and sobriety. She wouldn't really have an affair with him, she wouldn't know how, but the sense that it was possible left her invigorated.

She'd considered sleeping with him so he'd take her on *Norvegia* and away from the factories, but she knew, sneaking a glance at him, that it was more than that. She liked him. She chided herself for being such a simple woman that the mere thought of an affair could wipe out the horror of the factory ship.

It would be better not to get further involved with a man as charming and likeable as Hjalmar. Surely she could cope? They'd finished with one factory ship and had two more to go. Away from the stink, the memory of it was losing its potency.

'Not one but two sunny days,' Hjalmar said, smiling. 'Make the most of it, ladies.'

Mathilde smiled wanly.

'There she is!' Nils, with his keen eye, pointed to a dark smudge in the ice.

As the men looked in the direction he was pointing, Ingrid gave Mathilde a rueful glance and squeezed her arm. 'Are you all right?' she mouthed.

Mathilde rolled her eyes. 'I wish it wasn't so bright,' she whispered.

'Oh, come on!' Lillemor, of course, had overheard and she stepped in between them and linked arms with both. 'You should have both had a big cooked breakfast.'

'I wish you'd told us the cure beforehand,' Mathilde said.

The three of them laughed. The capering for *Discovery* and their frank talk the previous night seemed to have altered something between them, Mathilde realised. She'd needed the chance to drink alcohol and laugh, even if the evening had ended rather strangely. Now, at least until the next factory ship, she could enjoy the sight of the icebergs in the sun and the way the water sparkled and how pleasantly cold and fresh the air was on her face. Perhaps she'd be able to forget the sight of the flensed whale, hanging high.

She stepped forward with Lillemor and Ingrid to join the men at the railing. The breeze of their motion was fresh and smelled of ice and brine. The sun turned the water a deep royal blue and the sky was azure at its zenith, lightening at the horizon.

Thorshammer took shape in front of them and as they drew nearer, Mathilde's nose wrinkled with the first hint of the smell, the same as it had been at *Solglimt*. The factory ship was lying quietly. There were no whales on the flensing deck and no catchers to be seen. Horntvedt blew a welcoming blast on the ship's horn that made them all jump and Mathilde could see the crew gathering on *Thorshammer*'s deck to greet them. She glanced again at Hjalmar. He was staring intently out to the port side.

'What are you looking at?' Ingrid asked him.

He turned quickly. 'Ah, Mrs Christensen. Just that big iceberg. I think there may be a seal on it.'

Mathilde peered in the direction he was pointing, but could see no sign of a seal. His voice sounded oddly formal. He and Ingrid didn't seem to banter in the way they had earlier in the trip, she thought.

'Lars says you have a better chance of finding land near here,' Ingrid said.

'Some of the catchers have reported shallower depth soundings than any we've taken,' he replied. 'I hope we'll find land close enough to take you ladies ashore.'

His expression had become bland. From below on the deck came a shout and they all looked down. Several of the ship's crew had come out to see *Thorshammer* and one of them was pointing out to the port side.

'Ah,' said Lars. 'There's a little humpback, I think.'

Mathilde's heart sank as she realised what it was Hjalmar had been looking at. Against the glassy surface of the sea it was easy to see the whale's back break through and its breath blast high, hanging in a mist on the air. Next to it, a second whale rose and spouted. A few moments later a tail emerged from the water and crashed down, sending spray in all directions. Raised voices came from the deck below them; an argument over who had spotted the whales first and could thereby claim a tip if a gunner eventually shot it. Mathilde looked down to see a couple of sly punches thrown, but the men were quickly pulled apart by the rest of the crew.

'I heard a lot about the humpbacks on the catcher,' Lars said. 'They're much smaller, so the gunners don't favour them, but they're often to be found when there aren't any blues around. They're quite friendly, apparently.'

The whales surfaced again, closer now, and one rolled slowly to its side, lifting an absurdly long, slender pectoral fin and slapping the water. The crew over on the factory ship started pointing too. The underside of the dark fin was white. Beside it, a strange black shape emerged from the water and Mathilde realised it was the other whale's head, as it manoeuvred upright on its tail. She could make out the barnacles on its skin, mottled white and grey.

'Do you think it can see us?' Mathilde asked.

'Of course,' Hjalmar said, and she could hear the tension in his voice.

Another shattering blast issued from *Thorshavn*'s horn and the whale lowered itself below the surface. Mathilde expected the noise would send them fleeing, but moments later both whales blew again, apparently unconcerned.

Thorshavn's engines went into reverse as it came close to

Thorshammer. There were no dead whales to buffer the two ships and Horntvedt was leaving plenty of room to spare.

'Here comes the catcher,' Lars said.

Mathilde gripped the railing. The engines of the two big ships idled while the catcher came steaming in, dragging its haul of five blues by their tails. From both *Thorshavn* and *Thorshammer* came raised voices and gesticulations in the direction of the two whales, which continued to play off the stern.

'Will they try for the humpbacks?' Lillemor asked eagerly.

Mathilde watched the whales with a fixed gaze, praying they would flee.

'Which one is it?' Lars said, shading his eyes as the catch was offloaded. 'Ah, it's *Torlyn.* Andersen's boat. He won't pass up such an easy kill.'

'Why don't you have a go at this one?' Hjalmar said and Mathilde turned to him in astonishment. 'It looks like an easier shot than your last one.'

Lars laughed. 'Indeed.'

'Did you shoot a whale?' Ingrid asked him.

'Tried to,' Lars said. 'It's a damn sight harder than it looks. You've got to aim exactly at the waterline as the whale starts to go down. Mine went too high by a mile. The gunner was kind enough to say anyone who hits a whale the first time is just lucky.'

'So why don't you try again?' Hjalmar said. 'The catcher's just here. It's only a humpback.'

Mathilde stared at him, perplexed. He refused to meet her eyes. She turned to Lars, who was scanning the decks below. All of the factory ship's crew, and *Thorshavn*'s own, were on deck, some three hundred men who'd be watching keenly. Suddenly she thought she understood. Lars was far less likely to succeed than an experienced gunner like Andersen. Hjalmar wanted the humpbacks to escape too.

'Not this time,' Lars said.

'What about you, Lillemor?' Mathilde said desperately. 'I thought you wanted to have a turn?'

Lillemor laughed. 'I'd like a few practice shots before I try in front of an audience. But I'd love to see how they do it. Here they come.'

The catcher chugged around the edge of *Thorshavn*'s bulk, swinging past the bow and emerging into clear water. The humpbacks surfaced and blew lazily, unaware of the danger. There was no escape now, Mathilde thought. She watched the narrowing distance between the catcher and the round patch of clear water marking where the whales had dived. Both the large ships had cut their engines, and the only sound was the throb of the catcher, pumping black smoke from its funnel as it crept forward. The gunner stood by the harpoon gun at the prow, its pointed tip clearly visible, the line attaching it to the boat coiled in precise loops at his feet. On *Thorshavn*'s deck below them the men watched in eager silence, leaning over the railing. The crew of the fuel tanker had few such excitements.

Mathilde's hangover expanded and blossomed, and the pressure behind her eyes increased. She felt Ingrid's hand on her arm.

'Don't turn away,' Ingrid said, close to her ear. 'All these people will think Lars was wrong to bring us down here.'

The catcher slowed to a halt. Not a voice spoke as they strained to see where the whales might rise. Then Mathilde heard an incongruous sound above the ticking of the idling engine. At first she couldn't make it out.

'I've heard of this trick,' Lars said.

On the back of the catcher, one of the crewmen crouched close to the waterline, his arms around something. As a plaintive sound travelled across the water to them, Mathilde realised he was playing an accordion. She recognised the haunting refrain of 'Gjendine's Lullaby', the song that Norwegian mothers sang to put their children to sleep.

That they could use such a song to lure the whales to their deaths!

She didn't make the decision consciously; her body reacted on its own. Her mouth opened and the sound emerged. Her voice, silent for so long, had returned.

At first her singing was soft, a plea. The men below looked up with astonished faces, and over on the catcher the accordion player leaned closer to the water, drawing out his notes and playing louder. By itself, her voice rose too, louder than the song needed or demanded, loud enough to be a warning, an entreaty to the whales to swim far and fast, to ignore this spell.

Like two great fists punching up out of the water, both whales broke through the surface with explosive breaths. There was a terrible pause. The whales arched their backs to dive and the crack of the harpoon gun shattered the air.

The accordion player broke off and Mathilde's voice trailed away. The whales dived down, their backbones arching, the vertebrae rippling. Down, down, but too slowly. The rope whistled as it uncoiled, the harpoon flew true. It struck with a concussive thud that made Mathilde gasp. Ingrid put her hand over Mathilde's on the railing and squeezed, in comfort or warning, she didn't know.

The line pulled taut as the whale dived. A second, deeper thud signalled that the harpoon head had exploded inside its body. The line went slack and then the whale surfaced. The catcher went hard into reverse, dragging the creature backwards, pulling the line tight as the whale thrashed and the water began to run red. The gunner was loading another harpoon.

'A bit low, I think,' Lars said. 'If the harpoon goes off in the lungs, it should kill the whale almost at once.'

The whale's tail rose in the air and came down in a sickening blow, crashing on the water. A red spray spouted from its blowhole, forming an eerie mist. Mathilde gripped the railing, the only thing holding her upright. Until this moment she'd thought the hanging whale on *Solglimt* would be the most monstrous sight of the trip. But at least that creature had been already dead.

The gunner fired the second harpoon. The blow was more sickening this time now that Mathilde knew what was coming and she gasped aloud, feeling a sharp pain in her own entrails. The whale lunged against the two lines pinning it and made a terrible sound, a mixture of groan and shriek. It heaved back and forth, lay motionless for a moment, then shuddered violently, gave a final red spray from its blowhole and was still.

Thorshavn's crew began yelling like madmen, jumping and shaking their fists. Lars smiled down at them.

Mathilde felt far removed from the scene before her. The bloody water, the catcher coming up to the carcass of the whale and beginning to pump its belly with air so the pleats expanded and distended in a grotesque balloon of flesh. She'd tried to warn the whales off, but failed, and now she was trapped in the middle of this crowd, mad with bloodlust. Norwegians had always been hunters, but she'd thought of it as an unpleasant necessity and presumed others did too. She'd been wrong. There was a fierce, violent joy in the kill that she could never share.

Once the dead whale was secure and inflated, the gunner waved in their direction.

'Give him a wave!' Lars said. 'A job well done, and not easy with an audience.'

Ingrid's grip tightened and she prised Mathilde's hand free of the railing and raised both their arms. Mathilde was trapped in the forced gesture, but she refused to smile.

'Will they go for the second one too?' Nils asked.

'They say a male won't leave a female, even if she's dead, but a female will leave a dead male, so it depends which one they got,' Lars said.

Mathilde freed her hand from Ingrid's grasp. Hjalmar was scanning the horizon and she saw his face relax.

'I expect the other is far away now,' Ingrid said.

'I expect so,' Hjalmar answered, and pulled his pipe from his mouth. It had gone out.

'Well,' Lars said, looking around at them. 'That was a bit of excitement. Let's have a drink with *Thorshammer*'s captain, shall we? He's just preparing to come on board. Ladies, after you.'

Lillemor stood back to let Mathilde go past first. Below their feet was some scattered clapping.

'They like your singing,' Lillemor said to her.

To Mathilde's horror she realised the applause was for her.

CHAPTER 28

Lillemor braced her hips against the ship's railing and sighted along the rifle at a blue hole in an iceberg about twenty metres off. She squeezed the trigger and the gun fired with a satisfying crack and thud of the recoil against her shoulder. Chips of ice flew up from the hole.

'Good shot,' Nils said. 'You've got a keen eye, Mrs Rachlew. But there's a lot to remember. If the whale is close, you have to aim at the waterline as it starts to go down. If it's further away, you have to aim higher than where you want to hit, as the weight of the harpoon makes it drop. It can all change depending on the direction the whale is travelling. It takes a lot of practice.'

'Where are all those penguins when you want them?' Lillemor said. She smiled at him and took aim again. Another shot, this one making the water spurt at the iceberg's base.

'Nice one.' Lars was walking towards them from the cabin. 'Ingrid's getting her coat. Are you right to leave?'

Lillemor turned to him, lowering the gun. 'Ready.' She didn't miss the quick, almost unconscious glance he gave her outfit. She'd dressed in slacks, topped by a white fur coat with a hood, under which she'd tucked her hair into a tight white fitted hat. Every man on deck was staring at her, openly or surreptitiously, fascinated.

'We'll be leaving the rifles, unfortunately,' he said. 'When the whalers are working, they don't want to be distracted by us shooting seals. We'll go out another time for them.'

Lillemor handed her rifle to Nils. 'Fine with me. I'm not interested in a seal when there's a chance for a whale. I'll take the camera instead and get some snaps.'

She saw Ingrid emerge from her cabin and head down the catwalk towards them. She was also dressed in slacks, for the first time Lillemor could remember. She looked good in them, though Lillemor knew they suited her own taller, slimmer figure better.

'Did you tell Mathilde we were going?' Ingrid asked when she reached them.

Lillemor nodded. 'She went straight to bed and covered her eyes.'

'I don't suppose she'd come, anyway,' Ingrid said.

Lillemor found herself grinning. She and Ingrid had convinced Lars to take them out on the catcher to try for a whale. The prospect of a hunt seemed to override his fears about taking them on the smaller boat. With the three of them going for several hours, Mathilde had the perfect opportunity to be with Hjalmar. Lillemor winked at Ingrid. 'She might appreciate a chance to be on her own. Do you need a practice shot?'

Ingrid shook her head. 'Shall we go?'

'Let's,' said Lars. 'They've hooked up the basket to lower us into the catcher – it's the quickest way. They're keen to get moving.'

The catcher, *Torlyn*, was bobbing in the water alongside *Thorshavn*, the resupply ship's newness making the smaller vessel look even grimier. Streaked with soot, old blood and blubber, it carried the same thick stink as the factory ship. The harpoon mounted on its prow left no doubt as to its purpose.

The captain, Andersen, and his crew had the engines running and as soon as the three of them had been lifted over in the basket, the engines dug into the water and the smaller boat sped away into the ice field. In minutes they were out of sight of the ship.

They were almost down at water level and for the first time Lillemor had a sense that she was truly in Antarctica. As they passed icebergs, towering high above them, and slid through the broken-up brash ice, it seemed real in a way it hadn't from *Thorshavn*'s deck. Penguins plunged in and out of the water and Lillemor found herself laughing at their antics. They startled a seal resting on an iceberg, and as the creature roared and flapped to get away from them Lillemor managed to get her camera steady in time to take a shot.

'Wish I had my rifle,' Lars said.

'You've bigger things to shoot today,' Andersen said. 'Come up the front and I'll show you how to use the harpoon.'

Lillemor put the camera down and jumped to her feet, the first behind Andersen as he led them forward. They climbed the ladder up to the forecastle, where the harpoon stood on a swivelling mount on the catcher's prow.

Lillemor forced herself to be patient as Lars went first, taking hold of the handle and squinting along the sharp-tipped head with its folded-back barbs. Buried out of sight in the metal was the explosive device that caused the barbs to spring out in the whale's flesh, lodging themselves and ensuring the whale couldn't pull free. The harpoon was attached to a coil of thick rope.

Sensing Ingrid's hesitation, Lillemor went next, spinning the gun on its axis. Its weight and size were greater than any weapon she'd ever handled and she liked the smooth way it rotated on its stand. The motion was completely different from using a rifle, and she saw that it might not be an easy thing to shoot accurately at first.

Ingrid stepped up next and squinted down the sights. 'I'm not sure I'll be any good at this.'

Lars smiled up at her. 'Have a turn anyway. You never know.'

'The main thing is to aim higher than you think,' Andersen said.

The wind was icy at the front of the boat and they clambered back to the rear to wait in relative comfort. Lillemor scanned the horizon intently for the first sign of a whale's breath. Or a glimpse of the continent, for that matter.

'Do you think there's land nearby?' she asked Lars.

He glanced around at the gunner. 'What do you think, Andersen? Are we near land here?'

The gunner shrugged. 'Can't be too far away. I'm thinking about whales, not land, so I don't keep an eye out.'

'*Blaast*!' the lookout yelled above them. Lillemor was on her feet in a heartbeat. She could see the mist in the air, starting to disperse, and the dark curve of the whale's back. The boat swung around for the pursuit.

Andersen was already out of the cockpit and on his way to the front of the ship. Lillemor was hard behind him and she could hear Lars and Ingrid following. At the bottom of the forecastle ladder, Andersen turned to them.

'Who's going first?' he asked.

Lillemor held her breath. It wouldn't be her, she was sure.

'You go,' Lars said to Ingrid.

Ingrid smiled at him, took hold of the railing and climbed up to the forecastle, dreadfully slowly it seemed to Lillemor.

'Shall I help you?' Lars called up to her as Ingrid took up position in front of the gun and turned it back and forth to feel the heft of it.

'No, let me do it,' she said.

The lookout yelled again and the boat accelerated and shifted course.

'It's a blue,' Lars said excitedly.

Lillemor followed the line of his pointing arm. The whale had risen much closer this time, and was less than a hundred metres away. She had a sudden, vivid sensation of its size as it sank underwater.

The boat slowed and they waited. The water in front of them was still and glassy. The next explosive exhalation of breath was so close and loud that Lillemor jumped.

'There!' she cried. The creature had risen for breath right in front of them, huge and seemingly oblivious, the mist of its blow hanging heavy in the air, sending a briny scent over them. The curved back presented an easy target, Lillemor thought. She saw Ingrid swing the harpoon around as the whale began to sink.

'Now!' Lars called out.

It seemed to Lillemor that Ingrid hesitated. She heard the crack of the gun firing and the hiss of the rope spinning out of its coils. There was a splash and a muffled explosion. Whale and harpoon disappeared.

'What happened?' Lillemor asked.

'Missed,' Andersen said. 'Bad luck, Mrs Christensen. A close thing.'

Ingrid stepped back from the harpoon. Lillemor wondered if she'd truly tried to hit it, or lost her nerve at the critical moment. Ingrid came down the ladder and Lars patted her on the back as Andersen clambered up and started reeling in the rope to retrieve the harpoon.

'Will we get another try at that one?' Lillemor asked him.

'Doubt we'll see him again,' Andersen said. 'We'll find ourselves another. Are you next, Consul?'

Lillemor tried not to show her eagerness.

'Do you want to try again?' Lars asked Ingrid.

She smiled at him. 'That's sweet, but you should have the next shot.'

He nodded, then turned to Lillemor. 'I know you're keen, Mrs Rachlew. Want to go next?'

Lillemor felt a rush of excitement. She could see the look in his eyes, the gleam of a man on the hunt. It was generous of him to offer another the chance at a shot in the grip of this feeling. She gave him her best smile.

'I'd love to.'

Ingrid and Lars decided to sit back in the cockpit out of the wind, but Lillemor stationed herself to wait by the harpoon as she knew the gunners did. She didn't want to miss the chance at a shot if a whale rose unexpectedly close by. It turned out to be nearly an hour before they found another. By that time Lillemor's face was scoured by the wind, and the sleet was hurting her eyes. Her fingers were numb inside her gloves, her nose had gone beyond dripping and had frozen, and she had a new respect for the fleet's gunners. But when the lookout finally called '*Blaast*!' she forgot the cold. She gripped the harpoon gun and marked where the whale had risen.

Again they closed in on the whale; again there was the tense, silent wait for it to surface near the ship. The wind was picking up, Lillemor noticed with part of her mind, and it was icy. But her being was focused on the harpoon, her body poised to react. This was why she adored hunting, this hyper-awareness of her own body, the animal and the weapon.

'There!'

The whale surfaced and Lillemor spun the harpoon. The creature was in her sights, and close. She waited a heartbeat for it to come to the top of its rise.

Lars had come up from the cockpit and was standing below her on the deck. 'Aim low,' he said, his voice intense.

Lillemor dropped the gun a fraction, took a breath and fired. This time it happened in a flash. The harpoon flew out and hit the whale below the dorsal as it started to dive.

'Fish fast!' Andersen bellowed, leaping up beside her, tying off the rope and starting up the winch. Lillemor couldn't help a cry of excitement as the boat went into hard reverse to pull the line taut. She had a powerful image of the great creature below them pulling hard to escape while the ship fought to drag it backwards.

It was all noise and yelling and engines. Lars was beside her. She understood, in the flurry, that Andersen was loading the harpoon for another shot. She wanted it to be hers so much that she ached with it, and when Lars stepped forward she had to force herself to give up the gun.

He leaned down to it and waited with the same intensity. They were joined in it, like sex, as she crouched next to him.

The whale flew out of the water, lunging, and Lars fired, sending the second harpoon deep into its underside.

'Good shot, Consul,' Andersen said. 'That's it.'

The whale stayed on the surface, thrashing. Lillemor hoped its death would be quick. Watching the animal suffering wasn't part of her pleasure. She felt herself tensing up and then relaxed as the whale stiffened and went still.

A cheer went up from the crew and Lillemor turned to Lars. Their eyes met and she saw in them the hunger, the thrill, the satisfaction and the eroticism. He wasn't a married businessman right then, and she wasn't the younger wife of the naval attaché. They were humans who'd hunted, and the success of it was the fierce joy of survival.

He nodded his head. 'Well done.'

'And you,' she said. She put out her hand and shook his firmly. Nothing for anyone to see that suggested impropriety.

She'd had sex with less intimacy than the moment they'd just shared, but no one would know.

She looked over at their quarry again. It was far bigger than the humpback had been. As the boat manoeuvred alongside, she could see it was almost two-thirds the length of the catcher. One of the boys jumped nimbly across to the whale with a flensing knife, slashing footholds as he landed, as tiny as a tick bird on an elk's back. Someone tossed him a hose and he made a slit and fed it into the whale. As they pumped the air, the pleats of the whale's belly slowly ballooned, turning inside out.

Ingrid was waiting for them as they jumped back down into the cockpit.

Lillemor was still shaking with excitement. 'I thought he'd get away. I was sure I'd gone too low.'

'I knew you'd hit him, but I thought maybe he'd pull it out, and did you see how the line went hard – you wouldn't want an arm or a leg caught in that!' Lars said.

'No! My God, it'd rip it straight off. You know, that was like the best part of hunting and the best part of fishing – you get to shoot the thing and reel it in.'

'Did you get in a shot too?' Ingrid asked Lars.

'I fired the second harpoon,' he said. 'We killed it between us.'

Lillemor realised she had her hand on Lars's arm; she'd gripped him in the excitement of the moment. He hadn't noticed, but she felt Ingrid's eyes on her. She let go of him, making sure the movement was casual.

'Is there time to go for another?' Lars asked Andersen.

He shook his head. 'Factory's been on the radio. Blizzard coming, I'm afraid. We'll have to head back straight away. Don't want the ladies to get cold.'

'Sounds quite exciting,' Lillemor said. She'd stopped feeling the cold, and in her exhilaration, the challenge of a blizzard sounded appealing.

The dead whale was inflated until it floated freely and the boys attached a chain to its tail, ready for towing back to the factory.

'It's a good eighty feet,' Lars said. 'Do you agree, Andersen?'

He glanced along the length of the whale. 'Seventy-five, I'd say.'

Lillemor hoped there'd be some kind of trophy to take home, a piece of bone or tooth. A shout interrupted her thoughts. One of the catcher's crewmen was pointing at the whale and gesticulating. Lillemor got to her feet and felt Lars stand beside her.

'What?' Ingrid asked.

Lars clambered over to the side where he could see and Lillemor followed. Five huge dorsal fins rose from the surface of the water and Lillemor saw a flash of black and white, moving so fast she couldn't follow it.

'Orcas,' Lars said. 'They try to eat the tongues, I'm told.'

They were lunging at the carcass of the whale, rising out of the water to attack, and Lillemor climbed higher for a better view. Down low, almost in the water, the whale's shape was oddly distorted. It was a foetus hanging there, Lillemor realised, like the one they'd seen on the deck of the first factory ship. The dead whale was giving birth, in some kind of muscular spasm after its death. The orcas, with their instinct for an easy meal, were lunging and tearing at the foetus as it emerged.

She and Lars stared silently and then by common, unspoken assent, turned and climbed down again. Lillemor thought Lars looked a little pale as he faced Ingrid.

'What's wrong?'

He shook his head. 'Just some orcas. But best you don't look.'

'Why not?' Ingrid asked.

'The whale was pregnant,' Lillemor said.

The stink was spreading over the boat, as though the creature had died a week ago and not a few minutes earlier. The engine started and the catcher shuddered and began to move.

Lars took his wife's hand and Lillemor turned away from them. It was no use being sentimental now. Lars should be pleased – this one would bring in plenty of oil.

She looked up at the sky. An Antarctic gloom hung low on the horizon and the wind was starting to groan and whistle around them. It began to snow.

CHAPTER 29

Mathilde cocked her head to one side. Was that a knock on the door? The wind was groaning and whistling around the ship, and the bone saw whined without respite. But the sound she was hoping for didn't come and she slumped down again. She picked up her glass, but it was empty. She shook the aquavit bottle but it was empty too. Had she drunk it all? She couldn't remember how full it had been.

She'd locked herself in her cabin, trying to shut out the world. The short moment of beauty she'd experienced that morning had been destroyed. But neither the small space around her nor the alcohol had been enough to block her vivid memory of the humpback's death. She could still hear the whistle of the harpoon, the impact of it hitting living flesh, and the sound the whale made before it died, a shriek growing in intensity in her memory rather than receding. It was now mixed in with the scream of the bone saw, which was probably at that moment slicing the humpback into pieces. She'd wanted to drink herself into insensibility, but the alcohol had run out and she was still awake. She shook her head and put her hands over her face. What a fool she'd been to think she'd cope better with the second factory ship. It was worse. And her first song since Jakob died had helped lure the whale to the harpoon.

An hour ago a storm swept over the two ships. The temperature dropped, the wind picked up and flurries of snow began surrounding them. As she'd closed the curtains she'd seen the men on the factory ship working under spotlights. Ice had gathered on the ship's surfaces and some of them were labouring to chip it away from the stays and railings, a joyless job by the look of it.

She scrabbled on the floor for Lillemor's cigarettes and lit one with trembling fingers. Her belly turned at the taste, but at least it blocked the smell of the factory.

She was alone. No Hjalmar coming with his soft knock at the door to see if she was coping. No Ingrid or Lillemor to jolly her along, or even to mock her. She wished she'd gone to the sanatorium as Ole and Gerd had threatened rather than coming on this trip. Here, everyone acted as though the slaughter of whales was a sane activity, and she the only one disturbed.

She inhaled hard again and then coughed out the smoke with a convulsive sob. Perhaps she was mad. Perhaps she was the only person in the whole of Norway who thought this was wrong and cruel.

No, not the only person. Hjalmar disapproved of it too. She never felt mad around him. When they were together, she felt they made an island of sanity in the midst of craziness. Why didn't he come?

She stood up and opened the curtain a crack again. She could hardly see the flensing deck through the flurries of snow and ice, but every so often the murk lifted enough to reveal snow-covered figures moving about their tasks. Nothing seemed to stop them; nothing halted the bone saw's whine.

She heard the door rattle and started back from the curtain, a movement so sharp that she lost her balance and swayed. The door flew open, sending in a gust of wind and snow and two human figures. It was Lillemor and Ingrid, their outer clothes crusted in ice.

'Mathilde!' Lillemor's voice rang out, shattering the cabin's silence. 'Are you partying alone?'

She tried to focus on the two blurry figures before her as they came into the cabin. 'What?'

Lillemor laughed. 'Have you finished *all* the aquavit? You're a wild one. Or did you share it with Hjalmar?'

The door closed, shutting off the sound of the wind. 'Are you all right, Mathilde?' she heard Ingrid ask.

No, she wanted to say. No, not all right at all. She opened her mouth but couldn't form the words.

Lillemor and Ingrid stripped off their outer layers and hung them by the door.

'Lucky I've got another stash; I need something to warm me up,' Lillemor said. She crossed the cabin, opened a little drawer in her wardrobe case, and pulled out a bottle. 'I'm glad you didn't find this one.' She poured three drinks and handed them out. 'We bagged ourselves a blue,' she said, raising her glass. 'To the world's biggest hunting trophy.'

Mathilde's fingers felt slippery but she craved another drink. Perhaps this one would put her to sleep. She raised the glass and touched it to theirs. 'You're disgusting,' she said, and swallowed it.

'What did you say?' Ingrid stared at her.

'I don't know how you can do it.'

'Well, you see, Mathilde,' Lillemor leaned forward, 'we wanted to give you some time alone so you could be with Hjalmar. We did it for you, my dear. I hope it was worth it.'

Mathilde felt her knees wobbling and sat down on the bunk. The cabin seemed to be rocking back and forth.

'So did you?' Lillemor asked.

'What?'

'Have your little fling with Hjalmar? You look drunk enough.'

Mathilde shook her head, a movement that caused the cabin to rock more violently. 'How dare you?'

Lillemor laughed aloud and sat back. 'All prim and proper suddenly, Mrs Wegger?'

Mathilde looked at her with distaste. Lillemor had a soft side, she knew, but mostly she showed her ability to sense weakness and zero in on it.

'Oh, leave her alone, Lillemor.' Ingrid's voice sounded weary.

Ingrid would be pleased to know Hjalmar had rejected her, Mathilde thought. She felt a rush of anger and nausea.

'You're no different!' she said. 'You'd prefer to keep Hjalmar hanging around you like a dog than let someone else have him. You with your perfect marriage and your beautiful children and all your money.'

It was a thought she'd kept buried, but it was out in the open now. Mathilde didn't care that Ingrid was staring at her in shock. The words seemed to rush out of her without stopping. 'There's never a moment when you're not watching him. You just want him for your own.'

'For God's sake!' Ingrid got to her feet. 'Maybe he just doesn't find you attractive.'

It felt like a slap across the face. 'Fuck you,' Mathilde snapped.

Lillemor laughed. 'You sound like one of the flensers now. What's happening to you, Mathilde?'

Mathilde stood up, swaying slightly, her eyes fixed on Ingrid. The woman was determined to bring her down, by any means she could. 'I'm here against my will!' Her voice rose. 'You don't care how many whales you murder or how many people you tread on to get your own way.' She brought her face close to Ingrid's. 'First woman on Antarctica. Ha!'

Ingrid put a hand on Mathilde's shoulder and pushed. 'Get away from me. You've drunk too much.'

The shove was surprisingly hard. Mathilde staggered, any sense of balance upended. Her fury surged. This was the woman who would help Ole and Gerd take her children. She hit out at Ingrid, arms flailing. Her volley of slaps and blows landed on Ingrid's head and shoulders. It was richly, horribly satisfying, and she didn't notice Lillemor coming up behind her until the woman managed to grab one of her arms, pinning it. Mathilde turned her head to protest and Ingrid stepped forward and slapped Mathilde on the cheek.

The fierceness of the slap just inflamed Mathilde's desire to hurt. She balled up her free hand into a fist and drove it towards Ingrid's face.

It was an inexpert punch, but it landed in Ingrid's eye and the woman made a noise of pain and clapped both hands over her face, staggering backwards. She collided with the side of the bunk, slipped and fell. Mathilde heard the crack her head made as it struck the floor.

'Oh Christ,' Lillemor said, letting go of her. 'What have you done now?'

CHAPTER 30

There was a long moment of pain and disorientation, and a roar seemed to assault Ingrid's ears. She could feel hands on her and she twitched.

'Ingrid?' It was Mathilde's voice, sounding frightened.

'Are you all right?' That was Lillemor.

Ingrid managed to open her eyes. She was crumpled on the narrow floor beside the bunk, her head throbbing viciously. Lillemor crouched next to her and Mathilde was peering down over her shoulder, her eyes wide.

'Are you all right?' Mathilde asked.

Ingrid flinched at the sound of her voice. 'Get away from me.'

Mathilde's face disappeared. Ingrid put her arms out and scrabbled until she found a handhold on the bunk. She pulled herself up to sitting. Her head swam and for a moment she thought she might faint.

'Don't get up yet,' Lillemor said, putting a hand on her shoulder.

'Get me away from her,' Ingrid managed. She got to her knees and slowly pushed herself into a standing position, with Lillemor's help. She couldn't tell if the dizziness was her own head or the boat's swaying, and she wondered if she was going to be sick.

'Ingrid, I'm so sorry.' Mathilde was at the far side of the cabin, her face stricken, but Ingrid didn't care.

'Get my coat,' she said to Lillemor.

'Maybe we should call the doctor,' Mathilde said uncertainly.

'Shut up, Mathilde,' Lillemor said, putting her arm around Ingrid's waist. 'You've done enough.'

'Take me to my room.' Ingrid leaned on Lillemor, who helped her across the cabin. Mathilde stood still, her face dead white. When Lillemor opened the door, the wind hit Ingrid like another punch. They staggered the few steps to her cabin and Lillemor helped her inside. Ingrid leaned on the wall as Lillemor pushed the door shut. Her hands were shaking.

Lillemor examined her face.

'How bad is it?' Ingrid asked.

'You'll have a shiner, I'd say.'

'Let me look.'

Lillemor helped her to the mirror and Ingrid took a deep breath and raised her eyes. Her left eye was swollen where Mathilde's punch had landed. She touched the puffy flesh and flinched. On the side of her head a painful lump attested to whatever she'd hit on the way down. Her hair was wild and there was a graze on one cheek.

'I'll get the doctor,' Lillemor said.

'No!' Ingrid put her hand on Lillemor's arm. 'I'm fine.'

'You were knocked out!'

'Only for a moment. I just want to be alone.'

'I don't think that's a good idea.'

Ingrid tightened her grip. 'I'm not asking you, Lillemor. Lars will be coming to bed soon. I don't want you to mention this to anyone, understand?'

Lillemor eyed her uncertainly. 'Are you sure?'

'Imagine if they think we women have had a fight. How shameful! Not a word. Mathilde is raving drunk, that's all.'

'Can I help you to bed at least?'

'No. I'm fine.'

She waited until the door closed behind Lillemor before she turned to the mirror again. The image in front of her swam in and out of focus. A middle-aged woman with lines under her eyes and a body wearied from bearing children. Ingrid felt a rush of exhaustion. At all costs she mustn't have another one, not conceived in this bloody place. It could indeed be a child to run a whaling fleet, and the idea sickened her. She thought of Cato and Soren running down the dock at Sandefjord, laughing and fair-haired. Every flenser, caked in a season's whale viscera, had been such a boy once, sweet-smelling and innocent.

Her eye throbbed and she put a hand to it. What on earth had made Mathilde angry enough to hit her? She must be desperately in love with Hjalmar to react so.

Ingrid lowered her eyes. It was true; she couldn't bear the thought of Hjalmar and Mathilde being together. Was it really because she wanted him herself? He understood ambition; he was a man whose life was built on beating other men to remote places, doing what was needed to get there first. He was strong and proud, not beholden to anyone. An adventurer, like Amundsen.

That's why she liked him so much.

There. She'd thought it. She stared in the mirror. It had come to this between Mathilde and her, and partly she was glad of it. Mathilde had stepped across a line, a demarcation between their usual world where such violence would be unthinkable, and this world of the factory ships, where blood and guts were all. Ingrid felt a strange satisfaction looking at herself. Inner and outer suddenly matched; the chaos of her feelings writ large on her body.

She washed her face, wincing, stripped off her clothes with still-shaking fingers, pulled on her nightwear, climbed into the bunk and pulled the covers around her like a cave. Outside the blizzard shrieked.

❄

Waking was like swimming up from far down underwater through increasing layers of pain. When Ingrid's head broke through the surface, headache gripped her skull and her eye throbbed.

The curtain dragged on its tracks with a squeal. She opened her eyes. Lars was standing at the porthole looking out. When he heard her stir, he turned. The smile faded from his face as he saw her. He was by the bunk in two strides.

'My God, what happened to your face?'

'Oh,' Ingrid said. 'A bit of an accident. I fell.'

He bent over and looked at her closely. His fingers ran lightly over her cheek and touched her eyebrow. She flinched.

'I haven't been in a fight since school,' he said. 'But this is usually how they looked afterwards.'

Ingrid felt a sob rising up inside her and her chin began to tremble, an awful feeling as if she had no control of the muscles of her face. Lars stroked her hair, concerned. When his hand found the bump near her temple, she drew her breath in sharply.

'Tell me,' he said.

That was it, two tender words. Ingrid's throat convulsed. 'She hit me,' she managed to say, like a child telling a parent. He gathered her into his arms and pressed her face to his chest, rocking her back and forward while she clung to him.

'You have to tell me what's going on,' he said.

Ingrid snuffled and drew away a little. He pulled out a handkerchief and she blew her nose and wiped her face.

'Mathilde is quite beside herself. She can't stand the factories. It was a mistake to bring her.'

'What's that to do with your face?' he asked.

'We had a disagreement and she punched me. I hit my head when I fell.'

'What!' Lars shook his head. He shifted her so she was leaning back against the pillows and he could look at her face. 'Ole warned me she might be unstable, but this is outrageous.'

Ingrid blinked, confused. 'You never told me Ole said that.'

He peered closely at her face. 'I'll have to deal with this. Is there anything else I should know?'

Ingrid didn't want to face Mathilde again. She'd thought Lillemor was the more unpredictable but Mathilde was just as dangerous. She might throw herself on Hjalmar's mercy, force him to take her on *Norvegia*. She couldn't bear the thought of it. She felt herself coolly calculating her next words, observing in a detached way what she was capable of.

'Mathilde's got some foolish notion of falling in love with Hjalmar and she's lost her sense of propriety. She's quite out of control.'

'What do you think we should do?'

'I think you must confine her to her cabin for a little while. Perhaps until we drop Hjalmar at *Norvegia*. I'm sure once we're heading home she'll be better.'

'I never expected it to get to this.' He sat back and shook his head. 'I'll get Stevensson to give her a sedative.'

'I doubt she'll take it,' Ingrid said.

'We'll see about that.' He stroked her head again. 'Do you have something to cover up that eye?'

'I think so.'

'Get ready for breakfast. I'll sort this out.' He stood. 'We'll keep this quiet, eh? There's quite enough unrest about you three as it is.'

Ingrid watched him leave, his brow furrowed. She hadn't mentioned the way she'd slapped Mathilde's face. It wasn't really violence. That was what one did for hysteria, wasn't it?

CHAPTER 31

The sun had set, but not far enough below the horizon to bring darkness, and the evening colours of mauve and purple lingered and intensified. By the time Lillemor got back to the cabin, Mathilde had rolled herself into bed and was facing the wall.

She got into her own bunk and switched off the light, but sleep didn't come easily. That moment when Ingrid's head cracked on the floor kept returning. It was just a foolish spat, a child's tantrum, a few hits thrown. If Lillemor had managed to pin down both Mathilde's arms, it would have been just that, and they'd have never mentioned it again. But Ingrid had an egg on her skull and a black eye that would take some explaining, and somehow the whole sorry incident had tipped into something much more serious.

Damn Hjalmar! How hard would it have been for him to slip into the cabin when he had the chance? A bit of happiness that would have meant much to Mathilde.

In truth, the punch was meant for her, Lillemor knew. Ingrid had been fairly kind to Mathilde, all things considered. But Lillemor had used her mercilessly, had toyed with her feelings, and then taunted her about them. No wonder the woman had reached breaking point.

She squirmed uncomfortably in her bunk and hit the pillow a few times to get it into shape. She didn't like feeling guilt. But there was no avoiding what had happened and her own part in it. Lillemor didn't fall into a fitful sleep until after light started to filter through the curtains.

It felt like just a few hours later that a heavy knock on the door woke her. It was the sort of knock a person would expect after the night they'd had, a knock loud with accusation. She looked over at Mathilde, who hadn't stirred. The woman would have a monumental hangover. The knock came again, demanding. Lillemor scrambled out of bed and into her dressing gown then opened the door a slit.

Lars pushed in and past her without a word and by the time Lillemor had gathered her wits he'd already reached Mathilde's bedside. He was carrying a mug of something steaming.

'Mrs Wegger.' His voice was low and frightening. Lillemor shivered.

Mathilde's eyes opened. She stared at him uncomprehendingly.

'I understand there was an unfortunate incident last night,' Lars said.

Mathilde sat up and looked around, confused. 'What?'

'My wife has a black eye and a lump on her head this morning.'

Lillemor could almost see Mathilde sorting through the confused memories until an expression of dread spread across her face. 'Oh God.'

'Indeed.'

Mathilde pushed back her hair and Lillemor felt sorry for her. Lars wasn't a big man but his air of authority was absolute. Lillemor was glad it wasn't her under his heavy stare.

'Things got out of hand … an accident … I'm so terribly sorry,' Mathilde stammered. She tried to pull herself together. 'Please let me come and apologise to Ingrid in person.'

Lars shook his head. 'She doesn't want to see you. I have a duty to make sure you're not distressed, Mathilde. It would be best if you stayed here in your cabin for a day or two until your mental state improves. Ingrid says you find the factory ships disturbing, so best you don't look at them.'

'As you say,' Mathilde stammered.

He offered her the cup and she took it. Lillemor could see her hands shaking.

'The steward will bring your meals, and the doctor will look in to see if there's anything you require.'

Mathilde was staring at the coffee. Lars waited and the silence was unbearably tense.

'When you've finished, I'll take your cup back,' Lars said.

Mathilde gulped down the drink and handed him the empty cup. He strode back to the door, gesturing for Lillemor to follow. He stepped outside the cabin and she followed him.

'This is most regrettable,' he said in a low voice. 'I'd prefer word of it didn't get around the ship. Mrs Wegger is resting for a day or two, that's all.'

Lillemor marvelled that the day before she'd felt they were of one mind. His eyes were now icy cold. She hadn't seen him angry before. Ingrid had more to deal with than Lillemor had realised.

'I want you to lock the cabin once she's asleep,' he said. 'It won't hurt Mathilde to think she's in serious trouble.'

'Asleep?'

'There's enough sedative in that coffee to knock out a horse.'

Lillemor stared at him in shock. 'What?'

'You might not have known but Mathilde is unstable,' Lars said. 'Her family thought this trip might help, but it seems it's too much for her. Stevensson agreed a sedative was for the best. He'll be along shortly to check on her. I'd be obliged if you'd wait for him.'

Lillemor felt her gut tighten. 'Very well.'

Lars looked out at the factory ship. 'We're about to cast off from *Thorshammer*. I think we'll find land today or tomorrow.'

'Wonderful,' Lillemor said.

Lars turned back to her. 'My wife will be the first woman to see Antarctica. No matter who is on the bridge. I hope that's clear?'

'Quite.' Lillemor turned from him. 'If you don't mind, I need to get dressed.'

She went back into the cabin and shut the door hard behind her. Whatever he'd sedated Mathilde with was already taking effect. She was lying back on her pillow, her eyes closed, breathing deeply. Her face was stripped of colour, and curiously vulnerable.

Lillemor found herself shivering.

CHAPTER 32

Ingrid positioned herself next to Lars at the far end of the bridge where her face was away from the light, for in spite of her careful application of foundation powder, the bruised eye shone through. The worst part was she knew no one would comment or ask about it directly. There'd be rumours instead, of God knew what. She dreaded anyone thinking that Lars might have hit her.

Thorshavn blew a farewell blast on the horn as it steamed away from the factory, the crews of both ships lining the decks to wave. *Thorshammer*, with newly drained tanks, faced another six weeks of hunting and processing whales until the season turned and the sea started to freeze. The faces of the crew were already lined with exhaustion and Ingrid was sure some of its men watched with longing as they steamed towards the pack ice, bound for exploration and then a return to sunny Cape Town.

Fiddling with her camera, Lillemor was uncharacteristically quiet. Hjalmar, who'd looked at Ingrid piercingly when she arrived on the bridge, stationed himself far away from her. Horntvedt was, as usual, grim. Nils was the only one who didn't seem aware of any tension, cracking jokes and calling for coffee so often that Tobias was constantly running up and back from the galley. Ingrid drank cup after cup without noticing when one finished and the next began.

As the stench of the factory receded, Ingrid felt a weight lift from her. She wanted to put the memory of what had happened with Mathilde behind her and recall the real purpose of the journey – Antarctica.

The ship was moving closer to the continent, sliding slowly through the brash ice, which slid and scraped and clattered along the hull, a chiming symphony of ice and snow and metal. Small, pure-white snow petrels fluttered around the ship and the sea was alive with penguins, whose small, fat bodies flew through the air and plunged in and out of the water like miniature porpoises, unexpectedly graceful. It felt a world away from the gore of the factory ships.

Icebergs were scattered in the ship's path, seemingly impenetrable. Hjalmar watched the ship's course through them intently, consulting the chart from time to time.

'There,' he pointed at last. 'That's the lead we followed yesterday.'

Ingrid could see a narrow opening in the ice ahead of the ship. It was hard to judge the scale. The lead could have admitted *Thorshavn* easily, or been as small as a canoe.

'What do you think?' Lars asked Horntvedt.

He shook his head. 'I wouldn't have taken a catcher in there.'

'That's the only lead we found,' Hjalmar said.

There was silence for a moment. 'Then take us along the ice edge,' Lars said.

Horntvedt increased the throttle and turned the ship. He said nothing, though it seemed to Ingrid the lines on his face deepened. The aspirin she'd taken was wearing off too quickly. There was little conversation on the bridge and *Thorshavn* progressed at a frustrating pace.

'Why so slow?' she murmured to Lars after a while.

'Come,' he said. He led her to the control panel and pointed at the depth sounder. It was pinging on three hundred and seven metres.

'Most of the factories have been operating at about three thousand metres,' Lars said. 'Last night we got as shallow as one hundred and sixty-seven. It might just be a shoal or a bank, but along this edge of the ice it seems consistently shallow, which suggests land is close.'

'There's just the eternal problem of finding a way through the pack ice to get near it,' Nils said. 'It might be just out of sight.'

'How would you know?' Lillemor asked Hjalmar.

'You hope for a high landform you can see from a distance, like a mountain or a cape, with nunataks,' he answered.

'Rock sticking out of the snow,' Nils explained. 'But large icebergs throw shadows that can look just like nunataks, and some icebergs are dark and you'd swear they were land. Last trip we spent six days looking for the Nimrod Islands. They were supposedly discovered a hundred years ago, but no one's ever been able to find them again. So even the best explorers can be fooled.'

Ingrid was relieved when he fell silent and she could step away. She moved close to the window. The icebergs ahead of them were curiously jumbled together.

Hjalmar pointed. 'Captain, that looks like a shoal to me.'

Ingrid looked at the depth sounder. It had risen to two hundred and forty-nine metres. 'What does he mean?' she asked Lars.

'Those icebergs ahead look to be resting on rock.'

'Quiet on the bridge.' Horntvedt was curt. 'Consul, I require instruction.'

Lars went to stand next to him at the wheel. 'Yes?'

'I cannot take responsibility for an accident if we go further. You can see we're surrounded by shoals and icebergs, and the ship has a half-cargo of oil. If you want me to proceed, it's under your instruction and at your risk.'

There was a long silence as Lars weighed it up, but it was respectful. These men would trust him, Ingrid realised. There was no right or wrong here, no clear-cut trade-off, just risk and luck.

'I think Amundsen, God rest him, would be disappointed in us if we called it a day already,' Lars said at last. 'I'm looking for something to name after his ship. She needs to win some friends before she falls to pieces. I want you to proceed past the shoal, Captain, at the speed you judge to be safest.'

'I'll issue a lifeboat alert first, if you don't mind,' Horntvedt said.

Lars nodded. 'If you think it's necessary.'

Horntvedt picked up the wireless handset and switched it to broadcast. Ingrid could hear his voice booming across the ship as he instructed the crew to be prepared for an abandon ship. She wondered if Mathilde, in her sedated sleep, heard it. Lillemor looked at her anxiously, and Ingrid turned to Lars and raised her eyebrows in a question.

'It's just a formality, don't worry,' he said.

It was true; in the warm confines of the bridge the prospect of the ship foundering felt as remote as a dream. Ingrid buckled on a life jacket as if it were simply another layer of warmth. Nils stationed himself by the depth sounder and called out the readings. '206 … 180 … 246 … 173 … 80.'

At eighty, Lillemor crossed the bridge and stood next to Ingrid. 'If we run aground, will there be time to get Mathilde?' she whispered.

'I advise we don't go any closer,' Horntvedt said. 'It's clear there's a bank under there. It's probably worthy of a name.'

Lars nodded and Horntvedt drew the engines into reverse to bring *Thorshavn* to a halt. Ingrid tried to picture the ocean floor beneath them, a series of underground mountains rising up towards the surface, shallow enough that the icebergs were grounded there.

Tobias handed the little glasses of aquavit around and Lars waited till they all held one, before lifting his glass.

'Here's to our first discovery of the voyage,' he said. 'I hereby call this "Fram Bank", in memory of Roald Amundsen and Fridtjof Nansen, who sailed the faithful *Fram*. Let's hope we can find that ship a safe home before she rots.'

Everyone raised their glasses. Lars made a show of being merry, but Ingrid could sense his disappointment. An underwater bank, no matter how shallow, had nothing of the glory of land about it.

It occurred to her that seeing Antarctica itself, even landing on it, might be just as disappointing. Such a fuss was made about the first footfall, as though there was a mystical moment when foot met earth and the reverberations pulsed through the bedrock and rippled across the land. She would have liked to ask Hjalmar what he thought, but there was such a distance between them now that she didn't know how to broach it.

Horntvedt brought the ship around and they continued along the edge of the ice. Within a few minutes the reading on the depth sounder showed one thousand metres, then fifteen hundred, then twenty-five hundred.

'We're off that shoal at least,' Nils said.

'Pity,' Lars said. 'It was our best bet so far.'

'Just as well.' Hjalmar pulled out his pipe. 'There's a snowstorm coming. Best not to be in eighty metres when that hits.'

Ingrid saw that a squall was making its way towards them, blotting out the pack ice in a grey blur, pulling the world down around them. It suited her mood.

Lars looked at his watch. 'A late lunch, I think. It looks like that's our excitement for the day.' He turned to Horntvedt.

'You're back in full command. I'd like you to continue along the edge of the pack ice and send for me immediately if you see anything interesting.'

Hjalmar drained his aquavit and made a mock bow. 'Excuse me, gentlemen, Mrs Christensen, Mrs Rachlew. I'm staying here. I need to see as much of this territory as I can.'

His eyes raked over Ingrid, and though his expression didn't change she felt revealed, as though he could see every blow laid in her fight with Mathilde, not only her black eye, but also the hard slap that Ingrid had laid on Mathilde's soft cheek and how she'd contrived to have her locked up and sedated.

The blizzard overtook them as they ate lunch, hurling and shrieking around the ship, spattering the windows with ice. The engine dropped to idle speed as the continent's white fist closed around *Thorshavn*. Ingrid couldn't shake the feeling that Antarctica was furious at them for coming so close.

She picked at her food, feeling the very marrow of her bones aching. Lars was cheery and loud, keeping the conversation flowing with his natural charm, deflecting attention from her. As soon as it was appropriate, he excused them, saying they were heading back to the bridge.

'Why don't you rest?' he said quietly as they pulled their coats on before going outside. 'You look terrible. It'll probably be a whiteout all afternoon and we'll have to sit it out here. I'll send for you the moment there's anything to see.'

Ingrid nodded and squeezed his arm. She could see how worried he was that he'd ordered the ship into this treacherous area, this uncharted edge of an unexplored continent where a collision with an iceberg could sink them.

He opened the door and they stepped out into the sudden force of the blizzard. Ice particles smacked Ingrid's face and she shut her eyes.

'Shall I take you back to the cabin?' Lars asked, close to her ear.

'Don't be silly, I'm fine.' Ingrid dropped his hand. 'I'll see you later.'

She turned away from him and began making her way out on the exposed catwalk. Antarctica came at her with flailing wildness, threatening to throw her from her feet as she inched along the catwalk, clutching at the railing. Ingrid's face began to freeze and her fingertips were becoming numb inside her gloves. The shriek of the blizzard filled her ears until she clapped her hands over them. She knew exactly why Antarctica screamed. Surely every man on board could hear her wordless fury that they dared to come with their harpoons and boilers, and slaughter her children in her own waters, where they had been safe for all time.

She staggered in the direction of her cabin, found the door, shoved it open, entered and shouldered it closed behind her, shutting out the blizzard She shrugged out of her coat, already starting to drip melted ice on the floor, and hung it up. A glance in the mirror confirmed she looked as wild and desperate as she felt. Any makeup she'd been wearing had been scoured off by the wind and her face was frightening in its wide-eyed rawness, her still-darkening bruise revealed.

CHAPTER 33

Lillemor stepped over the sill into the cabin and shut the door behind her. She dreaded going inside, but wanted to check on Mathilde before dinner. The blizzard meant the ship wasn't going anywhere, and the feeling of being trapped was strong within her.

She set her shoulders and turned to face Mathilde's anger. But Mathilde was still fast asleep. Lillemor tiptoed closer. It looked like she hadn't moved at all. Her breathing was slow and regular, her cheeks white, and she was lying in exactly the same position.

She felt a stab of concern. Damn Lars! What had he put in that cup of coffee, and how much? There was no hospital nearby if Mathilde needed help, only a doctor who'd agreed that involuntary sedation was the best option. And now Lillemor had to be her unwilling guard.

She wondered if she should try to wake Mathilde. How far would the Christensens take this? Ingrid had shown no concern about Mathilde when the lifeboat alert was raised. If they'd hit something or run aground and been in danger, how would Lillemor have got Mathilde awake, into her clothing and out to a lifeboat in time?

She hoped Mathilde wasn't doomed to sleep through their remaining time in Antarctica, waking at its end as if from dreams of ice.

It was a moment that should be captured, Lillemor thought. She had a sense of needing evidence of what happened. She got up quietly and went to her cupboard. The Beau Brownie was heavy in her hands as she carried it back across the room and took aim. It was like hunting, she thought, as she looked at Mathilde's unconscious face through the viewfinder and pressed the lever, though the success was delayed. She wouldn't know till she got back to London if she'd caught her quarry.

She put the camera away and went to the porthole. There was no horizon visible. The ship crept forward in the inky water. Stately icebergs appeared out of the fog and slid by silently. The brash ice clanked against the hull. No wonder men had once thought they'd sail off the edge of the earth. What courage it would have taken to keep sailing in such waters, not knowing what abyss may await, or what krakens might reach up to catch them.

Lars had looked so different that morning with his stern face and his eyes like chips of ice. He was short and stocky, too long in the jowls to be handsome, but his face was pleasant and genial most of the time. The way he'd dispatched the problem of Mathilde with such cool brutality was chilling.

Lillemor missed Anton suddenly. He was always on her side and she had no ally on board. Lars and Ingrid would cleave to each other; Mathilde would join herself to Hjalmar or remain aloof. Lillemor had no one to call on, for what loyalty had she shown anyone? She'd seen it in Lars's eyes when he came to sedate Mathilde, the reminder that no matter what she might long for, in the end it was his choice what happened and who took part and what was remembered or recorded later.

She felt utterly insignificant. Antarctica reminded you of that, she thought, by showing her size and power in relation to your own.

If he were here, Anton would have stood by her and even if she didn't get her way, his love would have buffered her each night, his touch would have soothed her disappointment, his regard and his desire would have been a balm on her self-esteem, letting her float across the feeling that no one really liked her. Some of the men desired her – she hadn't lost that ability – but none looked at her with simple, frank liking and neither of the women did either.

It was her own fault. She'd played them off against each other, teased and pricked them, needled them, divided them. In the end, for all her machinations, it wasn't worth it, for Ingrid's husband could simply wave his hand and say *this is how it shall be.*

She longed, for a moment, to crawl into the bunk beside Mathilde, to lay her head in the hollow where Mathilde's neck met her shoulder, bury her face there and close her eyes, feel the simplicity of warmth and contact.

She shook her head. She should go to the saloon and have a coffee, or onto the bridge. She should indulge in human conversation, laugh a little, flirt a little, get out of this dark frame of mind. The gloomy weather would lift soon, the water wouldn't be so black, the sun would come out and these dark imaginings would go back where they belonged.

A knock at the door made her jump. Mathilde didn't move and Lillemor felt a moment of concern as she went to answer it.

It was Dr Stevensson. 'How's the patient going?'

Lillemor stood aside to let him in. She could smell alcohol on his breath as he passed. 'I'm worried. She hasn't moved.'

He took Mathilde's pulse, opened an eyelid and shone his torch inside, repeated it on the other side. 'She's fine,' he said, his voice horribly hearty. 'I'll call in again before dinner.'

'I don't think you should give her any more,' Lillemor said.

'Don't you worry. I'll be the judge of that. She'll be so much better after a rest.'

He stopped by the door and lifted his gaze from her chest as though it were an effort. 'Coming up for a drink before dinner, Mrs Rachlew?'

'It's been a difficult week,' he said when she didn't answer at once. 'Not surprising Mrs Wegger's had trouble coping. Some upsetting sights.'

'I suppose so,' Lillemor said.

'Can I walk you upstairs?'

His hunger was palpable and Lillemor felt herself retreating. It was one thing to inflame men with desire in London, when you could get into a taxi afterwards and go home. It was another in this queer world where every action and gesture took on its own significance and there was so much time to brood. She may need to be more careful, she thought.

'I'll follow shortly,' she said, and gave him a bland smile.

After the door was safely closed behind him, Lillemor went back to Mathilde and sat on the side of the bunk next to her. She reached out and stroked a stray hair back from her forehead. Mathilde wasn't beautiful, but in sleep her lips were soft and full, her eyelashes long, the corners of her mouth sweetly dimpled. She looked terribly young. Was this what Hjalmar saw in her? Were he here now, would he lean down and press his lips softly against the fullness of hers?

Lillemor took her hand away and stood up. It was time to get out of the cabin.

CHAPTER 34

Ingrid woke in grey no-time. The engines were off and a deep quiet hung over the ship. Lars shifted in his sleep and swallowed. The sound of it, magnified in the silence, made her shudder. She extricated herself from the bunk without waking him, tiptoed to the porthole and put her eye to the crack in the curtain. All she could see was white. She got into her coat, noiselessly squeezed the door handle open and stepped outside.

The ship lay unmoving in dark, glassy water, surrounded by mist. The blizzard had blown itself out and the world was lit with a flat, white illumination that seemed to emanate from all around them. The exhausted crewmen, free at last from the tank scrubbing that had dominated their time in Antarctic waters, were not to be seen. It must be some very early hour of the morning, Ingrid surmised. Nothing moved around them and the surrounding icebergs towered above the ship.

She could have been in a fairy tale where the world had been put into an enchanted sleep. It made her think of the Snow Queen and Ingrid shuddered, not only from the cold. It seemed she had somehow turned into the brutal Snow Queen herself on this trip. Her longing to go to Antarctica had been an innocent one at the start, but now it felt tainted. She didn't like who she was becoming.

Determined to shake the idea, Ingrid went downstairs to the deck and crossed to the railing, her breath blowing icy clouds on the still air. She ignored the cold, as it tried to work its fingers inside her collar and around the edges of her sleeves, and slowed her breathing down until it was almost soundless. Her eardrums sang.

There she was, at last, away from the factory ships, away from the stench of dead whales and the boilers working furiously. The smell still permeated her clothes, but compared to the stink that surrounded the factory ships, it was mild. Away past the bergs and the scattered pack ice, the ice barrier reared up in a towering cliff, as if some mighty axe had cleaved off the edge of the continent. Aptly named, it prevented further incursion.

Ingrid stared at the white line against the grey sky. Would she ever truly feel Antarctica, observing it from a ship? It was always a blur of white in the distance, as much of a dream as it had been back in Norway. It always kept her out.

She heard an explosive exhalation of breath across the water. Above the glassy surface a mist of vapour rose from a whale's blast. A moment later a second, smaller mist rose and she heard the second whoosh, loud in the silence. She wanted to clap or shout, somehow scare them off. Hadn't one of their kin warned them to stay away from metal ships and throbbing engines? But with no engine running, there was nothing to alert them.

Ingrid pressed her hand against her chest to slow the pounding. They were far from the factories now and none of the catchers had followed them this distance into the pack ice. Perhaps she could watch the whales without fear this time, with no one on board pointing and jostling for a gunner's tip, and no one to see if she smiled at the kill.

The ripples from their rising spread in large circles, moving out wider until they reached the ship's hull and splashed against its indifferent sides. Ingrid stared until her eyes burned, trying to guess where they might emerge. Then there was another breath, so loud and close it made her jump.

Against *Thorshavn*'s flank she could see a whale. It was smaller than she expected – was it a humpback? Most of the whales she'd seen were dead, and from their grossly distended shapes it was hard to discern distinguishing features.

The whale stayed on the surface and blew a second time and the fishy scent of its breath rose to Ingrid's face. She leaned over, wishing she could see through the water to the bottom of the icebergs and the mysterious creatures that swam among them. What was down there? Ingrid looked at the small whale again, and then blinked. Underneath it, the water was turning a brilliant blue, as turquoise as the inside of an iceberg. The shape rising from the depths was so vast she thought she'd conjured a monster from her own imagination. She drew back with a gasp as it broke the surface and the breath was so explosive this time that she thought for a moment some catcher, waiting, invisible, nearby, had fired.

It was a mother and her calf, Ingrid saw, and the mother's body ran alongside *Thorshavn* and out of sight. This could only be a blue whale and to the marrow of her bones Ingrid felt its size in comparison to her own. The creature looked big enough to flick her tail at *Thorshavn* and send them crashing into the ice barrier. Much bigger, it seemed, than the blue whale they'd shot from the catcher.

The calf arched its back and dived out of sight, but the mother lingered and after a moment Ingrid dared to come again to the rail and look down. The whale manoeuvred her huge body in the water, her tail sinking down out of sight as she raised her head the way the humpbacks had done. Her breath hung on the air and the mist of Ingrid's breath intermingled with it.

She can't see me, Ingrid told herself. It was impossible. The whale's eyesight would surely be as blurred in the open air as Ingrid's own would be underwater. Yet the whale pivoted, turning her body to the side and revealing a dark, round eye that seemed to be looking straight up at her.

The whale held her gaze as if it sensed that the ship carried the essence of her kin in its hold, the boiled-down oil of whale – blue, humpback, sperm and minke alike – distilled and mixed in its tanks.

The calf rose again and the mother began to sink back into the water. Ingrid leaned perilously over the railing. The whale turned her eye away as she went down and Ingrid wanted to cry out in anguish, wishing for a way to express remorse for the two thousand whales whose oil lay under her feet.

The whale disappeared, leaving a bubbling whirlpool behind her, a dark tunnel leading into her underwater realm. Ingrid's face was wet with tears that froze to her cheeks in the cold air, making the skin stiff. She hung there for a long time, until some slight movement caught her eye and she straightened up. Hjalmar was standing above her on the catwalk, holding his pipe. She could hardly bear him to see her at such a moment, laid bare.

The moment seemed to stretch out as wide as the ice. At last he took his pipe from his mouth. 'I'd give up some of my greatest discoveries for what you just had,' he said, his voice low.

Footsteps rang out; the day was beginning. Ingrid could see Tobias bustling along the deck – shortly he would be at her elbow with hot coffee. Her moment was gone and its passing was almost unbearable. She gripped the rail and tried to come back to herself.

'I was just coming to wake you,' Hjalmar said. 'Captain Horntvedt says we'll be coming out from the ice barrier and land isn't far off. I presume you and your husband would like to see it.'

❄

They gathered on the bridge again as the sheer edge of the ice barrier gave way to the familiar mess of pack ice. Ingrid stared into the shapes of ice and sky and water while the depth sounder pinged. The chaos of her feelings matched the chaos of the ice and she was equally without landmark or chart to orient herself. She was relieved that Lillemor, standing beside her, was silent.

It seemed the encounter with the whale had endowed Ingrid with some new appeal, for when she glanced up, Hjalmar was observing her. She steeled herself against whatever he might say, but he kept his peace and Ingrid was relieved. The chatter on the bridge was setting her teeth on edge. She wanted to be still and quiet, to press her ear against the hull down in the tank and hear the sounds of the whales singing in their ancient realm.

'Klarius Mikkelsen, one of my captains, found land in this area on his last trip,' Lars said to Ingrid and Lillemor, intruding on her thoughts. 'He said it was near sixty-eight degrees east, a good tall headland, clearly visible. If he was accurate, we should be close.'

'Excellent,' Lillemor said, when Ingrid didn't answer.

Lars had found time for his grooming before reaching the bridge, and he was immaculate. Ingrid knew why. Hjalmar had bestowed names from the Norwegian royal family on mountains and bays during previous discoveries, but Captain Klarius Mikkelsen, perhaps wanting to build favour with his employer, had named the entire stretch of coast after Lars. Ingrid knew the pleasure Lars felt at his name being laid down on the shoreline of ice and rock, and how he kept his pleasure close, not wanting to appear vain.

'Weather coming,' the first mate said.

The chatter dropped and everyone looked in the direction that Atle indicated. The familiar muffling of white was approaching them.

Lars frowned. 'After this we'd best get out of here. I've taken enough risks with the ship.'

Ingrid nodded and he patted her on the arm. 'I hope we find land today, for then you'll truly be the first woman to see it. Apparently there's a very beautiful cape there. I'd like to name it after you.'

'No.' Ingrid's instinctive response surprised her and Lars looked down at her inquiringly. Lillemor was looking at her too, but warily, it seemed.

'I want to at least step foot on land named after me,' Ingrid said.

Lars smiled. 'Understandable, I suppose.' He tucked her hand into the crook of his arm. 'You're cold! Do you need some more clothes?'

'Just a coffee,' Ingrid said. Tobias was bringing up the inevitable tray to the bridge and he came to the three of them first, his fair hair falling into his eyes as he proffered it. Ingrid wrapped her numb fingers around the already cooling cup.

'I must get my camera,' Lillemor said, and weaved through the press of bodies towards the door.

Sleet began to slant down and the visibility dropped. Ingrid could feel the windows being buffeted by Antarctica's winds as *Thorshavn* slowed to a crawl. The depth sounder beeped and she realised that beneath their feet the ocean floor was beginning to rise.

The jokes died away as the water became shallower and everyone began to watch the windows. The ship moved with infuriating slowness, Horntvedt steering with stiff shoulders, his eyes darting from one window to the next. The clouds dipped maddeningly; visibility rose and fell in a heartbeat.

'Consul Christensen –' Horntvedt started.

'There!' Nils stabbed a forefinger at the glass.

Lars squeezed Ingrid's arm excitedly and then let her go. There was a scramble as everyone tried to see what Nils was pointing at. The cloud dropped like a hammer, blanketing them in white and Horntvedt put the engines into reverse to stop the ship.

'Something dark, I'm sure of it,' Nils said, turning to Ingrid and Lars. 'Keep watching in that direction when the clouds lift.'

Ingrid felt a moment of intense claustrophobia. She stepped away from Lars, who was too engrossed to notice, crossed to the far side of the bridge and rested her forehead against the glass. Such a thin layer to protect her from Antarctica's might. She looked out at the swirling shapes in the fog. She wanted to go home, suddenly, where she understood night and day, summer and winter, north and south. She wanted to be alone. She wanted to be away from the vexed problem of Mathilde. She raised her hand and placed her palm against the glass. Her breath fogged the outline of her fingers and when she peeled her hand away, the place where her skin had pressed on the glass was clear and bright. Antarctica in the size of a handprint.

She turned to look at her companions, crowded against the windows, jostling each other for the first sight of the continent. There'd be a chorus of exclamations when they sighted it, and cheering, no doubt. Their backs were to her, and she was close to an outside door. She edged over to it. Only Hjalmar looked up. Ingrid sent him a silent plea to stay quiet as she slipped out the door. His answering gaze was unreadable.

It was bitterly cold as she walked away from the bridge and pressed herself into a niche that afforded a little shelter. From inside Ingrid could imagine a snowstorm as a quaint thing, its swirls of sleet making pretty patterns on the windows. Facing it directly, as with anything in Antarctica, was a different matter. She tucked her hands inside her coat sleeves and hunched her neck so that her collar sat high around her cheeks. She'd thought herself warmly dressed when she left her cabin that morning but Antarctica made a mockery of that.

It may have been foolish but Antarctica persisted in Ingrid's mind as a woman. She held them back or let them close; she drove her blizzards on them in anger or closed the leads in the ice like a woman drawing the folds of her skirts around her. She threatened to crush them, but so far had let them live. It should have made Ingrid feel some kinship with her. But she was afraid that here, so close to their goal, Antarctica would be merciless. *Thorshavn* was moving slowly ahead and land was close. They were navigating blind.

A strong wind gust hit her. The whiteness swirled and changed, and Antarctica's capricious fog rose like a curtain lifting. *Thorshavn* was facing a headland that reared up above them, its rocks deep black against the white ice. Birds wheeled around its upper reaches, tiny specks giving scale to its immensity. For a precious moment the first sight of Antarctica belonged to her.

Ingrid had wondered, beforehand, if somehow Antarctica could sense the first arrival of humans. But she saw in a moment what an ignorant notion that had been. The place needed no human gaze to bring it into existence. It made fools of them for competing to get there, for attempting to chart and define its outlines, for thinking that anyone could own it. It was indifferent to them.

The headland rose skywards as if it grew up straight from the ocean floor. Ingrid could hear the distant clamour of birds and the scent of their rookery. It was an acrid smell, but an uncomplicated one, unlike the stench of the factory ships. She took a deep breath, welcoming it, and suddenly wanted to land with an intensity that hurt. She wanted to feel Antarctica against the soles of her feet. To go ashore there, to impose her minuscule humanity onto that mighty place – the thought was exhilarating and terrifying.

The door to the bridge opened and Ingrid heard voices. She turned. Lars was leaning out, gesturing.

'There you are! Come in. It's your big moment.'

Ingrid turned her back on the headland and walked to the door. Her fingers and nose were freezing and there was a lump in her throat. Her first sighting was over. It was hot and stuffy in the bridge and the rabble of voices hurt her ears. She'd only been outside a matter of minutes, but coming back in to the crowd of bodies and faces felt like crossing a threshold between worlds.

Lars held out his hand to her, smiling. 'Horntvedt says this is part of Lars Christensen Land, named by Captain Mikkelsen last year. Is the aquavit ready?'

Tobias, who was standing by with a tray of shot glasses, moved around the bridge handing them out. Ingrid took hers and steeled herself in readiness for their odd ritual. It seemed such an unnatural response.

'A historic moment,' Lars announced. 'The first time the Antarctic continent has been seen by female eyes. I'd like to propose a toast to my wife.'

As they raised their glasses, there was a stir near the other door and Ingrid turned. Lillemor was leading Mathilde onto the bridge. She looked dreadful. She'd obviously dressed in haste and her hair was wild. But her eyes were worse, dull and staring, surrounded by dark circles. She looked like some creature from Bedlam as she shuffled forward.

Ingrid froze, waiting for Lillemor to turn and denounce her in front of them all.

'How good to see you, Mrs Wegger,' Nils said, going to her side. 'I hope you're feeling a little improved?'

'Yes, thank you,' Mathilde said softly.

'It's wonderful you could join us,' he continued, oblivious to the tension, or ignoring it. 'The first women to see Antarctica. We're just about to toast you.' He gestured to Tobias, who hurried over with the tray. Lillemor and Mathilde took their glasses and everyone turned to Lars again, in uncomfortable silence.

Lars lifted his glass high. 'To my wife, Ingrid, and her companions Mrs Rachlew and Mrs Wegger. *Skaal*!'

Everyone repeated his words. They drank and then Lars gave Ingrid a look and made a subtle movement with his head. She knew what he meant. She crossed the bridge to Mathilde's side, put her hands on her shoulders and moved in to touch her cheek to Mathilde's. Ingrid felt the stiffening in her body and willed her not to pull away. Their cheeks brushed, cool and smooth, and then Ingrid drew back.

'I'm so glad you could see this,' she said.

In Mathilde's eyes Ingrid read a matching fear, that everyone knew Mathilde had punched her and been punished for it. Now they each had a secret to keep. Neither of them would accuse the other aloud. Ingrid took a breath, weak with relief.

Lillemor turned Mathilde to the window and gestured to the cape. Her camera case was slung over her shoulder and she opened it and drew out the camera.

Mathilde moved closer to the glass, her mouth slightly open. Ingrid came to her side. She didn't dare to take Mathilde's arm but they stood close and looked out. Ingrid couldn't think of anything to say. She felt disconnected, cut off from the land outside, her experience slipping away in moments, melting, disappearing, just as if a fog was coming down and cutting it off.

'Time for a photograph, ladies,' Lillemor said. 'By the window, to show the continent. Nils, would you mind?'

Lillemor joined them and the three of them faced Nils as he pointed the camera. 'Smile!' he said.

Ingrid managed some kind of grimace as Nils pressed the lever.

'Consul?' Ingrid heard Horntvedt say to Lars.

'Yes?' Lars crossed to look at the charts and Ingrid left Mathilde and Lillemor to join him.

'We must start making our way to *Falk*,' Horntvedt said. 'I don't want to linger here.'

'What about a landing?' Ingrid asked.

Horntvedt looked from her to Lars. 'Every hour we spend here is risky. It's the job of *Norvegia* to make landings. I doubt even a small boat could find a way through to land here, even if there was a place.'

'That's a pity,' Lars said. 'I'd like to name this cape after my wife, but she's made me promise to bestow her name only if she lands.'

'Never mind,' Ingrid said, and turned away. Her own name, imposed on this place, was unthinkable. The fact that the whole stretch of coastline carried Lars's name felt strange enough.

She went back to Mathilde and Lillemor and together they looked up at the headland. *Thorshavn* drifted gently and the bridge fell silent as they gazed at the sight so few would ever see.

Hjalmar came to Mathilde's other side with a coffee and handed it to her. 'You should feel better after that,' he said matter-of-factly.

Ingrid tensed, wondering if he'd say something else. But Lars, alert to the situation, came up behind her protectively, and Hjalmar was silent.

It wasn't till dinner that he played his card.

CHAPTER 35

She had been under the sea ice, frozen fast, trapped, while around her the ice groaned and cracked and shifted. Far above, on the surface, she had heard footsteps, a murmur that might have been voices, but Mathilde was buried too deeply for them to reach. She had wondered if she was dead. Was this what it was like, the icy cold and the sounds of life like a muffled roar in the distance? The ice had held her as tight as a coffin, its arms wrapped around her, its cold lips on her brow.

One noise had become more insistent, separated itself from the rest, increased in volume. If she could have moved she would have blocked her ears. Her jaw was locked, her eyelids crusted shut, and always the light behind them was blue, iceberg blue, crevasse blue.

For God's sake, Mathilde, wake up.

She had flinched at that voice and found her body could move. She felt hands upon her and she shrank from them, curled in upon herself, brought her knees up like a foetus curled in the womb.

'Please, wake up.' The voice was gentle, gentler than she'd heard it, and Mathilde felt a tightening in her throat. Her mother had spoken like that, when she'd been a little child, and it felt like a lifetime since anyone had been tender with her.

'Mathilde?'

She willed her eyes to open. They were heavy and uncooperative, and forcing them was like lifting a bodyweight.

'Yes, that's it,' the voice encouraged, and at last she managed to open her eyes. The face in front of her was blurry, and she blinked. As it slowly came into focus she realised it wasn't her mother and the sadness of it was crushing. She could feel tears forming and then there was a hand on her forehead, warm and alive.

'Can you sit up?'

It was Lillemor. Mathilde was still on the ship; she hadn't escaped. She must still have been dreaming because Lillemor's hands couldn't possibly be so gentle. Last time they'd caught her by the wrist and pinned her so that Ingrid could hit her. This Lillemor, the dream one, whispered in her ear and her hands were soft as they helped her sit up.

'We need to hurry,' Lillemor was saying. 'We're here, Mathilde.'

She was tugging at her more insistently, trying to get her to stand. Mathilde's thoughts were frozen too, heavy and unmoving. 'Quickly. Don't you want to see Antarctica?'

Mathilde didn't want to hear that word again. Antarctica, where forever some part of her would lie frozen in the fast ice. Lay me under the stones, she thought, build a cairn of rocks over the top of me; I will be a memory in this country.

But Lillemor was firm and it had been too hard to resist the force of her motion. Mathilde found herself moving on unsteady legs across the cabin, out the door and onto the catwalk. When they reached the door of the bridge and Lillemor put out a hand to open it, memory suddenly sluiced through Mathilde's body. She'd hit Ingrid. Punched her. Knocked her out. And Lars had been angry.

Her knees locked. 'No.' She pulled back.

'Yes!' Lillemor's voice was firm. 'You're going to see it, Mathilde. Up here with everyone.'

'I don't want to.'

'Don't worry. No one knows what happened.'

Mathilde tried to pull away, but her muscles were watery and useless. Before she could resist, Lillemor had opened the door and drawn her inside, and the eyes of everyone on the ship, it seemed, were upon her.

One face stood out: Ingrid's. Her left eye was shadowed and she looked strange and wild. Mathilde felt their gazes lock.

'How good to see you, Mrs Wegger.' Nils was suddenly at her side. 'I hope you're feeling a little improved?'

Lillemor's arm was in hers. She didn't know if the pressure was terrifying or comforting.

'Yes, thank you,' she said to Nils.

Mathilde hadn't looked outside yet and beyond the faces it was all a blur. She took a glass obediently when it was offered, fumbling to wrap her fingers around it.

'To my wife, Ingrid, and her companions Mrs Rachlew and Mrs Wegger. *Skaal*!'

Mathilde managed to get the little glass to her lips and take a sip, though the taste made her gag. Then Ingrid was coming in close and fast so that Mathilde wanted to run. Ingrid pressed their cheeks together and stepped away. The look she gave Mathilde was piercing and there was no forgiveness in it.

'Come on, have a look before the fog comes down again,' Lillemor said. She'd kept Mathilde's arm linked through hers and now she led her to the window.

The bridge swayed under her feet as she stared out, blinking. She could feel Ingrid on her left and Lillemor still holding her arm on the right. Gradually the details took form. A dark, rocky headland, striped with ice, rising to a white peak far above them. The background sound resolved itself into the distant shrieks of birds, wheeling around the cape. Pale blue icebergs stood off the shore, cold and grim. She realised the tiny black shapes at their edges were penguins and suddenly Mathilde understood the scale of what she was seeing. Her mouth fell open. At this moment there was no past, no factory ships, no home and no journey. Just a landscape that felt utterly inimical to human life.

Ingrid walked away, across to Lars and the captain, and Hjalmar stepped to her side. He didn't say anything, and for that Mathilde was grateful. She could hear laughter and murmurs around the bridge, but for the most part people seemed to be mesmerised by the first sight of the continent.

'What do you think?' he asked her quietly.

She tried to find a word to describe what was before her and found herself shrugging helplessly. 'I don't think it's a place for people.'

He smiled. 'Coffee?'

A simple offer, but behind it was a world of unspoken understanding and she nodded gratefully. He touched her hand for a second, disappeared, returned with a cup. 'You should feel better after that.'

The coffee was strong, black and thick with sugar. Mathilde could feel it flooding through her veins, waking her. She remembered the last coffee she'd had, handed to her by Lars, with its strange, bitter taste and how she couldn't remember anything clearly after drinking it.

Lars had loomed over her with that drink while she was in bed and she'd been afraid of him. But he was actually very short. A middle-aged man, thickening around the middle, with a bald patch.

She slipped her arm out of Lillemor's and stood straighter. She'd been afraid of him before seeing Antarctica. Compared to that immense landscape, he was almost laughable.

❋

Mathilde was conscious of Hjalmar's eyes on her as she sat down next to him at the captain's table, and she felt flustered. She was a creature of Lillemor's devising that night, and it was a revelation to see how the men looked at her differently. Lillemor had brushed her hair and twisted it into a soft coil on the nape of her neck. She'd taken Mathilde's chin, tilted her head up, and inspected her handiwork. Her eyes had narrowed.

'Lipstick,' she'd said, and rummaged in her bag.

Mathilde had watched her. The effects of whatever she'd been sedated with were still in her body, and she felt floaty and disoriented. She'd have been happy to eat a few biscuits and go back to bed to sleep it off, but Lillemor was adamant that she come to dinner.

'It's easier for them to treat you like a criminal if you act like one,' she'd said, leafing through her dresses and selecting one that was a deep purple. She'd held it up against Mathilde. 'Aubergine. All the rage in London. What do you think?'

Mathilde stood in front of the mirror. 'It makes me look pale.'

'It makes you look interesting. And a bit vulnerable, to make sure they feel guilty. It's perfect.'

Mathilde was nervous that Lillemor's kind-heartedness might disappear at any moment. She told herself to remain aloof, to stay firm in shutting Lillemor out. But when Lillemor told her about the sedative and stroked her hair sympathetically, Mathilde knew it was useless. In the face of such kindness she was powerless and she let Lillemor dress her and make her up without resisting.

Thorshavn had steamed away from their brief sighting of land and they were back in the world of water and brash ice and icebergs. It was cold and still outside, but the saloon was so warm that Mathilde was sweating. As she smelled the rich scent of dinner on the air, she realised she was ravenously hungry.

Hjalmar poured her a whisky and soda and she was still sipping it when the pea soup arrived. He seemed nervous, fidgeting with his napkin. She wondered if he knew what had happened.

Lars had put on a suit for the occasion and Ingrid was also dressed smartly, with heavy makeup that almost masked the bruise around her eye. She was unusually talkative as the rest of them ate.

'You've a hard job, Captain Horntvedt,' Ingrid said as the steward and Tobias cleared the soup plates and began to lay out the main course and pour the claret. 'You must have little sleep.'

'No, not much rest,' he said, and rubbed a hand over his forehead. 'I nearly forget what night is.'

'Do you miss it?'

He shrugged. 'I get used to it. I can snatch sleep anywhere and any time.'

'What about you?' Ingrid asked Hjalmar.

'It's an explorer's lot, to have too much light, or none,' he answered. 'Men who winter here spend months in darkness, just like going to the North Pole. Me, I prefer the light.'

'Me too,' Lillemor said. 'I love it in summer when you only sleep a few hours at a time.'

'When you get home to spring, the dark will be nearly gone from Norway too,' Hjalmar said to Mathilde.

Mathilde shuddered and bent her head to her meal. She, too, longed for at least a few hours of dark to punctuate the days. She didn't know how her countrymen in the north of Norway tolerated the unrelenting light of summer.

'It's been a great day, don't you think, Captain?' Hjalmar went on. 'Confirming Mikkelsen's discovery and being present for the first official female sighting of Antarctica.'

'Official?' Lillemor asked.

'Well, you know about Olga, of course.'

There was a moment of silence. Ingrid and Lillemor both stared at Hjalmar and Mathilde felt her shoulders tense. Oh, he knew something of what had gone on, no matter what Lillemor thought. She wished he wouldn't say any more.

Lars gave a broad smile. 'Olga?'

Hjalmar sat back with an expansive smile. 'All the men working the catchers know the story, so I presumed you were familiar with it. Olga the stowaway, who hid on the factory ship *Christianna* when she left Sandefjord for the Antarctic with her whale catchers. By the time they discovered her in the fore hold, it was too late to turn back, so they were forced to take her with them.'

'What happened?' Ingrid asked. Mathilde saw that she had stopped eating.

'The captain put her to work. He didn't have much choice. But even though he kept her for long hours in the galley, she stirred up no end of trouble. She was pretty, see, blonde with blue eyes, and a sharp girl. All the younger crew preened like peacocks to catch her eye and there was nearly a brawl. The captain was passing by South Georgia to drop off provisions for some Scandinavians living there. He knew there was a woman on the island, the doctor's wife, and the captain left Olga in her care till he could collect her on the way home.'

'So she didn't see Antarctica,' Lars said.

Hjalmar raised a finger. 'She wasn't going to be stymied so close to her goal. She gave the wife the slip the night the boats were leaving. Stole some men's clothing and managed to sneak on board one of the catchers. She hid in a lifeboat all night, freezing cold and seasick, and only staggered out again when they were far from land. The captain was so furious he refused to let her back on the factory ship. She spent six weeks on the catcher in miserable conditions. The captain felt it was a fitting punishment.'

The whole table was staring at him. He smiled and took another mouthful of his meal.

'So?' Lillemor asked at last.

He finished chewing. 'So she made it to Antarctica, they say. She's not officially recorded. It might be a legend for all I know. But all the men know the tale.'

Ingrid laid down her fork, her face grim. Lillemor's expression was unreadable. Mathilde wished she were anywhere but at the table. After seeing Antarctica, who could quibble about such a thing? It was irrelevant.

Hans Bogen cleared his throat. 'I'm sure that's just a story made up by lonely sailors. I've no doubt you're the first women here, and your names will be remembered by history. I've never heard of this Olga girl. You'll need better proof than that, Hjalmar.'

'If she came from Sandefjord, we'd all know of her,' Lars said. 'She must be a legend.'

'No doubt,' Hjalmar agreed. 'Interesting tale though. She would have needed the courage and determination of a man.'

Ingrid shook her head. 'That's the trouble with legends, isn't it? Can anyone ever live up to them?'

Mathilde felt sorry for Ingrid. Hjalmar was being cruel to her, as well as to Lillemor who so desperately wanted to be first. Lillemor had buried her head in her food and Mathilde couldn't see the expression on her face.

'How soon do we rendezvous with *Norvegia*?' Lars asked, in an obvious effort to change the subject.

'Four or five days, all going well,' Horntvedt said. 'After we resupply *Falk*.'

'And then we turn back for Cape Town. We'll be back there in less than a fortnight and onto the liner to London a few days later,' Lars said.

'How much longer will you be on *Norvegia*?' Ingrid asked Hjalmar.

'It depends on the ice,' he said. 'We'll be trying to chart the coastline to the west of here. I'd say we only have another month, perhaps six weeks. The days are getting shorter and it's like at home. Once the season starts to change, it's rapid.'

'Home,' Mathilde said. 'I like the sound of that.' She glanced at Ingrid, who gave her a look so cold that Mathilde found it hard to imagine they'd ever been friends.

She felt Hjalmar shift beside her and the thought of another offensive, delivered with the pretence of charm, was unbearable. She had to escape. She turned to him.

'Captain, I'm still a little shaky,' she said, forcing a smile. 'Would you mind escorting me back to my cabin?'

'Not at all,' he said, pushing his plate away and standing. 'Captain, Consul and Mrs Christensen, Mrs Rachlew, excuse me please. I'll take the chance to do some more observations on the bridge. Good evening.'

He stood aside to let Mathilde go first through the door, and as she passed him, he put his hand on her back to direct her.

CHAPTER 36

Lillemor almost felt sorry for Ingrid. The expression on her face as she watched them leave; the way she tried to hide it and force a smile. Whatever had driven Ingrid to come down south, Hjalmar's announcement about Olga had shaken her. If there were reason to be kind to Ingrid, Lillemor would have told her the truth about Olga there and then. But she remembered the photograph she'd taken of Mathilde's unconscious face, pale against the pillow. The image imprinted on her brain as well as on the strip of film hidden in her cupboard. Their trip had a dark underside and that episode had revealed it.

She was content to allow Ingrid to suffer. For Olga was a piece of fiction.

Lillemor had stopped herself smiling when Hjalmar began his story, and pretended to be upset. But there was no such ship as *Christianna*, which Lars, the shipping man, should have known. Olga's story had appeared in a book published the previous year, purporting to be the adventures of a young whaler who'd joined a whaling ship in New Zealand and heard the legend of Olga from one of his shipmates. When Lillemor had read the first edition, her own disappointment had been as acute as Ingrid's was now. But she'd asked around, and Anton had a friend check the shipping records. There was no vessel by the name of *Christianna*. As she was sure Hjalmar knew.

When they'd left the bridge after seeing the continent that afternoon, Hjalmar had detained her with some spurious question and when they were alone, had asked directly about Mathilde. It wouldn't hurt, Lillemor had thought, for someone else on board to know how vulnerable she was, and so she'd told him what happened – the fight, Ingrid's fall, Lars arriving with the sedative and his instructions to keep Mathilde locked in the cabin.

He hadn't said much, but she'd seen the muscles in his jaw tighten and a hardness creep into his eyes. No explorer succeeded without a ruthless streak for it was by nature a competitive endeavour and coming second – unless you were Robert Falcon Scott and died on the way back to earn your place in history – wasn't good enough. For all his apparent charm, Hjalmar was an explorer, and he must have made ruthless decisions of his own over the years. Now, it seemed, he'd decided to twist the knife on his own benefactors. It was risky, and the only way was to act as if he was reporting a known fact.

Lillemor looked around the table. Mathilde, having gone with Hjalmar, was safe for now from the Christensens. Ingrid had slipped away without excusing herself. Lillemor had seen Lars lean in to talk to her, seen the tight set of his body, and she wasn't surprised when he stood a few minutes later and made his farewells. The main game for him was surely to see Antarctica for himself and now he'd done it. He was the type of man who'd want to celebrate.

They'd been married – how long? Must be fifteen or twenty years. Good luck to them if their marriage was still passionate. You wouldn't think it from the outside with their easy companionability, but outer appearances couldn't tell you everything about a marriage bed, she knew that.

She turned to Hans. He was looking after Ingrid with a peculiar yearning on his face and Lillemor remembered seeing it before, early in the voyage. She leaned across the table towards him.

'So, Mr Bogen, does Ingrid go into the history books today as the first woman to see Antarctica?'

He adjusted his glasses nervously. 'Well of course I'll have to investigate this tale of Hjalmar's and see if there's any truth in it. Sounds like some sailors' legend, but I'll have to verify it before I write about Mrs Christensen.'

'Have you known her a long time?'

He smiled. 'Oh yes. I remember her wedding day. I was only a boy at the time, but everyone talked about how enchanting she looked and what a beauty she was. And still is now, of course.'

Lillemor sipped her wine, amused. Hans's feelings for Ingrid were stronger than she'd imagined.

'And you got to know her later, when you'd grown up?'

'Yes,' he said. 'Not a close friend, Mrs Rachlew, I wouldn't presume that, but she always made me welcome at Ranvik. Lars is a very lucky man, to have a wife as bold and fearless as Ingrid. Most men who wish to explore must leave wives or sweethearts at home, but in this case, the two of them are completely united in their goals. It's extraordinary.'

'Indeed,' Lillemor said.

'She has the wonderful ability to brighten up a room when she walks in, don't you think?'

Lillemor nodded. For most of this trip Ingrid had blown into a room like a cold wind. Hans must be deluded.

'Are you married, Hans?' she asked.

He blushed like a boy and dropped his head. 'I've not been fortunate enough to meet the right woman yet. My work keeps me very busy.'

Lillemor slid her elbow closer until her arm was touching his sleeve. She judged – correctly – that he'd be too startled to pull away.

'We were all part of history today, in a way,' she said. 'How many people have seen Antarctica? A mere handful, and now we're among them. Will you list all of us in your book, Hans?'

He glanced at her. 'That would make a very dull history, Mrs Rachlew. I hope to do more than provide lists. The first person to arrive somewhere is history; the others fit somewhere else. Perhaps within journalism? I'm sure some magazine would be interested in hearing about the first women to reach Antarctica together, even if Ingrid was the first to see it.'

She moved her arm slightly so it wasn't touching his. Of course, he was Lars's man, wasn't he? It would take more than a rational argument to sway him. More than words to ensure she'd be memorable.

'Say my name,' she said, pushing both hands down on his chest and tightening her thighs, gripping him so he couldn't move.

'Lillemor,' he gasped.

'Again. Open your eyes.'

His eyelids flickered open; his hands were on her hips trying to move her. 'Lillemor. Please.'

She had drawn on her usual techniques to seduce him, adapting them to suit the Antarctic conditions. The suggestion of a walk around the deck after dinner. The exaggerated shiver that prompted him to give her his coat. The iceberg that conveniently floated by at the right moment so she could sigh about Antarctica's beauty and let her hand drop on top of his on the railing. The cold air that made the approach of a warm body so much harder to resist. She used his surprise to her advantage.

The hardest part was taking the stray thread of guilt she felt about Anton and tucking it away where it couldn't bother her.

This was an act in service of a higher cause, and as such, didn't qualify as infidelity.

And she was looking forward to sex. It had been three weeks since she'd said goodbye to Anton, and she was a woman of appetite. The conquest, even of such a man as Hans, was exciting. His response – aroused, shocked and terrified – was a thrilling reminder of her sexual power.

However, from his first fumbling kiss she realised he was desperately inexperienced. After she'd undressed herself and then him, he embraced her and groped briefly between her legs, knowing that he should do something down there, but apparently having no idea what. Lillemor was sure he was too old to be a virgin, but she'd been with virgins who showed more composure. She felt a flash of envy for Mathilde, probably experiencing a sexual awakening in the capable arms of Hjalmar. As Hans began to press against her she closed her eyes and called up her current secret fantasy, one that could take her to readiness in moments. It involved a certain Miss Earhart.

But she'd need more than just readiness, she realised. Hans had to have a sexual awakening of his own. And so she rolled him over and moved on top of him. When he made a startled outburst, she put her finger to his lips. 'Let me,' she said, and began to slide down his body. Judging by the way he was quivering and his uneven breathing, she didn't have long. She'd spread out the pleasure, she decided. Once like this, and then the second time, when he had more staying power, inside her. She had time to spare. Mathilde might be in their cabin with Hjalmar, and Lillemor didn't want to disturb them.

'Oh God,' Hans groaned. He gripped her hair so hard it hurt. 'What are you doing?'

There was no answer to that, except to continue. And hope she'd driven all thoughts of Ingrid from his mind.

CHAPTER 37

Ingrid saw Mathilde glance back once from the door as she left. She looked ethereal with her large, dark-rimmed eyes and her hair framing her pale face.

Hjalmar's hand brushed the small of Mathilde's back as he held the saloon door open and the grateful inclination of her head, the way her back yielded to the touch of his fingers, the invitation and its acceptance, were as blatant as a slap. Ingrid blinked. Was the whole party staring? But after briefly rising when Mathilde stood, everyone sat again and they were eating or talking, oblivious to what had just unfolded.

Only Lillemor was watching, with that damned knowing look in her eyes. But there was no wink or grin this time, no complicity. The lines of loyalty had shifted. Ingrid was on her own and Mathilde and Lillemor seemed to have joined forces.

Next to her, Lars leaned in close. 'That story is a nonsense,' he whispered. 'Don't let it upset you.'

Ingrid shrugged, but didn't trust herself to speak.

'You are the first woman to see Antarctica,' he said.

She turned her head to the side so Lillemor couldn't see her lips. 'Before Mathilde, even.'

'Yes, before her. She did the wrong thing and she knows it. We can forget it now. It's over.'

Lillemor was still watching and Ingrid moved her body away from Lars and directed a smile at the table at large. Her head was pounding and the strain of keeping up a flow of cheerful conversation was exhausting. She longed to retreat to her cabin, to hide in the only safety on board, her bunk.

She was disappointed, she told herself, that after all Olga had been the first woman to see Antarctica.

But in truth, the bitterness in her belly was having witnessed Mathilde's seduction of Hjalmar. She'd done it that way deliberately, Ingrid was sure, to enrage her.

Ingrid felt the spotlight of Lillemor's attention blazing on her. The nuances of interactions between men and women were Lillemor's speciality, and Ingrid knew the woman would be analysing any visible reaction on her part.

She'd thought of Hjalmar as her friend, but this night he'd twice undone her – firstly over the matter of Olga and then, following on hard, with his seduction of Mathilde right in front of her. Before this trip she'd thought their friendship a firm thing, strengthened by their shared grief over Amundsen. Now she wondered if it was all an artifice. Perhaps the appearance of friendship was only that, and all he really wanted was the means to explore Antarctica.

Mathilde had said Ingrid wanted to keep him around like a dog. The unfairness of it stung at the time, but she'd been pleased when Hjalmar divorced and came to their home first when he returned from exploring. She liked being the first woman to welcome him, to draw him a bath, to bring him a meal. She'd thought of him like a younger brother, she'd told herself. But it was a decidedly unsisterly feeling she was having now, imagining him and Mathilde together.

With his revelation about Olga, he'd robbed her even of the consolation of Antarctica, no matter what Lars said.

She pushed her plate away and wiped her mouth. She'd had enough. The pounding in her temples threatened to descend

313

into a searing headache. The confines of the saloon suddenly seemed stuffy and airless, the smell of the food nauseating.

'I'm going to bed,' she whispered to Lars.

He turned to her. 'I'll come with you.'

The intensity in his demeanour was unnerving. 'Don't make a fuss,' Ingrid said softly. 'I just want to slip away.'

He nodded. 'I'll follow.'

Ingrid waited a few minutes until the conversation was loud and Lillemor had been distracted by Hans Bogen, then rose and slipped away from the table. She didn't look back from the door. Let them think her rude.

It was bitterly cold outside. So close to the continent, the wind carried the chill of thousands of miles of empty ice in its breath. It was after midnight. The sky was a deep, translucent purple with a slash of orange light down low on the horizon. It would stay that way for an hour or two before morphing into a long, bright dawn that made it hard to fall asleep.

Lars came out. As she turned to him, he stepped forward and kissed her, his lips demanding. He took her hand and led her to the cabin. Inside, he came up close behind her, reaching over her shoulders, taking her coat by the lapels and sliding it off. He put his face to Ingrid's neck and kissed the skin there, pressing his body against her back.

'Time to try for that baby,' he whispered.

Ingrid's heart sank. She'd never felt less like making love. Just feet away, Mathilde and Hjalmar were probably doing just that and at that moment she hated them. But there was little enough time left in Antarctic waters and her bargain with Lars still stood.

'I'll get ready,' she said, grateful he couldn't see her face.

'Don't be long.'

In the toilet there was a long streak of red when Ingrid wiped herself. Her cycle had run off course with the travel and the disorientating effects of the light. The feeling of unease in her belly resolved itself into a dull menstrual ache. She leaned back in relief. A reprieve.

Lars had undressed, got into bed and turned off the light by the time Ingrid assembled belt and cloth and pins and put them on. She slipped into her nightgown and came in beside him.

'You took so long.' He rolled towards her, crushing their bodies together.

'I'm sorry,' Ingrid whispered. 'My monthly has come early.'

She expected him to roll back and let her lie against his side, her belly pressing against his hip, as she often did when bleeding. But he shifted on top of her, his lips urgent, his eagerness hard against her.

'Lars, we can't make a child,' she said, turning her head away.

'I don't care.' He fumbled at her nightgown, his breath fast. 'Please,' he said hoarsely.

Behind her closed eyes she saw Mathilde and Hjalmar together and the image infuriated her. In spite of herself, her desire rose, full of rage and jealousy.

She pulled at the nightdress and her underthings and reached down for Lars. He was in her hand, hot and alive, groaning out loud with his own need. She manoeuvred him on top, opened herself and took him in, deeper and deeper until it felt like she was splitting in two.

This was Antarctica, hard and bloody and full of need, longing and repulsion, fury, competition and jealousy, bargains made and payments extracted, everyone implicated, everyone faced with their own desire and brutality.

Mathilde had given her the word for it, a word Ingrid had never used even to herself to describe this act. Tonight it was the only word to describe it. Lars fucked her, and in her despair and bloodiness, Ingrid fucked him back. She thought the whole ship full of men would sense the animality of their coupling, the very continent would feel it, the vibrations rippling out from the ship underwater, so the whales could hear it and know that the steel monster floating above them contained living things like themselves. They fucked, and below them in *Thorshavn*'s tanks the essence of two thousand whales stirred and slid noiselessly.

She hoped Mathilde heard them.

The pounding reverberated through her sleep and woke her. It was loud enough to drive her straight to sitting with a jolt and for a few moments she looked around, confused. Lars shifted beside her and their surroundings shifted into familiarity.

The sound came again. Now that she was awake, she could identify it as a knock, not some portent of impending disaster.

Lars groaned and rubbed his eyes. The night before came rushing back to Ingrid and she felt embarrassed. As he rolled over and out of the bed, she lay back down and pulled the covers up to her chin. She was naked, and from the stickiness between her legs, surmised that she'd bloodied the bed. She couldn't remember the last time she'd allowed that to happen.

Lars found a dressing gown and wrapped it around himself before opening the door, sending in a blaze of daylight that made her blink. It was Nils, who glanced in and then drew back, blushing.

'What time is it?' Lars asked, rubbing his tousled hair.

'After ten,' Nils said. 'I'm sorry to wake you, but we've made contact with Mikkelsen.'

'About time!' Lars said. 'Where is he?'

'Eighty miles away, off the coast. Horntvedt's heading that way now. There's some news.'

'Yes?'

Nils hesitated. 'Captain Mikkelsen went ashore. He took his wife with him. I'm afraid Caroline Mikkelsen has become the first woman to land on Antarctica.'

CHAPTER 38

Mathilde woke slowly, luxuriously. She'd slept so deeply that for a long moment she wasn't sure of her whereabouts. The throb of *Thorshavn*'s engines soon reminded her. Eyes still closed, she rolled on her side and put a hand flat on the wall. Her bunk wasn't much bigger than a child's bed but it felt safe and cosy.

She heard the sound of footfalls and the rustle of fabric. Who was in the cabin with her? She cast her mind back to the evening before. She hadn't come back to the cabin alone.

'Awake, lover girl?'

Mathilde's eyes flew open. Lillemor was standing beside her with a mug of coffee. She was still dressed in her evening wear, hair wild, mascara streaked.

'You seem surprised.' Lillemor put down the mug. 'Expecting someone else?'

To Mathilde's relief Lillemor turned away and sat at the dressing table. She opened a jar of cold cream and began applying it to her face.

Mathilde propped herself up on a pillow and took a mouthful of warm coffee. The distance between their cabin and the galley ensured that coffee in bed was never hot. But Lillemor had loaded it with sugar and the sweetness was delicious.

She had a memory that was equally sweet and she wanted to hug it to herself. She couldn't bear Lillemor to turn it into something cheap.

Hjalmar had taken her arm when they left the saloon the night before and his touch was so comforting that she'd found herself leaning on him as they walked along the catwalk. He hadn't seemed to mind; in fact he'd squeezed her arm and held it more tightly as they walked.

They'd stopped to admire the sky. Although the sun was down and the light was deep blue, it was still quite bright, a state called civil twilight, Hjalmar had explained, with still enough light to read by.

Then he'd pointed out to the black water. 'Penguins. Emperors by the look of it. We call that porpoising, for obvious reasons.'

Mathilde followed his finger. The penguins looked more like fish than birds as they dived in and out of the water. What would it feel like to move in such a way, she wondered, effortlessly leaping from water to air and back?

A squabble broke out among the huskies on the forecastle and there was a flurry of snarls before they fell quiet.

'We'll be meeting *Norvegia* in a few days,' he said, keeping his eyes on the horizon.

'I suppose you'll be taking all the dogs?'

'They've got work to do.'

'That's a pity,' she said. 'They're the most uncomplicated creatures on board. I'll miss them.'

'I'm sure they'll miss you too.' He took out his pipe. 'There's not much softness once they're on the ice.' He glanced at her sideways, the stem sticking out of his mouth. 'Do you mind?'

She shook her head and he struck a match and held it to the bowl. The smell made her think of the factory ship and she wished the association was more pleasant.

'I'm worried for your wellbeing on the way back,' he said.

She shook her head. 'Don't be.'

'I heard what they did. Unless Mrs Rachlew was trying to stir me up.'

Mathilde felt calm. 'It won't happen again.'

'How do you know?'

Mathilde took a deep breath. 'I'm not afraid of them any more. I think it makes all the difference. And Lillemor seems more disposed to look out for me.'

He snorted. 'Don't trust her.'

'Don't worry about it, Hjalmar,' she said.

He puffed again. 'I wondered if I should take you with me. Only, it might cause you even more trouble later.'

Mathilde felt a small smile creep up on her and she turned her head slightly so he wouldn't see it. 'That's kind of you. But I really will be fine. I just want to get back to my children.'

A gust of wind swept over them, blowing sparks out of Hjalmar's pipe. Mathilde shivered at the sudden chill. 'I'd like to go to my cabin.'

He took her arm again and they hurried out of the wind. At the door he stopped as she reached for the handle.

'Mathilde?'

She opened the door and turned back to him. 'You've been a good friend to me, Captain Riiser-Larsen.' She held out her hand.

He looked at her for a long moment.

She could sense there was an invitation there, and it was tempting, but some other part of her held to an unswerving resolve.

'Goodnight, Hjalmar.'

He reached out for her hand, bent and placed his lips on her knuckles. 'If there's anything I can do ...'

She smiled. 'Nothing. But thank you.' She slid her fingers out of his grip and stepped back.

'They say Antarctica changes you,' he said.

She had closed the door and a moment later heard his footsteps retreating. He was wrong. Antarctica hadn't changed her at all. She felt more herself than she ever had, more solid, more present, less afraid. She'd undressed and climbed into her bunk. Its embrace had felt as warm as a lover's and she'd snuggled down under the covers, feeling suddenly, unexpectedly, happy.

She'd seen Antarctica and in truth it was even grander than they said. Back home, she'd thought her grief for Jakob boundless. It was the biggest thing in her world, dominating all else, crushing her. But here, in the face of Antarctica, she knew her grief was really a small thing. It was human-sized. That thought had followed her into sleep.

Lillemor finished cleaning off her makeup and swivelled around to face her. 'I stayed away so you could have some privacy. I hope it was worth it.'

Mathilde smiled. 'I had a very good night, thank you.'

Lillemor eyed her closely. 'Good. I'm pleased to hear it.'

She was waiting, Mathilde knew, to hear more but she sipped her coffee and smiled. Let Lillemor think what she wanted.

'We might see land again,' Lillemor said at last. 'I'm going up to the bridge. Want to come?'

'Love to,' Mathilde said, and threw back the covers.

They stopped just outside the bridge to watch the huskies cavorting in the snow on the forecastle. Babyen tilted his head on the side, looking so comical they both laughed. Mathilde was still laughing as they pushed open the door, laughter that spilled out of her easily, as if it had been hidden there all along.

Her laughter trailed off. There was a furious silence, though the bridge was crowded. Mathilde saw a row of grim faces and, in spite of her brave words to Hjalmar the night before, she felt a shiver of fear. Something had happened. 'What's the matter?' Lillemor asked.

There was a pause and finally Nils, the peacemaker, spoke up. 'Ah, Mrs Rachlew. We've just had some rather unexpected news from *Falk*.'

Mathilde wished she could flee. The happiness she felt suddenly seemed a fragile thing and she'd rather not have it snatched from her so quickly.

'Oh?' Lillemor responded.

'Captain Mikkelsen and his wife landed on the continent yesterday.'

Mathilde could feel Lillemor stiffen beside her and without thinking she reached out and put a hand on her sleeve. Under her touch, Lillemor's arm felt like steel.

'His wife?'

Hans Bogen walked over to them. 'Something of a surprise,' he said, stopping in front of Lillemor. 'No one knew his wife was travelling with him.'

Lillemor made a small, choked noise. Mathilde saw that Ingrid appeared surprisingly calm.

'We'll be meeting *Falk* by dinnertime if all goes well,' Horntvedt said. 'Now that we know conditions are suitable for landing there, I'm sure it will be possible for you ladies to go ashore.'

'And if it's not,' Hjalmar said, 'then I'll take you up in *Qarrtsiluni*.'

Mathilde gave him a small smile.

CHAPTER 39

Just like that it was over.

In the distance Lillemor could see the outline of the last factory ship, the one captained by that damned Klarius Mikkelsen, a triumphant Amundsen-like figure, while they, like Scott's tragic party, had arrived too late.

Her eyes blurred again and she wiped her nose with her glove. Crying was inconvenient when the tears froze on your eyelashes. She didn't want to go inside, not yet. In a few hours they'd be making fast to the side of the factory ship and meeting Klarius and his wife. There was only so much pleasant conversation she could make today, and she had to save that for when it was needed.

Having yesterday become the second – or third – woman to see Antarctica, Lillemor had imagined she knew something of what Scott had felt, approaching the South Pole and seeing the black tent and the Norwegian flag appearing over that featureless horizon. But she realised now she'd had no idea.

Seeing a mountain through the window of *Thorshavn*'s bridge a few minutes earlier or later than Ingrid was more of an anticlimax than anything. She'd consoled herself with imagining them finding a landing place where she would leap from the landing boat the way both Carsten Borchgrevink and some junior officer claimed they'd done on Henrik Bull's expedition, stealing his glory and forever confusing the claim for first footstep on Antarctica. But now even that fantasy, silly though it was, was dead. A woman had landed on Antarctica a matter of hours before Lillemor could make the attempt. It would have been one thing to get off the boat a few moments after Ingrid, at least being in the first party of women. But Caroline Mikkelsen's separate landing put her squarely at the front of this race, such as it was.

Lillemor had wanted to leave the bridge at once and go somewhere to be alone with her disappointment. The brutal cold would have been a suitable companion. But she was curious to know how Lars's own employee could have beaten him to the moment and so she stayed to hear the details.

Lars's loyal Captain Klarius Mikkelsen and the factory ship *Falk* had been out of wireless range and hadn't made contact. While Lars and Ingrid had kept their plans to take women south a secret until Cape Town, Klarius hadn't thought to mention to Lars that he was bringing his own wife along for the trip. Apparently he'd given no thought to the implications of putting her in the landing boat that set out for the continent. Caroline had gone along for the ride and become the first woman to land on Antarctica by accident. Some chit of a thing, still in her twenties, had beaten them all.

Lillemor didn't believe for a moment that Klarius was innocent of what it meant, and she was pretty sure Lars wasn't buying it either, but the truth or otherwise was immaterial. It was done; the foot had been placed. They'd laid a depot, raised a flag and even had a picnic and a cup of coffee. Didn't know the significance? Rubbish.

Lillemor wiped her eyes, trying to regain her self-control, but she couldn't seem to stop crying. She looked up at *Qarrtsiluni*. She wished she could hide inside and stay there through the whole of their stop at the factory ship. Would anyone really notice?

'There you are.' It was Mathilde coming up behind her. Lillemor swallowed hard and sniffed, trying to bring her trembling lip under control as Mathilde came to her side.

'Oh, Lillemor,' she said, and put her hand on her arm. 'Did it mean that much to you?'

Lillemor swallowed again and shook her head. 'It was silly anyway. It's not as if we got here under our own sweat. We're of no significance. So what does it matter if we get to land?'

'That's right,' Mathilde said. 'It doesn't matter at all.'

Lillemor looked up at the plane again. 'It's just I wanted to do something special, something no other woman had done before. Why is that such a terrible thing?'

'I don't think it is,' Mathilde said. 'But maybe it's got to be something you can do yourself, without relying on others.'

'And how, tell me, can a woman get to Antarctica herself?'

Mathilde shrugged. 'I have no idea.'

'Exactly. Do you know how hard I tried? Do you think I would have come as a passenger if I could have gone as an expeditioner with Mawson or even Hjalmar? He was this close to taking me, he'd agreed on it, and ...' she stopped.

'And?'

Lillemor lowered her voice. 'He'd agreed to take me as a photographer. But Lars forbade him, so his own wife could be the first. It damn well serves them right that Caroline's beaten them to it. I could have come here as an equal, with a job. Not like this.'

'I'm not sure about that, Lillemor,' Mathilde said. 'I think you'd never be an equal on a boat full of men.'

'What do you mean?'

'Men can't keep their eyes off you. And you encourage them.'

Lillemor was glad she hadn't told Mathilde about her seduction of Hans. 'I wouldn't need to attract their attention like that if I was an expeditioner with a proper job.'

Thorshavn's horn blasted and they both jumped. 'Time to meet the Mikkelsens,' Mathilde said. 'Will you be all right?'

Lillemor shrugged. 'No. But what choice do I have?'

'None of us seem to have many choices,' Mathilde said.

'Aren't you wise all of a sudden?' Lillemor snapped.

Mathilde stepped back. 'I'm just trying to help.'

Lillemor regretted her words, but couldn't bring herself to apologise as Mathilde turned away.

'Don't forget,' Mathilde said over her shoulder, 'if you behave yourself, you might get to be on the flight with Hjalmar. I doubt Caroline will get an invitation.'

She walked off. Lillemor stood still, watching *Falk* loom larger as they approached. Amelia Earhart had only been a passenger on her first famous flight. Perhaps there was still a chance to salvage something.

CHAPTER 40

The two ships drew slowly together, pushing at the inflated whale corpses chained to the side of *Falk* to buffer their joining. It was windy and the inevitable stench wafted over them. This time Ingrid hardly noticed it. She stood beside Lars on the prow of the ship feeling an unexpected lightness. She'd wanted to feel Antarctica, feel space and purity and wilderness, feel herself alone on the ice. The roar of *Thorshavn*'s engines and the babble about discoveries and landings and the squabbling and disagreements between the three women had driven it from her mind.

Emotions had run high after the news of the Mikkelsens' landing. Lars was furious, not only that Ingrid had missed out on being first, but that his own employee had snatched the honour from them. Lillemor appeared devastated. Hjalmar, perhaps remembering his own disappointments, had been his old kindly self towards Ingrid all morning.

Lars expected Ingrid to be as disappointed as he was, but in truth she was relieved. Now when she did land, it would be for the pleasure and wonder of it. She'd have the chance to feel Antarctica on her own terms, not pretending she wanted to land first, not trying to claim it or name it.

For they were hungry to name things, these men, and she realised now that the urge came out of fear. A named mountain could be marked on a map and found again. Moving, as they were, through seas covered in pack ice, dotted with icebergs many times the size of the ship, over a sea floor that dropped and fell like a mountain range beneath their hull, was frightening. There was nothing to grasp. She had been oblivious to the constant undertow of fear on board. No wonder Horntvedt was perpetually curt. He, Atle, Hjalmar and Nils were perhaps the only ones who understood the level of danger they lived with each day. Of course they wanted to name everything they saw; of course they wanted to chart landmarks on the maps and know when they were likely to meet them again.

The crew tossed heavy cables across the bodies of the whales to pull them close. Ingrid strained her eyes to see Caroline Mikkelsen. Klarius had married his much younger Danish wife fairly recently and Ingrid remembered the gossip that he kept her close, jealous that she might attract male attention.

'There they are,' Lars said, his voice still heavy with anger.

Ingrid followed his gaze. She could see a large man standing on the deck, heavily bundled in warm clothes. Beside him, a slight figure who must have been Caroline. The man raised an arm and waved and Lars, after a moment, waved back.

'Don't be too hard on him,' Ingrid said. 'It doesn't matter.'

'Of course it matters!'

'Look at it this way. The first women in Antarctica have all come this season on your fleet.'

He shook his head and for a moment the disappointment on his face was that of a boy. 'I wanted you and I to land together and you to be the first woman.'

'We can still land together.' Ingrid raised a hand to wave and after a moment the smaller figure waved back. The ships jostled together, the corpses packing close into a solid mass between them. The wind was picking up, cutting through their clothes, though the sky was clear.

'Don't make a fuss of it,' Ingrid said. 'You'll just embarrass us.'

'I think we're pretty embarrassed already, aren't we? Beaten to the goal by my own employee. How foolish we look.'

The ship jerked and they staggered to regain their balance. Ingrid was glad that the moment was broken. The basket was already rigged up to swing them across to the factory; they wouldn't be picking their way across the whales' bodies in such a wind. As soon as the two ships were fast, the first mate called out to them to come down on deck.

Hjalmar was waiting to help them, but Lars waved him away, climbed into the basket and sat down awkwardly. It was an uncomfortable way to be shifted from one ship to the next, like a piece of cargo, and Ingrid could see it was adding to his humiliation. She stepped to the side, leaned in and kissed him on the cheek.

'Be generous,' she said softly and stepped back.

His eyes were on her as the basket rose in the air, rocking in the wind. She waved and managed a smile. He didn't smile back, but she thought his face softened a little. She hoped the short journey would be enough for him to calm down. He was the most powerful man in Sandefjord, and with such power came the responsibility not to terrify those beneath him.

'How are you bearing up?' Hjalmar asked.

Ingrid turned away from the sight of the basket in the air. 'What?'

'You're hiding your disappointment well,' he said. 'Lillemor won't even show her face on the deck.'

'I don't really care, Hjalmar. I'd just like to land somewhere.'

He gave her a smile and it seemed the first one for weeks. She remembered how much she liked him, and how she'd missed his friendship.

'If that's true, then you're a better person than I,' he said. 'I still remember the disappointment of getting that cable from

Lars on my last trip saying I couldn't claim that land for Norway. Being the first man on it was incredible, but that spoiled it.'

'But you still had the feeling of being on land no one else had visited.'

'I try to remember that. But it's the problem with being an explorer. If you're not first, then you've failed by definition.'

The basket came swinging back across from *Falk* and landed on the deck next to her. Hjalmar steadied it and offered a hand to help Ingrid climb in. She clambered awkwardly over the side and settled herself down.

'I know things have been a little strange with having us women on board,' she said. 'I'm sorry if it's affected you.'

'It's not me who's been affected.' Hjalmar gave her a rueful smile.

'Some things have been … regrettable,' Ingrid said. The basket lurched. 'I hope we can still be friends, Hjalmar.'

He said something in reply but she was rising so quickly that the words slipped away and then she was airborne. The basket danced in the wind and she felt suddenly free of *Thorshavn*'s heaviness. Too soon, in just moments, she landed with a bump on *Falk*'s deck. Lars was waiting to help her out and she took his hand and climbed over the high side, jumping down to land on her feet.

As Ingrid righted herself, the Mikkelsens stepped forward. She could feel their hesitation and wondered what Lars might have said to them while she was being lifted across.

'Captain Mikkelsen,' she said, holding out her hand. 'And you must be Caroline.'

Klarius bobbed his head, not knowing, it seemed, if he should bow, kiss her hand or shake it. His colour was high.

Caroline drew back her hood and Ingrid knew at once why Klarius wouldn't leave her at home. The blonde waves of her long hair were drawn back softly and her eyes were an extraordinary shade of green. She had the kind of devastating beauty that would turn any man's head and she was clearly innocent of it.

Ingrid blinked and realised she was gaping. She stepped forward and reached for Caroline's hand.

'Mrs Mikkelsen, congratulations.'

Caroline took the proffered hand and Ingrid could feel her trembling. She glanced over at Klarius, who was fiddling with his cap. The two of them no doubt regretted the impulse to make an unscheduled landing on the continent.

She let go of Caroline's hand and turned to her husband. 'Captain Mikkelsen, you've done such valuable work in charting these coastlines. Lars has told me many times of your discoveries and what they mean for the fleet's safety. We're in your debt.'

'Thank you, Mrs Christensen.' He put his cap back on his head. 'It seems our latest discovery has been rather unfortunate.'

Ingrid waved her hand dismissively. 'Not at all. We're so proud that the first woman to land on Antarctica was part of my husband's fleet.'

'You ladies are still the first women to see Antarctica,' Klarius said. 'My wife only saw it for the first time at our landing, after you'd seen it yourselves.'

Ingrid shrugged. 'It doesn't matter. Anyway, you've found a landing place for us – that's excellent news. We haven't yet found any other area where we could put ashore, so we're most grateful.'

Caroline's pretty face flushed and Klarius coughed. 'I wish that were the case, but last night's storm has shifted the pack ice,' he said. 'We sent some men out in the catcher earlier but the lead in to our landing place has closed up completely. I'm afraid there's no way we can get there, even in the lifeboat. We had to shift the factory to get out of the way when the ice started to move.'

Ingrid's heart sank and she looked at Lars. His face was set. 'A great pity,' he said.

'Mrs Christensen, there's something that may make up for it.' Caroline's voice was as innocent as her face. 'We wanted to tell you ourselves.' She glanced at her husband and he nodded for her to continue. She turned back to Ingrid and smiled nervously. 'The last time he discovered new land, Klarius named it after your husband. But this place he's named for you.'

Ingrid stared at Caroline. 'What?'

Klarius made an expansive gesture with his arm. 'We've named this entire region "Ingrid Christensen Land". It's on the proclamation we buried at the landing site.'

Ingrid felt the blood rush from her head. Lars took her arm and she leaned on him, trying to compose herself.

'What a lovely idea,' he said. 'I've been looking for something to name after Ingrid, and a whole region is most appropriate.'

The irony of the situation wasn't lost on her. Just minutes ago she'd told him to put aside his own anger. Now she had to do the same. How dare they apply her name to something so beyond human understanding? Her name was her own, a personal thing. Klarius and Caroline had taken it from her and made it public. She hated the idea of it.

Klarius gestured over the railing. 'There is a good stretch of clear water further out. Perhaps you could ask your pilot to show you Ingrid Christensen Land from the air.'

Lars squeezed her arm. 'Excellent idea. It's about time *Qarrtsiluni* made a flight.'

Ingrid forced herself to smile and nod.

'Oh, and we have a gift for you,' Klarius said. He nodded to a crewman nearby with a cloth-wrapped bundle. Klarius took it from the man and handed it to Lars. 'To celebrate the growth of our industry. Careful, it's fragile.'

Lars unwrapped the bundle, revealing a sealed glass canister with a wooden base. Inside, in clear fluid, a perfect pale-skinned whale floated, its eyes closed.

'A blue whale foetus. Rare to find one so well formed at that size,' Klarius said. 'There wouldn't be another three like this in the world, I'd say.'

Lars held the canister aloft and the creature bobbed up and down. 'A most memorable gift,' he said.

Some response was expected from her, Ingrid felt. She reached out her hand and her fingertips brushed the glass. It felt cool and slippery. She hoped, with all her being, that there'd been no hiccup in her cycle. The sight of the foetus made her feel sick.

She waited till they were by themselves before telling him. She'd make this flight without him, without the other women, by herself. Hjalmar would pilot *Qarrtsiluni*, but the other three seats would be empty.

Lars hadn't understood. He wanted them to go together for this first flight over the continent and she'd struggled to find words to explain why she had to be alone when she laid eyes on the land that now carried her name.

'Just give me this,' she said to him. 'You made me wait twenty years before coming to Antarctica. I want to see this land alone. It's mine, isn't it?'

She expected they would fight, but instead Lars looked hurt and turned away from her.

'I don't understand you any more,' he'd muttered. 'Go then.'

Some fundamental difference had opened up between them. When Lars's name had been given to Antarctic land, it became bigger than him and he expanded to match it, accommodating the breadth of the land within who he was. But Ingrid felt robbed. Applied to a slice of the continent, her name ceased to be hers. From now on it would be written on maps, read by people who had no idea who she was, and who'd wonder, if they gave it a thought, what she'd done to deserve the appending of her name to such a place. She hadn't even landed there. It was shameful to only fly over it, she thought, but less shameful than not seeing it at all.

Lars couldn't understand that she needed to be alone to relinquish her name to something so much bigger. She had to see it without the weight of his presence beside her, and surrender something of herself. She didn't expect to enjoy it.

Everyone on *Thorshavn* came out on deck to watch Ingrid and Hjalmar climb into the plane. It was sunny, but a breeze reminded Ingrid how quickly Antarctica could turn cold. Lillemor, who was pale and red-eyed, pressed her Beau Brownie into Ingrid's unwilling hands and turned away abruptly. Mathilde just smiled, making no attempt to speak to her. Lars, his face expressionless, gave her a small Norwegian flag weighted by a heavy metal flagpole with a point on the bottom.

'I hope you can bring yourself to throw it down and mark your land,' he said.

She took it without making a promise. It was the last thing she wanted to do, but to refuse would just increase the distance between them. He leaned forward and kissed her on the cheek, a kiss so devoid of warmth that she wished he hadn't done it.

'Come back safely,' he said, and stepped back.

Hjalmar was already inside the plane. He extended a hand and helped her up the ladder and into the cockpit.

'I suppose you know your way around,' he said with a smile. 'Would you like the co-pilot's seat?'

She sat down and handed Hjalmar the camera. 'I've no idea how to use the thing. Could you take a snap or two, to please Lillemor?'

He nodded. He'd said nothing about Ingrid being the only passenger on this flight when Lars had instructed him. But she somehow felt he understood.

He tugged at the seatbelt to check the catch and then clambered into the pilot's seat and ran through the pre-flight safety check. Then the plane shifted as Hjalmar gestured for the bosun to lift her from the deck with the crane and lower her into the water. Ingrid was sorry, suddenly, to have hurt Lars. Part of his reluctance to let her go first was fear. *Qarrtsiluni* hadn't been airborne in more than a year and no insurance company in the world would cover her to fly down here. There'd only been a handful of flights ever made in Antarctica, not all of them successful.

It occurred to her that she might not come back. Ingrid Christensen Land would truly earn the name if Ingrid met her death there and she shivered. Her hand dropped to her seatbelt and for a moment she was so close to changing her mind that her lips began to move. The plane lurched and settled on the water, and before she could speak, the crane had been released and they were on their own.

'Let's go,' Hjalmar said, with a sideways glance. As the propeller started to spin, the roar drowned out any possibility of speech. He began to taxi the plane away from the ship into clear water for takeoff. He raised his thumb and then *Qarrtsiluni* began to move with purpose, shuddering as it accelerated. Ingrid saw the spray flying back past the window, until with a final bump they lifted from the ocean and were airborne.

In a few moments *Thorshavn* and *Falk* fell away below them, like toy ships. The people were insects and the dead whales crushed between the ships were herrings. The change in perspective was dizzying.

Beyond the little world of the ship lay Antarctica in her might. Hjalmar tilted the plane into a turn and a long, rocky shoreline came into view. Ingrid could see the ships were quite close to the land, but blocked from it by the pack ice and bergs. The sun sparkled on the ice-free areas of water, and she saw how easy it would be to become lost. She stared down, her heart beating, wondering how they would ever find the ship again amidst the floes of ice and icebergs. Who had thought to paint *Thorshavn* white?

The plane bounced and Ingrid gripped the armrest. She'd flown before, but in larger planes. *Qarrtsiluni* felt tiny, and every part of the machine shook with the effort of keeping them in the air. The ships had disappeared and there was nothing to give her perspective. The land below them was on such an enormous scale that it hardly looked real and she blinked and shook her head slightly.

Qarrtsiluni straightened out of the turn and Hjalmar dipped the plane's nose. Ingrid had expected the view of Antarctica to be ice and snow, white receding into an unfathomable distance. In the far edge of her vision she could see the ice plateau as expected, a white expanse disappearing into the sky. But before them was a jagged, rocky shoreline rising to low brown hills, criss-crossed with vivid black lines like some giant had dragged charcoal across the ground. Lakes of different shades of blue dotted the rocky hills and the pale blue sea ice that remained around parts of the shoreline was veined with fractures and freeze marks. Dozens of small bays and a confusion of islands traced the shore, making it difficult to see what was land and what was outcrop or archipelago. It was a modest land to be named after, some might say. There were no big mountains here, no majestic ice falls, no headlands that could be seen for hundreds of miles. It was also unexpectedly familiar.

Hjalmar scribbled and passed over a piece of paper. It said *Looks like the Vestfold!* and Ingrid smiled. She'd never seen their home county from the air, but even so she could tell the resemblance was striking.

They rose over the last line of hills before the plateau and then they were above white. This was what she'd expected from Antarctica and Ingrid pressed her face close to the window.

The wind had scoured the snow on the glacier into lines of sastrugi and she saw that, under the white surface, Ingrid Christensen Land was ice the colour of the sky. The long curve of the ice plateau sloped gently down until it became a glacier, carving its way through the old rocks and emerging at the dark blue edge of open sea. They were flying over ancient brown rocks criss-crossed with black dolerite veins, the sea ice in all shades of eggshell blue and the ice plateau striped with snow drifts.

It mattered nothing what it was called, Ingrid knew. She wiped her eyes, hoping Hjalmar wouldn't comment. He turned and caught her in the act and she saw in the look he gave her that he understood. She stopped trying to hide the tears then. She could give up her name for such a place.

CHAPTER 41

Mathilde felt the wind freshen on her cheek. Something about Antarctica drove you inside, she thought, and it wasn't only the snap of the cold's jaws at your extremities. It took a strong will to resist the seductive warmth of cabin and saloon and stay out. It was the immensity of the place that made you want to retreat to the safety of an enclosed space. An iceberg could look less than ship-size and not far off. Then a speck of penguin would appear beside one and its vastness would leap into relief.

The plane, by contrast, had turned gnat-sized within moments of leaving the water and she'd watched it for some minutes, a speck in the blue sky, hovering over an unimaginable wide land, before it disappeared from view.

Lars stayed out on the deck watching and though Mathilde felt her fingertips and the end of her nose becoming painful, she stayed too, ensuring she wasn't near him. The land was over there behind the ice, apparently, but Mathilde could see no hint of it. Their surroundings were the same as those of the past days: blue sea, brash ice shuttled back and forth by wind and wave, bergs looming towards them or standing so still that they looked like islands themselves.

One thing had solidified in her as she watched *Qarrtsiluni* pick up speed across the water, the spray flying from its skis until it achieved a miracle and lifted off. She'd not go anywhere in that plane. She'd let them think it was female timidity, but in her bones she felt the weight of its name. *Qarrtsiluni* had to carry not just one whale soul but thousands of them, all of those killed this season perhaps, or at least all those whose oil lay in the tanks below her feet. Those souls would draw the plane back down to join their brethren in the deep. She hoped it wouldn't be today, or any other time Hjalmar was in the pilot's seat.

She glanced over at Caroline, standing close by her husband's side. Compared to their own journey, Caroline had faced a far more gruelling experience, living on board the factory ship amidst the dismemberment and boiling down of the whales, without another woman to keep her company. There was no destination to her journey, only the drive of industry to kill enough whales to fill the ship's tanks with oil. By rights, Caroline should be begging to come home with them.

But she looked content with her lot. She held her husband's arm and Mathilde watched them exchange a few words. He smiled at her as if he couldn't believe his good fortune and she smiled back with an expression that seemed to light up the air around her. Mathilde wished Caroline was coming with them. A fourth woman could break the stranglehold of the triangle, the shift and play of loyalties that seemed to have trapped them.

She looked back at Lillemor and sighed. No, of course it wouldn't be so simple. Lillemor had turned away to the railing to watch the plane take off and manoeuvred herself far away from Caroline. She'd managed a grimace of a smile and a few strangled sentences when they'd been introduced, but Mathilde couldn't imagine her ever forgiving the woman.

Mathilde looked up again to see if she could spot the plane, and Caroline caught her eye with a hesitant smile. Mathilde smiled back and Caroline slid her arm out from her husband's and came over to join her.

'Mrs Wegger, how have you enjoyed the trip so far?' Caroline's voice was accented by her native Danish, adding, if it was possible, even greater charm to her demeanour.

'It's been very interesting,' Mathilde said. 'But nothing compared to yours! How have you managed?'

Caroline waved an arm, encompassing the ship and all that surrounded them. 'It's so lovely! I've grown used to the smell. Now I just notice the beauty.'

She looked incapable of subterfuge and Mathilde believed her, though she couldn't imagine such an uncomplicated relationship with the whole business.

'What was it like to land?' she asked.

Caroline's face lit up. 'We rowed for an hour to get through the ice leads, so far that we couldn't see *Falk* any more, nor smell it. I loved to feel land under my feet again. There were many penguins there and it was rocky all the way up to the hill from the bay where we landed. I couldn't stop smiling, Mrs Wegger. I'll never forget it.'

Her expression changed. 'But we have disappointed you ladies and I'm very sorry for that. Mr Christensen, I'm sure, thinks my husband did so deliberately and it's unfortunate, for there's no man more loyal. He didn't know you ladies were on board. He said to me, in Antarctica when a chance comes you must take it, for it might never come again.'

Mathilde laid a hand on her arm. 'Never mind. Nothing can be done about it now. And you named it for Ingrid. I'm sure she appreciated that.'

'I thought she would too,' Caroline said, frowning. 'But she seemed angry. I don't understand.'

Nor I, thought Mathilde, but didn't say it. She cast around for another subject. 'Do you have children, Mrs Mikkelsen?'

She shook her head. 'We haven't been blessed with them yet.

My husband is impatient, as he's not a young man any more. It's hard with his work, being away such long times. We thought I was pregnant before leaving and of course I wouldn't have come. But when it turned out I was wrong, he didn't want to lose another whole season of trying and at the last moment decided to bring me.' Caroline stopped and covered her mouth. 'Listen to me! You can tell I haven't seen another woman for a while. I'm sorry to babble so. Do you have children, Mrs Wegger?'

'Oh, call me Mathilde. Yes, two young ones.'

'You're lucky.' The smile left Caroline's face and she stepped close. 'May I ask you something personal?'

'Of course.'

'Did it take you long after you were married to fall pregnant?'

The fumbling night of her wedding came vividly to Mathilde's mind. Her own mother had told her something of what to expect, but the information hadn't prepared her for how elemental it would feel. To think that all the genteel married couples around her, even her own parents, closed their bedroom doors at night and came to each other panting and slick like animals! No wonder no one spoke of such a thing. At the heart of their civilised lives was this secret, the raw urges of the flesh that must be sated. She didn't know if she loved it or hated it sometimes, the way it reduced them to desperate need and transported them to pleasure and pain. Jakob's desire hadn't waned when she fell pregnant and she still felt ashamed that hers hadn't either.

It was so strange to have another person – a man! – witness the workings of her body. When she bled, she still had to lie beside him at night with a wad of rags between her legs, and in the mornings she was afraid he could smell the rich smell of her blood. Appalling that such a personal thing was no longer private. When she fell pregnant, he saw every swell and stretch, noticed her nipples expanding and darkening, cupped her belly in his craggy hands. Marriage allowed him access to all the secrets of her body. That he seemed to find pleasure in these things was perplexing and had taken her a long time to accept.

Caroline was still waiting for her answer and Mathilde shook herself mentally. 'Quite quickly,' she said, wondering if her colour was high. 'I was with child in three or four months.'

'We've been trying for two years,' Caroline whispered, glancing across at her husband. 'Nothing. Perhaps something is wrong with me. I hoped the change of air might help, but it hasn't yet.'

'Perhaps it will just take a little longer for you,' Mathilde said.

The wind blew a sharp gust and Mathilde raised her collar. Clouds were moving high in the sky above them and gusts darkened the surface of the water. The brash ice streamed past the edges of the large bergs. The Antarctic weather, it seemed, was changing with its usual speed. She couldn't see the plane. Next to her, Caroline began to scan the sky and Lars peered skywards too, shielding his eyes from the glare.

Thorshavn's engines shuddered under their feet as Horntvedt increased the throttle to keep the ship stationary against the wind. The temperature was dropping. Mathilde's nose began to run and her fingertips ached with the cold. She moved towards the railing. It could happen just like this, she thought with a shiver. The plane taking off, flying out of sight and never returning. How would they even know where to search for them? If Antarctica should turn on a blizzard, or even just a strong wind, it could snatch the plane from the sky and dash it on the ice.

She saw Lillemor stiffen and turned to follow her gaze. Yes, there was a speck in the sky and she took a deep breath of relief. She wasn't ready for another death; not yet. The plane quickly grew larger and began descending, bumping and swinging in the wind's grip. The brash ice was streaming past on the water around them and Mathilde wondered how Hjalmar would bring the plane down.

Qarrtsiluni turned in a wide arc and they all gathered at the rail to watch her come in, silent. The plane came down low over a clear patch of water, bounced once, twice, thrice, rocked on its skis and settled into a landing. It slowed to a near halt and then Hjalmar turned *Qarrtsiluni* around and began threading his way through the brash ice towards them.

Mathilde realised she was gripping the rail so hard that her fingers were numb. She let go and wriggled them, feeling light-headed. It wasn't today that the soul of the whale would avenge its kind.

CHAPTER 42

To return home having achieved nothing made her a tourist. Just a woman tourist, not even deserving of the term 'traveller'. A tourist with a few snapshots.

Perhaps she was jinxed, Lillemor thought. The ice leads had closed up around Ingrid Christensen Land (how it galled her to call it that) so no landing attempt from the sea was possible, even in a small boat. Ingrid had gone up in the plane to see Antarctica from the air and got back just as a change in the weather made further flying impossible.

Lillemor took to her bunk after *Qarrtsiluni* was grounded by the weather, unable to put on the requisite front needed to dine in the saloon with the Mikkelsens and hear about Ingrid and Hjalmar's flight. She stayed there all night and the next day, refusing to come out to say goodbye to *Falk* and its people when the refuelling was complete. *Thorshavn* was setting out to meet *Norvegia* and drop off Hjalmar, Nils, the dogs and the planes. Once that was done, they would turn back for Cape Town and Lillemor would leave with only those few tantalising glimpses of the continent she'd had already.

It wasn't until *Norvegia* appeared as a dark speck on the sea that Mathilde convinced her to come up on deck at last. The little ship, hardly larger than a whale catcher, had already circumnavigated Antarctica under the command of Captain Gunnar Isachsen and *Thorshavn*'s cargo included replenishment of her stores, the two aeroplanes and all that Hjalmar and Nils would need for landings and sledging trips.

Mathilde led Lillemor to the forecastle where the dogs were chained, avoiding Lars and Ingrid who were standing on the catwalk. Disturbed by the rush of activity on the ship, the huskies barked and howled, straining at their chains. Mathilde wandered among them, speaking soothing words and patting each dog, paying special attention to the puppies. Lillemor sat on a packing case and watched the crewmen carrying boxes and crates up from the cargo holds and stacking them on deck as the jaunty little ship approached. She couldn't imagine how *Norvegia* could carry such a weight back through the rolling seas off the bottom of Africa. Where on earth would the planes fit?

Norvegia manoeuvred towards them, oily black smoke rising from her stack. Hjalmar and Nils were waiting on the mid deck for the two ships to couple. To Lillemor's eyes they were filled with a new sense of purpose. They'd been passengers on another man's ship for five weeks, and in minutes would be in command of their own. How the inactivity must have strained them, she now saw.

With a volley of shouts and gestures, the two ships drew alongside. There were no floating whales to lie between them and cushion the bumps; it was down to the skill of the captains to join them without incident. Lillemor watched as they came together like whale and calf, the smaller ship nestling by the larger in the lee of the wind. As the coupling operations began, she turned away. Hjalmar, she saw, had taken the opportunity to come to the foredeck. He weaved through the dogs to Mathilde.

'Thank you, Mrs Wegger,' he said to her. 'It's hard to keep them under control when they're excited.'

She smiled up at him and Lillemor resisted the urge to roll her eyes.

Hjalmar bent down and scooped up one of the pups, the one that Mathilde had favoured. 'I'd like you to have Babyen.'

'Oh no!' She raised her hands.

He pushed the pup at her and let go so she had to catch it. 'He's too small to hold his own in the pack. Make sure he gets plenty of exercise. Your boy will have to see to it.'

Lillemor thought she might be physically ill. She wished she were anyplace but on *Thorshavn*'s deck, listening to their farewell. She turned away.

'Mrs Rachlew?' Hjalmar was approaching her.

'What?'

He halted in front of her. 'I'm sorry how things have worked out. I know you very much wanted to land.'

Lillemor was beyond trying to keep Hjalmar on side. 'Don't waste your sympathy, Captain. I know you don't like me. You don't need to be polite now.'

He recoiled slightly, then recovered. 'I understand your disappointment.'

'Do you?' she asked. 'I'm no explorer. I'm barely a photographer. A passenger, that's all.'

'Don't give up, Lillemor,' Hjalmar said. 'You're an intrepid woman. This isn't the only adventure around.'

Lillemor shrugged. 'You needn't concern yourself. Safe travels, Captain.'

'And you.'

Lillemor watched him walk off towards the stairwell. It wasn't until he reached the top that the idea occurred to her. She stayed very still, considering. The loading wasn't finished. She had a little time.

She forced herself to walk slowly along the deck and up the rear steps to the cabin. As the door closed behind her she pulled off her outer layers and flung open the drawers of the wardrobe trunk. She couldn't carry much; she'd have to wear some extra clothing. Extra socks dragged on, extra jumpers pulled over her head, gloves stuffed into her pockets, two hats jammed on her head, one under the other. She opened her small duffle bag and shoved in the first essentials that came to hand, throwing the camera on the top.

Lillemor had no plan, just the idea of Olga. She pushed a final few things into her coat pockets and opened the door. Lars and Ingrid were still standing out on the catwalk, watching the cargo being loaded. Lillemor strolled quietly down the stairs to the rear deck. A light snow began to fall and the wind picked up as she crept around to *Qarrtsiluni*'s door and cracked it open. She pulled the lever that folded down *Qarrtsiluni*'s steps and put her hand on the railing, ready to climb inside.

'Bad weather for flying, Lillemor.'

It was Mathilde, standing at the top of the stairs, her face expressionless. Lillemor stared up at her, caught. Shouts rose from the mid deck as *Norvegia* rose and fell on the waves beside them.

'You'd better hurry,' Mathilde said. 'They'll be coming for the planes in a moment.'

Lillemor stared up at her in entreaty. 'Mathilde. Cover for me?'

Mathilde gave a low laugh. 'Oh, you'll get your way. As always.' She turned and walked away.

Large, wet snowflakes started falling, piling up on the deck. They fell into Lillemor's hair and her coat, and flew around in flurries. With exquisite timing, Antarctica was giving her the camouflage she needed. She could hear the activity on the mid deck as smaller crates were passed from arm to arm, swung across and handed down to willing hands. Any moment the bosun would be bringing over the crane to lift the aeroplanes across.

Lillemor gripped the railing. Like Olga, she'd be strong enough to keep hidden until the two ships were far apart and

Hjalmar had no choice but to take her. Perhaps he'd even hinted as much in his last comment. Never mind stepping onto land for an hour – she'd be the first woman to explore in Antarctica. She would do something worthy of respect.

She climbed the steps, pulled the stairway up, closed the door and curled up on the floor in front of the seat, pulling her coat over her face. Outside, Antarctica's winds sang.

Just minutes later, Lillemor felt the plane move as the men released the ropes lashing her into place. Loud kicks and thumps ensued as one of them scrambled up the plane's sides to attach the crane. Orders were yelled, the crane groaned, and suddenly they were off the deck, rising aloft. *Qarrtsiluni* moved sharply, swinging over the deck and out across the water, rocking as if she wanted to break free and fly in the teeth of the wind. Sleet hit the windows, helping to hide her. Lillemor hunched low as the men of *Norvegia* snared the plane and lowered it to the deck. The sound of them lashing it down was only inches from her ear. She heard the crane lift the other plane across and the crew lash her down next to *Qarrtsiluni*, and then the sounds of loading faded.

The cabin became icy cold and Lillemor started to shiver. She wondered if she risked freezing to death. She rolled herself into a smaller ball to conserve her body warmth. She could manage a few hours.

A farewell lunch was planned, she remembered, in *Thorshavn*'s warm saloon, a final luxury before Nils and Hjalmar gave themselves up to *Norvegia*'s spartan comforts. They'd be there now, the windows steamed up, the table loaded with hot food. Would Mathilde reveal her?

The crack of the door opening made Lillemor jump; she hadn't heard approaching footsteps. She thought it was cold inside, but the air that streamed in was frigid. She closed her eyes more tightly and tried to stay still.

'Lillemor,' Hjalmar said.

She burrowed down and pulled the coat further over her head.

'You can't,' he said.

'Mathilde told you, didn't she?'

'No.' His voice sounded sad. 'I just had a feeling when I couldn't see you anywhere.'

A sob was rising up inside and she fought it, not wanting to weep in front of him. 'Just let me be like Olga, for God's sake. Pretend you don't know I'm here.'

'Come on,' he said.

Lillemor sat up. 'You hate me, I know.'

'I don't hate you,' he said. 'I just don't understand why you act the way you do with us men.'

The desire to cry disappeared in an instant. Lillemor raised her chin. 'You men keep us out of here as though you own the place. We don't have many weapons at our disposal, Hjalmar. Why won't you give us a chance?'

He said nothing for a long moment and then gave her a small smile. 'Come, Lillemor. The weather's bad so we're not staying for lunch. You can slip back across while they're still loading.'

He reached to help her get out and when she put her hands on his shoulders she found herself gripping him, and the pain of leaving did make her weep. For a few moments he held her and patted her back. Then under the cover of the falling snow he helped her down and took her bag. She followed him across the gangway. In her pants and heavy coat, with her hood pulled down, she was just another anonymous figure among the others loading the ship.

CHAPTER 43

Ingrid moved closer to Lars as the wind gusted harder. Soon one of Antarctica's blizzards would be upon them. Men were gathered on the deck, snow covering their shoulders and heads. All the small cargo had been transferred and the crane was lifting the last of the coal sacks across.

Lars scanned the deck. 'Where's Hjalmar?'

Ingrid wondered where Lillemor was. Surely she'd come to say goodbye? Mathilde was standing nearby and she returned Ingrid's questioning look without expression. Then Ingrid saw Hjalmar and Lillemor coming up the deck towards them.

'There you are,' Lars said to Hjalmar. 'Horntvedt wants to get us out of here as soon as loading's done. The weather's getting worse, and it's a bad place for bergs.'

'We're ready,' Nils said with a grin and Hjalmar nodded agreement. Both men shook hands briskly with Lars.

Nils turned to Ingrid and bobbed his head. 'Mrs Christensen, it's been such a pleasure to be on board with you. We'll miss female company on *Norvegia*. Congratulations and safe travels home.'

'Safe travels,' Ingrid echoed, with a pang of sadness. Of everyone on board, Nils was the most uncomplicated.

Over his shoulder she saw Hjalmar take Lillemor's hand, bend down and kiss it formally. Then he turned to Mathilde and did the same, though the action somehow seemed completely different. Ingrid strained to read the gesture. She still couldn't tell if they'd been lovers.

Hjalmar let go of Mathilde and turned to Ingrid. As they faced each other, the wind whistled and hissed around them. Ingrid extended her hand and he took it, but instead of bending his lips to it, he shook it, with a palm-to-palm grip, as if she were a man.

Ingrid felt offended, but Hjalmar's expression was appraising, and she had the impression she had somehow measured up. She wanted to say something – anything – about the journey, but every phrase that came to mind seemed inadequate.

'We'll miss you,' was all she could manage.

He nodded. 'It's never easy coming here. It tests you in ways you never imagine.'

He released her hand and stepped back. Captain Isachsen was waiting at the foot of *Norvegia*'s gangway for them to come across so he could hand over his command, and *Thorshavn*'s crew was ready to cast off the ropes.

Hjalmar saluted in the direction of the bridge, stepped onto the gangway and ran across with light, firm steps. Nils followed. Ingrid thought she heard a muffled sob from Mathilde. She watched the huddled conversation between the captains as Hjalmar took control of the ship and Isachsen relinquished it before stepping out on the gangway. As he reached *Thorshavn*, two crewmen unlashed the gangway, dragged it back onto the ship and tied it in place. Someone shouted an order and *Thorshavn*'s crew cast off the ropes. Hjalmar gave a single wave, and Ingrid could see his grin of delight even through the blowing snow. His voyage was beginning, at last, while she was about to turn for home.

The two ships began to draw apart and Ingrid felt her chest constrict. They'd be turning north shortly. In a few days, a week at most, they'd be clear of the pack ice and *Thorshavn* would start rolling again as they crossed the miles of empty ocean, all the way back to a bustling Cape Town summer. It was done; it was over.

'Let's go,' Lars called. 'It's freezing!'

She turned from the rail, blinking.

'There's a hot lunch waiting to celebrate the fifth ship to sail around Antarctica,' Lars said to Isachsen. 'Congratulations, Captain.'

Captain Isachsen smiled like he'd forgotten how. His beard was caked with snow and Ingrid doubted he'd washed during his voyage.

'I need a clean-up before I can dine with ladies,' he said.

Lars waved at Tobias, who'd been hovering. 'Our lad will show you the way.'

Ingrid turned for a last glimpse of *Norvegia* but she was already almost invisible in the blowing snow. She found herself instead looking into Mathilde's iceberg eyes.

'After you,' Ingrid said, gesturing.

'Oh, really?' Mathilde said, and passed her. Lillemor followed without a word.

Lars came beside Ingrid and took her arm. 'Home, now. I think it's time, don't you?'

Antarctica's wind slapped her in the face. Ingrid blinked and the ice on her eyelashes blurred her vision.

'Try to make friends with them,' he said. 'It's a long way back.'

The Antarctic gloom was still there the next morning, the mist obscuring the heights of the ice barrier. Ingrid leaned on the railing alone as *Thorshavn* sliced through the brash ice as if it were a woman's white thighs parting.

The first woman to see Antarctica. Perhaps. Even aside from Olga, that claim would always carry the recollection of how she'd treated Mathilde during the voyage. The ruthlessness she'd found buried in herself was unnerving, a discovery she couldn't leave behind.

A movement caught Ingrid's eye and she turned her head. Mathilde was on deck, but she'd stationed herself near the front, her hood pulled tight around her face.

Ingrid knew if she walked away now, any hope for reconciliation was probably lost. Perhaps she could patch something like a friendship together again. She took a breath and set off across the snow-slicked foredeck. As she approached, she saw Mathilde was holding one of Hjalmar's puppies beneath her coat.

'Mathilde?'

Mathilde turned her head slightly. 'Yes.'

The one word said it all, like the ice barrier looming before the ship, impenetrable.

'Please,' Ingrid persisted.

Mathilde didn't deign to answer.

'The three of us are still the first women to see Antarctica,' Ingrid said.

'What about Olga?'

'She's just a sailor's story.'

Mathilde turned to Ingrid. 'I really don't care. I just want to go home and get my children back. If you have any compassion at all, don't try and stop me.'

'What do you mean?' Ingrid asked, confused. 'Why would I try and stop you?'

'Please, don't pretend,' Mathilde said. 'I know why Ole asked you to take me.'

'Because he was worried about your children?'

'Because he wants my children, as you well know!' Mathilde snapped. 'I can forgive you most other things from this trip, Ingrid, but I'll never forgive you for helping him.'

Ingrid stared at Mathilde as everything she'd understood about her during the voyage shifted perspective. When Mathilde started to turn away, Ingrid reached out and put a hand on her arm.

'I know nothing about that. All I know is he wanted you to have a rest and feel better.'

Mathilde whipped her arm out of Ingrid's grasp. 'Give me one good reason why I should believe you!'

Ingrid hesitated. It was true, she'd betrayed Mathilde more than once on this trip, but not the way Mathilde thought.

Mathilde was looking back at her, framed by the ice behind her rising in fantastic jumbles. She gave a grim smile.

'Exactly. Now if you don't mind, I want to be alone.'

Ingrid backed away. Something had changed in Mathilde in the past days, and she felt sure that she and Hjalmar had been lovers. What else could account for the new strength within her?

She walked away. There were degrees of cold and degrees of freezing. She was learning more of them than she had imagined existed.

The brush caught in Ingrid's hair and she pulled it hard to clear the tangle. She'd washed her hair, and its drying was a slow matter. She leaned forward to examine herself in the mirror. The first flecks of grey were starting to show through the long red strands and her heart sank at the sight of them. How long till she was an old woman, grey all over, invisible?

She heard Lars at the door and tensed. Lars hadn't forgiven her for taking the flight without him and Ingrid thought they'd carry that tight knot of resentment back to Norway like a thing conceived out here, not the child he'd hoped for but something that would develop and grow and perhaps one day thrust them apart.

Instead of turning to greet him she glanced into the mirror and found his reflection. She saw at once that something had happened. Ten years seemed to have come off his face and she hadn't realised how disappointment was etched there until she saw its absence.

'What is it?' she asked.

He came to her side and picked up a necklace, fiddled with it, let its links run through his fingers.

'Hjalmar has radioed,' he said. 'He's flown over Lars Christensen Land and Klarius Mikkelsen Mountain.'

He paused again and Ingrid waited, her knuckles tight on the hairbrush. When it seemed he would say no more, she recommenced brushing with long, firm strokes.

'The ice has opened up and there's a wide, clear lead going in. We could be there by morning.' He put the necklace down. 'There could be a chance to land.'

Ingrid kept brushing. 'I'm glad. You deserve a landing.'

He put his hand over hers and stilled the brush. 'It means nothing to me unless you come. Do you still not understand that?'

Ingrid stared at their reflections in the mirror. For a moment she felt ashamed of herself in the face of his generosity. He didn't understand why she'd needed to go alone in the plane, but he was willing to put it behind him.

'We must do this together,' he said, and then let go of her hand. 'Unless you don't want to.'

She saw the flash of fear in his eyes, as if he thought he'd lost her. She reached for him. 'I'm amazed you can still bear to take me.'

He shrugged. 'I thought I wouldn't. I was angry with you. But this is the last chance and I want us to take it.'

'Just one thing,' Ingrid said. 'We all go. Enough of this nonsense of first and second. It's irrelevant now.'

Lars stepped back, his smile fading. 'For once on this trip, I'd like something just for you and me. You had your flight. This is our moment, Ingrid. Can't it just be us?'

Ingrid hesitated. This was a fragile peace between them and she was wary of shattering it. But she was resolute. 'Mathilde and Lillemor and I all come, or none of us.'

She could see in the mirror that Lars had clenched his fist, but when he spoke, his voice was calm.

'Very well,' he said. 'Whatever you want.'

She smiled at his reflection. 'Thank you.'

He didn't return the smile. 'I'm going up to the bridge.'

Ingrid had planned to ask Lars about Ole, but it wasn't the right time. She'd talk to him later about the bargain he and Ole had struck over Mathilde, she decided.

And she wouldn't tell Lillemor and Mathilde about this landing. She'd let it be a surprise. The lead might close after all, a blizzard might blow in, any number of unexpected dangers might arise before morning and there'd been enough disappointment already. Mathilde seemed to care nothing for it and Lillemor cared too much. It was better they didn't know.

CHAPTER 44

The engines dropped to idle speed and hollow thunks and clunks, the sounds of ice against the hull, echoed through the cabin. Lillemor raised herself on one elbow to look at the time on her wristwatch in the half-light.

'What is it?' Mathilde's voice came from the other bunk.

'We've stopped.' Lillemor got up and crossed the floor in her bare feet to twitch aside the curtain. She couldn't see anything unusual, and let it drop back.

The knock at the door made them both jump.

'It's one in the morning for God's sake,' Lillemor said. 'What passes for the middle of the night round here.' She wrapped her dressing gown around herself as she went to the door. 'Yes?' she asked, without opening it.

'It's Ingrid.'

Lillemor glanced over at Mathilde. She'd just as soon not open the door to Ingrid. She felt like ignoring her and going back to bed. She'd drunk too much at dinner with *Norvegia*'s captain and her head throbbed.

'May I come in?'

Lillemor sighed and opened the door. Ingrid stepped inside, heavily dressed in outdoor clothing and dusted with snow. She pushed back her hood and smiled.

'Well, ladies,' she said. 'Our moment has come. There's an open lead in the ice and we think it runs all the way to Klarius Mikkelsen Mountain. It's time to try for our landing.'

Lillemor stared. Her first impulse was to push Ingrid back outside and slam the door. It was too late, now, for the three of them. Didn't Ingrid know that?

'Don't you want to go alone again?' Mathilde asked from her bunk.

'I want us all to go together,' Ingrid said.

Lillemor thought she saw a faint tremble in Ingrid's lip. 'It's a bit late for that now, isn't it?'

'Once we land, the rest doesn't matter any more,' Ingrid said. 'It's one of life's great experiences. I'd really like us all to go.'

'And what you want, you usually get,' Lillemor said. She walked back to her bunk, twitched open the curtain again, peered out into the grey light and let it fall, trying to gather her thoughts. She felt like getting back into bed, pulling the covers over her head and shutting the whole thing out.

She sat down on the edge of the bunk. 'Do you think Scott felt it was one of life's great experiences when he was the second to reach the Pole?'

Ingrid was silent. Mathilde got out of bed, came over to Lillemor and put a hand on her shoulder.

'You're not Scott,' she said. 'You're not Hurley. You're a person who's come across the world to see something. Don't ruin your chance. Go with Ingrid and be glad of it.'

'I just feel like a tourist.' Lillemor felt a wave of frustration and pounded her fist on the bed. 'Just a silly bloody tourist. I hate it.'

'You've fought to get here,' Mathilde said. 'That's enough. Now go.'

'Please, Lillemor,' Ingrid said. 'Now there's no question of going first and we can all go together.'

The appeal on Ingrid's face seemed genuine, Lillemor thought, and she had a sudden flash of Freda. She wouldn't sit sulking in the cabin. She loved to climb and she climbed whenever she had the chance. Lillemor knew what Freda would ask her: did she truly want to land, or only want to land first?

'Oh, all right, I'm coming,' she snapped, and stood up. In spite of herself, Lillemor felt a flutter of excitement. Her lips twitched as she fought back a grin, not wanting to look too eager. 'We'd better get dressed, I suppose?'

Mathilde went back to her bunk and got into it. 'Not me.'

'What do you mean?' Lillemor demanded. 'After you've gone all wise-woman and talked me into it.'

'I never wanted to go to Antarctica in the first place. As Ingrid knows. So why should I join your nice little landing?'

Lillemor was taken aback. When had Mathilde become so assertive?

Ingrid looked at Lillemor and shrugged helplessly. 'We're casting off in twenty minutes,' she said. When no one answered, she walked out of the cabin, closing the door behind her.

Lillemor marched over to Mathilde's bunk. 'What's going on?'

Mathilde rolled over. 'Ingrid only wants us to come so she can say something good about Antarctica when she gets back. She saw it first because I was drugged and locked up. She flew over it first because she refused to let anyone else on the plane. Neither of those things look good for her. Now that she's not the first woman to land, she wants to report that we all landed together, as friends. As though everything is all right now. Well damn her.'

'Now it's your turn to listen to me,' Lillemor said. 'What would your children think of you? That you can't be bothered to get out of bed to see Antarctica? You've persuaded me, and now I'm telling you. The three of us are going, just as Ingrid's offered. So get up.'

Mathilde sat up. 'Oh, all right then.' Then she smiled. 'Lillemor, of course I'm coming. I just wanted Ingrid to suffer a little. She's too used to getting her own way.'

It took Lillemor a moment to understand. 'Do you mean you were making a joke?'

Mathilde threw back the covers and got up. 'I suppose I was.'

Lillemor grinned broadly this time. 'My my, Mrs Wegger. Aren't you coming along?'

They came out on deck into the biting cold. Lillemor could see three dark mountain peaks over the top of the ice. It was impossible to gauge their distance in the dim pre-dawn light. The cloud was heavy over their heads and a light snow was falling. A group of people stood on the lower deck above a lifeboat that had been lowered into the water.

A deep rumble boomed across the water as she and Mathilde reached the group.

'I don't like this,' Horntvedt was saying. 'Very poor conditions.'

'It's not far, Captain,' Ingrid said. 'Just across the water.'

'It's four nautical miles away,' he snapped. 'A very good distance if something goes wrong.' He turned to Mathilde and Lillemor. 'Ah, the rest of the ladies. Are you two willing to risk your lives for this?'

Lars smiled at the captain. 'Now Horntvedt, don't worry yourself. We're going with Atle, who's the best first mate of the whole fleet. I have total faith in him.'

'It's nothing to do with faith!' Horntvedt said. 'It's dangerous.'

Lillemor couldn't bear one more disappointment. She drew herself up taller. 'Let's get going.'

'Suit yourself, Mrs Rachlew,' Horntvedt said. 'You're braver than I. Or more foolish.'

'Fine,' Lillemor snapped. She looked at Lars and Ingrid. 'Are we going to stand around talking about this or are we going to do it?'

Another long, low rumble reached their ears.

'What's that?' Mathilde asked.

'Let's find out,' Lillemor said. She moved closer to the basket that was to lower them into the lifeboat and gestured to Ingrid. 'We'll follow you.'

Ingrid nodded, seeming to understand Lillemor's sudden urgency. Lars helped her into the basket and waved up at the bosun in the crane. The basket carrying Ingrid rose into the air and then over the side of *Thorshavn* and down into the lifeboat below.

Snow began falling thickly, piling on the deck. As the basket came swinging back for Mathilde, Lillemor wondered why the light was so gloomy. The sun must have been below the horizon, she thought, or the cloud cover very thick. Mathilde climbed into the basket and it rose, leaving Lillemor standing by Lars.

'It seems you're going to get your wish, Mrs Rachlew,' he said.

'And you,' she replied.

'I'd like my wife to step from the boat first.'

Lillemor shrugged. 'It means nothing now.'

'It means something to me. You'll have your chance at landing and you'll have to be content with that. Do I have your word?'

The basket landed on the deck in front of them and Lillemor put her hand on it to climb in. 'My word is a strange concept in such conditions.'

She passed the camera to Lars, clambered over the edge, sat down, and put her hand out for it. 'They're still unsure who really was the first man to land on Antarctica,' she said as he handed it to her. 'On Bull's expedition, they say Alexander von Tunzelmann, a junior seaman, jumped from the landing boat to hold it steady and thus snatched the honour of the first landing from his superiors.' She waved at the bosun. 'Luckily we needn't concern ourselves with such things, as the matter is irrelevant now.'

The basket lifted her up and if he answered, she didn't hear him. She shook her head. She couldn't help herself baiting him, but she'd probably regret it.

The deep roar came across the water again and this time she could see what caused it. A slab of ice was falling from an iceberg, the slowness of its descent betraying its size. It hit the water and even at a distance she could see the wave rolling out from the impact. She glanced down at the lifeboat. Such a wave, close by, could swamp them. But it was too late to go back now.

The basket bounced into the lifeboat and someone helped her out. She couldn't see who it was until the person tilted his head back and she realised it was Hans. He dropped his hand from her arm as though it burned and his cheeks were red even through the snowstorm.

Of course the historian would be coming; it made sense. She hadn't said a word to him since their night together and it had taken on the quality of a dream. She wondered why she'd thought sleeping with him would make him write something different about who landed on Antarctica. What a foolish reason to throw away her own fidelity. She'd make sure she was never alone with him again.

She settled herself where indicated in the front of the little boat. Six men were holding oars to row them ashore and a small sail flapped from the boat's mast. It was a long way to go in such a small vessel.

The basket was coming down again with Lars, the last one to board. He clambered out of it and took the seat next to Ingrid. There was no shelter and they were packed tightly together. There was a yell as the basket rose. The men cast off from *Thorshavn* and bent their backs to the oars. The sail flapped and filled and the little boat began to move.

CHAPTER 45

Ink-black water. The splash of oars, rattling in their rowlocks. Shards and chunks of brash ice scraping the boat's hull.

The gloom and the falling snow and the rhythmic dip of the oars stilled any urge to talk. Snow fell, soft and silent, transforming them into white-coated figures. A spell seemed to have fallen over them, a trance in which the six crewmen would row forever.

A splash in the water nearby startled Ingrid. A sleek, glossy back arched and disappeared. A moment later a head popped up and round dark eyes stared at them curiously before the seal slid underwater. Five penguins passed them, diving in and out of the water in an effortless, streamlined motion.

Ingrid pulled her hood close and wriggled her fingers and toes to stave off the chill. *Thorshavn* was too comfortable, she thought. She'd grown soft. She was shivering already and they hadn't even landed. It would be better to explore on a ship like *Norvegia* where your resilience couldn't be eroded by luxury. She adjusted herself on the hard bench. Her bottom hurt, her toes were starting to ache with the cold, her nose was streaming and freezing. She could hear the faint cries of seabirds as they moved deeper into the ice.

She was looking back when the crack came, much louder than the others. The sound of roaring reached her as the face of the berg behind them gave way and started to slide into the sea. The first mate, Atle, looked over his shoulder once to see how far away it was, and rapped out a curt order to turn the boat to face the coming wave. From the speed at which they manoeuvred, Ingrid understood the danger, and she reached for Lars's hand. If the boat capsized, life jackets would be no help. They'd be dead from cold within a matter of minutes.

The impact wave was coming fast and Ingrid tensed, trying to judge its size.

'Hold tight,' Atle said, not wasting words.

Each of them gripped the nearest seat or gunwale as the wave hit and the prow of the lifeboat tipped up. Ingrid heard a cry of fear and wondered which of them had uttered it. They rose higher and then they were over the wave, sliding nose-first down into the trough. They hit the bottom and the boat bounced once, twice, throwing them against each other before righting itself. The following waves, smaller, rocked them again.

They were all silent. Ingrid took a few deep breaths. She was careful not to look at Lillemor or Mathilde. Should she call a halt? Would Lars?

Atle looked at Lars with a raised eyebrow and, when Lars nodded, ordered them to turn the boat again and continue. The boat slipped through the water, the snow kept falling and no one spoke.

Then they rounded the edge of the lead. Everyone gasped as the vista opened up. They were facing a dramatic string of peaks that formed a half-ring around the edge of a wide bay. The mountain closest to them rose straight out of the water, its sides dark and forbidding, specks of seabirds circling its summit. The boat rocked as they all tilted their heads back to try and take in its size.

'Welcome to Klarius Mikkelsen Mountain, on Lars Christensen Land,' Atle said. 'Discovered by men of the Christensen fleet in 1931.'

It was completely different from the place Ingrid had flown over with Hjalmar. This formation would be visible from hundreds of miles away in the air, unlike the more modest land carrying her name.

She looked across at Lillemor and Mathilde. Lillemor was lining up the camera to take a photograph and Mathilde's expression was one of awe.

'Where are we going to land?' Lars asked Atle. 'I can't see anywhere.'

'There's lots of penguins,' Atle said. 'We might find a spot where they scramble ashore.'

Ingrid could see brown specks around the shoreline. There were thousands of penguins, claiming every ledge and outcrop.

'Why are they that colour?' Mathilde asked.

'The brown ones are the chicks. They're not fledged yet,' Atle said.

Atle called a halt and got to his feet. He stood, examining the shore keenly. At last he pointed and the men started to row again.

'What did he see?' Ingrid asked.

'Some penguins just went ashore,' Lillemor said.

The boat came closer to shore and Ingrid saw a gouge in the rock forming a passageway that led high up the side of the mountain. At its base, a group of adult Adelie penguins stood on the rocks, watching them with surprised, white-rimmed eyes.

'It's the only place I can see to try,' Atle said to Lars. 'I'll go first.'

They manoeuvred in close. The water rose and fell, lapping over a tiny, slippery-looking ledge and washing back with a sucking sound. It would be a tricky business, Ingrid saw, waiting till the wave washed back from the ledge and then jumping across. Atle crouched and leaped. He scrabbled on the ledge, fell to his knees, and quickly recovered. He was up before the next wave could catch him, clambering to the rocks above the ledge, scattering a group of watching penguins that squawked indignantly.

Another crewman tossed the rope over and Atle pulled the lifeboat close to the shore and tied it to a boulder. He straightened and gave them a thumbs up.

The little boat rose and fell with the swell. Water washed over the rock ledge, drained away, covered it again.

'What do you think?' Lars asked Ingrid. 'Can you do it?'

Ingrid looked at the ledge again and up at the forbidding slope of the mountain. It seemed so close, she could reach out and touch it. That swelling strip of black water, that rise and fall, that slippery ledge, were all that stood between her and Antarctica.

'I'll go first and then you can decide,' Lars said.

Of course there'd be no stopping him so close to his goal. If Atle could make the leap, Lars would try. And so would she, she realised. It was a waste of time considering the question. Everything in her life had been leading her here, to a rock ledge by a restless shore at the foot of Antarctica.

She gave him a quick kiss. 'Good luck. See you over there.'

Lars stood up, two of the crewmen crouching by his sides. Atle climbed down close to the ledge and bent his knees, ready.

'Watch the waves a few times to get the rhythm,' he said.

The swell came in, lifting the boat, rushing over the ledge, and then sucking away, letting them drop. It surged in again. Ingrid was suddenly aware of the smell of bird droppings, sharp and ammoniac.

'The next one,' Lars said.

The crewmen braced. 'I'll count for you,' Atle said.

Ingrid gripped the gunwale and glanced at the others. Lillemor and Mathilde were holding hands, their eyes fixed on

Lars's back. Hans had shut his eyes. The wave rose, swelling over the ledge. Two penguins shot out of the water, landing on their feet in the very spot where Lars was headed, startling all of them. They scrambled out of the way, followed by a rush of chicks, their beaks gaping. The wave started to recede.

'One, two, three!'

Lars crouched and leaped across the chasm, scattering the penguins. He balanced himself, reached for Atle's outstretched hand and pulled himself up next to the first mate as the next wave started to come in. A spontaneous cheer rose from the boat as he turned back to them, his face split in a wide grin. Ingrid felt a surge of love for him as she clapped. Even the penguins seemed to hoot their approval.

'Coming?' he asked, holding his hand out to her.

Ingrid stood, steadying herself against two of the crewmen. Lars was holding her with his gaze, his arm outstretched. Atle was ready to jump down on the ledge to catch her, and still she hesitated.

'Go on, Ingrid,' Lillemor said.

Ingrid turned her head. Lillemor was clutching her camera on her lap, her face pale, her eyes wide. Even her freckles seemed to have disappeared. She wanted to be the first so badly, Ingrid thought. Would it hurt her to give up this turn? It didn't really matter now, not after Caroline.

'You can do it,' Lars said, from across the other side of the world. 'Come, Ingrid.'

'Think of the Valkyrie.' Lillemor's lips were trembling and Ingrid thought she could see tears glistening, but in the cold it was impossible to tell.

Ingrid was about to offer the younger woman her place, and then she glanced at the shore again and saw Lars watching her silently. He knew what she was thinking.

She looked up at the mountain, towering above them. Lillemor wouldn't even be there if it weren't for her and Lars, she thought. Ingrid had waited since she was a teenager to get there. Why shouldn't she go first?

'Are you ready, Mrs Christensen?' Atle said, his voice urgent.

Ingrid turned and locked her gaze on to Atle's. At his count, the crewmen boosted her up. For a moment she was in the air, flying across the gap and then her boots landed heavily on the ledge. Atle caught her around the waist and Lars reached down from his perch and gripped the shoulder of her coat. The two of them swung her up as the next wave came rushing in below her feet. She landed beside Lars, wobbled, then gained her balance. A cheer came from the boat.

Lars threw his arms around her. 'We're here!' he said into her ear. 'At last.'

He held her so tight that it hurt and when they drew apart, Ingrid saw that his eyes were wet. He wiped his nose on his glove. 'I wish my father was alive. He would have loved this.'

Ingrid stroked his cheek and cupped it for a moment. 'I'm sure he knows.'

Lillemor was standing up to make the leap and Mathilde sat behind her expectantly. As they waited for the next wave, Ingrid felt the cold coming up through the soles of her boots. She was standing on the continent, at last, her feet pressed against the stone.

'One, two, three!'

Lillemor landed with both hands on Atle's shoulders, but her feet skidded on the wet rock. There was a collective gasp as he braced himself to take her weight and Lars reached down to help. They might all end up in the water, Ingrid saw, her own muscles tightening.

Scrabbling, Lillemor started to fall to one side. Atle bent lower and threw out an arm to get a better handhold. The Beau Brownie looped over her shoulder swung around on its strap and hit the rock shelf with a clunk. Lillemor groaned, but as if galvanised by the sound, found her footing, reached up to grasp Lars and swung up from the shelf just as the wave swept in. Atle, a moment later, got his feet wet for his trouble.

Lillemor was panting as she landed. Ingrid reached out to grab her arm and could feel her trembling. 'Are you all right?'

Lillemor's cheeks were flushed. 'Fine. Thank you, gentlemen. I only hope the camera survived.' She pulled it close. 'Come on, Mathilde,' she called down.

Mathilde, standing ready, hesitated. Ingrid wondered if she'd change her mind. She'd never wanted to come, not really. The risk of jumping might be too much for her, but Ingrid wanted all three of them there.

'Imagine telling Ole and Aase about this,' she called, projecting her voice.

Mathilde took the arms of the crewmen. Atle counted and she jumped with surprising determination, landing squarely and making the step up to the rock next to them easily.

She laughed upon reaching them. 'My God. We're here.'

Ingrid reached to Mathilde and Lillemor and grabbed their hands. They raised them and shook their joined fists at Hans, still miserably huddled in the boat.

Hans refused to make the leap, insisting he'd wait in the boat and watch from there. The other crewmen came ashore and after a sustained cheer when the last one landed, they all climbed up from the ledge and into the rock crevice, which seemed to rise to the mountain's top, disappearing out of sight above them.

Atle directed the crew to collect rocks and deposit them on a ledge above the water, ready to build the cairn. They'd tossed over a stout wooden box and a flagpole from the lifeboat and these waited by the growing pile of stones.

'The university will be pleased we landed,' Lars said, looking around. 'We'll get some proper geological samples this time.'

Ingrid watched him talk to Atle and recruit several men to start chipping at the walls of the rock chute. Lars was proud of the scientific work done by his expeditions, and all his ships were charged with bringing back samples and observing weather and ice conditions, under the guidance of the University of Oslo. But the crewmen looked bemused as they wielded their picks. She wondered how they knew what to gather.

'Where's Mrs Rachlew gone with that camera?' Lars asked, coming back to her.

'Hunting for rocks, so she said.' Mathilde pointed.

Ingrid looked up the crevice. She could see Lillemor's white fur coat standing out against the brown rock about fifty yards up, almost hidden behind the boulders.

'I'll get her,' she said.

'Can you?' Lars said. 'I'll have one more go at talking Hans into coming. I want to get the flag ready.'

Ingrid began to climb. It was steep and she used her hands to pull herself up, watching carefully where she placed her feet. Making the leap back into the lifeboat with a broken ankle wasn't something she wanted to try.

Even just a short distance up the mountain's shoulder, the view of the bay and the mountains was panoramic. Seabirds wheeled around the cliffs above Ingrid's head, at least three different species she thought, their cries loud on the still air. Underfoot, desiccated white corpses littered the ground; penguin chicks that hadn't survived. In this climate they might have lain there for three months or thirty years.

She stopped below the boulder where she'd glimpsed Lillemor and sat down. She was grateful for the chance to spend a few minutes alone, away from the flurry of the landing site.

Ingrid had spent the voyage down dreaming of ice, but in fact they'd reached bedrock. No ice was accessible from their landing place, not without climbing the full height of the mountain. It was rock that confronted her, a mountain of it, hard and real, brown and black.

Mostly. When she looked down among the pebbles scattered at her feet, she saw a chunk of pale green, which at first looked like a piece of ice. She bent to look closer. It was a small translucent rock, of some kind of crystal structure. She picked it up and held it on the palm of her glove to examine it. This one she'd take home, she thought, and not for the university. A piece of Antarctica for herself.

She'd bargained with Lars to take back something even smaller than that – a few cells in her belly, the start a child. But her blood time had come and that was the last time they'd …

She felt a rush of shame thinking of it. There was still a chance of conceiving, on the way home. She'd be fertile again in a few days. Perhaps she shouldn't try to avoid it, she thought. Men put their names on extraordinary places to make their mark. Explorers came home with maps and muddy, blurred photographs. What if she were able to carry the essence of this place home in her own belly, a child with white hair and eyes of iceberg blue?

Ingrid wished the sun would break through the heavy clouds. She needed the Antarctic light now, but it remained resolutely gloomy. This was the moment she'd hoped to find what drew her south, but there was no dazzling sunlight to help her see.

She closed her eyes and the sounds around her sprang into relief like parts of an orchestral score. The chittering of seabirds;

the chink and chock of the men stacking the rocks for the cairn, the ring of stone and metal connecting as they chipped samples from the cliff. The swell rose and fell over the rocky shoreline, clattering loose stones under the surface. Below her, voices rose: a muted laugh, a snip of conversation, a shout. Ingrid could hear the sounds of her own body, her breath moving in and out of her lungs, the ringing in her ears. Beneath it all, there was something else.

It took her a while to realise that it was the quiet, palpably present. She'd thought it an absence of sound, but it was its own sound, carrying the immensity of the silence that lay over the whole continent, a silence that could hold the land's sounds without being obliterated by them.

An image began to form behind Ingrid's closed eyelids. It was Alfhild, she thought, seeing a sweep of alabaster skin. Then the image wavered, and she realised she wasn't seeing her mother. It was a child, with Alfhild's skin and aquamarine eyes. The child Ingrid might conceive, if only she would allow it. She wanted to reach for him, but sensed if she strained too hard, he would disappear. She squeezed the stone and tried to still her mind.

Yes, there. A cheekbone. His face turning slowly so she could see the delicate whorls of his ear, and his hairline.

His hair was red.

Ingrid recoiled. Her ice child would have blond hair, wouldn't he? Not the red of the flensing deck; not the stain of blood spreading on the water after the humpback was harpooned. For her to come here, whales had died in numbers so high she couldn't envision them. The whale that had risen in its turquoise glory to look at her would die too, next season or the one after, in all likelihood. She didn't want a red-haired child to remind her of that.

Then the child opened its eyes and Ingrid saw that it wasn't a boy, but a girl. Not a nameless girl, but Ingrid herself, her own child self with her Viking red hair and eyes the colour of the sea.

The recognition was a physical shock, reverberating through her body. Ingrid felt like an old woman now, tired and garrulous, worn out. But that child before her, that younger Ingrid, glowed. A person with such life blazing from her could have found her own way to Antarctica, not as someone's wife and not on the bounty of the whales. Where had that light gone?

Ingrid remembered the deep groan and lilt of the whale echoing through the oil tank. It felt like her own lament, for all the light she'd somehow lost.

The image disappeared and Ingrid opened her eyes. Tears were freezing on her cheeks and prisms of ice had formed on her eyelashes. Out across the water, snow was starting to fall. Leaving her name in Antarctica would be a reminder of this, she thought. She'd remember it was her own self she'd seen in the light.

It came to her that Alfhild had been seeking the same thing when she went out in the snow. The self she might have been, untainted, glowing, out of reach.

A snow petrel flew past her, tilted, turned and flew back again. Another hurtled past, and another, making a scolding sound. She wondered if she was sitting near a nest.

'Let's hope we don't get a blizzard while we're here,' a voice behind her said. 'We'd be in trouble.'

It was Lillemor coming around the side of the boulder, shattering the quiet. There should be a vow of silence in Antarctica, Ingrid thought, the way these same people wouldn't dream of speaking out loud in a church. Her moment was gone. She closed her fingers tight around the green stone so Lillemor wouldn't see it.

'Lars wants you to come down. He'd love you to take some pictures,' she said.

'Oh, sorry about that,' Lillemor said. 'I was looking for some specimens.' She looked down. 'Here comes your husband now.'

Ingrid followed her gaze and saw Lars climbing nimbly towards them.

'I've found something he might be interested in,' Lillemor said.

'Oh?' Ingrid didn't really want to start a conversation.

Lillemor stood silently beside her as Lars approached. He heaved himself up over the last boulder and stood next to them. The ledge felt crowded.

'Ah, Mrs Rachlew,' Lars said affably. 'Isn't this something? We must record this moment – thank goodness we have a photographer with us.'

Lillemor smiled. 'It's extraordinary. And there's something around the boulder you simply must see.'

CHAPTER 46

'Hold him tight, Mrs Wegger,' Atle said. 'He's slippery!'

Mathilde put her arms out and then staggered as he deposited the penguin into them. They swam as if they were streamlined, but away from the water, the creature in her arms was rotund and surprisingly heavy.

'Got him?'

Mathilde nodded, and then the penguin squirmed and freed himself from her grip, landing hard on the rocks at her feet. He bounced up and shook himself, unperturbed, then waddled away.

'What about a chick?' Mathilde asked.

Atle shook his head. 'They'll try to peck you for food. The adults are more docile.'

He approached another one. It stared up at him, seemingly unafraid. Atle crouched, let the penguin approach, then pounced and grabbed it. The penguin wriggled once or twice and then gave in.

'Here, Mr Bogen, you hold it so Mathilde can stroke it,' Atle said.

Hans, who Lars had finally convinced to make the leap ashore, took hold of the bird and grunted under its weight. Mathilde pulled off her glove and let her bare fingers run over the penguin's feathers. It felt nothing like a bird and more like she imagined a seal might feel.

'Bring me that box!' Atle called down to one of the boys,

who scrambled for a crate sitting near the ledge and carried it up to them.

'What are you doing with it?' Mathilde asked.

Atle took the penguin from Hans and bundled it into the crate. 'The Consul wants to take a few home. He thinks he could establish a colony in Spitsbergen. It wouldn't hurt tourism up there.'

'Goodness.' Mathilde stared down at the bird as it paddled its flippers. How would it survive the long trip back?

'How many are you taking?' Hans asked.

Atle shrugged. 'We'll probably take a dozen Adelies and hope we've picked enough females. The Consul would love to find a pair of emperors, but they don't nest around here so it's unlikely.'

'But what if you take one that has a chick?' Mathilde asked.

'The other parent can feed it, this late in the season. And if not,' he gestured at the bodies littering the ground, 'another handful dead won't make a difference.' He looked up. 'Here they come. Good.' He called out to the men hacking at the cliff face with ice picks. 'Let's get on with it. We don't want to linger here.'

Lars, Ingrid and Lillemor clambered down towards them. They reached the pile of rocks that had been assembled for the cairn and halted next to Mathilde.

Hans brushed his hands on his trousers and gestured for Mathilde to go first. They squeezed onto the ledge where the flagpole had been jammed in a small pile of rocks. It was a tight fit.

'Are you going to read the proclamation?' Hans asked Lars.

Lars looked uncomfortable. 'I'm just going to say some thank yous and raise the flag. Mrs Rachlew has come across something rather disappointing, I'm afraid.'

His voice and his expression were grim, Mathilde thought. Lillemor, on the other hand, had a slight smile on her lips.

'What do you mean?' Hans asked.

'There's a cairn and a depot up there laid down by Sir Douglas Mawson,' Lillemor said. 'Dated February 13th, 1931. He's named it Scullin Monolith, after his prime minister. We're standing on Mac.Robertson Land, according to the proclamation he's left there. The Australians have claimed this entire coastline.'

There was silence. 'But weren't your men here before that?' Hans asked Lars. 'This is already named.'

Lars nodded. 'Several ships in my fleet explored here in January and February 1931, including the one Klarius was on. This area was named Lars Christensen Land in January, weeks before Mawson saw it.'

Hans shook his head. 'There'll have to be some investigations. They can't keep claiming lands we've discovered!'

'Consul,' Atle said. 'I'm sorry, but we need to be getting back. The weather is unpredictable today.'

Lars coughed. 'You're right.' He stepped forward and waved at the two men who'd been holding the flag ready. 'We'll still raise the flag, of course.'

As the men began pulling on the rope to raise the Norwegian flag, everyone took off their hats. Lars cleared his throat again and stood up straighter. His gaze fell on Ingrid.

'I'd like to thank all of you for coming,' he said. 'And most of all I'd like to thank my wife, who's patiently waited twenty years for me to bring her here.'

Ingrid smiled and stepped forward to take the hand he was holding out.

'My dear Ingrid,' he said, 'I'm sorry it took me so long to keep my promise.'

Lars nodded to another of the crewmen who started pouring out coffee from a Thermos into tiny cups and handing it around.

It steamed and started to cool at once. Mathilde put it to her lips, glad of the warmth. The cold was starting to feel oppressive.

'I also formally put on the record that this place has been christened Klarius Mikkelsen Mountain, recognising that Captain Mikkelsen was the first to discover this area and name it Lars Christensen Land,' Lars said. 'He has done much for Norway's scientific research in Antarctica.'

Lars bent down and closed the wooden trunk. Two men picked it up and put it next to the flagpole. Everyone moved forward to heap the rocks around it.

'Mrs Rachlew,' Lars said, 'could you take some photographs?'

Ingrid and Lars posed together in front of the flagpole. Lillemor fiddled with the camera for a long time, holding it in front of her and looking down into the viewfinder. Lars and Ingrid began to look awkward.

'I think it's damaged,' Lillemor said. 'I'll try, but the picture doesn't look right. Stand still, the two of you.'

She took a couple of shots, and the lever jammed after the third one. 'That's it, I'm afraid.'

'Oh, Lillemor,' Mathilde said. 'There isn't one of you!'

Lillemor shrugged. 'We'll just have to remember.'

'Back into the boat, please,' Atle called.

They clambered down towards the rock ledge. The tide had shifted while they were there and the water level was creeping up the ledge.

'Quickly!' Atle stationed himself near the ledge and two of the younger crewmen nimbly jumped across. Atle started a chain, swinging a person or a piece of cargo across with every receding wave until Mathilde thought they looked like a stream of penguins flinging themselves into the water.

Everyone was focused on the crossing and Mathilde hung back. When she was sure no one was looking, she crouched down on the ground and slid her glove off. She must have gained weight on the boat, for her wedding ring was tight on her finger again and she had to twist hard to remove it. She held it in the centre of her palm for a moment, feeling its cold against her skin, then lifted a small rock, laid her ring on the ground underneath it, and put the rock back over the top.

'Mrs Wegger, next please.'

Mathilde stood up, shoving her glove back on. Before she could blink, Atle had helped her down to the ledge and she was leaping across the water to the boat.

She was glad of it. Antarctica was too big. Too many sights, too many sounds, too overwhelming. It was no place for humans, she thought, but big enough to leave feelings there. She was ready to go.

CHAPTER 47

The mist and snow came down quickly once they pushed off and within a few minutes the land was hidden, as if it had never been. The Beau Brownie seemed heavier on her lap as they turned away from the continent. Lillemor didn't know if she was infuriated with the thing or secretly pleased it was damaged. There was no evidence now that she'd ever landed. No record of her standing on Scullin Monolith – a name she was happy to use in her own mind rather than linking the Mikkelsen name any more closely with the continent. The place would never be Lillemor Rachlew Mountain, or Cape Mathilde Wegger, that much was certain.

All she had was the rocks, clacking in the pocket of her coat. She wished she'd thought to ask Marie what to look for, but the idea had only come to her once they'd landed and she'd seen the crewmen chipping at the cliffs. She'd climbed out of their sight, picked up as many rocks as she could comfortably carry and stuffed them in her pockets. Hopefully she'd chosen one or two that would be of interest to Marie.

She was cold. They all were, she could see. The few sips of coffee on shore had given them some respite, but the snow was coming down again and some of them were wet from jumping back into the boat. Hans was visibly shivering, and she could see Atle stamping his feet, though he appeared unconcerned. She glanced at her wristwatch, but it had stopped. They must have been gone three hours or more from the ship, she thought.

Normal time didn't apply out there. They might have been rowing forever, the men straining at the oars, the snow piling up on their shoulders and thighs and on the floor of the boat. Icebergs loomed up out of the mist, frightening in their sudden appearance. They were dangerously close, Lillemor knew. Sharp cracks and creaks and distant rumbles issued from the mist, their sources invisible. Atle's face was impassive but the tension in his body betrayed his concern. He put one of the oarsmen in the prow as a lookout as the boat crept slowly through the water.

Lillemor wondered if she should have kept quiet. She'd been scrambling upwards in the crevice, searching for a rock seam of the sort she'd heard Marie describe, when she came around the corner and saw the cairn. The flag was gone, torn away by the wind she presumed, but the flagpole still stood wedged into the rocks, and she could see the corner of the box poking out at the side. She could have called for Lars then, but damn him, it was her discovery. It had been hard work to pull away the stones covering it and open the box. She'd pulled out a bundle of red fabric and unrolled it. An Australian flag, the maritime ensign, with its five bold stars making up the Southern Cross.

Lillemor thought she'd be disappointed at the evidence someone had beaten them there, but to her surprise it was exciting. The great Mawson had placed the box there himself, had stood over it and read the proclamation claiming the land for Australia, then rolled the paper up and placed it inside, along with a jacket, some pemmican, a block of chocolate and the flag. She was, in all likelihood, the first person to open it since it was laid down.

Scullin Monolith, on Mac.Robertson Land. Or Klarius Mikkelsen Mountain, on Lars Christensen Land. Four men vying for the honour of having their names appended to this continent. Two young nations, Norway and Australia, trying to prove themselves on the world stage as forces in their own right, independent from Sweden and Great Britain.

She'd closed the box, stood up and turned around. If she walked out from around the boulder and said nothing, in all likelihood no one else would climb that far. It could be her own secret. She didn't have to spoil their landing. If Mawson and the Australians had claimed that land, Lars would know about it soon enough.

Then she thought of how he'd spoken to her that morning as she was sitting in the basket. *I'd like my wife to step from the boat first.* Even when it didn't matter. And what he was prepared to do to Mathilde to keep her out of the way. He was ruthless. Why should she be any different?

She had enjoyed the look on his face when he saw the depot. He wasn't used to failing and she was pleased he now had some idea what it was like. Feel that, she thought. Feel what it's like to have Mawson not bother replying to your application. Feel what it's like to be refused a berth on the ship for no good reason. Feel what it's like to come second, or last, or not be included in the race at all.

On the other side of the lifeboat, Lars had his arm around Ingrid's shoulder, keeping her close to his side, presumably for the warmth. Lillemor thought to find him grim-faced, but as she watched, a little smile played around the corners of his lips.

Mathilde shifted next to Lillemor and moved closer. 'It's cold,' she murmured.

Lillemor put an arm around her so their bodies were pressed together. 'That's better,' she said.

Atle called a halt and stood up. He rotated slowly, trying to find a way through the mist. The snow was falling more heavily and the visibility was only about twenty metres.

Atle bent down and picked up a loud hailer from under his seat. He put it to his lips and bellowed so loudly that they all started. '*Thorshavn*!'

The snow muffled the sound and it seemed to stop dead. The silence around them pressed in, broken only by the soft slip-slip of the snow falling. In the distance came a rumble and somewhat closer an ominous cracking.

'They should be here,' Atle said to Lars. He put the loud hailer up again. '*Thorshavn*!'

There was no answer. He directed the men to keep rowing slowly and remained standing.

It was impossible to see, but they must have rounded the edge of a berg, for a sudden gust of wind hit the boat and it rocked. Atle sat quickly. The men kept rowing, blind. The snow was blowing sideways and they were pushing into a swell, the boat moving up and down.

'We're out of the ice lead,' Atle said to Lars. 'They can't be far away.' He picked up the loud hailer again and called into it.

Lillemor felt to her bones what a lonely sound it made, unanswered. It was all very well to visit Antarctica. They could stand around on the rocks drinking coffee, they could read their proclamations, they could raise flags and lay down names, and by such acts feel themselves in control. But a single storm could bring them undone, no matter how close *Thorshavn* might be. Scott and his men had died only eleven miles from the depot that could have saved them, caught in their tents by a blizzard that raged for days. Twenty years ago, Mawson had made that last hundred-mile run alone and Lillemor suddenly had a sense of his fear. It was ridiculous; they'd only travelled four nautical miles from *Thorshavn*, but if they couldn't find the ship again or if they capsized, fifty yards was as good as a hundred miles.

How fast and how silently fear took over the boat. No one spoke. Atle called for the ship every few minutes, the men bent their backs and rowed, though to what purpose Lillemor didn't know. They were out of the bay, they couldn't see, they might be rowing away from the ship with every stroke for all they knew. The crewmen kept their faces impassive, as did Atle. The snow blew around them, the wind first on one cheek then on the other. Atle must be taking them in circles, she surmised. At least they weren't simply rowing blindly out to sea.

Mathilde reached over and gripped her hand. Lillemor could feel her shivering, with fear, or cold, or both, and her face was deathly white. Lillemor tried to smile, but she could feel her face grimacing.

'Is there any more coffee?' Ingrid asked.

Lillemor shook her head in disbelief. They were lost, didn't Ingrid realise? Their lives were at stake and she was asking about coffee!

But Atle called a halt and they put up the oars then one of the men bent down, scrabbled under the seat and came up with the basket. He opened a Thermos flask and poured out tiny cups of coffee. The warmth of the coffee staved off the cold but Lillemor realised how hungry she was. She patted her pocket. She'd taken Mawson's chocolate from the depot, intending to carry it back to Norway. She pulled it out and looked at it. The wrapper said *Mac.Robertson's*. Mawson had named the land after a piece of confectionery.

'Ah, some chocolate. Good thinking, Mrs Rachlew,' Atle said. 'May I?'

He took the chocolate from her, unwrapped it, broke it into pieces and handed it around. Lillemor made sure she took it last, and stuffed the wrapping back into her pocket.

Ingrid was no fool, Lillemor realised. The injection of chocolate and the heat of the coffee raised everyone's spirits a little. Eating and drinking, even in the blowing snow with the boat pitching up and down, was a trace of normality. Of course they'd find their way back.

'I'm sorry you're getting cold,' Atle said to the passengers at large. '*Thorshavn* must have moved position, but she can't have gone far and she'll be looking for us too. I think we should all yell together so we're louder. On the count of three, all right?'

Shackleton had been lost in far more desperate circumstances, Lillemor recalled. His ship *Endurance* – Ingrid's old *Polaris* – had been crushed by the ice and had sunk. After making it to Elephant Island with his men, he'd set out on a boat not unlike the one that carried them now, and had managed to sail across eight hundred miles of open sea to South Georgia. If *Thorshavn* were crushed, where would they go? They'd have to try and find one of the whaling ships, or *Norvegia*, but they were many miles away. Lillemor couldn't even see the nearest iceberg.

Their calls sounded desperate, and Lillemor thought that after a few repetitions they'd end up panicking and shrieking it.

'I've an idea,' she said, shifting to loosen her grip on Mathilde. 'Let's sing a song. Mathilde can lead us.'

Mathilde shook her head. 'I can't,' she said, through chattering teeth.

'Yes you can,' Lillemor said. 'That one you sang the other day. We know it. What's the name?'

'"Gjendine's Lullaby".'

Lillemor nodded. 'We'll all join in.'

She squeezed Mathilde's hand hard and leaned close to her ear. 'We need you.'

Mathilde took a deep breath.

The first note came out, resonant and true, and swept over them like relief. They opened their mouths to join in, one after another. Mathilde's voice soared and they followed, more or less in tune. One of the crewmen dropped into the tenor harmony, laying down a bed of sound below Mathilde's voice, one that supported all of them. The sound rose up and into the snow, snatched and carried off by the wind.

Lillemor saw that Hans was crying, or perhaps his eyes were just streaming with the wind. They all had streaming eyes, she saw, the tears crystallising on their cheeks. The crewmen had stopped rowing and were leaning on their oars, some of them tucking their hands under their arms or in their jackets to try and warm themselves, but all of them, every last one, singing.

Mathilde held the last note long after the rest of them ran out of breath and trailed off. The sound was so pure that Lillemor felt her chest constrict. It was a sound that could lift you above grovelling fear and make you face death with some kind of pride. There could be worse ways to die, she thought.

'Lifeboat ahoy!' The faint call came floating to them through the snow, directionless, joining the final breath of Mathilde's song. An exhalation of relief washed over the boat and suddenly there were smiles again. They were going to make it.

'Thanks,' Lillemor said to Mathilde, pulling her close.

Atle tipped his cap to Mathilde solemnly. He put his mouth to the foghorn and called. The reply from the ship came back at once, from over to the left, Lillemor heard, distant but audible. The crew turned the boat in its direction and began rowing with renewed vigour.

'You saved our lives,' Hans said. 'Thank God.'

Mathilde shrugged. 'Not at all, silly. Look how close by they were. It was a good way to pass the time, that's all.'

She gave Lillemor a small smile. She quite possibly had saved their lives, Lillemor thought, but it sounded crass to repeat it and so she just smiled back. Now that she'd stopped singing, Mathilde's teeth were chattering again and Lillemor felt herself shivering too.

Thorshavn's white side appeared through the mist, suddenly close by. Lillemor saw the relief on Atle's face. They wouldn't have lasted much longer, she thought, for all that Atle acted calmly.

'We'll need to go up the ladder,' he said. 'It's too rough for the basket.'

The ship and the lifeboat were both moving up and down in the swell and it would be a tricky job to get onto the ladder hanging down *Thorshavn*'s side. It took some time to manoeuvre the lifeboat alongside the ship and Hans was looking queasy by the time they made fast. Atle hurried them up, timing it so that each person stepped up when the wave was at its highest point. Mathilde, by common consent, went first, then Ingrid, then Lillemor. The cold slowed them, so they crawled stiffly up the ladder with numb fingers that refused to grip properly.

At the top, Horntvedt helped each of them over the gunwale. His own face was white and his mouth was a grim line.

When Lars reached the deck he gave the captain a smile. 'We landed!' he said. 'What an experience!'

'I hope so,' Horntvedt said. 'That was the worst morning I've had at sea. Not only did you go missing, but the depth went from two hundred and sixty metres of water to fifteen. The last hour nearly came for the ship and for all of us. Four metres to spare, Consul!'

Lillemor felt her stomach turn over. She could picture, vividly, coming back to find *Thorshavn* holed and sinking. With the wireless they could call for rescue, perhaps, but if the weather deteriorated, no one could get to them.

Lars clapped Horntvedt on the shoulder. 'Things tend to work out.'

Horntvedt shook his head. 'I'm afraid I can't be so relaxed,' he snapped. 'I want us out of here at once. It's too dangerous.'

'Of course, Captain,' Lars said.

He turned to the rest of them. 'Let's celebrate,' he said. 'Dry clothes and hot breakfast.'

Hot breakfast, thought Lillemor. As if it was a morning like any other. And she supposed it was, in its way.

CHAPTER 48

Thorshavn turned for home, sailing north through the brash ice, which scraped and clattered down the ship's side like a Morse code pattering of dots and dashes, tapping out a secret message Ingrid couldn't decode. It was a deep, resonant sound, ice on metal, echoing through the hull.

She avoided the bridge and instead dressed herself warmly and stood outside for long hours in the empty place where *Qarrtsiluni* had been lashed, watching the snaking pathway they carved through the pack ice, a line stretching all the way back to the continent. She had until they reached home to gather the unravelled strands of herself and twist them back together into a person she could recognise. She wondered if it would be long enough.

Lillemor and Mathilde had clearly teamed up for the return voyage, strolling arm in arm, laughing and talking, sitting side by side in the saloon to take their meals, playing with the puppy and the penguins. Although they'd landed together, Ingrid still felt distant from them. She avoided them when she could, made polite chit-chat when she couldn't.

After four days *Thorshavn* cleared the pack ice. The air temperature suddenly rose and the ship began to roll. They were back in a world ruled by open sea, and Ingrid's fancies became strange in the constant motion. She imagined the undersea world dropping away, an upside-down night with large and small creatures flapping through its skies. She thought the ocean's denizens must look up through the membrane separating the worlds and wonder what was up there. That membrane was a violent place. Birds pierced the sea's surface and speared fish. Leopard seals came from below to snatch penguins from the air. And humans sent down their harpoons like arrows from the gods to snare their prey.

Ingrid wondered if humans were as mysterious to the gods as the whales were to humans. Would she one day be flensed and boiled in some unimaginable manner, her human essence liquefied for the gods' pleasures?

Everything she had came at a price, Ingrid thought, and now she knew what it was. Their comfortable lives, Ranvik's graceful lines on the grassy slope at the edge of Sandefjord, the hunting lodge, the servants, the motor vehicle, the food she put into the children's mouths. It was paid for in blood that spouted into the air and hung in a red haze, blood that clouded the water and spread, blood sluiced off the flensing deck to float suspended in the water, attracting orcas – just as the smell of an abattoir hung in the air above it and attracted carrion birds.

Time became a blur, and as they steamed north into the world, Antarctica felt more and more like a dream. Ingrid feared she'd lose every memory. Perhaps that was how the continent held on to its secrets.

Lars left her to her musings. He seemed distracted and absorbed in his own thoughts, and spent most of his time on the bridge. Ingrid still hadn't found the moment to ask him about what he and Ole had agreed about Mathilde. But one morning she came in from a long stint outside, cold and stiff, to find him sitting heavily on the bunk, his head in his hands. The whale foetus was on the floor in front of him. It was the first time she'd seen it – Lars had brought it back to the cabin and packed it away in his luggage after the Mikkelsens presented it to him.

'What's wrong?' she asked, alarmed.

'Those bastards,' he whispered, and Ingrid felt a rush of fear. 'What?'

He lifted his head. 'A wireless has come. Unilever has found some loophole in our agreement. They say they won't buy the oil.'

'They can't do that,' Ingrid said, uncomprehendingly.

'No,' he said. 'The contracts are watertight. So I thought. But they have bigger and better lawyers than mine to fight it.'

Ingrid shook her head. 'They've pre-bought the oil. They can't simply change their minds.'

'I won't know the details till we get to Cape Town,' he said. 'But this is very bad.'

The ship rose and Ingrid grabbed his shoulder to steady herself. 'We'll fight it. Tooth and claw. They can't do this to you.'

'Of course we'll fight it,' he said. He put out a hand and rested it on the glass canister. 'But I'm afraid that may be our industry. Stillborn.'

Ingrid heard the tremor in his voice, over *Thorshavn*'s engines and the groans and creaks of every joint and rivet. The ship rolled, and the Southern Ocean crashed against the hull and the whale oil slick-slicked in the tanks and the foetal whale rocked in the canister as if it were still in the womb. Lars was afraid, and Ingrid had never known him to be afraid without good cause.

The light had turned dark grey outside, the first hint of night's return. He was a good man, this husband of hers. What had she to comfort him? Only her body and the chance of one success after all, a child conceived down here. Not a child to run a whaling empire. Just a child.

Ingrid drew his head to her belly. She bent her knees and rocked with the ships rhythm, holding him close. Then she manoeuvred him around to the bunk, drew them both down and pulled him close.

'I can't, my dear,' he said, when she kissed him.

'Never mind,' she whispered back, 'Just lie with me; just hold me.'

But she was duplicitous. She moved against him and touched and held and kissed, she took off her clothes piece by barely noticed piece, draping her cardigan over the baby whale to block it from her view. At last Lars was stirred and they made a sad and rocking love, riding *Thorshavn*'s pitch and swell so that the ship was a third presence with them, rising and falling, holding them safe, carrying them across the Southern Ocean, away from the ice and homewards.

CHAPTER 49

Lillemor stepped out of the cable car, smiling her thanks at the conductor and his assistant. It was cool up there. Clouds drifted over the mountain's edge, tipping up their skirts to reveal Cape Town spread out below, and then dropping again, blotting out the city.

She strode up the steps to the lookout, leaving behind a gaggle of English tourists rummaging in their bags for hats and gloves, shocked at the change in temperature. The cold braced Lillemor. She wanted that chilly southerly wind on her face to blow away all of Cape Town's humidity.

The ground was shifting and swaying beneath her feet, her blood still singing to the rhythms of ship and sea. *Thorshavn's* throb had been her companion day and night for six weeks and her bones still reverberated with it.

She'd almost staggered down the gangway early that morning. The air was chokingly hot and the smells were vivid: sweat, hair cream, fuel and some kind of vegetation she couldn't identify. Her nostrils flared, not only with the competing scents, but with the delicious humidity. Breathing it in was a sensation like eating when hungry, as if she'd only then realised how the dry Antarctic air had desiccated her.

She had searched the blur of faces to pick out Anton, but couldn't find him. When her feet touched the ground and she stopped moving, the dock shifted alarmingly to one side and Lillemor staggered.

A flash popped nearby, blinding her momentarily. She felt Mathilde's arm slip into hers as photographers gathered around Lars and Ingrid, and several journalists advanced, notebooks and pens ready.

'Consul Christensen! Was it a successful trip?'

Lars smiled broadly. 'Very successful. The whaling season is going extremely well and we're very grateful to Cape Town. Without your port it would be impossible to resupply our fleet.'

There was a babble of questions, from which one rose clearly. 'Consul, did your wife land on Antarctica?'

'She did,' Lars said, smiling down at Ingrid. 'Four Norwegian women travelling in my fleet landed on Antarctica this season, bringing great honour to their country. One of the landing places has been named "Ingrid Christensen Land" after my wife.'

'Mrs Christensen, how did it feel to be the first woman down south?'

Lillemor couldn't see Ingrid's face and it was hard to hear her words over the roar of sound on the dock. Something about it being beautiful.

'Where's your husband?' Mathilde asked her, pulling the puppy close to their ankles.

'I don't know.' Lillemor felt a moment of fear. What if she'd lost him somehow?

They'd taken a small fleet of taxis to the Mount Nelson Hotel, where bundles of letters were waiting for them in neat pigeonholes. Lars had checked them in to their suites and handed out the envelopes. Lillemor shoved hers into her handbag, fearful of what they might contain.

When the checking-in was done, Lars had looked at the time. 'It's early. Let's rest for the day. We'll go to Kennedy's tonight for a meal together.'

They had dispersed in moments, going their separate ways to their rooms.

Mathilde gave Lillemor a peck on the cheek.

'I'm going to sleep,' she said. 'I'm exhausted. See you tonight.'

Lillemor went up to her suite, followed by a porter who wheeled in her trunk and left it in the corner, bowing as he left the room. As soon as he was gone, she opened the first of the letters, the one from Anton.

He'd waited as long as he could, he said, but urgent business at the embassy called and he had to take a liner back to London. *You won't mind? I know how strong you are. I've been counting off the nights and lying awake longing to have you home. You've no idea how I've missed you.*

Lillemor was exhausted suddenly, but with a brittle, buzzing exhaustion that she knew wouldn't let her sleep. Every time she moved her head the world moved a beat later and the effect was slightly nauseating. She was sweating and restless; she longed for cool, moving air. It was then she'd remembered the cableway and the mountaintop, and decided to go there.

She was close to the top now, but the rocks still seemed to shift and move around her. She put out her hand for support and misjudged the distance, scraping her knuckles. She stopped and took a long, shaky breath. Voices were coming towards her up the path; she didn't want to talk to anyone. Sucking her grazed hand, she pushed herself forward, scrambling and slipping, willing herself not to cry.

At last she made the top, but she could see nothing. The capricious mountain winds blew the clouds in her face, blotting out the harbour.

'Excuse me, Miss. We're on our honeymoon. Do you know how to use a camera? Could you take a photograph for us?'

They were English, and the man's florid face was no match

for the Cape Town summer sunshine. He was holding out a Beau Brownie, just like Lillemor's own, though the cover was elaborately patterned. She nodded and took it from him, feeling the familiar size and weight of it in her hands.

She'd given her damaged camera to one of the men in the engine room and he'd managed to fix it on the return journey. She'd taken some photos of Mathilde and Ingrid holding the penguins, which due to handfeeding had become tame as dogs and provided much-needed entertainment when they were out of the ice and there was nothing but grey sea to every horizon.

But in truth, Lillemor had lost her heart for photography. She wouldn't know till she got back to London and had the film processed if any of the pictures had worked out, but the camera had failed at the very moment it was most needed – the landing on Antarctica. She'd shrugged it off that day, but coming back with no proof that she'd ever stood there gnawed at her. The Mikkelsens had taken photographs, Klarius told them, and had promised to send some. Lillemor would burn them if they ever turned up on her doorstep. She still couldn't think of Caroline's landing without a rush of anger.

'We're ready,' the man said, bringing her back to the present.

Lillemor positioned the Brownie to frame the couple, holding it in front of her belly with both hands and looking down into the viewfinder. She'd have guessed they were on their honeymoon; they looked as though they couldn't wait to get back to their hotel. She pushed the lever, wound the film handle and handed the camera back to them. Their smiles at her were distracted and fleeting, as though she barely existed.

As their voices faded down the path, she turned again. The wind was playing with the cloud, lifting it and letting it fall. She found herself standing on tiptoes as if the extra inches would somehow help her see through it. Why on earth did it matter? She had no idea, but when the clouds swept back at last, giving her a straight view down the mountainside, over the city to the docks, her throat tightened. Far below, *Thorshavn* was unmistakable, its size and white colour making it stand out against the blue sea. She had to bite her lip to make sure she didn't cry. The voyage had been anything but what she expected, but she'd lived in that ship. It had carried her to another world and brought her safely back.

She longed for Anton with an intensity that hurt. He understood her, she realised now. She'd thought she was the one who snared him, but in truth he saw it all – her desire to be remembered, her competitive streak, her flirtatiousness, all of it. She hadn't fooled him about a single thing and he loved her anyway.

The cloud dropped again, sudden as a curtain fall, and she was staring into white nothingness. The rocks of Table Mountain fell away steeply and disappeared below her. In the blankness Lillemor realised she understood something new about explorers like Hjalmar. He could never win the place. He might achieve his goal, might sledge to the Pole or walk an unknown coast or find a mountain range, but he'd be hungry again for that moment of rapture and silence, that moment of understanding the immensity of that land and his own insignificance in the face of it.

For Hjalmar, and perhaps now for her too, going once wasn't enough. For the rest of your life you'd dream of ways to get back there. You'd invent expeditions, you'd find new goals: this coastline to be mapped, that unknown area to be flown across and named. You'd stow away if you had a chance, in a plane or on a whaling ship, and if, like Olga, you were foiled, you'd try again. Always there'd be something more to do and always the hunger to return, no matter how bitter it was, no matter what success or failure, no matter if you made it to your own South Pole or not.

Lillemor shivered and wrapped her arms around herself. Tomorrow they'd sail for London on the *Warwick Castle,* a passenger liner so large and impersonal, so unlike an actual ship, that Lillemor could scarcely remember a thing about her.

She had packed her rocks for Marie, but still had to buy a present for Freda. She longed to see her again. While Anton knew her, perhaps better than anybody, Freda understood this particular feeling, this mixture of elation and grief. The second envelope had been a letter from her. Lillemor took it out of her pocket and unfolded it again.

Don't be surprised if you feel rather strange, Freda had written. *God knows, it can be more depressing getting back from an adventure than not going in the first place. You'll find me in the usual chair at the club, but hurry. I'm going back to Australia in the spring. Oh yes, and I found a quote I thought you might like. Your Miss Earhart said in the papers* 'I want to do it because I want to do it. Adventure is worthwhile in itself.' *I liked that.*

'Madam?'

The conductor had come up the steps so quietly she hadn't heard him and at the sound of his voice she jumped and brushed at her cheeks to hide the tears.

'Madam, I'm sorry, but the last car is leaving.'

'Yes,' she said, swallowing. 'Thank you. I'll be down in just a moment.'

He stepped back and left her. She strained for one last view of the ship as the clouds rose and fell. Yes, there she was. Lillemor knew the lines of her like a lover.

She'd take Freda some cigars from Cape Town, she thought, as she turned to head back down the path.

CHAPTER 50

The brown envelope was heavy in her hands, covered with stamps, addressed with a firm hand. Mathilde turned it over. It was from Lillemor. She cut it open and a sheaf of photographs slid out like something from another world.

On top was the image Anton had snapped of the three of them leaving Cape Town, just before *Thorshavn* had pulled away from the docks. Mathilde's face was thin and drawn, and the fear in her eyes was writ large. Lillemor was obviously delighted, and Ingrid just seemed confused. But for all that, it was an innocent photo, before any of them knew what was to come.

The next image showed Ingrid and Mathilde standing on the deck as the ship sloped alarmingly and a wave washed over behind them. They were blurred, but obviously smiling. Then a shot of *Thorshavn* tossing in heavy seas, which made Mathilde feel unsteady. It had taken a month for the ground to finally stop moving under her feet after she'd arrived back in Norway, and she wasn't taking dry land for granted.

Lillemor had included a photo of Lars and Ingrid standing in front of the cairn at their landing site at the foot of Klarius Mikkelsen Mountain, but it was so blurred it was nearly impossible to make out. There was a shot of Mathilde and Hjalmar standing near *Qarrtsiluni*. He was pointing up at it, describing something to her, and she was smiling at him. She hadn't known Lillemor was taking that shot. She felt exposed, and flicked past it.

Then there was a picture of her holding a penguin, taken on the way home. She was smiling down at the penguin, and her hands on it were tender. The photo reminded Mathilde of the weight of its firm, round body and the smooth slickness of its feathers. She wondered where it was now.

The final image Lillemor had taken as *Thorshavn* approached Cape Town. Hans Bogen, Lars and Horntvedt lined up along the veranda, flanking Mathilde and Ingrid in the centre.

Another photographer might have tossed that photo, but Mathilde understood why Lillemor had included it. Lars had his hands behind his back and was staring out into the distance. Ingrid's eyes were shut and her arms hung awkwardly by her sides. There was something terribly vulnerable in her face, caught just before she'd readied herself. Mathilde was staring at the camera, her own face solemn, her eyes seeming to hold the whole story of their journey.

Mathilde flicked back to the start, pulled out the first photo and held the two of them together. The person in the final picture looked like someone else, Mathilde thought, not the woman who'd left Cape Town for Antarctica as if going to her own execution. By the time of her return, she was someone not to be trifled with.

That was what Ole and Gerd had seen when they came to the docks at Oslo to meet her. They'd been disappointed. Their smiles had wavered slightly when they caught sight of her disembarking. Their upraised hands had faltered a little.

The children had responded instantly to the change. They came running across the dock to meet her, screaming in delight, and had thrown themselves on her. She'd crouched down and wrapped her arms around them and for a long time the three of them had been one large tangle of arms and hands and lips. It was a homecoming of something else altogether.

When she finally stood up and approached Gerd and Ole and their fixed smiles, Mathilde knew her suspicion at the start of the voyage was true. They hadn't wanted her to recover. They'd have preferred she came back worse than when she left. They could have kept the children for themselves and put her quietly away somewhere.

But the children were holding her hands as though they'd never let her go again, and when Mathilde stopped in front of Jakob's parents, she felt a moment akin to triumph. Let them try to take her children!

Mathilde flicked back through the photographs again. There was one of her alone, sitting on the wooden deck, smiling up at the camera as though she was a woman with no care at all. It was happiness blazing out of her, no doubt of it, though she hadn't known at the time. She couldn't remember when Lillemor had taken it, or what part of the voyage it had come from. Surely she would have remembered such a moment?

There was more in the envelope. She slid her hand inside and withdrew a book, and a page clipped from a newspaper. She unfolded the clipping. The headline said 'By wireless from the *Discovery*, written specially by Sir Douglas Mawson'. Lillemor had circled a passage towards the end of the article.

A PLEASANT SURPRISE

On one occasion, emerging from a belt of sparkling pack, we came upon two vessels lying side-by-side, coaling in a calm ice-girt pool. This prosaic business provoked little interest but as we drew near enough to distinguish those on board, much astonishment was excited by the dramatic appearance on their decks of three women attired in the modes of civilization. Theirs is a unique experience, for they can make much merit of the fact that they are, perhaps, the first of their sex to visit Antarctica.

Surely Lillemor would have written? Mathilde felt in the envelope again for a letter but couldn't find one. She picked up the book and saw there was a bookmark. She opened to that page. Lillemor had underlined a sentence.

In my own marriage I paid such a terrible price for sex-ignorance that I feel that knowledge gained at such a cost should be placed at the service of humanity.

Mathilde turned back to the title page. The book was *Married Love* by Dr Marie Stopes.

She found herself smiling. 'Oh, Lillemor,' she said out loud.

At the sound of her voice, Babyen thumped his tail. Then he cocked his head, jumped to his feet and barked.

'Mama!' Ole came thundering down the hall. 'He's coming!'

Mathilde put the book down. 'Really?'

Aase was close behind him. 'He's nearly at the gate!'

Mathilde stood and smoothed her skirt. She'd barely thought of him on the trip, not really. But once she was home, the summer afternoons seemed long and she found herself walking to the gate and looking down the road when she was sure no one would notice. Five weeks had gone by and he hadn't come.

She took off her apron, closed the book and slid it back into the envelope. She carried the photographs over to the mantelpiece and propped them up.

'He's at the door!' Aase squealed.

'Stay in here,' Mathilde said. 'Hold Babyen.'

She walked the length of the corridor. The front door was open to let in the summer breeze and she could see his silhouette. He was wearing an open-necked shirt and his face was pleasantly tanned. He had a bundle tucked under his arm and a nervous expression on his face.

'Mr Lund,' she said, and she couldn't stop herself smiling. 'It's been some time.'

He looked straight at her. He really did have very nice eyes. 'I thought you'd need some time to settle in,' he said. 'After your big adventure.'

'I'm quite settled now, thank you,' she said.

He extended the bundle in her direction. 'I brought you some fish.'

'That's very kind of you.'

Hans stood still, his arm outstretched. 'I wondered. Perhaps you and the children would like to come for a swim? It's such a hot day.'

A muffled squeal came from the kitchen, instantly hushed.

'We'd like that very much,' Mathilde said.

A smile started to spread across his face.

'And when we get back, perhaps you could fillet that fish,' Mathilde said. 'It would make a nice dinner.'

CHAPTER 51

The afternoon was so long and light that she could almost have been back in Antarctica, if it weren't for the warmth. Ingrid threw a raspberry into the bucket, pushed her hair back from her forehead and stood up, putting her hand in the small of her back to ease the ache. Faint shouts and laughter drifted her way from lower down the slope, where the younger children were eating more raspberries than they were picking.

A voice said her name, familiar but at odds with the setting. It took Ingrid's mind a moment to make the connection. He was standing with the sun behind him when she turned, and she blinked in the brightness.

'Hjalmar,' she said automatically, as though nothing had happened. She felt a rush of embarrassment and wished she'd greeted him more formally.

But he said 'Ingrid,' the same way, like a person in a strange country who had found someone from home. He looked haggard, she saw, when he stepped to the side and the light fell on his face, picking out areas of tender pink skin where frostbite had caught him. He'd lost weight; his cheeks were gaunt and his clothes hung loosely.

'When did you get in?' she asked.

'This morning,' he said. 'You know my news, of course.'

She nodded. 'Terrible, Hjalmar. I'm sorry.'

Word had come as they were on the way from Cape Town to London. *Norvegia* had set Hjalmar and Nils down on the ice for a sledging run along the coast, with an arrangement to pick them up in another location. But they'd sledged onto a loose ice shelf that broke away. All the dogs had been lost, along with most of the gear. Hjalmar and Nils had survived, but it had been a near thing.

'Lars will be glad to see you,' Ingrid said. 'He was terribly worried.'

'It will be good to talk to him,' Hjalmar said. 'It makes all the difference that he's been there and knows how easily disaster can strike. We still managed some mapping from the plane. It wasn't a total loss. I've a plan for the next expedition.'

'I thought you nearly died,' Ingrid said. 'Would you go again?'

'Of course,' he said, and for a moment the old Hjalmar was looking at her with a boyish grin. 'Wouldn't you?'

It was true, she realised. 'Yes, I would.'

She didn't want to tell him that the chance wouldn't come again. Locked in a legal case with Unilever over the purchase of the season's oil, Lars was considering pulling out of the whole whaling business. He'd made a settlement offer, a closely guarded secret, to sell Unilever his whole fleet at a knockdown price. Ingrid hated to think how they'd live in Sandefjord if such an offer became known, let alone if it became a reality. Bjarne Aagaard champion of the whales, was perhaps the only one in Sandefjord who would be pleased with that outcome. She'd managed to avoid reporting back to Bjarne so far, but she knew she couldn't put it off much longer.

'Will you stay for dinner?' she asked instead.

He looked at her steadily. 'I'd like that.'

The moment lengthened between them and Ingrid was aware of the sun beating on her face. 'I know some things changed down there,' she said, and stopped.

He reached out and put a hand on her arm, and she felt a shiver that she hoped he didn't notice.

'It's in the past,' he said. 'But there's one thing I need to tell you.'

In the field below the children were absorbed in picking and eating. If they saw Hjalmar, there'd be a stampede, and no chance for them to speak privately.

'Let's go down to the beach,' she said.

He carried the berry basket for her, eating a few along the way. She led him around the edge of Ranvik's sloping lawn, not wanting Lars to see them from his study. He followed her down the steps and onto the sand.

'Take your shoes off,' she said.

'Bare feet. What a thought.' He bent down, unlaced his shoes, slid them off and pulled off his socks. Then he stood up and his face changed.

'My God!' he said, staring.

A line of Adelie penguins was waddling towards them. They'd taken up residence on the beach and seemed quite happy in their new home.

Ingrid took her own shoes off, hitched up her dress and waded into the water. The penguins threw themselves into the tiny waves and porpoised behind her, hopeful of fish. Hjalmar gave a short laugh and followed.

'Incredible,' he said. 'It's good to come back to summer. Although I'd love a long, dark night.'

He'd have that soon enough, she thought. 'Have you seen Mathilde?' she asked, as though she'd just thought of it.

'Yes,' he said. 'I went around this morning.'

Ingrid felt a rush of jealousy, almost as strong as it had been on the ship, that he'd gone to her first.

'She has the last of my dogs,' he said. 'I need to see if he's worth breeding from. Mathilde looks very well, I thought. She said she's happy.'

'I must invite her over,' Ingrid said. 'Would you like her to come tonight?'

He shook his head. 'Remember what it's like when you first get back?'

She did remember. Everyone asking how the trip had been, everyone wanting to know what Antarctica was like. Too many people at once, all of them too loud, the whole thing too much. She and Lars had shut themselves in for the first weeks and seen as few people as possible.

'What is it you want to tell me?'

He ran his hand through his hair. 'After we left you, there were good conditions for two days, so I did as much flying as I could.'

She nodded. 'I remember. When you radioed us about the lead in to shore.'

'Right. I also made another flight over Ingrid Christensen Land. I was able to go fairly low and I saw where the Mikkelsens landed.'

He paused. 'It was on an island, Ingrid. Four or five kilometres offshore.'

She didn't realise what he meant at first, and looked at him quizzically.

'Your party was the first to land women on the continent itself,' he said. 'For what it's worth.'

Ingrid laughed. So far from Antarctica the notion seemed ridiculous. After a moment, when she didn't stop, Hjalmar joined in. They stood facing each other in the water, shaking with laughter.

'Oh dear.' Ingrid wiped her eyes. Then she grew serious. 'Hjalmar, don't tell anyone.'

He sobered. 'But you're the first woman to land on Antarctica. Presuming you got off the boat first.'

'Oh, I did,' she said. 'But I don't care for it. Caroline thinks she was the first; Lillemor is heartbroken that she wasn't the first. Don't stir it all up again.'

'Your husband might have a different idea about it.'

'Don't tell him either.'

'You don't mean that.'

She waded closer to him. 'I do, Hjalmar. It's finished. I don't want to be drawn into a public discussion of who got off where, how many hours earlier, and how many miles closer or further away. Leave it there.'

'Don't you want your moment of glory?'

She shook her head. 'If it had been Lillemor off the boat first, I wouldn't mind. She'd be thrilled. But this will just upset her more.'

He shook his head. 'If that's what you want.'

'Promise?'

'Promise.' He looked down at his feet in the water. 'I'd best see your husband. There's lots to discuss.'

'You go up,' Ingrid said. 'I'll stay here a few more minutes.'

She watched him dry his feet on the grass, climb the stone steps and set out across the lawn barefoot, his shoes dangling from one hand. Let Lars tell him there'd be no more voyages on *Norvegia*. He was already planning to sell the little ship to shuttle tourists to Svalbard for bear hunting.

Ingrid waded out of the water and walked across the sand to the rocks. She clambered up, hand over foot, to the top of the low headland. The afternoon sun was starting to slant over the fjord as she sat down, facing south.

The ground had stopped rocking under her feet, though it took a few weeks. Day and night were circling around and coming back into alignment in a way her body understood. But some inner compass was still spinning, and Ingrid wondered if she'd ever find equilibrium again.

The house was full of Antarctic memorabilia. The penguins that hadn't survived the voyage had been stuffed and mounted and were ready to go to the Whaling Museum. The rooms downstairs were crammed with samples for the University of Oslo.

Ingrid had put the foetal whale in its glass canister inside her wardrobe while she decided what to do with it. Lars had been kind, assuring her he quite understood if she didn't want it in the house, and he'd send it to the museum for safekeeping.

'It's only fair other people should see such an extraordinary thing too,' he'd said.

But Ingrid wasn't ready to give it up yet. When she looked at the creature, bobbing in its sleep as if still in the amniotic waters of the womb, the smells and the sounds and the cold of Antarctica came back in a rush. She remembered the embrace of her bunk as the ship rose and fell, how that seemed at times the only place she could surrender to it, held safe in the ship's belly as *Thorshavn* battled the sea on her behalf.

There was nothing sleeping in the fluids of her own belly. She hadn't fallen pregnant. She was relieved, and strangely, it seemed Lars was too.

'I don't think there's going to be whaling for my sons to take over,' he'd said when her monthly time came. 'I'm going to train Lars Junior in shipping instead. So never mind, my dear.'

Ingrid had made the decision on the voyage back not to ask him about Ole and Gerd unless trouble arose when Mathilde arrived home. But Mathilde was living with her children and

Ingrid was inclined to think she'd exaggerated the possibility of losing them. At any rate, it was a relief to let it go.

She and Lars were tender with each other after their return. They'd become again like an old married couple, Ingrid thought. They were affectionate, as they'd always been, but there was a deeper side to it; what they'd seen of each other on the journey. That they still loved each other seemed a small miracle. She didn't mind that the passion evident on their voyage had faded. It was something from that place, not from this one.

Hjalmar had been right; she'd go to Antarctica again in a heartbeat. But it wouldn't be the same. Before going south, the dream of Antarctica had been the promise of a place so different, so transporting and transforming, that nothing would ever be the same again. She'd find her essential self there.

It was true, she had found something essential. But in finding it, she'd lost something else. The Antarctica of her imagination, that mystical, wondrous place, was gone. In its stead was the real Antarctica, at once smaller and larger than she'd imagined, at once more wondrous and more ordinary. It was a place indifferent to humans. It was itself, no more and no less.

The dinner bell clanged across the lawn, and she heard the children's voices in the distance. They'd be gathering up their baskets, stuffing the last few berries into their mouths, grabbing shoes and hats and running to the house. They'd be hardly able to eat dinner, she knew, and she smiled. It was time she started to work on Lars about Sofie. Her youngest daughter would be as capable as Lars Junior of running a shipping empire, and she was old enough to learn something about it.

Ingrid stood up and looked out one last time over the water, blinking against the light. She put her hand to her chest and felt the hard knot of the small green stone tucked into her bodice. Since she'd got home, there had been no further appearances of her mother, or of any child floating in her mind.

The only thing she could see was the baby whale, lying in its glass womb, its flippers tucked close to its body, its eyes closed, dreaming of the south.

AFTERWORD

About the novel

Chasing the Light is a work of fiction, inspired by the travels of Ingrid and Lars Christensen and Ingrid's female companions, Mathilde Wegger and Lillemor Rachlew.

I have taken the liberty of using many real names, but the characters in the novel are works of speculation. The voyage described in *Chasing the Light* is loosely based on events that took place during Ingrid's four real-life trips to Antarctica in the 1930s with her husband Lars on board *Thorshavn*.

There is no evidence that Ingrid, Lillemor, Mathilde and Caroline were competing to be the first woman to land on Antarctica and, in fact, discussions with Ingrid's descendants suggest the matter was of little interest to them. Neither is there any contemporary suggestion that Lars wanted another child.

I chose to make this an exploration story not only as a tribute to Ingrid and her companions, but in memory of the thousands of women who longed to travel to Antarctica and were largely prevented, a state of affairs that continued from the start of the twentieth century through to at least the 1970s.

Dozens of women applied to join Antarctic expeditions during the Heroic Era – including those of Shackleton, Scott and Mawson. Marie Carmichael Stopes met Robert Falcon Scott in circumstances similar to those in the prologue and was refused a place on his expedition, in spite of her impressive scientific credentials. When Mawson was preparing for the

1911–14 Australasian Antarctic Expedition, he received a letter that asked:

> *Will you take me as your cabin boy, a servant, on your antarctic*
> *expedition? I am a girl in the twenties, strong, healthy and fearless,*
> *& could make up as a boy perfectly. You will find the nimbleness*
> *of youth combined with the knowledge of a woman, a very useful*
> *factor. Yours truly Marjory Collier Alias Jack Sëall*

Eighteen years later he proved no more amenable, refusing the twenty-five submissions from women who applied to join his British, Australian and New Zealand Antarctic Research Expedition (BANZARE) in 1929, though acknowledging some of them had the required expertise. In 1937, the extraordinary number of 1300 women applied to join the proposed British Antarctic Expedition.

But of all the aspiring female explorers who attempted to join Antarctic expeditions between 1904 and 1937, none were successful. The only women who managed to reach the Antarctic mainland before the mid 1940s were those Norwegians who went in association with Ingrid and Lars Christensen as part of the Norwegian whaling fleet.

One possible exception is 'Olga', whose adventure was recounted in the 1932 book *Harpoon* by Henry Ferguson. But I have found no evidence to show that her tale is true.

Ingrid Christensen's voyages

It was a photograph that first sparked my interest in Ingrid Christensen. I was looking through a book on the subject in the reading room of Sydney's Mitchell Library and came across a black and white image of Ingrid and Mathilde sitting on the deck of a ship, bound for Antarctica in early 1931. Mathilde was looking down, but Ingrid gazed out at me across continents and decades.

Ingrid Christensen and Mathilde Wegger on board *Thorshavn*, 1931.
(Image provided courtesy of Sandefjord Whaling Museum)

When I went looking for more information about this enigmatic woman, there was little to be found. I discovered that Ingrid went to Antarctica four times during the 1930s, travelling with her husband Lars on *Thorshavn*, the resupply ship for Lars's whaling fleet. This was in the heyday of Antarctic deep-sea whaling, when up to 40,000 whales were killed each season in the Southern Ocean, mostly for margarine and soap, and leading eventually to the collapse of those populations. The Norwegian historian Bjarne Aagaard was campaigning against the pelagic whaling activities of Norway and other whaling nations on the basis that such rapid expansion would bring about the extinction of the larger whale species and wipe out an industry that had operated sustainably for hundreds of years.

In January 1931, the time of her first voyage, Ingrid was thirty-eight, and the mother of six children. She left them all at home. This was surely unusual, even in progressive Norway and even in the relatively liberated 1930s. For Ingrid, like Louise Arner Boyd, it was wealth that gave her freedom. Lars personally funded much of Norway's Antarctic exploration and his nickname in Cape Town was 'the Whaling King'. Ingrid, and her companion on that trip, the widow Mathilde Wegger, travelled in relative comfort. They carried Captain Hjalmar Riiser-Larsen and Captain Nils Larsen, and the planes *Qarrtsiluni* and *F18*, to rendezvous with the exploration ship *Norvegia*.

After refuelling the whaling factories and offloading their whale oil, *Thorshavn* went looking for the Antarctic mainland. On 5 February 1931, they found a headland and named it Bjerkö Head. The surrounding area had already been named Lars Christensen Coast by one of Christensen's whaling captains earlier in the season. On that date, Ingrid and Mathilde became the first identifiable women to see the Antarctic mainland (an unnamed female shipwreck victim possibly saw it in 1839). But travelling through unknown territory, in a large ship loaded with whale oil, meant landing on the continent was a tricky endeavour and a suitable site wasn't found.

It's likely Sir Douglas Mawson saw Ingrid and Mathilde on the first voyage, as he was sailing the area in *Discovery* on the second year of his BANZARE expedition and there are no other women known to have been in Antarctic waters at that time. In quoting part of the article he wired back to *The Sydney Morning Herald* in the closing chapters of *Chasing the Light*, I took the liberty of adjusting the number of women he reported seeing from two to three.

In 1932, the entire whaling fleet was laid up in Sandefjord due to negotiations with Unilever, and none of Lars's ships went south.

In early 1933, Ingrid and Lars travelled to Antarctica for the second time, again leaving their children at home. This time Ingrid's companion was Lillemor (Ingebjørg) Rachlew, a Norwegian who'd been doing charity work in the London slums in the aftermath of the Wall Street crash. She had recently become the wife of Cato Rachlew, the Norwegian naval attaché in London, who left his wife and three children to marry Lillemor just a few months later.

Lillemor Rachlew on *Thorshavn*'s 1936–37 voyage to Antarctica with the captain's dog Bello. (Image provided courtesy of Sandefjord Whaling Museum)

Lillemor kept a lively diary of their trip, took photographs (some of which were later published in the French journal *L'Illustration*), hunted seals with a rifle, and by her own account, participated energetically in the voyage. Lars quotes extensively from her diaries in his own book about their travels and I have used one of these quotes in the novel, in the scene where Lillemor reads from her diary. These quotations from Lillemor's diaries are possibly the only surviving female descriptions of visiting Antarctica prior to 1947, when Edith Ronne and Jennie Darlington spent the winter on the continent with their husbands. Unfortunately I've been unable to find any remaining trace of Lillemor's original diaries.

Thorshavn also carried a large team of huskies for Hjalmar Riiser-Larsen, ready to offload for sledging exploration. Due to the heavy ice conditions, they instead transferred Hjalmar to the whaling factory *Thorshammer*, to look for a suitable landing site once the resupply ship was ready to leave the Antarctic. His expedition came to grief when the sudden break-up of the ice barrier sent it floating out to sea on a small ice floe. He lost all fifty dogs and much of his equipment before being rescued by one of Lars's factory ships.

Ingrid went to Antarctica for the third time in 1933–34 on the refuelling vessel *Thorshavn*, accompanied by Ingebjørg Dedichen. Once again they didn't manage a landing, though they circumnavigated the entire Antarctic continent. A wealthy heiress in her own right, Dedichen became known for being the long-term lover of Aristotle Onassis, who she met on the luxury liner *Augustus* while returning home with Lars and Ingrid from Buenos Aires, after their Antarctic voyage.

By 1934 Ingrid had made three trips to Antarctica, but not managed a landing. Lars set about writing his book on their travels, *Such is the Antarctic*, and the following season, the 1934–35 austral summer, Ingrid and Lars stayed at home.

Another woman headed south that year. Danish-born Caroline Mikkelsen had recently married one of Lars's whaling captains, Klarius Mikkelsen (the man who'd discovered and named Lars Christensen Coast in 1931). She was around twenty-eight years old, much younger than her new husband, and was considered a beauty – too beautiful, perhaps, to be left at home unattended. So she joined Klarius, who was that year the captain of the resupply vessel *Thorshavn*. After completing transfers of oil and cargo with the whaling ships, *Thorshavn* followed the Antarctic coastline until it was approximately five nautical miles off a snow-free coast that ran to the southwest.

According to the expedition report, 'The weather was splendid, with light winds from the east'. Caroline was in luck – conditions were ideal for landing. Her husband launched and manned a lifeboat with his wife and seven crewmembers, and set out for shore. They landed in a small bay with a freshwater lake and a steep rocky hill, on the slopes of which were young Adelie penguins in an extensive colony. Caroline raised the Norwegian flag and a depot was laid under a stone cairn. Klarius named the area Ingrid Christensen Land and the party had a meal of sandwiches and coffee, took photographs and collected rock samples.

Caroline Mikkelsen's was the first female footstep on Antarctica. But there was little fanfare. Her landing wasn't mentioned in the English translations of her husband's reports in the geographic journals of the day, nor in the report of the landing in the *New York Times*. Lars Christensen doesn't mention it in any of his writing. The Norwegian historian Hans Bogen reported it years later in *Main Events in the History of Antarctic Exploration*, but Caroline herself remained silent about her adventure. Two years after the landing her husband died. Caroline remarried and, with a new name, made a decision not to talk about her Antarctic experiences 'to spare his feelings'. She stuck with that decision for decades, only going public again in 1995 when Australian Antarctic researcher Diana Patterson tracked her down in Norway.

What Ingrid thought about being pipped at the post – if she thought anything – was never recorded. But she did return to Antarctica one last time, in 1936. Lillemor Rachlew went again as her companion and this time Ingrid took her youngest daughter, Augusta Sofie ('Fie'), who was then eighteen. Another woman, Solveig Wideroe, wife of the aviator on the ship, also joined them, making the 'four ladies' for whom an underwater bank near the continent was named. Hans Bogen, who later described Ingrid as 'spreading the Sunday sun over the working week' and has having an 'incredibly bold, fearless personality', travelled with them. The aim of the trip was for Lars to carry out full aerial mapping of the Antarctic coastline to 'lay the foundation of the coastal lands discovered by Norwegians in the East Antarctic'.

Ingrid had the chance to fly as a passenger over the land that had been named for her two years earlier, and she dropped the Norwegian flag out of the window. She sent a wireless from the plane back to her husband on the ship that said, 'Greetings to the Consul from his wife … I bless my land and baptise it with my own hand'. With that flight, she became the first woman to see Antarctica from the air, including previously undiscovered areas. Lars and Lillemor Rachlew went up in the plane immediately afterwards.

After the flight, the weather was fine and sunny and Lars thought it time to try for a landing at last. But it was not to be:

We got into a motorboat we had brought for the purpose, but before we had rounded the bow of the Thorshavn *the sea turned rough and waves broke on the boat, drenching us to the skin. So quickly does it change in the Antarctic from idyllic calm and sunshine to storm. We thought better of it, and turned back to* Thorshavn, *where we had not a little trouble getting on board again, on account of the heavy seas.*

Caroline Mikkelsen's landing

It seems like Ingrid's efforts to land were jinxed and according to most recorded history her Antarctic story ends at that point. Even later writers who attempted to flesh out the record of women who travelled to Antarctica failed to follow Ingrid any further. Caroline Mikkelsen became known as the first woman to land on Antarctica and Ingrid was more or less forgotten.

It wasn't until 1998 that an Australian polar researcher, Ian Norman, and some colleagues went back to the original records and sketches of Klarius and Caroline Mikkelsen's 1935 landing site to examine Norwegian explorations in relation to contemporary Antarctic investigations and politics. They referred back to the original ship logbooks, sketch maps and historic accounts, including those in Norwegian, as well as later Davis Station logbooks and field reports of travels to the site.

After combing through the evidence in these documents they looked again at the map sketched by Caroline's husband showing their landing site as being on the continent. Contrary to the sketch, the flagpole marking the landing spot is on the largest island of the Tryne group, a few kilometres from the shore. Although some have disputed this conclusion, no firm evidence has been found to prove Caroline Mikkelsen ever landed on the mainland.

Ingrid Christensen's landing

Initially it was difficult to find out if Ingrid Christensen had actually landed on Antarctica. None of the scholars I'd been reading mentioned her doing so. In his 1937 address to the Norwegian Geographical Society, Lars described his own landing, but didn't mention if Ingrid or the other women on board were with him:

> On the 30th of January 1937, at two in the morning, I experienced the unique pleasure of setting foot on the Antarctic mainland, where we made a depot. Klarius Mikkelsen Mountain was a remarkable one, with precipitous, crevassed sides. The stillness was almost uncanny: only the rhythmic beat of the waves and the unceasing, soft chatter of the penguins broke the solemn silence.

Norman's article refers briefly to a landing made by Ingrid and her friends, as does the work of Hans Bogen. However, the sketchy information about the women's landing remained buried. No later writers correctly picked up on the story and no history books had been adjusted.

The Sandefjord Whaling Museum holds Lars Christensen's personal 'logbook' diaries from his second and fourth voyages. It appears he didn't keep a diary of his first voyage (or it has been lost) and the diary of the third voyage is in the keeping of one of his grandchildren, who only discovered it three years ago in a box when her own mother died. The diaries are handwritten in Norwegian and their existence isn't widely known.

So it was with a sense of discovery that I had the relevant section translated. And there, in Lars's personal description of what it felt like to finally land on Antarctica, lay the answer to which woman landed first on Antarctica:

Firern *came at around midnight. There was considerable rumbling (hollow echo sounds) and booming, a dim dusky twilight, a little layer of snow and a two-and-a-half-hour trip. So it was in fact uninviting, but ashore I wanted to go. Captain Mikkelsen was feeling uneasy. He had telegraphed advising that only I attempt to go ashore, that it was bad over there – and we came, six of us who all dreamed of going ashore.*

We had coffee, daylight started to break, it stopped snowing and the wind settled a bit. So our spirits started to rise gradually. We come high up on the mountainside and pass first two reefs which signals uncharted waters. The walls of the mountain jut straight up approximately 500 feet with a small plateau down towards the water. Here sit dozens of penguins watching us. Firern *is stopped quite close to land and the lifeboat is lowered onto the water.*

Ingrid and I along with Mikkelsen are the first.

The swell heaves Braaten up and down and the only place we can land is at a slippery ledge on the mountain. Mikkelsen jumps ashore, slips and nearly ends up in the sea so it looks frightening. He has a line behind him and he calls out, telling me to jump. I did and took the line with me upwards so the others had something to hold on to.

Ingrid came ashore well and the others followed one by one. We had a flag with us which was raised over the depot and there was a sense of ceremony in the air when we bared our heads and I, in a short speech, thanked the people who had allowed this land to bear my name …

… The whole thing was one of life's big experiences and it was so good that Ingrid and Fie were there on shore too. Every southern trip I've dreamed about Ingrid and me setting foot on land, on the very South Pole continent, and today at two in the morning, the 30 January, 1937, we succeeded.

Ingrid Christensen and her three female companions landed on the Antarctic mainland at Klarius Mikkelsen Mountain (now known as Scullin Monolith) on 30 January 1937, with Ingrid being the first ashore.

On the way back to *Thorshavn* after the landing, it began to snow heavily and the wind and swells increased. Lars described it as being like searching for a needle in a haystack as they shouted into the foghorn for the ship. It was some hours before they found it again. While they were gone, the depth sounder suddenly showed only fifteen metres of water below and the captain said he believed their last hour had come.

In Lars's diary of the 1937 trip, he's glued a photograph of their landing. It shows Lars and Ingrid standing in a rock chute in front of a large Norwegian flag. It's a disappointing shot, slightly blurred, distant and rather underexposed, and one of only a few from the landing (a fact that gave me scope for fictional speculation).

Sir Douglas Mawson landed on the same spot six years earlier, on 13 February 1931, left a depot and named it after the Prime Minister of Australia, James Scullin. In January of that year, a few weeks before Mawson, men from Lars's fleet had also landed there and named it Mount Klarius Mikkelsen. The highest point of the outcrop is still called Mikkelsen Peak.

Because it is an important and unique seabird breeding site, Scullin Monolith is an Antarctic Specially Protected Area and according to its terms of management, no access is allowed except for compelling scientific or management purposes.

Until now, no one has been aware that the landing site of the first woman to reach the Antarctic mainland lies somewhere there. Ingrid's landing place is still undiscovered.

The area of coastline where the Mikkelsens landed is still known as Ingrid Christensen Land.

Research sources

I am indebted to the following authors and publications:

Anon. (1929, 6 July). Mawson Antarctic expedition: 25 women applicants. *The Times.*

Anon. (1937, Saturday 3 April). Women want to go to Pole – 1,300 applications – 'No,' says leader. *The Argus.* Retrieved from http://nla.gov.au/nla.news-article11053800

Antarctic Heritage Trust. The first landing on the Antarctic mainland. Retrieved 8 December 2011 from www.norwaysforgottenexplorer.org/english/first-landing/

Bogen, H. (1957). *Main events in the history of Antarctic exploration.* Sandefjord: Norwegian Whaling Gazette.

Chipman, E. (1986). *Women on the ice: a history of women in the far south.* Victoria: Melbourne University Press.

Christensen, L. (1935). *Such is the Antarctic* (J. EMG, Trans.). Great Britain: Hodder and Stoughton.

Christensen, L. (1936–37). *Dagbok ('Logbook').* Unpublished manuscript, Sandefjord.

Christensen, L. (1937). *My last expedition to the Antarctic.* Oslo: Johan Grundt Tanum.

Ferguson, H. (1932). *Harpoon.* Oxford: Jonathan Cape.

Norman, I., Gibson, J. A. E., & Burgess, J. S. (1998). Klarius Mikkelsen's 1935 landing in the Vestfold Hills, East Antarctica: some fiction and some facts. *Polar Record,* 34 (191), 293–304.

Norman, I., Gibson, J. A. E., Jones, R. T., & Burgess, J. S. (2002). Klarius Mikkelsen's landing site: some further notes on the 1935 Norwegian visit to the Vestfold Hills, East Antarctica. *Polar Record,* 38 (207), 323–8.

Parker, A. (1977). Is Tryne Island the correct landing site of Karoline Mikkelsen the first woman to land on mainland Antarctica? Unpublished report.

Patterson, D. (1995). The Vestfold Hills: the Norwegian connection. *ANARE News*, Spring/Summer 1995–96, 43–4.

Ringstad, J. E. (2005). *Bjarne Aagaard and his crusade against pelagic whaling in the late 1920s.* Paper presented at the second symposium on whaling and history, Sandefjord.

Williams, R. (Writer). (2011). Antarctica, Glossopteris and the sexual revolution [Radio]. In B. Seega (Producer), *Ockham's razor*: ABC Radio National.

Wireless from the *Discovery*. (1931, Saturday 14 March). The *Discovery* – rich whaling industry – women in Antarctica. *The Sydney Morning Herald.* Retrieved from http://nla.gov.au/nla.news-article16762092

ACKNOWLEDGEMENTS

The Australian Antarctic Division (AAD) has run an arts fellowship program since the early 1980s, sending artists of all kinds, including writers, poets, filmmakers, photographers, artists, musicians and dancers, to visit Antarctica. It has been an exceptional program resulting in a significant body of creative work over some three decades. I thank the AAD for running this program and for awarding me the 2011–12 Antarctic Arts Fellowship, enabling me to voyage for six weeks on *Aurora Australis* and visit Ingrid Christensen Land, where Davis Station is located.

AAD marketing and events manager Kristin Raw cheerfully encouraged me to apply for three years running and was most helpful before and after my voyage. I am grateful to Antarctic expeditioner Dave Hoskin, who took me on an unforgettable field trip in Ingrid Christensen Land (including a visit to Caroline Mikkelsen's landing site) and allowed me to use some of his photographs. Outgoing Davis Station leader Graham Cook was happy to spend hours while we sailed back to Australia discussing conspiracy (and other) theories about where the women landed. Voyage leader Sharon Labudda and deputy leader Leanne Millhouse made the trip a pleasure, along with the friendly crew of *Aurora Australis*, the expeditioners heading down to Antarctica for the 2011–12 summer, and those hardy souls who had spent the previous winter there and returned on the ship with me. Photographer Tui De Roy was also on the ship and inspired me to improve my photography, as well as allowing me to use some of her images. Thanks to Margie Law and Jane Wasley (AAD scientist) for putting me up in their house in Hobart, which I'm sure felt like the Antarctica halfway hotel by the end of the season.

I wrote *Chasing the Light* as part of a Doctor of Creative Arts in the Writing and Society Research Centre at the University of Western Sydney (UWS). I am very grateful to the university for supporting my research for three years with a scholarship. Thanks to my supervisor, Gail Jones, who headed me off at the pass when I was going in a wrong direction and saved me a lot of heartache with her wise feedback and warm encouragement. Thanks to staff members Melinda Jewell and Suzanne Gapps, who helped with admin and travel plans, arranged fabulous food at all the group's events, and organised a brilliant series of seminars and workshops over the three years of my candidature. UWS librarian Susan Robbins went beyond the call of duty in helping me settle in to university life, find a Norwegian translator and track down tricky historical details. Academic staff at the centre and my fellow candidates were encouraging and inspiring – I will miss being part of that group.

In 2011, I travelled to Norway to research Ingrid Christensen in more detail. Thank you to Ingrid Wangen, granddaughter of Ingrid Christensen, who spent several hours talking to me about her grandmother and showing me the diary/photo album from Ingrid's third voyage.

Thanks to modern-day Norwegian Antarctic adventurer Liv Arnesen (the first woman to ski solo to the South Pole), who put me in touch with Wanda Widerøe and Turi Widerøe, daughters of Solveig Widerøe who went to Antarctica on Ingrid's final voyage in 1937. I spent a wonderful afternoon with Wanda and her husband, Kaare, eating waffles and strawberries and drinking champagne at their summer house near Sandefjord while discussing women and Antarctica, as well as the mating habits of elk.

Staff at the Sandefjord Whaling Museum in Norway gave me access to Lars Christensen's diaries and other materials during my visit, and have been most generous with permitting me to use historical photographs from Christensen's voyages in talks and publications. Thank you to museum curator/historian Jan Erik Ringstad, curator/historian Dag Ingemar Børresen and photo and film consultant Øyvind Thuresson (who introduced me to Ingrid's granddaughter). Polar researcher Susan Barr from the Fram Museum made time to meet me and answer my questions.

Two people helped me with translations from Norwegian into English. Thanks to Tonje Ackherholt for answering all my questions so promptly, as well as for translating longer documents. Thanks to Eva Ollikainen, cabin mate on my first trip to Antarctica with Aurora Expeditions, who translated the critical 'Who landed first?' entry from Lars Christensen's diary minutes before we flew out of Oslo in different directions.

Ingrid Christensen's grandson, Thor Egede-Nissén, heard about my project and sent me fascinating documents including the transcript of a journal kept by his mother 'Bolle' in 1931 and 1932, in which Bolle wrote about her frustration at Ingrid, with all the vehemence of a rebellious teenage daughter. Thor also advised me that Ingrid's mother, Alfhild, was committed to an asylum in Ingrid's youth and spent the rest of her life there.

Thanks to Howard Whelan and Rosy Whelan for encouragement and Antarctic contacts, and to Elizabeth (Elle) Leane of the University of Tasmania for several conversations about women and Antarctica over the course of the writing. Stephen Martin, then the Antarctic specialist at the State Library of NSW, gave me early advice and encouragement. Alice Giles and Arnan Weisel from the School of Music at the Australian National University organised an inspiring conference 'Antarctica – Music, Sound and Cultural Connections' in 2011, which was very helpful for my research.

Diana Patterson, one of Australia's first female station leaders in Antarctica, wrote about Caroline Mikkelsen's landing site and managed to track down Caroline in Norway before she died. Thanks to Diana for meeting me and talking about the landings. Polar researcher Ian Norman and his colleagues John Gibson, Robert (Bob) Jones and Jim Burgess wrote two fascinating articles in the *Polar Record* journal analysing where Caroline Mikkelsen landed in Antarctica. Any change to the historical record about the first woman to land on the Antarctic mainland is thanks to their extensive efforts.

I joined a humpback whale research voyage with Wally and Trish Franklin of the Oceania Project in 2009 which helped me understand the impact of 1930s pelagic whaling on creatures in the Southern Ocean.

I have greatly enjoyed meeting and/or corresponding with other Antarctic writers (many of whom travelled south on AAD arts fellowships) including Robyn Mundy, Alison Lester, Hazel Edwards, Favel Parrett, LA Larkin, Tom Griffiths, Karen Viggers, Craig Cormick, Lucy Jane Bledsoe, Diana Patterson, Emma McEwin, Elizabeth Leane and Leslie Carol Roberts.

Thanks to my agent, Sophie Hamley, and publisher HarperCollins, particularly Jo Butler, Sue Brockhoff, Kate O'Donnell, Kate Burnitt and Jane Finemore.

The Northern Rivers Writers' Centre in Byron Bay has been an ongoing support since I moved to Byron Shire more than a decade ago and I thank the centre's past and current staff.

My writing group read and commented on several drafts

of this novel. Thanks to Hayley Katzen, Sarah Armstrong, Amanda Skelton and Emma Ashmere for your friendship, constructive suggestions, delightful humour and title ideas.

Thanks to family and friends for all your support and encouragement, especially Sally, Marg and Aimee who provided a welcoming second home during many of my travels.

And thanks to my partner, Andi Davey, who absolutely hates the cold but has nevertheless supported me with steadfast love and great coffee for the past three years while my mind has been in the snow.